BY J. R. SALAMANCA

The Lost Country
Lilith
A Sea Change

A Sea Change

Alfred A. Knopf · New York · 1990

Alfred A. Knopf · New York · 1969

A Sea Change

J. R. Salamanca

THIS IS A BORZOI BOOK
PUBLISHED BY ALFRED A. KNOPF, INC.

Library of Congress Catalog Card Number: 76–79330

Acknowledgment is gratefully made to the following for permission to reprint from their works:
   Norma Millay Ellis—for the lines from Sonnet XXVI of "Fatal Interview," from Collected Poems, *by Edna St. Vincent Millay, Harper & Row. Copyright 1931, © 1958 by Edna St. Vincent Millay and Norma Millay Ellis.*
   Western Publishing Company, Inc.—for the quotation from Birds of the World, *by Oliver T. Austin, Jr. Copyright © 1961 by Western Publishing Company, Inc.*
   Holt, Rinehart and Winston, Inc., The Society of Authors as the literary representative of the Estate of A. E. Housman, and Jonathan Cape Ltd.—for the lines from "A Shropshire Lad" (Authorised Edition), from The Collected Poems of A. E. Housman. *Copyright 1939, 1940, © 1959 by Holt, Rinehart and Winston, Inc. Copyright © 1967, 1968 by Robert E. Symons. For the lines from "They say my verse is sad: no wonder," from* The Collected Poems of A. E. Housman. *Copyright 1936 by Barclays Bank Ltd. Copyright © 1964 by Robert E. Symons.*
   The Macmillan Company, the Macmillan Company of Canada, and Mr. M. B. Yeats—for the lines from "The Lady's Second Song" from Collected Poems of W. B. Yeats. *Copyright 1940 by Georgie Yeats; copyright renewed 1968 by Bertha Georgie Yeats, Anne Yeats, Michael Butler Yeats.*

Manufactured in the United States of America

This book is for Rick

Who order'd that their longing's fire
Should be, as soon as kindled, cool'd?
Who renders vain their deep desire?—
A God, a God their severance rul'd;
And bade betwixt their shores to be
The unplumbed, salt, estranging sea.

—MATTHEW ARNOLD

Part One

Part One

My family, which is distinguished chiefly for the virtue of its women and the austerity of its men, has not produced any literary figures that I know of in its entire history—a set of facts which makes me a defector in a double sense. My paternal great-grandmother, a particularly pious woman, did indeed publish her convictions from time to time, but only in an intramural way, and with a view much less toward entertainment than exhortation. They took the form of samplers—the opportunity to combine inspiration with industry was never overlooked in our family—and were, even for so exact a medium, very much condensed, being limited, all of them, to a single apocalyptic word, the name of a cardinal virtue, spelled out in threads of striking colors, which time has greatly subdued. Three of these—PITY,

CHARITY, and LOVE—survive, and are still, for reasons which this book may help you to appreciate, distributed at strategic points about my house. They constitute my major inheritance, both material and spiritual.

I grew up in the shadow—perhaps I should say the light—of those invocations. Originally there were five of them; I remember that when I was a boy they used to decorate the five adjacent panels of the entrance hallway of our old house in Georgetown; but FAITH and HOPE have been misplaced, or have perished, somewhere in the intervening years—whether due to someone's negligence (ah, whose!) or the natural depredations of time, it is difficult to say. The old pieces of handiwork were framed and covered with panes of glass, as the surviving ones are still, and arranged symmetrically above a Gothic prie-dieu that my mother had shipped home from an antique expedition to Newmarket. Their panes reflected the light of the evening sun which entered our hallway through the fanlight above the door; and I remember, as a very small child, being held up to them and allowed to touch the polished rosewood of the frames or to trace with my tender fingertips the shape of those exemplary words, while my father, in whom rectitude and sentiment were equally combined (as is so often the case), would recall to me in a somewhat constricted voice how he, as a child, had witnessed their manufacture, and how he had devoted the balance of his life to their maintenance. Pity, Charity, Love. It is strange, is it not, that anyone instructed from infancy in their history and significance should have come so grievously to misconstrue them?

The samplers, all incongruity notwithstanding, I inherited; and the samplers only. I remember thinking at the time that the prie-dieu should have been bequeathed to me along with them, as an almost indispensable accessory; but this, together with the old house and the rest of its furnishings, went to my younger brother Maurice, by an explicit and ironical provision of my father's will. A circumstance which may require some explanation.

My father, like all the male members of my family for three

4

generations, was the small-scale manufacturer of an unusual, and as far as I was concerned, a somewhat disconcerting commodity. In a small brick workshop that my great-grandfather had built beside the Potomac River he produced prosthetic devices, chiefly artificial arms and legs. This great-grandfather, himself a wounded veteran, had founded the business on his return from the Civil War, his preoccupation with his own disability leading him to invent what I believe was the first articulated artificial limb to be regularly produced and marketed in this country. It was certainly a commendable enterprise, founded from the most humane of motives and conducted with a degree of dedication that would have done credit to a missionary; and there was as well something very satisfying to me in the notion of contributing so directly to the correction of the world's deformities. Yet I had, from the earliest time I can remember, a profound antipathy for the trade. I didn't like the look of the things. As a child, my father's shop window used to fill me with dread: a strange advancing legion of dismembered arms and legs, limping forward on a kind of monstrous pilgrimage, or else retreating in wounded mechanical rout from some awful universal catastrophe, the broken remnants of mankind. They filled my nightmares.

Later, this distaste was translated into more philosophical terms. As a student, I began to form the opinion that to capitalize on the misfortunes of mankind, to make a profit from them, however humane the motives of my great-grandfather may have been, was morally improper, and indefensible in an amateur of the arts—in the direction of which my interests were at this time turning. It could be objected that there was something overly fastidious in this attitude, a kind of callow prudery, rather than the idealism whose name I had decided to give my childish terror. The observation is welcome, if you want to make it. We will call terror almost anything but what it is; my own has gone under many names, and this is probably the most innocent of them all. At any rate, my aversion for aluminum arms and legs developed into a philosophical conviction sufficiently firm to liberate me from the obligation of making any more of them. I made this known to my father on the occasion of my graduation from college with a grandeur born of desperation, for it was one thing to hold convictions inimical to his interests and affection, and another to pronounce them. He received my declaration with the impassivity for which he was famous and feared, polished his glasses for some time in silence, and left the room. I was astonished; I even dared to believe that he was reconciled to my departure from the family tradition. I was very much mistaken. I began very shortly to perceive, in the coldness of his relations to me, that he was gravely disappointed in my decision; but the full extent of his displeasure he managed to conceal from me until his death, when, at the reading of his will, it was revealed that my younger brother Maurice, who had succeeded to my abdicated post as executive partner of the firm, was to receive not only the total income from that establishment, but the family house, the furniture, all of my father's investments, and a considerable acreage which he had owned in Montgomery County—in short, the whole of his estate, with the exception of the three tattered bits of needlepoint already described. I don't remember the exact terms of the provision, but its essence, set forth in saturnine and stately language, took the form of congratulations on the delicacy and independence of my nature, and wound up with the observation that anyone so admirably endowed by God for his battle with the world could not need very much help from man. The samplers, however, were to be left for my continued contemplation—as a prescriptive measure, no doubt, which anyone of such an idealistic temperament could not fail to appreciate. It was, as far as I was concerned, a fair enough exchange; for of the forfeiture of the entire estate I regret alone that of the house.

Although I don't ever hope to exercise the passion in strict accordance with my father's criteria, I feel it fair to say that I loved that house. Of course it is relatively safe to love inanimate things: one's devotion works no visible change upon them, their response to it is predictably composed and constant, and there is a great natural probability that they will outlast one. (This isn't always true: many of the things that I have loved—including the house—have been destroyed to provide for supermarkets, Bowl-O-Ramas, Pan-O-Ramas, used-car lots, and Tastee Freeze establishments.) Still, I don't discredit on this account my affection for the house, nor what I conclude to be my reasons for it: it was old, it was made of stone, it had a garden, and it endured that most disconcerting of all phenomena—the intimacy of man—while continuing to provide him with shelter, comfort, and a sense of sovereignty. What else in this world could there be so deserving of man's love?

It had been built, like most of its Georgetown neighbors, in the late part of the eighteenth century, and managed, as Georgian houses do, to be both small and stately. The garden was in the rear, to the south, surrounded by an ancient wall of bulging rose-colored brick, which was cloaked in ivy and Virginia creeper. In the center there was a stone fountain and a lily pool, where two enormous indolent carp lived for as long as I can remember; I used to peer down between the lily pads and see them suspended dimly in the dark green water. There was a boxwood tree as well, which I often climbed, and where I would sit for hours with a cat in my lap, my legs dangling down toward the cool slate squares, watching for a landfall across the waters of blue, spice-scented seas, or perhaps murmuring verses to the sad-eyed Persian lady who used to appear mysteriously from time to time and feed pomegranate blossoms to the carp, trailing her pale fingers in the dark water.

So much for the house. I'm going to say just a few more words about my youth and then close the wretched subject forever; it is of little importance to my story.

My brother Maurice I played tennis with, and that was virtually the extent of our relationship. He was tall, vigorous, assertive, and completely assured on the few subjects which he found worthy of his attention: batting averages, motorcycles, model railways, and the probable virginity of various female acquaintances. Only on this last category did our interests coincide at all, and there my speculations were so different from and so much more tentative than his that it left us little grounds for concord. He had bright blue eyes, huge hands, and a harsh, hale voice—the absolute antithesis of myself. When I think of him at all, which is not very often, I see him striding along beside me on a Sunday morning to the public courts in Montrose Park, his pockets bulging with tennis balls, a racket under one arm and an air of morbid anticipation settling over him as we approached the court, for although he was two years younger than I he beat me with a viciousness and regularity which no one should be expected to forgive. He long ago, and for a tremendous profit, sold the house, the garden, the spice islands, the Persian lady, and the dreaming carp, and in their place there stands a gasoline station which dispenses motor fuel in seven different octanes. He is married now to a woman of considerable beauty and great ambition, who has produced for him three very handsome children. Every Christmas I receive from them an expensive greeting card with their three signatures and the words: Merry Xmas to Uncle Michael. This is the only remaining contact which I have with my family, and it is curious to consider that my single thought on reading this annual message of affection is how really disgusting a combination of sounds the words "Uncle Michael" produce; a phrase which nature never intended to be uttered.

I have hesitated to say anything here about my mother because I failed ever to make the acquaintance of that lady. That my father loved her I have the assurance of my family shibboleths; and that this was the great misfortune of her life, the evidence of my senses. For my father's conception of love, as far as I could make out from his relations with my mother, was a combined punitive, sacrificial, and purgative measure in which two persons sharing no common regard, compassion, tenderness, or joy whatever endured one another's presence and intimacy until the more enterprising member fled, went mad, or died. My mother herself tried all of these expedients, succeeding only in the last. Her first venture was a weekend visit to her cousin Clara in Philadelphia which was extended indefinitely until, after the fourth month of her absence, she was fetched home by my uncle Roderick in a black limousine. After this she became very vague, gradually withdrawing her attention from all worldly and domestic affairs, with the single and passionate exception of antiques. For the remainder of her life she pursued and collected these objects with a really demented fervor, until our home had the appearance of a warehouse or museum. This took more years than may be realized, for although she bought them in prodigious quantities, her tenure over them was greatly limited by the constant exercise, on my father's part, of his two most distinguishing characteristics: his lack of grace and his religiosity. The more fragile of her purchases he broke almost immediately; those that were frivolous or nude—categories whose vastness first awoke my admiration for the past—he sent back indignantly, and collect, to their purveyors. Only in those that were suitably devout or sententious by nature did he indulge her; these he had framed, stuffed, gilded, or mounted upon pedestals—interpolations which helped, I think, to inspire her final, and successful, act of insurrection; for after several years of seeing her treasures so tastelessly and arbitrarily disposed of, she managed, with a really unusual show of initiative, to contract pneumonia and die.

As I was only eight or nine at the time, my memory of her is almost entirely of her later years, that unfortunate period of distraction during which, on the few occasions when our paths crossed, she always seemed a little perplexed as to my identity, although very gentle and solicitous. She rose very late, had breakfast alone, and retired almost immediately to a little third-floor drawing room where she ordinarily spent the balance of the day, absorbed in auction lists and antiquarian literature. Whenever I wandered into that quarter of the house—which was seldom, as it was out-of-bounds to my brother and me—I would come upon her, poring over these publications through a gold lorgnette which she held delicately between her thumb and index finger. She would lower the lorgnette and smile at me sweetly.

"What a lovely little boy. What pretty eyes. Have you had lunch?"

"Yes, ma'am."

"If you haven't, I want you to go right down and ask Martha to make an oyster salad for you. I believe in feeding children oysters."

"I've had lunch, ma'am."

"Oh, you have." (A pause.) "What's happened to your velvet suit? It seems to me you used to wear a little pair of velvet breeches."

"I don't remember, ma'am."

"We'll have to get you some, I think. Little boys look so sweet in velvet."

"Thank you, ma'am."

"Now I'm afraid I'm very busy just now; but you can come back tomorrow and talk with me. Will you do that? I'll have a piece of marzipan for you."

"Yes, ma'am."

"What a lovely little boy."

She would lift her lorgnette and turn back to the clutter of periodicals, smiling wistfully.

At the time my father died I was twenty-seven years old, had been engaged for several months in what is still my occupation, and was about to enter into the relationship which is the subject of this book—my marriage with Margaret. Perhaps I'd better tell you how we met.

But first—you'll have to indulge me in this—I'd like to take you on a little tour of her room. I think it will tell you a good deal about her nature; more, perhaps, than a necessarily prejudiced description of my own.

Owing to the circumstances of our separation, which were haste and humiliation, and the fact that we were abroad at the time of it, many of her personal possessions are still here. Some I brought back from Europe with me, including one or two mementos which she acquired on that fateful trip, and have distributed in what I believe to be characteristic attitudes about the room. Of the rest, nothing has been altered since the morning we left, just over three years ago, to take the *Nieuw Amsterdam* for Le Havre. I'll simply point them out, one by one, and you can make what you will of them.

As you can see from the draperies, the toile coverlet, and the upholstery of the Victorian chaise longue by the window, blue was her favorite color (it matched her eyes); and if you will open the copy of Yeats, there on her writing desk, to the poem entitled "The Lady's Second Song" (page 344) you will find, in keeping, a pair of pressed violets which she picked in a meadow near Antibes on a May afternoon. You may notice as well that she has bracketed the second verse in the curious violet ink she always used; it is worth reading:

> *He shall love my soul as though*
> *Body were not at all,*
> *He shall love your body*
> *Untroubled by the soul,*
> *Love cram love's two divisions*
> *Yet keep his substance whole.*
> The Lord have mercy upon us.

There on her dressing table, in a silver frame, is a photograph of myself at the age of twelve, which, judging from my expression—which she interpreted as spiritual, and in which I never corrected her—indicates that my father was closely supervising the event.

If you will open the center drawer you will find, in a blue velvet box, thirteen small identical garnets—one for each year of our marriage—which were my anniversary gifts to her. She was to have had them strung into a little bracelet when there were fifteen of them; that would have been two years ago. There are also a dozen or more left-hand gloves of various colors, which she wore to conceal her disfigurement.

The pictures on her walls are what one might expect from the balance of the room: a Fragonard print of a shepherdess bound up in acres of pink muslin, one of Degas' ballerinas, and an infant's head, by someone I have forgotten. One, however, is her own work, and therefore of more interest. In spite of its inexpertness and the transparency of its symbolism, I have always found it troubling. It shows, as you see, a farm girl with a blunt peasant face and very beautiful hands, dressed in a long skirt and apron in the style of the eighteenth century, standing at a gate and staring off down the road that winds past her farm. Her expression could be called mournful, yearning, exalted, or maudlin, according to one's own disposition and the depths of one's charity.

The whole effect of the room, as you see, is one of conventional gentility; nothing very bold or imaginative, and yet nothing in evident poor taste. The room of an educated matron of moderate sensibility, slipping quietly into early middle age.

But the parcel! you exclaim. What about the parcel?

Oh, yes; the parcel. There it is, to be sure, lying in the center of the bed; a small square parcel wrapped in silver foil and tied with a blue ribbon, under which is tucked a small white envelope. I am afraid I cannot tell you what is in it. I have never dared to open it. Hope, perhaps, so long ago misplaced. About the contents of the envelope, however, I can report; for recently —this very morning, as a matter of fact—I did, at last, work up the courage to open that. You may read it yourself, if you like. It is a very good sample of her handwriting: a ragged, girlish scrawl, in which she never improved:

> *Dear Mickey:*
>
> *This is for you to open when you get back, when you know (I know already) whether we found what we needed. It isn't very much, but it's all I can afford right now.*
>
> *With all my gratitude for everything you ever gave me, or tried to give me,*
>
> *Mickey*

But I see the experiment has not been a success. You are impatient; you feel imposed upon; you want these things construed. Very well. As a matter of fact, it was less for your sake than for my own that I brought you here. But I have learned nothing. I understand no better—as is invariably the case, although I wander into this room five or six times a day in the hope of doing so. I had better begin with the meeting.

It took place on an April afternoon. It was raining lightly; I was a student, twenty-six years old and immersed, at the time, in Caroline poetry—a very fertile combination of circumstances. Near George Washington University there was a tavern named Bassin's where students used to convene after classes to discuss the major problems of existence—some of the most urgent of which, due to the amount of beer consumed and the intimacy of the atmosphere, were solved quite magically, on the spot. On the afternoon in question I was seated here with a group of fellow-students, engaged in a discussion of the possible validity of mystical evidence for the existence of God. This is a topic which used to be of great concern to me. A good deal of passion had been generated; a friend of mine named Zugsmith had reached unusual heights of rhetoric, accompanied by equally formidable gestures, one of which knocked a mug of ale onto the floor. As I was seated nearest to the aisle in the booth we occupied, I reached down to pick it up; at that moment a girl who happened to be making for the door collided with my shoulder, dropping several books and a pack of cigarettes.

"Oh, I'm sorry."

"Never mind," she said. "It was my fault, anyway."

I gathered up the books—one of which, I saw, was a freshman textbook in philosophy—and returned them to her. She took them from me with considerable difficulty, due to the fact that one of her hands, which was concealed in a fawn-colored glove, seemed to be of very little use. The natural embarrassment of the circumstance prolonged the operation, and in my concern to appear impervious I focused my attention on the

title of the textbook, with which I was fortunately familiar.
"You're taking Philosophy I. Do you have Boughtmann?"
"Yes."
"I had him last year. How do you like him?"
"He seems to be very good."
"He's good on the Greeks, all right. I suppose you haven't gotten to the Metaphysicals yet?"
"No."
"Listen, that's what we're talking about right now, as a matter of fact. Blake's concept of Energy. Why don't you join us?"
"I just ran in to get a pack of cigarettes. I haven't got much time."
"Oh, you've got time for a beer. You'll get some good ideas to throw at old Boughtmann. I owe you a beer for banging into you, anyway."
"All right. Thank you. Maybe I have time for just one."

Between these last two speeches was interposed a swift but comprehensive look of mine, the first which I had had the opportunity of taking, and on the basis of which I am suprised that she accepted my invitation so readily, for I am afraid that it was not entirely appreciative. Margaret herself denies this, and for the sake of her dignity we ought to consider the matter in a separate paragraph.

If this were a romantic novel I would not hesitate to assure you that she was beautiful, and that this, and my destiny, I perceived instantly and simultaneously. But it is not; it is—or aspires to be—a novel about love; which is, of course, a very different matter. Because I have come to love her, I call her face beautiful; but that it would meet any very universal criteria for beauty—or indeed my own, at the time of our meeting—I have very little faith. What, then, did she find in my look? In her own words: "Everything that I needed to know." Feminine nonsense, one is tempted to reply. And yet she used the phrase, and several similar ones, more than once. "From the moment we saw each other," "The first time you looked at me"—this is the kind of thing she often used to say. What is it, if not love, that a woman is able to interpret so auspiciously in a man's first glance? The potentiality of love, perhaps; a certain fallow look, one might say, which she feels the impulse and the prerogative to cultivate. Very likely. It will serve, at any rate, to sustain her feminine dignity. The perceptive reader, however, will have sensed that I am skirting the genuine issue; that I have deliberately avoided introducing the word "pity," because of the morbidity of its implications. Considering my background, however, it is unavoidable.

Was it pity that she saw in my glance? A woman would deny it, of course; she would reject any such feeling toward her as humiliating, as being a less noble, less comprehensive one than love, as constituting an implicit confirmation of her disabilities, spiritual or physical. Yet the natural reaction to human disability is pity; and in myself, in whom it was no doubt compounded by reason of my family profession, one might well expect it to be more than ordinarily intense. This is very possible; yet having Margaret's assurance for its inaccuracy, I am willing to drop the matter.

"All right. Thank you. Maybe I have time for just one."

She sat down; introductions were furnished; the discussion resumed. It had taken, as I have indicated, a metaphysical turn. Blake had been introduced—with a certain amount of cunning, as well as reverence, on my part—he being a person whom I could quote at some length, and perhaps effectively. I was charmed by her attentiveness and, progressively, by her ease, reserve, and tact. She contributed to the discussion without either embarrassment or ostentation, making an occasional observation framed with just the degree of humor, modesty, and discernment most becoming to the novelty of her status among us. She had, as well, several curious personal mannerisms which I found oddly attractive; for example, she would sometimes dip the tip of her cigarette into her beer, draw sharply through it, and then lingeringly exhale, blinking with a kind of mild, experimental awe. This sounds very strange indeed, now that I have set it down; but the impression it gave was a most intriguing composition of childishness, adventurousness, and sensuality. Women have been loved on less grounds. When greatly absorbed she would tug at a strand of her hair, so sharply that it would incline her head. Her laughter I thought especially appealing; soft and soundless, and terminated by clenching her lower lip gently with her teeth.

We talked for perhaps thirty minutes; forty, at the most; then, fearing that the time at her disposal—which she had declared was limited—must have very nearly expired, I announced that I must leave.

"Oh, so must I," she said, looking at her watch.

"Good. I'll walk along with you, if I may."

She gave her permission; we took leave of our companions and left the tavern together. I have said that it was raining; so it was: a very light spring rain, scarcely more than a mist, which beaded her lashes and cast a silvery rime upon her hair. I walked with her through this conspiratorial rain for several blocks.

"Did you like them?" I asked.

"Yes, they were very nice."

"Did you enjoy the conversation?"

"They talked a great deal about death, didn't they?"

"Yes, but it's interesting, don't you think?"

"No. I think it's inevitable, and therefore boring. Only things about which there is a great degree of probability are really interesting to me."

"Give me an example."

"Oh, anything that we can change the course of. Anything that we can affect with our personalities. What are you going to do now, for example?"

"I am going to accompany you as far as possible and then go home and read Plotinus."

"And what would you have done otherwise—if you *hadn't* met me?"

"I would have gone home sooner and read with a greater degree of concentration."

"There, you see how interesting that is? These are the things that ought to occupy us more."

"I'm beginning to be persuaded," I said. "What are you going to do?"

"I have to go to the hospital. I work there every Thursday."

"It sounds like one of those dull, inevitable things you speak of."

She laughed in the pleasant way I have described. "No, not dull; but inevitable, I'm afraid."

"Are you a nurse?"

"No, I'm a Visiting Lady."

"What does that mean?"

"I visit the children's ward. I read them stories and play games with them."

"Are you particularly interested in children?"

"In afflicted children, yes."

We had crossed half the width of Pennsylvania Avenue and stepped onto one of the narrow concrete islands in the center which offer haven to prospective streetcar passengers. I waited with her until her car arrived; and although without speaking further for some time, in perfect comfort. I regarded this as an auspice. The mist freshened our faces; the wind blew her hair slightly. She turned to me and smiled.

" 'The angel of silence has flown over us,' " she said; which I was delighted to recognize.

"That's Chekhov," I said.

"Yes." Her smile was sustained by my discovery.

"Will I see you again?"

"I hope so."

"What time do you finish tomorrow?"

"At three."

"Will you meet me in the Student Club?"

"Yes."

Her streetcar was approaching.

"Good-bye until tomorrow, then."

"Good-bye, Michael."

It is a memorable thing to hear one's name pronounced for the first time by a woman one admires.

Having stimulated the reader with this bit of romance, I feel it my duty to calm him with a dash of philosophy. Cherished reader, you have, no doubt, in the course of your scholarly life, had reason from time to time to make use of the facilities of the Manuscript Division of the Library of Congress in Washington. Your application, if it happened to concern Early Arabic or Middle Eastern Liturgical Works, will have been attended to by a Dr. Pritchard, whom it is reasonable to suppose you have forgotten. Let me help you to recall him: a man in his early forties, of middling height, with thin, reddish hair, a soft academic style of speech, and the rather humble and abstracted air of a man who has been brought much more recently than tradition normally requires in a man of his age, to the contemplation of his own infirmities. He will have listened to your request with a melancholy which you may have mistaken for concentration, lowering his head occasionally to adjust with his fingertips the frames of his reading glasses and periodically encouraging you with a murmur. Eventually he will have disappeared into the stacks, returning with a truckload of dark red manuscript boxes whose contents he will have produced and spread before you with a curious decayed kind of elation which twenty years ago would have been recognizable as reverence. During this operation you will have detected about him the faintly corporeal odor of a man who frequently forgets or neglects to set out his laundry box before leaving for work, from which you may have intelligently deduced a certain amount of disorder in his domestic life —that loss of fastidiousness, perhaps, which characterizes widowerhood. Only in this last observation would you not be entirely correct. Well, now: do you remember him? No, I thought not.

At any rate, you may suggest, a person of not unreserved charm. He is not, no. Yet, gentle reader, I am afraid you must learn to put up with him, for, such as he is, he is the hero of this tale, the romantic devil of the tavern—myself!

I see it is a mistake to have burdened you with philosophy at so early a point in our relationship. Please dismiss the matter, with my apologies. Apparently I have not so much calmed you as alarmed you. Let us have a bit more romance.

Second meetings are very precarious occasions. A reaction has set in. There has been time for certain misgivings to develop. The image of the enchantress has blurred somewhat on the inward eye, and one is not at all sure if it was as fair as one imagined. The male of the human species, at any rate—I am not sure if it is equally true of the female—while his first impulse is to conquer at all costs, has a second, and apparently equally powerful, impulse to escape at all costs. He approaches the rendezvous warily, with a vague sense of having been tricked and a host of reservations.

In this ignoble frame of mind I entered the Student Club on the following day at the hour of my proposed meeting with Maragret. A somewhat cynical and yet strangely excited survey of the room discovered her to me, sitting forward on the edge of her chair, her elbows on the table, her legs crossed, the toes of one foot lodged prettily behind the ankle of the other, studying a notebook while she sipped Coca-Cola through a straw. Oh, how swiftly the phantoms of doubt are dispelled by the actual presence of a woman!

I don't know how many miles we walked that day, how many cups of coffee we stopped to drink, and let grow cold between us, how many shop windows we paused to look into with that bemused, effortless, and tender interest in the world's radiant miscellany which you may remember, gentle reader, but if you are my age will never experience again; or how many things we discovered about each other; but they must, in every category, have been many. We walked, I should think, for three hours through the city of Washington, down avenues, through parks, and past memorials, monuments, and fountains which since have been removed or else so greatly altered that I no longer recognize them. All this in a fine spring rain, hatless, and carrying something like ten pounds of textbooks.

I have never understood the passionate curiosity which newly acquainted persons of the opposite sex display toward one another. I consider it the most phenomenal of human instincts. They cannot learn enough; every detail of one another's lives, hopes, feelings, habits, dreams, opinions, attitudes, distastes, and desires is solicited and consumed with an avidity which is really frightening. It is as if by learning everything there is to know about a thing, they could possess it. Perhaps this is true; perhaps by seeking to understand the world we seek to possess it. Which throws the instinct into a rather sordid light, reducing, as it does, man's noblest impulse—the desire for understanding—to that ancient "mania for owning things" of which Whitman despaired. The misgiving, however, did not occur to me on that particular afternoon. I asked her a thousand questions, I am sure; some of them witless and whimsical, others very solemn. And her answers, however trivial, however capricious—there were few such!—were like rain on parched earth.

"Look at the little flowers. They're crocuses, aren't they?"

"Where? Oh, yes! Oh, aren't they lovely!"

"Do you like crocuses?"

"Yes, I love them. I think they're almost my favorite flower."

"Really? Why do you like them so much?"

"Because they're the first to come up, I suppose. I think it's amazing that they are: they're such frail, shy little things. You'd think they'd be terrified. But still, that's very much like the world, isn't it? The people who really break ground, who do the real exploring, are often like that: shy, humble little people, who don't do well in midsummer or in crowds. Don't you think so?"

"It never occurred to me. Who do you mean, for example?"

"Oh, all my favorite people are like that, I think. Keats, Blake, Rilke, Emily Brontë, Emily Dickinson, A. E. Housman. But most of their names we've forgotten, or we never knew, because they don't particularly care about being famous."

"And you admire that?"

"Yes. More than anything. 'Modesty is heaven's greatest gift.' Do you know who said that? Sophocles." A church bell was tolling somewhere. She listened, smiling.

"And the worst sin of all?"

"Oh, vanity."

"Where do pigeons go when they die?"

"Heaven, I suppose; if they've been good."

"No, I mean where do their *bodies* go? There are so many thousands of them in every city, but you never see a dead one. What happens to them?"

"Maybe they don't die, at all. Maybe they ascend directly to Paradise."

"Oh, I hope not. They're such awful birds. I'd hate to think of heaven being all cluttered up with them."

"You don't like pigeons?"

"No, they're awful."

We were sitting on a wet bench under bare, dripping elms in Dupont Circle. "It's lovely here, isn't it? Except for the pigeons?"

"Yes."

"So wet and cold."

"Yes. Would you rather walk?"

"Not right away. I really love it." The tower clock chimed again. She asked suddenly, "Were you in the war, Michael?"

"Yes."

"You don't wear one of those little button things, so I wasn't sure."

"Oh. No. I sent it to the cleaner in one of my suits, and it never came back."

"What was it like?"

"The suit?"

"No, the war, idiot."

"Dirty, bloody, swinish, inexcusable. But there were some wonderful moments."

"What were they?"

"Oh, flying over the Owen Stanley mountains on a clear morning. Swimming in the Tontouta River in New Caledonia. And being aware of sacrifice for the first time. I never was before. That was the most wonderful thing, I suppose. Terrible, but wonderful. All that useless bravery."

"Why do you say it was useless? It was necessary, wasn't it?"

"I don't know. I don't think so."

"Michael, it *was*. Most wars aren't necessary, I know; but this one *was*. Someone had to stop him, didn't they? We couldn't just let him go on enslaving helpless people, debasing and murdering them."

"I suppose not. Somebody's always got to stop somebody. Would you like to have a cigarette?"

"No, don't be cynical like that, Michael. Tell me, please: don't you think it was necessary? If you don't, then we've failed *you*, you see—those of us who didn't go. We have to make you believe it was necessary. That's our part of the job."

"Well, you've got quite a job."

"I don't mind that." She looked at me with rare and utter sincerity.

"You really care, don't you?" I said. "It really matters to you, how I feel about it?"

"I have to care, or there is no such thing as civilization. If we can accept their sacrifice—all those men who died and were maimed and permanently horrified—and not really care; and just go on making money, building our own careers, joining clubs, and having babies; then there is no such thing as civilization. The whole idea of society is just a cheap joke unless we care and remember. I have to care."

"Yes, I can see that. I don't know how many more there are who do; but it's nice to know there's one, at least."

"Oh, there are many."

"Just one is enough."

"What are you studying for, Michael? What are you going to be?"

"Well, I got my B.A. in Business Administration, before the war; but I couldn't stand it. I'm taking my M.A. in English now, on the G.I. Bill."

"And what are you going to do? Write, or teach, or what?"

"Well, I thought I'd try a bit of both, you know; the way most people with English degrees do. But you know what happened to me not long ago?"

"No."

"I went down to the Library of Congress one day to do some research on a paper, and I fell in love with the place. Have you ever been there?"

"No."

"It's a wonderful place. A great old rococo palace, like the Vienna Opera House or something. And then the main reading room is this huge circular vault with a gigantic dome for a ceiling, and marble galleries all around the top. And there's such a wonderful smell: old leather and mahogany and India paper. I think libraries and bakeries are the two most wonderful-smelling institutions in the world. And it has these quotations written everywhere: all over the ceiling vaults and at the tops of columns and everywhere. That's another thing that gets me: quotations. Do you like quotations?"

"I don't know very many."

"They have a really idiotic effect on me. All I have to do is see a quotation printed somewhere—it doesn't matter what sort of nonsense it is; something like, 'Gentlemen, in fifty years Swiss cheese will bring forty-nine shillings a pound.—Ruskin,' and I start feeling an idiotic glow, like the first sip from a martini, or something. I suppose that's the pedant in me."

"I haven't noticed any pedant in you."

"I keep it well concealed, ordinarily; but give me a copy of Bartlett, and I go berserk."

"And would you like to work there now?"

"I really think I would. Although it appeals to my two very worst instincts, I'm afraid: pedantry and reclusion."

"What is the reclusion part?"

"I don't know; a feeling of wanting to get away into some quiet corner with books or paintings or music—imitations of life, I suppose—rather than going out and getting mixed up in life itself. It's a kind of renegade thing, I think; a respectable way of defaulting on life."

"Oh, that's silly. Where would the world be without people like that: scholars and philosophers and poets?"

"I don't know. Do you think it really pays any attention to them?"

"Of course it does. Look what's happening in India right now. Do you know what Gandhi has based his whole nonviolent revolution on? An essay by the greatest American recluse of all, Henry David Thoreau. He even uses Thoreau's title—*Civil Disobedience*—for his campaign."

"That's true, isn't it? I hadn't thought of that. Do you think he'll win?"

"Of course he'll win."

"I hadn't really thought of that. It's a rather comforting idea. Old Thoreau dreaming away by Walden Pond, making a blueprint for revolution for a nation of five hundred million people. Maybe it was a good idea to give up the Business Administration, after all."

"I should hope so. Why did you ever study it, anyway? I can't imagine you as a businessman."

"My father wanted me to. He has a small business, and it was always sort of assumed that I'd take it over; I'm the eldest son. But I hate it. I always did."

"What sort of a business?"

"He makes—well, small appliances. The place would be

bankrupt inside of a month if I took it over. He ought to be glad I'm not going to, but he doesn't see it that way."

"Does he mind that you're not?"

"I think so. He doesn't say a lot about it, you know; but I know him pretty well. I didn't tell him till I got my B.A., just before I went in the army. I hadn't really made up my mind. Lord, I'll never forget that day."

"Was he angry?"

"Well, my father is a spectacle-polisher. Do you know the type?"

"Oh, yes. Very quiet and deadly."

"That's it. And virtuous. That's a really scary combination. You know, if there's one thing in this world that scares me to death, it's silent Yankee virtue."

"Me, too."

"Really?"

"Yes. I had an aunt like that in Kansas. Not Yankee, but Midwestern, which is probably even worse. I used to stay with her sometimes when I was a little girl, and you know what she used to do? She used to sew my panties on, so I couldn't get them off. Isn't that awful?"

"What was the idea of that?"

"Well, I guess she wasn't taking any chances on my natural experimental impulses; or else she didn't trust the local little boys, or something. Every time I wanted to go to the bathroom I had to come galloping home and have her cut them off. I was a pretty nervous little girl, anyway, and that made me even worse, wondering if I'd make it back to the house in time. And of course the more nervous you get, the more often you have to go. I had a reputation for being very high-spirited, because I used to spend my life galloping across Kansas with a wild look in my eye."

"How are the books?"

"They're getting pretty wet. Especially the Higher Verte-brates. They're really soaked."

"They deserve it, most of them."

"What's all this Logic and everything? I knew you had Boughtmann, but are you majoring in philosophy?"

"No. I'm just taking it so I can learn to think straight. I can't think straight yet."

"I don't know, it seems to me you think pretty straight for such a small, wet girl. What is your major, then?"

"Well, Spanish, I guess. That's an awfully fakey major, isn't it? But I had an idea I'd like to work for a relief agency— UNRRA or CARE, or something like that; and I thought the languages would be a help."

"That would be a perfect job for you, I think."

She looked at me a little apprehensively. "Are you making fun of me?"

"No, of course not."

She stared at the fountain wanly for a moment. "It sounds awful, doesn't it? Like one of those cheap movies—the beautiful American heroine dispensing vaccines in a plague-stricken city, wearing one of those cork helmets and jodhpurs. That awful professional nobility that you see advertised in all the women's magazines."

"I didn't say anything of the sort."

"Well, you thought it."

"I didn't—"

"I don't really have any pretensions of nobility, at all. But, you see, I can't help being a bit that way—"

"Honestly, I didn't think anything of the sort."

"I'll have to think of something else to be, entirely. A barmaid."

"That's even nobler. Dispensing alcohol in an anxiety-ridden society."

"Oh, Lord. You're an awful man. You'll have to buy me some, for that."

"Some what?"

"Alcohol. I'm chilly, all of a sudden."

"All right. What would you like?"

"I don't know. Some kind of a big green drink. Are there any kinds of big green drinks?"

"We'll find one."

We sat in a small dark cocktail lounge on Connecticut Avenue, looking through the wet window at the rain in the street. The window was tinted a miraculous blue. Margaret sipped a huge mint frappé through a green-striped straw.

"Do you feel better?"

"Yes. It's very green though, isn't it?"

"It certainly is."

"I'm not sure I wanted one *this* green. And look at that street out there, Michael. Does it seem to you to have gotten all blue all of a sudden?"

"It's the window; they've tinted it."

"Why in God's name would they do that?"

"To make you *feel* blue, I suppose. So you'll drink even more."

"What a sinister idea. Don't we live in an awful age? How are we ever going to discover what reality is? With all these blue windows and everything?" She was a little tipsy, a condition becoming to only a very few women.

"Well, we have your Logic here. We must hang onto that."

"Oh yes, we have the Logic, don't we? Michael, look in there under *Frappés, Mint,* and see if it gives an antidote."

"It says, 'Frequent long walks in the rain with cynical young men.'"

"That can't be right; that's what got me into this state."

"Perhaps it works both ways."

"Anyway, you're *not* cynical. I won't have you say that."

"I didn't really think so."

"Do you know who's really cynical? All those awful old men who organize in the name of everything but self-interest and send all the young men out every twenty years to get blown up, and then accuse *them* of being cynical, because they're honest enough to admit that there are things like death and disaster and natural indifference, and that there may not be any God at all."

"Don't you believe there is?"

"Oh, Michael, don't ask me that, after two of these things."

"All right."

She stared at her drink for a few moments and then said shyly and uncertainly, "Yes, I do believe He exists, and I love Him; but shall I tell you the absolute truth? I don't believe anyone has ever discovered Him."

"I know."

"I mean any of those people who think they know all about Him."

"I know what you mean."

I saw that she was going to cry.

"I believe in Him so much, and I want Him to show Himself so much, and He never does."

At this point I unwound her fingers from the stem of her glass and kissed them.

"Maybe He's just a bit late. It's a privilege of the Mighty."

She looked up at me in a hazy way and murmured something that I did not understand and that she would not repeat.

After we had walked for several blocks she took my arm and breathed in the cool moist air shrilly through her nostrils.

"Oh, that's better. That tastes so good. And things are their proper color again. Those awful drinks."

"And that window."

"Yes, that window. I think that was part of it. It destroyed my confidence, that window. Wasn't I horrid? Such a horrid, maudlin, blasphemous, ungrateful creature. Will you believe that I've never gone on like that before, ever?"

"I thought you went on very well."

"No, I was awful. But, you see, I had polio when I was a little girl. I was only ten, and I was terrified. My arm wouldn't move, and I was so frightened. I used to lie and look at it and pray. I couldn't understand why God would want to do that

28

to my arm, and I used to beg Him to make it work again. I was sure He would. I thought He only wanted to frighten me a little because sometimes I forgot to make my bed, and once in a while I didn't get home to dinner on time. But then one day the doctor came in and said, 'Well, young lady, I think you've done it. You look as fit as a fiddle to me.' I said. 'What do you mean?' And he said, 'Why, you're well; that's what I mean. You can get up tomorrow, if you like.' I said, 'What do you mean, I'm well? My hand won't work. I still can't make my hand work. And it's all funny-looking. *Why do you say I'm well?*' And he said, 'Oh, that may get a bit better, in time— with exercise and therapy. You're mighty lucky to be alive, you know.' But I didn't feel lucky, at all. And it didn't get any better, of course. And I could never understand it.

"That's what I was talking about, in there. I just wanted to tell you what it was all about. I never really wanted to tell anyone else. Well, thank heaven I've finished with *that*. It made such a strain."

"There wasn't any strain."

"There's always a strain. But the odd thing is, I never really cared very much before. I mean, with other men. I never really wanted to bother getting it *settled,* or something."

"Is it settled now?"

"Yes."

"Well, that's good."

"It certainly is."

I am not going to impose upon you the entire history of my courtship; I have reached—somewhat tardily—that period of life where I am less concerned with beginnings than with finalities; nor do I have, in any case, sufficient confidence in its originality to make such a demand on your attention. I feel, however, that it is necessary for you to have some understanding of our relationship in its early days, its flowering, in order that I may expect your sympathy at its confusion; and, above all, that you should see Margaret as I first saw her—in all the charm and grace and mystery of her young-womanhood; it is perhaps the single privilege which these pages are able to confer.

She *was* mysterious. It is an abominable word, of course, to use in connection with a woman, and Margaret herself would be furious, particularly since so many of the heroines of modern fiction whom she especially despised are given mistaken title to the distinction by virtue of their mere extravagance, their eccentricities, deformities, or abandon. By mysterious, in Margaret's case, I mean very nearly the opposite of this: that profound and luminous mystery which she shared with all things that are natural, temperate, excellent.

This is not to deny her a normal complement of those titillating inconsistencies which are so indispensable, apparently, to female charm, and with which women of even the gravest nature occasionally confound us. She had her share of those. As a matter of fact, the most successful way to go about presenting her to you may be to acquaint you with a single pair of such vagaries on her part: those inspired by my proposals to her.

I say proposals because there were two of them; a fact which the reader will no doubt accept with more equanimity than I, who have never been able to make it correspond either with my own determination or Margaret's statement that she saw at first glance "everything that she needed to know." How the devil could a woman, so far convinced of the credentials of her suitor, manage to refuse him in circumstances so wildly picturesque that they amounted to her being drugged? It will have to remain one of Margaret's mysteries; I dedicate it to the scientists among you.

The circumstances were those of a weekend cruise on a sailboat in the Chesapeake Bay through the sunlight of spring mornings, cool blue water, and the moonlight of a night as warm as one of Eden's. (We would both of us be idiots, she said, trembling adorably, to stake our whole lives on the reliability of emotions generated under such conditions. For the sake of our futures, and her own self-respect, she was obliged to refuse me: a very unexpected and provocative piece of logic.)

The boat belonged to a college friend of mine named Mitchell, who had several times the previous summer invited me to go along with him on day-sailing excursions of the bay. It was a little twenty-six-foot sloop with a two-berth cabin, very slim and fast, and in my opinion the most beautiful boat in the world. Her name was *Hyacinth*. I am not going to embarrass you here with a panegyric on sailing ships; I shall say only that of all things that men make with their hands I consider them one of the very loveliest, and sailing, one of the supreme experiences of my life. It is unfortunately a very expensive one, whose enchantments I have long ago had to relinquish in favor of those of domesticity; but although I have been able to enjoy them not more than ten or fifteen times, all told, I shall remember each separate occasion—and one particularly—as long as men make room in their memories for experiences of almost unearthly freedom, peace, cleanliness, and grace.

One day in early June of the following year, 1948, Mitchell offered me the use of his *Hyacinth* for the weekend. He had intended to sail her himself, as he did every weekend, but had to go unexpectedly to New York to attend the funeral of a relative; and feeling, like every true boatman, that it was a crime for a sailboat in full commission to sit idly at her berth over a summer holiday, proposed that I should take her out myself. I was too astonished by this stroke of fortune to reply sensibly. I simply stared at him.

"Don't you *want* to?"

"Good Lord, yes. Do you think it's all right? I mean do you think I can handle her all right?"

"You handle her as well as I do. I can't leave her sitting at the dock in this kind of weather."

"Lord, that's wonderful, Mitch. Listen, I have a date with Mickey; is it all right if I take her along?"

"Sure. You need a crew, anyway. Have fun." He gave me the keys to the cabin and the auxiliary motor and instructions as to where I should find charts, stove fuel, and other paraphernalia with an air of largesse that was well justified.

I had to sit through classes in Logic and Anglo-Saxon—subjects whose obscurity and prolixity I had never before suspected—before meeting Margaret for lunch. I was wearing, as I had been for hours, the bemused and hectic smile of a child at Christmastime.

"I think you've already had lunch," Margaret said. "A whole cageful of canaries, from the look of you. Why are you grinning like that?"

"We've had the most wonderful luck. Guess what we're going to do tomorrow, Mickey."

"Play chess in the park."

"No. It's something to do with the wind."

"The *wind*? What do you mean?"

"And bells."

"*Bells!* Oh, it sounds magical! What is it, Mickey? What are we going to do?"

I had intended to tease her by offering a progressively tantalizing set of clues to our good fortune, but I was too impatient to carry out the game. Reader, I ask you to believe this as a sort of basic premise for everything I have to say (I do not insist on its virtue so much as on its curiosity): there has never, ever in my life been anything I desired above the evidence of Margaret's pleasure. Her pleasure, in any of its degrees or extenuations: amusement, appeasement, contentment, triumph, ecstasy, delight, the assuagement of her hunger, her thirst, or the pain of any of her life's indignities—a blister on her heel, an aching tooth, an insult, loneliness, remorse, the death of friends, of pets, the breaking of a treasured figurine, her first gray hair, her very birth itself. And do you think, my agreeable reader, that this is an entirely generous, an entirely commendable, an entirely benign ambition? Oh, not entirely. Not entirely. I shall, a little later, give you solemn evidence of that. But at the moment, certainly, my impatience for her smile, the kindling of her eyes, the growing wonder in her face, was very unsophisticated, very new. And so, with my still innocent, but characteristic, impulse to delight her, I exclaimed:

"We've got a boat! All to ourselves! Mitch has lent us his boat!"

"Oh, how lovely, Mickey! How wonderful!"

I was not disappointed, for slowly her face assumed that series of infinitely critical adjustments, tensions, and suspensions resulting so magically in such radiance, that expression so sovereign in its power to inspire, so emblematic of consonance and splendor in the world: her smile. Margaret smiled. And added, immediately, "For how long?"

"For the whole weekend! Saturday and Sunday. Both days!"

And now, ladies and gentlemen, there came a pause in the day's occupation which cannot properly be called the Children's Hour, for I was obliged, by my own announcement, to consider the full implications of our fortune. And for the first time, if you will believe it; the obligation having been obscured by my excitement until that very moment. Now Margaret and I, while perhaps not satisfying in every respect the definition of maturity, were nevertheless full-grown, and we had, as I have already made clear, experienced passion. But passion only of that degree and kind which circumstances and the present stage of our relationship permitted. I say the present stage of our relationship to disclaim any extraordinary scruple or delicacy of feeling on our part, for we were very simply still in that enchanted phase of love which is, by its very nature, chaste. The Silver Days of Innocence, a more lyrical writer than myself might put it. As yet the most improvident of our impulses was simply to adore; to be witness to the voice, the breath, the rustle of clothing, the smallest gesture of the other was equivalent to consummation. We had, of course, held hands, we had kissed, we had stroked each other's hair, and in the crushed and redolent grass of Rock Creek Park our bodies, although fully clothed, had lain in lingering contact; but this was all, and it was exquisite, it was enough. We were aware, of course, of other modes of consummation—more gross, substantial, or exhalted (I leave it to the reader to determine)—to which Time should bring us; but the Time had not yet come. Nor, indeed, had the Opportunity.

Which may be the most important point of all. Opportunity, I am afraid, is the ancient enemy of innocence, of purity, of morality in general. How much of this world's virtue resolves itself to simple lack of opportunity I am embarrassed to reflect upon. In Margaret's and my case, for example, opportunity depended almost entirely upon privacy, and in our situation, as students, privacy was very hard to come by. Margaret lived on campus in a dormitory called, forbiddingly enough, Strong Hall, which had very severe regulations about entertaining. She was allowed to receive visitors in a clinical-looking common foyer on the ground floor until nine o'clock, providing it did not involve loud conversation, laughter, playing of phonographs, or stimulating beverages. She was subject, as well, to a ten o'clock nightly curfew, which was extended, on weekends only, to midnight. No male acquaintance of any description was to be allowed at any time in her own room. I, of course, lived at home, where there was no privacy of any kind and where the atmosphere was so little conducive to romance that had the house been lined entirely with vermilion plush, steeped in incense, and deserted from midnight until morning, a satyr would have hesitated to invite her there. Aside from our few hours spent in taverns, concert halls, or theaters and our weekend rambles in the park, there were few places where we could enjoy any sort of intimacy, and virtually none where we could be alone together. As a matter of fact, until the weekend of which I am writing now, we had never been.

There is little wonder, therefore, at the conspicuousness of the pause of which I speak. To be confronted for the first time with Opportunity in so consummate a form, with such utter and idyllic privacy, was enough, I found, to suspend not only the conversation, and momentarily the breath and heart, but apparently the reason itself, for when at last I broke the turbulent silence it was with a remark of strangely limited pertinence:

"Of course, it might rain."

"Oh, that would be awful, wouldn't it?" Margaret said.

"Yes."

"To spoil my first sail."

"Haven't you ever been before?"

"No."

"Not even in those little tiny ones—dinghies—or anything?"

"No, not even in those."

"Well, it looks nice enough right now, but you can't ever tell about the weather on the bay."

"That's what I've heard."

I was striving, by means of these mumbled inanities, to avoid any appearance of undue resolution in organizing our weekend, a thing which I realized would be very little becoming to me. Whether this best represented delicacy, cowardice, or total moral upheaval on my part, I am not sure; but I recognized, at any rate, that Margaret, as the compromised party, should be allowed the initiative, and I was determined to offer it to her. She accepted it, mercifully, only after my composure had further deteriorated during a pause of even greater dimensions than the first.

"Where *is* the boat?" she asked.

"In Annapolis."

"Oh. That's a long way, isn't it?"

"About an hour and a half by bus. We'd have to go over by bus, I guess."

"Well, it would be kind of silly to go over there on Saturday, and then come all the way back here on Saturday night, and then go back there *again*, on Sunday; don't you think?"

"It sure sounds silly."

"Well, what shall I do? Shall I try and get a weekend pass?"

"Can you?"

"Not unless I'm visiting relatives or something."

"Well, then, you can't, I guess."

"I can lie."

"Really?" It was a faculty of which I had actually never suspected her capable. "You really could?"

"Well, if you wanted me to. If it was important enough."

"Do *you* think it is?"

"Well, I think it would be an awful nuisance to have to come home right in the middle. I mean of the holiday. And then go back again."

"Yes."

"And anyway, if we're going to be on the thing all day long, both days, way out in the middle of the bay, I can't see what difference it makes if we're on it a few hours longer, at night."

"No, but other people might. If anyone you knew heard about it I'm afraid you'd be—ha— (I managed here a very imperfect imitation of a sophisticated chuckle)—compromised."

"Well, I'm twenty years old," Margaret said, giving a much firmer impression of urbanity than my own, "and if a girl hasn't been in at least one compromising situation by that time, she might as well give up."

"I think you're right."

"I am right. And anyway, if that's all people have got to worry about—criticizing other people for having a perfectly innocent good time—then it's a pretty miserable world we're living in."

"*That's* the truth," I said fervently, delighted at being able to fortify our somewhat specious argument with indignation. (This argument of ours followed what I have discovered since is the classical pattern for all successful rationalization: first to invoke the imaginary censure of Authority or Society by theoretically yielding to what one desires, and then, having brought down upon one's head the hypothetical wrath of a hostile and Philistine world, to react with an indignation so fierce that in its fever one is swept triumphantly away toward actual, untroubled self-indulgence. A technique at which it seems, in retrospect, that Margaret was remarkably adept.)

"The hell with them, then. It's just too bad if we can't have a wonderful weekend together."

"Absolutely. Well, you get the pass, and I'll find out what time the earliest Greyhound leaves in the morning. You'd better meet me at the station."

"What shall we do about food and things? Hadn't we better bring them along?"

"We can buy them in Annapolis." (Her decision had been made; there was no point now in jeopardizing it by itemizing such prerequisites as bedsheets, blankets, pillowcases, towels, and other necessities of such an intimate nature as to give one pause. These, I decided with silent cunning, I would provide myself.)

The ordeal over, we laughed.

And so, boarding a Greyhound bus in the magic dew-scented silence of a city dawn, Margaret and I were transported to Annapolis through a morning that has not been equaled before or since for the purity of its light or the brilliance of its prospects. Annapolis is a properly enchanted place for such an adventure to begin; a tiny, elegant eighteenth-century city of lovingly preserved brick and clapboard houses, Georgian churches with slender, slate-shingled spires, and ancient narrow streets which do not end, but wander inevitably toward a blue infinitude of bay and swaying masts. It has the cleanliness and the wonderful odor of seaside towns, its streets, squares, and buildings scoured by sunlight and salt air, spiced and speckled with the roses and heliotrope of its little gardens. The bustle of its miniature municipal harbor is comfortable, antique, and folkloric, rather than commercially maritime, like that of Baltimore: there is not the whine of cranes and scream of whistles, but the gentle bump of lopsided fishing boats nudging the piling of the wharves and the rhapsodic slap of halyards against nodding spars. Surrounding this Old World harbor (so much like those of the Mediterranean villages we were to discover so much later, in such very different circumstances) there was an old stone sea-wall, cracked, water-smoothed, and lined with velvet tidal slime; beyond it, in a foot-worn square, a marvelous reeking jumble of fish, crab, and oyster stalls, vegetable markets, and seafood restaurants. Among these we discovered what must have been a very close replica of an old ship-chandler's shop: a dim, dust-scented wooden cavern, from whose ceiling beams, on hand-forged iron nails, hung nets and gaffs and boat-hooks, coils of hemp line, oyster tongs, ship's lanterns, mooring buoys, anchor chain, and a hundred other richly emblematic items of seamanship. In this place, with much delighted and nonsensical conference, we provisioned ourselves for our adventure.

"I wish we could have a harpoon," Margaret said. "Don't you think we might need one? Mightn't there be a sea serpent or something. It would be such a lovely souvenir."

"And something to discourage albatrosses. No sense taking any risk with albatrosses."

"Oh no, we mustn't. What do they dislike particularly?"

"I don't know; but from the looks of this cheese here, in the case, it would discourage anything. This ought to put them off."

"Oh, Mickey, what *is* it? It must have come over on the *Mayflower*. It isn't cheese, is it?"

"I think so. Let's get a couple of pounds of it, anyway. We can always use it to caulk seams."

"And, Mickey, look at this wonderful old thing, with all the lovely brass knobs and doohickies all over it. What *is* it?"

"It's a confabulorum," I said, after a moment of fruitless examination. "But it's bent. We don't want it."

"A what?"

"A confabulorum. You run it up on the burgee mast to indicate mutiny."

"You know, I don't think you know anything about sailing at all. I think you're a fraud."

"Ask the man, if you don't believe me."

"I will not; he's sound asleep. I wouldn't wake him up for anything."

"He's just pretending. We're the first people who've been

in here since the Spanish American War, and he's sitting there with bated breath."

"Oh, the poor man. We've got to buy something. Buy that confabulorum thing. I think we're going to need it, anyway: from the way you're outfitting this ship, I'd say there's very apt to *be* mutiny."

"Let's not have any of that kind of talk. You know what happens to mutineers."

"What happens to them?"

"They're clapped in irons, keel-hauled, and sometimes kissed by the captain."

"Oh, dear. I don't know if I'm going to like this voyage, at all. I don't like the sound of that captain."

"Oh, you'll get to like him. He's mad about all his first mates."

"Is that me—the first mate? It sounds sort of connubial, doesn't it?"

"Very."

"And impermanent. As if I were going to be succeeded by thousands of others: second mates, third mates, ninety-fifth mates."

"Not succeeded; supplemented. Didn't I tell you about the others I'd invited?"

"Oh, yes! Who do you think you are, anyway? Blackbeard? You'd better get a cutlass and an eyepatch while we're in here."

"I am; absolutely. And gold earrings and a parrot. They're right here at the top of my list. Look: 'Aftershave, toothpaste, cutlass, parrot.' "

"Well, you'd better add tuna fish, because that's what you're going to eat."

"My God. Why?"

"Because that's one of the two things I know how to cook."

"Well, what's the other one? Couldn't we have it?"

"*Carbonnades de boeuf à la Flamande.*"

"And tuna fish."

"Yes."

"That's a pretty fascinating repertoire. How did you happen to develop it?"

"Well, I thought I'd choose something from each end of the scale, so I'd be prepared whether I married a prince or a pauper."

"How about a pirate? You haven't made any provision for pirates."

"You don't marry pirates."

"Oh? What do you do with them?"

"You wait and see."

She discovered, miraculously, the canned tuna fish, canned mushroom soup, canned pineapple, canned milk, a cylinder of propane for the stove, insect repellent, tanning lotion, and other odds and ends which she considered indispensable. All of these the proprietor, brought to reverent attention, wrapped up for us with brown paper and a piece of string in a little ceremony that was almost ecclesiastical in its gravity. Margaret was delighted.

"I think it was the major transaction of his career," she said.

"I know. I felt as if I ought to shake hands with him after it was over."

We found a liquor store in the square and bought three bottles of California red wine, an extravagance which Margaret defended by pointing out the indispensability of alcohol in the treatment of scurvy, a disease whose prevalence among mariners was notorious, she contended. Thus equipped for every hazard of the sea, we wandered along the docks in the sweet morning air to find the *Hyacinth*. She lay heaving softly at her docklines on the morning tide, her masthead sweeping across the sky, then pausing for a moment, then sweeping back in a slightly altered arc, in that gesture of grave ambiguous urgency on the part of ships which seems the desire to indicate a course, or star, or tract of heaven which will assuage the eternal faring of their masters —a gesture which only provokes it eternally. It is full of pity, that gesture, but of insolence, too; like a woman dancing nude.

I don't think any more consummate piece of sculpture has ever been produced than a ship's hull; her lines, next to those of a woman's body, are the purest, tenderest, and most invincible in the world; her movements the most graceful and passionate; and the pattern of her rigging, next to that of human nerves, the most delicate and complex, like a harp or loom, an instrument for the manufacture of songs, silks, or fantasies. We stood in the sunlight considering these things while we regarded our little vessel, bound in that kind of felicity with which only the common perception of something beautiful can bless a pair of people.

"Oh, Mickey, she really is lovely. I had no idea how lovely she'd be."

"Well, there you are, you see. I've been trying to tell you."

"I know. I had no idea. I've never seen a ship, you know. I mean except in pictures. There aren't any ships in Kansas."

"Then you're well out of Kansas."

"I am, indeed." She sighed in the strangely plaintive way I had learned to associate with emotion on her part. "Can we go aboard?"

"Yes."

I leaped onto the foredeck and reached to take the packages which she handed across to me merrily and fearfully, kneeling to do so, across the fluctuating chasm between the dock and deck.

"Now you jump," I commanded.

"Oh, my goodness. Do I have to?"

"Yes. I'll catch you. Jump."

"Oh, my goodness."

How ineradicably, with what ruinous clarity, do I see her standing there at the brink of this unknown adventure, her eyebrows twisted apprehensively, biting the tips of her fingers as she calculates (how rightly!) with what daring, glee, timidity, and vulnerability the risk of her plunge onto these strange seas with this fatuously assured and very amateur pirate. She leaped at last, with a little yelp and in a wonderful confusion of flying chestnut hair and yellow silk. I caught, captured, and submitted instantly to her fragile, pliant, lilac-scented slenderness and warmth. She shivered gaily in my arms, laughing at my sudden somber look of subjugation.

"When do you think you'll let go of me?"

"I don't know. I haven't thought about it, at all."

"Well, you'd better. We haven't even got the anchor up yet."

I released her, with wonderful restraint, and took her on the tour of the *Hyacinth* which she then demanded. It was a truly beautiful little sloop, handmade in Hong Kong of solid teak. She was worth admiring, and Margaret admired everything: the rich darkly glowing joinerwork of the cabin with its hand-carved ornamental dragons, matched paneling, flawlessly fitting drawers and cupboards and hardware of heavy hand-forged bronze; the magnificent teak-and-holly inlay of the cabin sole; the perfectly laid vertical-grained teak of her decks; the gleaming purity of her winches and turnbuckles; and the final grace-note of her brass-bound Oriental wheel which Mitchell, in a romantic extravagance, had installed in lieu of a tiller. Margaret poked about in the galley as she stored our supplies, exclaiming over the intelligence and compactness of its design, marveling at the way paneling could be folded down to make tables, shelves converted into hidden sinks, and stoves produced astonishingly out of exquisite little cabinets. She discovered what I had long rejoiced in and wished to surprise her with: that combination of ingenuity, comfort, and beauty which delighted her in the art of her Bach and Beethoven, so evident here in that of the shipwright as well. She sat in the cockpit, fondling the spokes of the wheel and smiling dreamily at the sea mist through the glinting shrouds.

"I'm sure I've lived before," she said, "and I was a skipper's daughter, born on a tea clipper, somewhere between Canton and New Bedford. And I grew up staring over a taffrail for hours at the sea; because it seems so familiar, and ancient, and comforting. I seem to know all about this ship, like walking into a house that I used to live in. It's really sort of ghostly. Am I a ghost, do you suppose?"

"Yes."

"Really? So that's what's the matter with me. I'm a ghost."

"Yes. I've known it for months."

"Have you? Were you scared?"

"Yes." I said this not entirely without sincerity. She withdrew her eyes from the sea for a moment and looked into mine with tender amusement.

"Poor Mickey. Alone on the wild sea with his ghost-girl."

"And you with the Gray Wolf of the Chesapeake."

"We're both very brave. We'd better go before we get demoralized completely. What do we do first?"

"Cast off the lines," I said. I leaped back onto the dock to do so, moving from one to another of the three lines that bound us, by bow and portside cleats, to the piles of the slip. I tossed them one after another to Margaret, then jumped onto the deck and called her to the bow.

"Now you're to sit up here and hang onto the pulpit. Stick your legs out and kick us away from anything I might bump into. I'm going to start the motor."

"The motor? I thought this was a sailboat."

"Well, it is, of course. But we have a little auxiliary motor to get us in and out of port."

"Oh, dear, I hope I'm going to be some use to you, Mickey. I can't do much, with my hand."

"All you've got to do is kick."

"Well, that's good. I'm a pretty good kicker."

She sat obediently in the bow, clutching the pulpit rails and making ready to fend off with her feet. The motor started with the first snap of the switch, which was fortunate, because it often did not. It made the wonderful overture-like sound of a marine motor: a muffled, gurgling, exuberant chuckle. I let it warm up for a moment and then put it into gear.

"We're off," I said, somewhat breathless.

"Hooray!"

The still flat surface of the harbor water swelled about her prow as she pressed forward, bent upward, then broke apart and flashed along the hull in a steady whispering bow-wave as she gathered way and slid out toward the channel, stately, erect, and shivering a little, full of tremulous energy, like an untethered mare. In the bow, Margaret looked back at me and laughed.

"Oh, I love it! It's so exciting!"

"I don't think we're going to hit anything. You can stand up now."

She stood up, holding onto the forestay and pressing her thighs against the pulpit rails. Her hair began to blow and her collar to flutter lightly as we gathered speed. In front of her a low green headland floated on the blazing mist, ornamented with tall pale farmhouses and softly burning cattle. Then, as I turned the boat into the wind, this background wheeled slowly away and she was presented to me against an enormity of sun-glazed water and sky, against which she looked infinitely fragile. I cut the throttle until we were no more than drifting, and then, although the sails were yet to be raised, I sat for a little while in the cockpit, simply beholding her, contentedly and fearfully, listening to the succulent sound of the water along our drifting hull and the wind humming sweetly in the shrouds.

"Are we stopping?" she called.

"I'm going to raise the sails. You'll have to come and take the wheel."

She came toward me cautiously, handing herself from shroud to shroud along the gently tilting deck, and stepped daintily onto the seat, then into the well, of the cockpit.

"First Mate reporting, sir," she said. "What are my duties?"

"Well," I said, after a moment of exaggerated approval of her appearance, "they are apt to be considerable."

"Nothing funny, now, Captain, or the Union will hear of it."

"Nothing," I said, "that any conscientious skipper would not require. You are to keep this ship clean and orderly. You are to be obedient. You are to prepare the food which I will provide for us. On summer nights you are to lean against the shrouds and sing chanteys in a voice of pure and haunting beauty. You are to take soundings over dangerous shoals, and to report to me all discontent aboard. You are to keep this ship safe from mutiny. You are to be strong in gales and resolute in the face of all adversity, and you are to comfort the crew of this vessel when they are uneasy, or injured, or ill. You are to watch for birds and islands. You are to mend your captain's clothing, and sustain him in his loneliness and uncertainty, and if we should pass the Sirens you are to bind him to the mast and blindfold him and stop his ears with wax. You are to conserve the salt and to search the apple barrel regularly for rot. You are to take very good care of the rum and to dispense it fairly but generously. And you are never, ever, to grow whiskers."

She leaned her head against my shoulder and sighed.

"It sounds very difficult."

"Oh, not for you."

I watched her breathing delicately, in a dream whose length I began to distrust.

"And the captain," she said at last. "What are his duties, then?"

So I was obliged to declare them, with a humility appropriate to their solemnity, I hope, but not without a certain awful pride: "He is to study the stars, and set our course by them. And to follow it steadfastly."

"Ah," Margaret said. "You have the worst of it, then. Will you really undertake that?"

"Yes."

She would say nothing else for the present, but bit me on the chin instead. Full of secret confidence, but pretending great injury, I instructed her in the mysteries of the wheel.

"Just keep her into the wind, so the sails won't fill while I'm raising them. This is the throttle; if she should fall off, press it down a little to give her more way, and bring her back. Do you see those little pennants fluttering from the shrouds? Those are called 'telltales'; you can read the wind direction from them. Line them up fore and aft and you'll be on the wind. Never trust the waves; they seldom run directly with the wind."

"You're so wise, darling. I love it when you're wise and gruff like this."

"And try not to say anything stupid. That's very important."

"Yes, darling. But suppose I hit an iceberg?"

"You probably will; you're the most ironical mate I've ever had."

I went forward, removed the stops from the rolled mainsail, and shook it out along the boom. Then I went to the mast, freed the main halyard tail, wound it twice around the winch, and heaved backward. With a splendid creaking and fluttering of sailcoth and purring of the winch the great white triangle of the mainsail climbed into the sky; towering taut along the mast, it snarled deliciously, thirsty for wind. Margaret made properly poetic sounds of appreciation. I fastened the downhaul, secured the halyard, and stood smiling at my work.

"It's beautiful, Mickey! Are we ready now?"

"No, there's the jib yet. Steady as she goes."

"Aye, aye."

I went into the bow, snapped the jib shackles to the forestay, and raised it. It luffed playfully, less majestic than the main; a lolloping cub at the foot of a mother tiger.

"I'm coming back now," I called. "Steady on."

"Aye, aye, sir."

I climbed into the cockpit and sat close beside her, encircling her with my arms and placing my hands beside hers on the wheel spokes.

"Now hold on. You want to feel this."

"All right."

Together we turned the wheel, hearing the cables grind. Then there was that most magnificent sensation: the soar of the bow to leeward as the sails filled and lunged against the mast, distended with power, and the leap forward of the startled hull. Whether in exuberance or anguish I have never determined, for a ship at that moment has such an afflicted look, heeling as if in pain, her mast shuddering and driven into her at such an excruciating angle, as if she were impaled with a freshly planted poignard. And yet the elegance of the passage which this wound—if it is a wound—inspires; such suavity of motion, which nothing but the flight of birds—and nothing else at all, available to man—can duplicate. Such a combination of the exquisite and the elemental is sailing. So enigmatic is it. Such hectic intuitions it invites. With such augury does it excite, and comfort, the heart of the equivocal beast who has invented it.

Margaret and I, surely, were subjects of that augury as we steered our little *Hyacinth* through the crowded harbor, past the tall moored sailboats, the glimmering headlands to our starboard, the buildings of the Naval Academy to port, the last of the heaving harbor buoys, and into the open vastness of the bay. Here the wind freshened over the unsheltered water, driving the *Hyacinth* to a deeper heel, stretching the sails to a shivering extremity and lashing our faces with the blazing strands of Margaret's hair. Half-blinded and with my lips stinging sweetly, I swung the bow deliberately into the wind and held her there with one hand on the wheel while with the other I tightened the sheets until she was as close-hauled as she would stand. The mast shuddered and dipped, the lee rail plunged until it sheared green water, the bow broke into a heaving hard-driven stride, smashing the crests and showering us with spray. It is unnecessary and perhaps dangerous to sail a boat this way, but it is very thrilling; and I was determined to introduce Margaret to the art in the most dramatic manner possible. It was also, I am afraid, an opportunity for bravura on my part that I could not resist. I took as tribute Margaret's gasps and little shrieks and cries of horrified delight.

We beat into the wind for a quarter of an hour, sitting almost vertically in the cockpit, our feet braced against the opposite seat, which lay almost directly beneath us, our faces wet with spray, our hair wind-snarled, and our fingers cramped on the wheel spokes, demented with exhilaration. Then we brought the bow to leeward, slackened sail, and as the wind fell abeam of us, felt the sudden astonishing declension of all that wild power into the mildness and leisure of a gentle reach. The lunging pitch of the hull softened into a lilting glide, the sails swung wide, the mast straightened, and it was quiet, blue, hot, idle, and luxurious.

Margaret shook her head slowly from side to side, her eyes wide with a kind of exhausted awe.

"Well, that was *something*," she said.

"Wasn't it marvelous?"

"Yes. At least I can't think of anything else to call it. Are we going to do an awful lot of it?"

"Didn't you like it?"

"I suppose so. It's sort of like asking Leda if she didn't enjoy the swan's little call. Wow!"

"Well, now you can relax. We'll make a long reach."

"I'm glad to hear that."

She stretched out on the leeward seat in the sun, staring up into the pale morning blue of the sky. She was thinking, happily. Sometimes her face reflected this with a gentle private smile. I hung my arm across the wheel to hold our course and watched her. Once a gull glided over us and her eyes moved to follow it in an idly appreciative way. After some time she stirred, adjusted her body languorously, sighed, and closed her eyes.

"I'm going to sleep," she said.

"All right."

I was delighted with her contentment, her indolence. I was jealous of nothing: not the privacy of her smile, nor her silence, nor her sleep. For I understood that they were dedicated to myself, all her secrecies. They contributed to our delight, as the shadows in a stone contribute to the passion of the sculptor who caresses it. They were not desertions or delinquencies, but the cunning counterpoints of love; she was singing to me with her silences, her sleep. I listened in a state of drowsy benediction, my arms draped upon the wheel, my back bent to the sun, and noted that the elements, too, with their huge hushed serenities, and our ship, with the rhythms and little wildering noises of her passage—the rustlings, the creaks, the plashings—all helped compose the hot, fugue-like contentment of that hour.

Then it was noon. How does that happen, when one is sailing? It invariably does; mornings at sea are as ephemeral as youth and of much the same quality: one stoops to free a line or clinch a sheet and, rising, perceives that it is no longer morning; the dazzle, the mistiness, the turbulence, the hilarity, are gone, and supplanted by something of an entirely different order: a passage. There is a kind of gravity upon the sea; the quality of light is different, and of motion: although it may be more violent than that of early morning, it is somehow less astonishing, less agitating, for one is now as familiar with every cadence of the voyage as with those of one's own body, and feels not so much the scarifying originality of things as the quiet joy of the initiate. In this second stage of appreciation we made a long calm reach across the glittering bay toward the Eastern Shore. A jeweled passage: shrouds of silver, the hull slavered with molten mercury, the bow at each demure descent dipping into diamonds, the great hot jewel of the sun hanging over us, and through our veins, warm gold flowing. After a while I saw that Margaret had wakened and was watching me.

"What are you looking at?" I said.

"You. You really love it, don't you? You're so happy; and it makes me happy to see you."

"I am," I confessed.

"You keep looking back toward Annapolis. Why do you do that?"

"I don't know. To see how far we've come, I guess. I never really relax until you can't see the land any more."

"Don't you?" She looked back involuntarily and smiled at the discovery that this afforded her. After a moment she asked, "Have you ever been in a storm out here?"

"Yes."

"Really? Does it get rough here, in the bay?"

"It sure does. I've talked to people who've sailed the North Atlantic and they say they've never seen anything there to compare with the bay when it's really rough. This is shallow water, you know; and shallow water gets very rough, very fast."

"It doesn't seem possible," Margaret said. "It's so gentle and bright right now." She returned her eyes to me from the mild water. "Were you scared?"

"Yes."

"Were you really, Mickey? What happened?"

"Mitch and I got caught coming down from Baltimore one Sunday just before the war. We thought we'd make it in about six hours, but it took us fourteen, the last half of them in total darkness. I really didn't think we'd make it. There were thirty-foot waves piling over us part of the time."

"I'm glad I wasn't there."

"Oh, you survive. If you don't, it doesn't matter; and if you do, you're all the better for it. It's a good thing to be frightened occasionally, I think. Storms are good for people once in a while."

"I don't mean the storm," she said. "That's not what I'd mind."

"What, then?"

"Oh, I don't know. Everything." She laughed at the inquiry in my eyes and then said with a hastiness and heartiness that were not quite natural to her, "I made fun of you back there in the store for being so grand and nautical, but I don't think I should have, at all. You're a born sailor." When I had grinned at her humbly, as I was intended to do, she added, "You look very natural, at the helm."

"Then why would you have been afraid to weather a storm with me?"

"You'd shout, and bully me, I guess."

"No, why?"

She saw my determination, and in a moment said, "I suppose because only amateurs have nothing to lose by making a mess of things; it's only funny, if they do. But if professionals, if talented people, do, it isn't funny. They have so much to lose."

I considered this for some time, tapping the wheel spokes with my fingertips. It was far too honest a remark to permit either indignation or entire comfort. In such cases I permit myself to be facetious; it is one of those reflexes left over from childhood—the giggle, when confronted by mystery—for which I have found continued use.

"You mean you don't trust my seamanship," I pretended to decide.

"I trust it too much," Margaret said. She had sat up, raised one knee, and was clutching it, staring down through the waves at the bottom of the sea with a certain look of rue at what she appeared to have discovered there. "I mean it would be a very intimate sort of experience. And I don't know if I'm prepared for that kind of intimacy, with you or anyone. You know, Mickey, I'm rather shy about life, and people."

I had nothing immediate to say to this. She accepted my silence as reproach, apparently, for she leaned forward and, reaching her arm below the gunwale, patted the *Hyacinth's* sleek hide, murmuring, "Oh, well, he loves you best. I know why, too."

This was entirely diversionary, of course, this pretense of jealousy; and I let it be seen that I was not deceived. Margaret stood up, on her very toes, reaching to a shroud for support, and stretched herself in the most surprisingly beautiful and abandoned manner possible, her back arched magnificently, whimpering with delight. She shook her hair loose in the sun and said in a mocking patois, "I'm goin' for'ard, Cap'n."

"Go ahead," I said. "I'm glad to get rid of you. You're a troublemaker."

And then, as if to provide me with an illustration of what she had been unwilling or unable to pronounce, she moved in a lurching unstable stagger toward the bow across the unfamiliar pitching of the deck, her hair spilling down, burnished, as she bent to clutch the grab-rail on the cabin roof. She was able to hold it only with her one good hand, shifting it quickly from place to place along the rail, the other folded uselessly against her breast, so that her progress had a halting, hobbled look: moments of security alternating with others of unaided vulnerability; and I saw that the sea, which compounded her beauty, compounded her frailty too.

When she had reached the bow she stood hanging to the forestay, rising and falling before me with the dipping of the bow, as if we were placed on the opposite platforms of a gigantic scale which was eternally engaged in weighing us, one against the other. We appeared to be of very equal gravities, or else the process was so infinitely delicate and protracted that we should never know its outcome.

"Can you turn this boat around?" Margaret called.

"Why? Do you want to go back?"

"No. I just wondered whether you could come and get me if I fell off."

"I could if I thought it was worth the trouble."

"Then we'll find out what you really think of me, because I'm going swimming."

And to my considerable astonishment and delight she began to take off her clothes, piece by piece, in a most matter-of-fact and methodical way, stooping to tuck the individual pieces under the chocked anchor to prevent their being blown away. When she had finished she stood completely naked, dazzlingly white and slender in the sun, and stretched again, her small breasts thrust against the wind, her thighs and buttocks hardening like marble.

"I thought you were shy," I said.

"Well, I am—about things that it makes sense to be shy about. Certainly not bodies."

"You look like a figurehead," I said. "I think we'll have to keep you there forever, nailed to the bow."

She laughed. "Do men ever do anything else with their women?"

She placed her outstretched hands together as if praying, lowered her head, and in that prettily awkward and childish way that women have of diving, plunged down into the blue water. She made a great splash, shattering the surface into a foaming cobalt mound through which, in a moment, reappeared her head, sleek as a seal's, the lovely wet brown hair glittering tight against her sculptured skull, her brows and lashes and the tip of her nose dripping little diamonds. Such a beautiful and merry face to appear suddenly, out of the depths of the cosmic chaos, laughing at the whole absurdity! A visitor to this universe could not have been more enchanted than I was at the sight.

"Oh, golly, it's *cold!*" she cried, gasping with delight, scattering diamonds from her jeweled head. She treaded water for a moment, apparently suspended by her shoulders, her body melting and flowing in some dazzling metamorphosis, marbled with burning veins of light through the clear rippled water.

"What are you turning into?" I said.

"Ice. But it's wonderful. Just feel." She raised her hand and, as I slipped past her in the gliding cockpit, showered me with bright cold spray.

"All right. You'll be sorry for that."

"You'd better come back, now! I'm sorry. Really I am, Mickey."

"We'll see. You hang onto this until I make up my mind." I lifted the hinged seat, took out a ring preserver and tossed it, with a pleasant smacking sound, onto the water.

"Oh, that's what I need. Thanks. I don't care whether you come back or not, now."

She swam to the preserver, wriggled her head and shoulders through it and began to paddle happily about, splashing her long ivory feet and cooing contentedly. I watched her growing smaller and more elaborately unconcerned as the sloop carried me away. She began, for some reason, to sing "The British Grenadiers," and her voice, faint but aggressively contented, came tinkling across the water.

"Good-bye!" I called. She sang louder than ever.

I gathered in the mainsheet and jibed the boat about, single-handed and not at all badly, considering the degree of my distraction. I had found a rope swimming ladder under the cockpit seat; I brought this out and dropped it over the transom as I approached her.

"I've decided I need you, after all," I said. "What's a boat without a figurehead?"

"Hah! If it wasn't so cold you'd have to do plenty of talking to get me back in that boat, believe *me!*"

"Now, listen. I'm going to come about and luff—just face her into the wind, so she'll die. Then I'll throw you a line. But if you take too long about grabbing it, I'll blow all over the bay."

"I'll try."

I did this, wheeling the *Hyacinth* about and letting out sheet until she languished to a halt, her canvas fluttering emptily. I tossed a line to Margaret which she managed, surprisingly, to seize on the first attempt, and hauled her, bobbing on her life-ring, to the transom. She lifted the preserver over her head and climbed up the swaying ladder into the cockpit, slim, long-legged, dripping, lacquered with sunlight, scalding me with her loveliness.

"You're sort of beautiful," I said, surprised to hear the statement issue in a whisper.

"Yes, I am," she said haughtily. "Would you mind getting me a towel, before I freeze?"

I went below, very shaken, to perform this errand, and on my return found that she had staggered back to the bow, where she sat shivering on the cabin trunk. I rolled the towel into a ball and hurled it to her across the cabin roof.

"Catch."

"Oh, thanks, Mickey."

I watched entranced while she dried her hair, chafing it, bundled in the towel, her head sweetly inclined, her face turned to the sky with lowered drowsing eyes, her mouth a little open, in an expression that was a winsome parody of some far more ancient, avid look of cunning or cupidity. A very strange look, cabalistic, utterly unfathomable, yet both comforting and exciting; I watched it almost every evening of my life for twelve years, when she came from the shower, sat naked on the edge of her bed, and dried her hair in the lamplight. Once, much later, on a summer evening in the South of France, I interrupted it by placing between her lips a cigarette she had requested me to light a moment earlier, and she turned toward me eyes of such astonishment, such nudity of spirit, such violation, that I dropped the cigarette in fear. Now, however, she was dressing on a sailboat, scowling as she tried to button her flapping blouse in the wind. I was madly in love with her. I began to mutter idiotically to myself, "My God, I love this woman. If this woman doesn't marry me I'll go out of my mind."

"What are you saying?" Margaret called. "I can't hear you."

"Nothing. I was just sort of praying."

"What on earth for? What's the matter?"

"Ghosts," I said. "This ship is haunted."

She laughed and began clambering back toward me on her hands and knees across the cabin roof. "But only by a very small, agreeable ghost, who is going to make you tuna fish for lunch. You don't have to start praying all over the place."

She went below and began to sing again and to rattle pans. We carried on a long, shouted catechism on the operation of a propane stove through the open companionway. Then, after sounds of cheerful enthusiasm, of consternation, of exasperation, of careful reassessment, of utter indignation, of dangerous, quiet, ultimate commitment, and finally of wild triumph, there issued the unmistakable smell of food. It was a mixture of equal parts of canned tuna fish and mushroom soup, very brown in spots, poured over a slice of bread on a paper plate, and decorated arrogantly with a sprig of parsley. We ate it in the cockpit with many reverent murmurs and cluckings and noddings of the head, intermittently gulping red wine out of paper cups.

When we had finished, Margaret stood a trick at the wheel while I lounged in the cockpit and admired her. She sat peering into the binnacle with frowning concentration, sometimes raking her blowing hair from her eyes with her fingertips, holding the course I had given her.

"Where are we going?" she asked once.

"Where do you want to go?"

"To Samarkand."

"Well, that happens to be just where we're going."

"Will there be princes waiting on the beach, with golden arms and wicked eyes and spice in their beards?"

"More likely there will be civil servants, with spectacles and inky fingers."

"And will we stay in a palace where you can look out and see the doves flying around the minarets, and hear the camel bells tinkling in the dusk outside the city gate?"

"No, probably in an apartment where you can look out and see the sparrows flying around the incinerator and hear the horns honking on the freeway."

She looked reproachfully toward me from the helm and said after a moment, with a certain note of defiance in her voice, "And shall we spend our mornings writing poetry, drinking wine, and making love on sun-drenched terraces among the jasmine gardens?"

"More likely at the laundromat or the supermarket or driving the children to the dentist in the rain. Maybe a bridge luncheon once a week, and on nice weekends a trip to Skyline Drive."

"This place sounds familiar," she said. "I think I've been there, already. It doesn't sound at all like Samarkand. More like Jersey City."

"Just so you're sure what it's like," I said. "I don't want to take you any place you don't want to go."

"Well, if it's going to be like that, I don't." She narrowed her eyes at me fiercely. "You're kind of horrible, aren't you?"

"I'm just philosophic," I said. "All we lovers of truth are despised by the self-deluded."

"Oh, really? Is that what you call truth? That miserable

little gray nightmare? That's not truth; that's a disease, or a symptom of one. And you sound so terribly proud when you're talking about it—just like somebody describing his colitis symptoms over the back fence."

I grinned, delighted with her indignation; but she was not to be mollified so readily.

"Honestly, you make me mad. Is that what mankind has been working toward, all these thousands of years? Is that the end result of civilization? Regular dental appointments and a bridge luncheon once a week? You'd better set another course on this thing right away, or count me out, if that's what you've got in mind."

"Listen," I said, "don't get so mad. I just don't ever want to deceive you about anything, that's all; especially about me. I don't want to brag, or hallucinate or anything, because it's too important."

"Well then, you'd better stop talking about dentists. And bridge. Ugh."

I was very pleased with both of us. I arose and began to kiss her on the neck and ears. But they were poor kisses, vaguely congratulatory, and I saw that they made her sad. I became sad, too, immediately.

"I don't know why anybody wants to get married, at all," she said suddenly and quite violently, "if it makes them start analyzing each other to death and getting so damned mean about everything. Why shouldn't it be enough for me that you're a nice, kind, generous, intelligent, and physically attractive young man? Why should I have to go poking and prying around into the innermost depths of your soul before I decide that you're good enough, before I deign to let you go to bed with me? What a nasty kind of spiritual snobbery it all is. And why the hell *forever*? Why can't we say, 'Well, it sounds like fun. Let's try it for a while and see how it goes.'? How much more sensible than a lot of perfervid promises about 'forever' or 'eternally' or 'until death do us part,' or whatever. Nobody on earth, in his right mind, can make a promise like that. Why can't we take whatever we have to give each other right now, gratefully and happily, while this moment is real for us, without a lot of crap about until death do us part? I may very well despise you tomorrow; as a matter of fact, if you go on talking like you have for the last few minutes, I probably will."

"I thought I was being pretty gallant," I said.

"Oh, yes; did you hear hearself? I wish you could have. You ought to just hear what even the *prospect* of marriage does to your imagination, your vitality, your sense of humor. It absolutely bleaches them out of you. You talked like a potato: 'I don't want to deceive you about myself. I don't want to brag or hallucinate.' *Hallucinate,* for God's sake. What kind of a word is that? You sound like Dr. Turner's Symbolic Sociology."

"I think that's where I learned it," I said. "I love it. I use it a lot."

"Yes, well don't use it around me anymore, will you?"

"Would you rather I did?" I asked. "Hallucinate, I mean."

"Certainly I would. Go ahead and hallucinate a little, like Shakespeare and Giotto and Emily Brontë. Or do you maybe think the purpose of existence is just to smell out the greatest little old insurance policy ever written and get yourself signed up for as much as you can carry? Honest to God." She shuddered and dropped her head.

"Mickey," I said respectfully. "What's the matter, anyway?"

"Oh, it's all this awful bargaining. They've ruined love forever, let's face it."

"Then," I said, trying to demonstrate some of the effrontery she seemed to require in a suitor, "it's up to us to restore it."

She smiled at me very sweetly. After I had kissed her in a manner which was far from congratulatory, she said in a drawn, legato voice, "Do you know what is the most terrible thing in all literature to me? Nothing from *Lear* or *Faust* or *Hamlet* or any of those big things, but an awful, quiet line from one of Shaw's prefaces to his plays: 'If people cannot have what they believe in, then they must believe in what they have.' I hate him—and love him—for saying that."

So we had our brief sadness. But because people so young have almost inexhaustible time and energy with which to expiate their errors, and correct them, and because the weather was absolutely glorious, and because our feeling was genuine enough to survive the negotiations necessary for its consummation, we could not be sad for long.

One of the great qualities of sailing is that it offers a range of accommodation to the human disposition that is unequaled by any other activity I know of. If one wishes to be idle, to loaf and dream, one can do so with a thoroughness that is unsurpassed. On the other hand, if one is inclined toward activity, toward a vigorous physical engagement with the elements, the opportunities are equally supreme. It was time now for activity, and so we embarked upon a condensed but comprehensive course in sailing, to the relief of both of us. All through that warm tranquil afternoon, whose light had darkened to amber and whose seas had softened to long, gelatinous, violet-colored swells, we practiced the principal points of sailing: beating, running before the wind, close and broad reaches, and the many points between. In spite of her handicap, Margaret showed an aptitude that was remarkable. I have always thought that the chief qualifications for success at anything are intelligence and interest, and she had exceptional shares of both. She handled the jib sheets, in tacking, with a zeal, alacrity, and sense of timing which sailors of many summers' standing might have envied. After some very elementary instruction and half a dozen trials, she discovered that exactly optimum moment, during the bow's sweep across the wind, when the leeward sheet must be let go and the windward sheet snatched free, winched and tightened; and before the afternoon was over she had developed a system and a rhythm for this operation that never varied, and that were uniquely hers. It is something that people who basically fear boats and the water never achieve. I nodded at her with professorial pride.

"You're good," I said. "You understand it. You have a style, already."

"I love it," she said. "What else can we do? I want to learn everything."

"Well, there's the spinnaker, which is a whole education in itself. And the genoas. But we have to leave something for tomorrow. Let's try wing-and-wing."

So I showed her how, with a whisker-pole, as it is called, the jib may be held open to starboard while the mainsail bellies out to port, giving a boat in fact a winged appearance and a lovely gliding motion, with the wind astern. This maneuver captivated Margaret.

"She looks like a swan," she said. "Have you seen them do that? Hold their wings out like sails and drift with the breeze across a lake? I have."

In this poetic manner we went coursing across an evening sea under a sky that deepened in the west from copper to orange to vermilion, with long slate-colored rifts of cloud lying cool across it, like shale. And the sun! A gigantic new gong was being forged, apparently, for heavenly effects: thunder, or possibly an imminent apocalypse. The enormous, red-hot disk of blazing metal was lowered slowly, millimeter by millimeter, into the quiet sea, casting a carmine stain across the surface, all shingled and shifting, like the scales of a scarlet dragon. In front of us, the low hills of the Eastern Shore appeared in the purple dusk; we stood and watched them with that startling surge of reconciliation in the heart that a landfall always brings. Margaret laid her head on my shoulder and sighed, staring across the hammered pewter water. We saw isolated farmhouses on the hills, telephone poles, a windmill, an abandoned automobile upside down in a field, its doors hanging open. Their beauty we commemorated, wisely, with our silence; and Margaret's single sigh.

We drifted down the coast to where a huddle of houses, docks, and fishing shacks gave promise of a harbor. There was a cluster of skipjacks, the lovely clipper-bowed oyster boats of the bay, rocking gently on the tide, their bows all pointing seaward, their rigging frail and stark against the lavender sky. Behind them a low breakwater ran out from a wooded promontory, enclosing the docks of a fisherman's wharf, where half a dozen workboats lay at berth, their skippers sluicing down their decks with a hollow clatter of buckets and brush-handles in the darkening air. Someone was playing a harmonica.

This was not Samarkand, but Gratitude; a more beautiful place, I think. I had been there only once before, many years ago, but it has always, since, been my favorite harbor on the bay. Margaret would not believe its name. All of her aesthetic and metaphysical instincts were stirred to the roots by it. She came and kissed me.

"Gratitude," she said. "We shall sleep in Gratitude."

"If we get around the point. We have to make the anchorage yet. It's narrow, and there's not a lot of water under us. You'd better get the chart. It's on the table."

She brought and spread it out for me on the cockpit seat and found the place with her wandering fingertip.

"Gratitude. There it is. On Swan Creek. How did you know about this lovely place, Mickey?"

"I was here once before the war. I've always liked it. Now, can you find the anchorage, around the point? It's called The Haven."

"Yes."

"All right. Read me the depths in the channel."

"Ten, nine, sixteen, seven. That's the lowest, seven."

"Well, that ought to be plenty, but you never know. This is an old chart, and there may have been shoaling since. You'd better get the lead line, under the seat. You're going to have to do some sounding."

"Aye, aye, sir," she said, delighted with this responsibility. She took the line and went forward to the bow, without difficulty now, for the breeze had fallen to the warm babybreath of evening, and we were gliding smoothly over glassy water.

"Throw it a little ahead," I said. "So you'll have a straight line from the bottom when we come up on it. Those little leather strips are feet; the big ones are five."

"Aye, aye, sir."

She tossed the line, the lead weight dropping with a chuckle into the glassy water. She looked very phantom-like indeed, standing on the bow in the twilight, reading the dripping line between her fingers.

"Twelve feet, Captain."

"All right. Throw it again."

"When do I say 'Mark Twain'?"

"You don't, anymore. They don't mark the line in fathoms now."

"Couldn't I say it anyway?"

"All right, if you really want to."

"*Mark Twain!*"

"Good," I said. "That sounded very authentic."

"Now I belong to the ages."

We drifted past the wharf and around the point, found the arms of the inlet and made between them, ghosting through the quiet water to the cove. The channel buoys hung strange and still, like night clouds, in the gloaming between the sky and water. We followed them into the tranquil blue silence of The Haven, where a dozen sailing vessels lay at anchor, their tall masts tangled in the twilight, their riding-lights already winking through the dusk.

"Stand by to lower sail," I said.

"Now how on earth do I do that?"

"Just unwrap the halyards from those cleats on the mast and let them drop."

"These?"

"That's right. Now: lower away."

She released the halyard tails and down came the sails, with a great soft sigh of the collapsing canvas. I went forward to help her bundle and strap the mainsail to the boom and tumble together the fallen jib in the bow. We were barely moving now, making a long smooth soundless V in the purple mirror of the water. I knelt to lift the anchor from its chocks and, leaning against the pulpit, lowered it slowly, the chain rattling up through the locker port with that hollow, oracular sound of conclusion, of achievement, of redemption, with which every voyage ends. The anchor caught and the *Hyacinth* trembled, in captivity. We stood smiling at one another in the fragrant glimmering darkness and reached out to take one another's hands.

"Oh, Mickey, this is heavenly. Thank you for this trip."

We stood and watched the cabin lights across the water, and the first stars above the hills and the tall phantasmal ships. There were martins hunting in the dusk, making a mournful winnowing sound in the dark air with their wings. Sometimes, from the distant cockpits, voices came with quiet clarity across the harbor. Beyond the black hills there was a pale glow in the sky where the moon was rising. We leaned against the mast to watch it come up, lighting the long shoals of cloud above the bay with milky radiance, breaking clear of the horizon at last and touching everything, the sea, the hills, the rigging, and our transfigured hands and faces, with a tender, luminous patina. Thus glorified, with platinum limbs and lunatic hearts, we idled for a long while on the deck and talked night-talk, moon-talk, sea-talk, in the course of which Margaret said this: "Mickey, please don't make me say, tonight. It isn't fair. How could I possibly say no, on a night like this? But how much pride could you possibly take in my saying yes? And would you really trust me, if I did? Under a moon like that? And would I really believe you meant to ask me? We'd be fools to risk our whole lives on a promise like that; people are fools enough to risk them on one under any conditions. Now, no more love, do you hear? I will not be made love to any more tonight. At least not on a permanent basis." She trembled adorably as she said it, as I have already reported.

Shortly after, she fled into the galley, where we exchanged our platinum bodies for copper ones in the warm glow of the cabin's kerosene lantern, and while she prepared our dinner I lay on a bunk considering the relative value and allure of these two varieties of matter, of which she appeared so curiously to offer me the latter. There was much to be said for platinum, or silver, those chaste metals of innocence; but at the moment, suffering great distraction by reason of her brazed and glowing arms and throat and shoulders, I have to confess that everything was leaning in the direction of the baser metals.

The dinner, which we devoured, was a mixture of equal parts of mushroom soup and canned tuna fish, decorated, for this more formal occasion, with a radish carved in the form of a little coronet.

"What is this we're eating?" I asked.

"It's called *Volaille de la Mer, aux champignons.* Do you like it?"

"Marvelous. It's something like what we had for lunch, isn't it?"

"Oh, no, that was very different; that had parsely."

"Oh, that's right. That's the marvelous thing about a cruise; the food is always so wonderful."

"Isn't it?"

"You get such new and exciting dishes all the time."

"Yes."

After we had eaten, and cleared the table, I conducted at her insistence a very elementary course in navigation—the only kind that I was capable of. Margaret loved learning of any kind; or perhaps I should say that she loved education, rather than learning, for she was not a scholar in any profound or exhaustive sense. What she was in love with was the poetry of crafts and professions, their paraphernalia and vocabulary. It is a very nice trait in a person, and I think what Gerard Manley Hopkins means when he speaks so lovingly of "all trades, their gear and tackle and trim." It was just this kind of infatuation that Margaret evinced when I produced the few and simple instruments of dead reckoning with which the *Hyacinth* was furnished: the charts, dividers, parallel rules, a compass rose, and a battered copy of Chapman's *Small Boat Handling.* She fondled and smiled over them, rapt. There is a formula for determining compass bearing (True Bearing ± Variation = Magnetic Heading ± Deviation = Compass Bearing) which boatmen traditionally memorize by means of the mnemonic phrase True Virtue Makes Dull Company; this piece of lore Margaret received with an especial delight, repeating the phrase voluptuously and mischievously.

"Now there's a really incomparably nautical turn of phrase. I can just hear those clipper captains murmuring it to themselves as they stared out of their cabin windows and watched the last picket fences of New Bedford fade out of sight; and then turned their bows toward India with a smile. The whole history of New England is in that phrase."

"The sea breeds truth," I said, producing an aphorism of my own.

"And such practical truth. I can't think of anything more useful for a girl to learn on her maiden voyage: True virtue makes dull company. I think we ought to adopt it for our motto. For all voyages."

"It sounds like a pretty dangerous principle for a long trip."

"Oh, no, it would help. I know it would help. It would have helped my mother and father. It would have helped almost everybody's mother and father I know."

I could not deny the truth of this.

"Well, just remember you said it," I said. Somewhat hectically, for we had finished our lesson, and set our course for the morning, and now it was time to put these principles to the test. I folded the charts very elaborately and gathered together the instruments in a meticulous and lingering way which Margaret mercifully ignored.

"Who makes the beds?" she said. "Is that the mate's job?"

"Ordinarily. But this is a pretty liberal ship. I'll make my own."

She accepted the offer silently, for which I was grateful since I realized that nothing but silence would have served to temper the air of nervous facetiousness to which I had so inappropriately committed us. (This kind of silence, delicate and articulate, was one of Margaret's most constant and distinguished claims to sensibility; with silence she was so much better able to restore or propagate an understanding, to correct my own extravagances or commonplaces, to create harmonies and intimacies between us, that I am able, through the enormous silence that divides us now, to have hope still.) I delved into my seabag and produced the bedclothes about which I had maintained a certain canny silence of my own. I tossed a pair of folded sheets and a blanket onto either bunk.

"Oh, you brought the bedclothes yourself."

"Yes. Mitch never leaves them aboard. They get damp and musty-smelling if you leave them in a closed boat."

"Why didn't you tell me? I would have brought my own."

"You had enough to think about."

I watched her make her bunk, tossing the white sheets in a cool, fragrant, billowing tumult, then smoothing and tucking them under. I was fascinated; I had never before seen a woman making a bed. My own mother had abdicated this chore since long before I could remember, and the maid who succeeded her in the duty had always sternly expelled me from the bedroom before she arranged it in the mornings.

"Get on with your bed," Margaret said. "What's the matter with you?"

"I like to see you do that."

"Why?"

"You look very pretty, making a bed."

"Well, don't stare at me like that. You're getting me all nervous."

She lifted her suitcase onto the freshly made bunk and began to unpack it, setting onto the blanket a pair of blue nylon pajamas, a hairbrush, a towel, a tube of toothpaste, and a toothbrush. From these articles, and from the open suitcase, there emanated into the little cabin the scent of the mimosa sachet she always used, a very sweet, candidly artificial odor, like the drugstore perfumes with which little girls saturate themselves. I was stricken by the poignance of it; a kind of tender mortification possessed me suddenly—something that the whole of Calvin's *Collected Sermons* could not have effected.

"You're sentimental, aren't you?" Margaret said.

"No."

"Yes, you're very sentimental. Who gets the bathroom first?"

"The strongest."

"I think it should be the smartest."

"All right. Go ahead."

She gathered up her possessions and disappeared into the litle cubicle in the forward passage, and during the time she took to prepare herself for bed—although very brief, it will do nicely —I am going to relate to you the history of my sexual adventures until that moment. They were two: one effected with a sixteen-year-old girl in a rented room full of empty beer bottles and sleeping fellow-airmen on the outskirts of Manila, and the other with a lady much nearer sixty under the shrubbery of a public park in Wellington, New Zealand: both in the course of leaves I was awarded while flying combat duty in the South Pacific. Perhaps they were sordid; I suppose they were (although I regret the term); however, I should like it understood that the girls— or females, rather—were not harlots, and were not, in my opinion, vicious or degraded, notwithstanding the casualness and primitivism of the circumstances; they were simple, generous creatures, bewildered, like myself, by a war they did not understand and for which they were not responsible; and while there was certainly nothing transcendental about either experience, they afforded a kind of bitter, melancholy excitement which corresponded very closely with my requirements at the time. Since this was virtually the only type of introduction to sex permitted by society during the period of my youth, I should say that my education in the matter was thoroughly traditional. With this traditional wisdom to sustain me, I awaited now a night of love with a woman I adored.

She emerged in a moment in her shimmering blue pajamas,

smelling of soap and toothpaste, her face, freshly washed, damp about the temples, pale-lipped, nude of makeup and of the equally cosmetic complications of midday which so infernally elaborate feminine features, bearing that startling elemental look of anonymity with which a woman's face is bleached by the revelatory glare of leisure or desire. Children's faces are like this. And animals'. And especially the faces of flowers, which, however intricate of feature, are ablaze with the same simplicity. She came and leaned against me lightly, laying her open palms against my breast, and I took this revealed face in my hands and studied its floral innocence for several minutes, lulled by the soft fluctuation of her breast against my own, and her breath that smelled of toothpaste.

"Oh, Mickey, you're lovely," I said. "I love you so."

"Then do," she said.

And so I did. I loved her indeed, in her bunk, in the cabin of the little vessel, on the waters of the dark seas that surrounded and sustained us and which seemed to merge and flow confluent with the great, grave, conjugal impulse that had borne us to this place, so happily called Gratitude. It was, truly enough, our wedding, as Margaret insisted, although she steadfastly refused to ceremonialize the occasion.

I woke an hour before she did, and lay in my bunk for that amount of time, watching her across the aisle, still sleeping in her own, feeling a huge, bereaved, and cruel joy in the discovery that the look of innocence and vulnerability with which, so few hours ago, she had so perilously invoked my manhood, was gone forever, and succeeded by one of contented ravishment. I studied every emblem of this transformation with a profound and mournful pride: her flushed and swollen lips, her tangled hair, her body, disposed so luxuriously under the crumpled sheets, as if, even in sleep, aware of its own delicious nakedness and power. I had, a few hours earlier, carried a soft anonymous child to the bunk where now lay sleeping a fierce, phenomenal woman. It had been, as a man, my grievous, beautiful, inabdicable duty. I lay in a patch of scalding sunlight that fell through an open porthole and considered the mystery of this most sovereign of obligations that life and manhood were ever to require of me.

When she awoke she opened her eyes quickly, as if nothing had separated these moments of consciousness, and smiled at me.

"Hello, darling."

"Hello."

We lay looking at one another across the aisle.

"You're beautiful," she said after a moment.

"No, you're the beautiful one. And I made you."

"You certainly did."

"That's not what I meant," I said with some confusion, captivated nevertheless by the poetry of the colloquialism.

"Are you going to get up or anything?" I asked her.

"No."

"You're just going to lie there forever?"

"I'm just going to lie here until you come over and make love to me again. And then I'm going to get up and fry ten thousand eggs and make six gallons of coffee."

"Are you sure? I mean are you sure you're all right?"

"I don't care whether I'm all right or not. Please, darling. Right away, please."

So we made love again, more excitingly this time, if less supernally, with an almost vicious excitement that left us trembling and exhausted; and then lay with our cheeks pressed together in the disheveled bunk, watching the hot white disk of sunlight wander about the cabin as the *Hyacinth* wheeled slowly at her anchor, listening to the creak of rigging and the mewing of gulls through the portholes, and smelling the salty perfume of the morning air, teak and tar and hot canvas.

Later I watched her tottering precariously on one white foot as she plunged her slender legs, one after another, into a pair of sharply pressed white cotton slacks. I saw the dark oaken sheen of her hair as she stroked it with an amber-handled hairbrush. I heard her watery and joyful burbling, from the tiny lavatory, of "Nessun Dorma." I drank in the look of smiling, utterly contented absorption with which, over the hiss and sputter of frying bacon and shining-yolked eggs, she prepared, in spite of her professions of incompetence, the most delicious meal I have ever eaten, and throughout which we exchanged greasy, gloriously spontaneous kisses. Still later we emerged from the dim, delicious privacy of the cabin into a shower of mid-morning sunlight, through whose golden pools on the warm teak she padded with little nude, caressing sounds of her bare feet. A weary yellow butterfly, blown out across the bay by the morning breeze, clung trembling to our rigging, a lovely fragile pennant to our enterprise.

When we lay at berth once more in Annapolis, our little ship secured, our gear assembled in the cockpit for departure, and drank the lees of our last bottle of wine, raising our paper cups with sad, valedictory gestures toward the sunburnt, lapping water of evening, I laid my hand against her glowing cheek and asked again:

"Why don't we get married, Meg? Really, why don't we?"

"We are married."

"No, I mean really."

"Do you mean why don't we do this every day?"

"I guess that's what I mean."

"Well, are you sure that has to involve marriage? I mean what else can we give each other, except children?"

"But I want to be sure you don't get away. I want to be sure it lasts."

"Oh, Mickey, how can you guarantee I'm going to go on loving you just by having a document tucked away in a drawer somewhere? Like a certificate of title you get with a new auto-mobile or a house, or any other piece of valuable registered property. All I can say is that I'll love you as long as I love you. And I'm not going to make a commodity out of my love. If it should end, no certificate of title to it would do you any good. Or me."

"Do you think it will?" I asked.

"I don't know, honestly. All I know is that I love you now.

More than anything. Why don't we drink to that? And to this lovely sea, that we were married on? Isn't that the best thing we can do?"

And, this being indeed the best thing I could do at the time, I did so; the full text of my toast you have before you.

At the end of that month I received my Master's degree, and in celebration of the fact we spent the following day on a picnic at Glen Echo. This is a spot that was reached in those days by taking a streetcar through Georgetown out into the Maryland fields and climbing down through beech forest and sumac scrub to the shore of the Potomac. On our way back we descended from the streetcar in Georgeown and walked for an hour along the ancient cobbled streets, beguiled by the old miniature brick and wooden houses with their iron gates and gardens, drowsing in the air of another century. One of these, with a FOR RENT sign in its parlor window, fascinated Margaret. It was a typical Georgetown house, one of legions that stand wearily along the narrow streets, shifting their weight, as it were, from one aching infirm pilaster to another. Margaret climbed up the worn wooden steps and leaned across the iron balcony to peer into the empty sunny rooms.

We stopped at a tavern and drank a glass of beer.

"If I could find a girl to marry," I said, "I could settle down very happily in a house like that."

"*I'll* marry you," Margaret said.

"I thought you said you wouldn't."

"Oh, well. I've changed my mind."

A month later I bore her up the steps of this little house. The ceremony, far from being perfunctory, had been replete with a bridesmaid (Susannah, a beautiful dark-haired girl who was a classmate of Margaret's and her dearest friend), a best man (Mitch), a pair of trembling, sunburnt Kansas flower girls, a contingent of rugged Midwestern aunts and uncles, a rented, ruinous tuxedo for myself, a distraught rendition of "Oh, Promise Me" by a gigantic mezzo-soprano from Elk Falls, acres of lilies, fern, and gladioli, and a prodigally passionate sermon on the part of a thin, inflamed, anxiety-ridden pastor, whose decline in his profession he had evidently chosen this occasion to reverse. I do not understand women at all. The fact may not strike the reader like a thunderbolt, perhaps; but to me, as an aspiring author, it is a matter of some concern. Still, having insisted upon the introduction of formality into our relationship, I suppose I had no right to protest; but I must confess I was startled by the thoroughness of Margaret's capitulation. Yet I enjoyed it. (I enjoy ceremony of every kind; it is no good pretending otherwise.)

I took a very humble job at the Library of Congress as a stack assistant in the Manuscript Division. At night I studied at George Washington for my Ph.D. Margaret contributed to our survival by working in a welfare agency, where she shepherded underprivileged children. They were years of the typical merry frugality of young married people. In a jumble shop we found a pair of purple china ducks with removable heads (you may have noticed them on the mantel-shelf in the bedroom), in which we deposited coins toward the purchase of an occasional pair of concert tickets. We had a great many friends. We gave parties and attended them. Every summer we went for a commemorative sail together on the *Hyacinth* (it was Mitch's perennial anniversary gift to us). Gradually, we prospered. At the end of five years I was awarded a Doctorate in Classics and was promoted to the grade of G-15. We took vacations in Maine at a cottage on Deer Isle, near the summer camp I had attended as a boy. We acquired a hi-fi set, a library of recordings of baroque music, a station wagon, an eight-place setting of Louis XIV silverware, a set of Johnson Brothers china. I would go into a great deal more detail about these early years of our married life, but for this fact: I suspect they are very much like your own. With the exception, perhaps, that we did not have children.

For this reason, I suppose, the house absorbed much of the devotion which is normally invested in one's heirs. We rehabilitated it with a passion and periodically redecorated it. It went through an Early American, a Georgian, a Spanish Provincial, and finally a Victorian period (one in which I am prepared, somewhat gnomishly, to end my days). The garden was Margaret's chief delight. (To look at it now, with its sundial shattered, its paving stones stained with the rust of the decaying garden chairs, its beds gone wild with fennel and plantain, you would not know that it had once been such a pretty spot.) She grew roses, peonies, cannas, marigolds, and iris, but her special passion were the moonflower vines she planted every spring against the old brick walls. On summer nights she used to get out of bed, steal down the kitchen steps, and sit for hours on the stones of the patio in her pajamas, to watch the white bells open in the moonlight. When we went to France she dried seeds from the blossoms, took them with her in an envelope, and planted them against the wall of our villa at Cap Ferrat.

It took us three summers to pave the garden floor with uncut flagstones, each of which weighs roughly eighty pounds and was hauled there in the trunk of a 1937 Plymouth from the Maryland fields. I remember that one evening, having tugged into its final resting place a particularly large, well-formed, and beautifully colored stone, Margaret said triumphantly, sitting down cross-legged on our prize: "Oh, what a lovely day! I do love stealing things, don't you, darling?"

"Yes, very much."

"It makes such a bond between us, don't you think? Being partners in crime?"

"I do, yes."

"Do you think we might pry a couple of the smaller ones out of the Washington Monument some night?"

"We can certainly have a try at it."

She studied the late evening sunlight on the moonflower vines against the soft rose-colored brick.

"I like to think of us," she said, "as a pair of marvelous gay corsairs, preying on the whole world together."

. . .

One evening, thirteen years later, Margaret paid me an un-expected call at my office in the Library. I had stayed late to work on the preparation of a new acquisition for cataloguing. This is a thing which I had begun to do with increasing fre-quency, but seldom with such unassailable intentions or genu-ine delight, for the material on which I was working in this case was the complete manuscript collection of the poetry of A. E. Housman. This magnificent addition to our shelves was a gift of Mrs. Gertrude Clarke Whittall, a lady of generosity and vision to match her means, who had made the purchase at auction and very recently presented it to the Library. It be-longed, by every right of tradition and sentiment, in the British Museum; but some of the passion and avidity of the True Col-lector—a fellowship in which I was by now irredeemably en-rolled—can be seen in the fact that I gave the consideration very untroubled regard indeed; I positively gloated over our good fortune. But, to do myself justice, for more than merely professional reasons, for Housman was a poet for whom I had had, since my high-school days, an unparalleled devotion. It was this devotion which had prevailed on our Division Chief to assign the manuscripts to me for processing, since they did not properly fall within my province, as an Orientalia expert. Those sorrowfully intractable verses, so deceptively tinkling out such cosmic themes, had haunted, comforted, and dazzled me as a boy, a young man, and now again—as I held them in my literally trembling hands and read, in his own handwriting, the burningly tender dedication to *More Poems*—now again, as a middle-aged, troubled, truant householder. *This is for all ill-treated fellows,* it said,

> *Unborn and unbegot.*
> *For them to read when they're in trouble,*
> *And I am not.*

And now I read them, holding them between my very fingers, in the slightly faded ink in which he had written them down, on the foolscap pages which his own hands had once shuffled into place! Troubled and unbegot I was; and smiled at the largess he cast to me from what I fervently hoped was his own now perfect and perpetual ease. That I alone, of all the billions of people on the teeming earth, should be privileged to sit alone, on this evening, in this vast silent room and hold these pages, so evidently dedicated to myself, in my own hands, was a turn of chance and fortune so awesome that, as I say, it made me tremble.

The manuscripts had come to us from the custody of the poet's brother, Lawrence Housman, who had arranged them in order of publication and by grouping into the contents of the three small volumes which made up his lifetime work, and the dozen or so incomplete or unsatisfactory verses and variorums which had never been published. This order I intended to preserve, with only the possible alteration of inserting the variorums alongside the stanzas for which they were intended as alternate readings, so that there was little to do in the way of classification or organization beyond numbering and card-indexing the pages. My chief occupation was in preparing the manuscripts physically for shelving. This consisted of enclosing each sheet in a film of Durtite, a thin, tough, transparent, light-polarized synthetic, and sealing it along all edges, so that the manuscript was contained in a moisture-proof, airtight, wear-proof, and fade-resistant envelope, preserved, to the best of technical ability, for centuries. I sat in the laboratory to do this, because the sealing required the application of an electrically heated clothes-iron-like device. It was not really a laboratory at all, but simply a divided-off section of the large communal office which was furnished with basic chemical and optical equipment for the restoration and preservation of ancient manuscripts. I liked working there alone at night, particularly on winter evenings when it became dark very early. In the huge, silent, softly lighted room, sealed off from the strident icy streets of the winter night outside, streaming with taxicabs and home-ward-bound pedestrians leaning against the cold wind, there was a sense of peace, seclusion, and warm eternal conversation with the past that I drank in like wine or firelight. I think Margaret resented this. She had a right, of course, to resent the delayed or solitary dinners that it forced upon her, and the other occasional disruptions of our daily life, such as hastily substituted theater companions or forfeited dinner invitations; but more than this, I think, she resented the privacy of my contentment there. It excluded her; and more than that, it did not require her; and even more (I shall stop at nothing) it may have been a refuge from her love. Love, I have found, if one is not absolutely equal to its responsibilities—and who is so divinely proportioned?—can lay on one (infrequently, of course, but nonetheless) a burden which, like the weight of any grace, must be shifted from time to time on man's imperfect shoulders. Women do not appear to understand this fact, and so I am going to take a moment of your time, ladies, to instruct you in it.

Man should never cease, of course, to seek perfection; but he should be sustained in the effort by the assurance that he will never find it. There should be, for a truly beautiful—though, of course, imperfect—world, in every orchard, one twisted, fruitless tree; on every street, one harlot; in every sky, one cloud; in every garden, one serpent; and from every day of love, one hour of liberty.

Now my own such hours of liberty were becoming, perhaps, a bit more frequent than the theory would normally require, but that may have been because Margaret yielded them to me somewhat reluctantly in the first place, and nothing is better calculated to make a man overstep his prerogatives.

Well, I was happy, then; as a sailor is happy only when at sea, but perfectly happy only when at sea and in possession of the knowledge that there is a woman in a warm Nantucket parlor dreaming of his return. I had loosened my necktie and removed my jacket and shoes, which gave me a wonderfully elemental feeling. I had brewed a cup of coffee on a hot plate I had recently installed in a service closet for the purpose. I had lit my pipe and set it carefully aside, since I detested it. And in the Faustian rays of the laboratory table lamp I had pored, for I don't know how many hours, over my priceless manuscripts, preserving them for generations I should never know. There was no door to the laboratory area, and the outer door to the division itself had evidently been unlocked by the janitor, because I did not hear Margaret enter. I was very startled to see her.

"Good God!" I exclaimed. "You scared the life out of me."

"I'm sorry," she said. "I tiptoed, because it seemed like such a holy place."

"It is," I said. "Just look at this. These are the Housmans."

She came to the table and peered down at them. "Oh, aren't they wonderful. Can I touch?"

"Yes. Touch this one that I haven't done. Touch the paper itself. You'll be the last person who does, for centuries."

"Oh, that's a lovely idea." She leaned down to read the lines, smiling at her privilege. It was a page that contained the three stanzas of the poem that is numbered VI in *A Shropshire Lad*:

> *When the lad for longing sighs,*
> *Mute and dull of cheer and pale,*
> *If at death's own door he lies,*
> *Maiden, you can heal his ail.*
>
> *Lover's ills are all to buy:*
> *The wan look, the hollow tone,*
> *The hung head, the sunken eye,*
> *You can have them for your own.*
>
> *Buy them, buy them: eve and morn*
> *Lovers' ills are all to sell.*
> *Then you can lie down forlorn;*
> *But the lover will be well.*

"Does it have to be that one?" Margaret said.

"Yes, they're in order. You have to take what you get."

"Oh." She put her fingertips down slowly onto the page

and ran them along the lines, lingering almost imperceptibly upon the last.

"Now I'll seal it up. You can watch. Sit on the stool, there."

She perched on a laboratory stool, hooking her heels on the rungs, and leaned forward to watch the operation.

"You've got your shoes off," she said.

"Yep."

"Do you always work barefooted?"

"Stockingfooted, for poetry. Barefooted for Vedas, Apocrypha; really formal stuff."

"You mean the more reverent you get, the more clothes you take off? That's interesting."

"Absolutely. Watch this, now. This stuff keeps out ultraviolet rays."

"It's sort of the way they seal up pork chops at the supermarket, isn't it?"

"Not even remotely. You've got to be a Doctor of Philosophy to do this."

"You've got coffee, too," she said, casting her eyes about.

"Oh, yes."

"All the comforts of home," Margaret said. "And some additional ones."

"Yes. Now I clip it, see, with this cutter. I have a feeling you're not entirely engrossed."

"I am. I was just wondering why you had a pipe. You never smoke a pipe at home."

"Academic formality. We have our code, you know."

"What is your code? I'd love to know."

"It's printed in full on the back of the washroom door, if you want to read it."

"Just tell me about it. What does it say?"

" 'Do not pour chemicals or other caustic materials in the sink.' "

"Oh. You have such delicate plumbing, then?"

"It gets a little upset," I said, "when exposed to foreign, irritating substances."

"Foreign, irritating substances."

"Yes. There, now. It belongs to the ages." I handed the processed sheet of manuscript to her. She held it by the edges and studied it, unsmiling.

"I don't like it," she said. "It's a really dreadful poem."

"Well, we don't rewrite them, you know. Our duties here are not primarily creative, but custodial."

"Like your domestic ones," Margaret said.

I stared at her for a moment and plucked the manuscript rather roughly from her hands, turning again to my table.

"How did you happen to pay me this delightful visit, anyway?" I asked in a moment.

"Well, it gets a little quiet around there sometimes, you know. And they seem to be doing all reruns on the TV. There was a 'Doctor Kildare' that I'd seen eight times, so I thought I'd just hop on the bus and see what was going on on the academic front. I thought maybe you'd take me out to dinner, if I could tear you out of the womb of the centuries."

"You haven't eaten yet?"

"No, just a pack of potato chips."

"What time is it, anyway? My God, it's nine o'clock. Aren't you starved?"

"Aren't you? Or does somebody usually run up with a sandwich for you about now? Some pretty little secretary or someone?"

"What the hell are you talking about, anyway?"

"I was just wondering what you did about dinner when you stay up here this late."

"You know what I do. I stop at that little place across the street, on Pennsylvania. Or I have a bite when I get home, if it's closed."

"Well, let's stop over there now, then. I love these little neighborhood places; they're usually so cosy, aren't they?"

"Some of them have that virtue," I said.

"Plus a large selection of really good food."

"Oh, yes."

"And congeniality, no doubt."

"Relative congeniality, yes."

"I can't wait to see it. I may start eating there myself."

I began to lock up my equipment and to put the manuscripts away in a silent, fastidious way which was intended as a very oblique rebuke to her. They went into a wall safe, where I installed them with a grave, solicitous care, implying vaguely that she was included in that world of philistinism from which I meant to protect them. I think she recognized this, since she gave a soft bitter chuckle of understanding. I locked the safe, spun the dial defiantly, and made several unnecessary, fussily ostentatious adjustments of pencils, rulers, documents, and boxes of paper clips on my desk-top (repairing the defilement that her intrusion had worked upon it).

"My goodness, how tidy you are," Margaret said. "Like a little old withered-up bachelor."

"I have a little old withered-up soul."

"You should learn not to advertise the fact."

"It is too generally known to conceal," I said.

"Oh, really? I didn't know there was such universal speculation about the state of your soul. On the part of your staff, no doubt. The secretaries must spend hours talking about it."

I took my overcoat off the tree-rack, struggled into it, and with no invitation to her to follow, walked across the length of the division office between the vacant desks and chairs, pausing at the corridor door to switch off gangs of area lights. She slid off the stool in a moment and came silently toward me.

"It's so lovely, going out to dinner with you," she said in the elevator. "One feels so infinitely desirable."

I stared in silence at the consecutively lighting and darkening floor buttons as we descended. The elevator contained our torment like a miasma. Outside, the cold air of the winter night was very little more congenial. At the curb I offered Margaret my arm with a gravity which intentionally approached parody. She accepted it in much the same spirit and we crossed the windy avenue with our heads bowed into the gale and our coats flapping; an experience which once would have been a laughing, exhilarating one, terminating, with reddened cheeks and a huge sense of comfort, in the warmth of a neighborhood coffee shop, where we would have talked for hours. It amounted, now, to a shuddering, bitter, obligatory campaign against the elements.

The coffee shop appeared to have been equally debased: the steam on the cold windows was speckled with grime; in the grim frosted bowls of the suspended ceiling lights lay the huge magnified shadows of the corpses of flies; from the kitchen came the suffocating reek of stale cooking fat; and the waitress was no pretty, impudently familiar wench, but a bleak, flat-breasted slattern with pale pimply skin and devastated eyes. This composition of horrors seemed to reassure Margaret somewhat.

"Well, you can't have gotten into much trouble in *here*," she said.

I very nearly assured her that most of my troubles originated at home; it was not mercy that forestalled me, but my wounded astonishment at the insolence of her insinuation.

We ordered veal cutlets, for the reason that this was the only item still in supply (I have for years been discouraged by the apparent inexhaustibility of veal cutlet in cheap restaurants). While we waited for it to arrive we sat, both, with elbows on the table and chins on our laced fingers, staring into the windowpane. I saw there our opposed images, identically reflecting despair, and closed my eyes.

"Are you tired?" Margaret asked.

"No."

"You look tired."

"Well, maybe I am, a little."

"I'm sorry if I was nasty, Mickey."

"All right."

"You're not in a very communicative mood, are you?"

"I *was*," I said.

"Oh. And I ruined it all, did I; with my vulgar observations?"

"It hasn't been improved," I said, "by anything you've said so far."

She made a movement with her lips, parched, feral, awful, as if she were about to say some truly unspeakable thing, and then said nothing. Only her eyes spoke, repeating the question she had asked all evening, constantly, with every word she uttered. That they had asked every evening, for months. For years, I am afraid. How does one reply to such a question? With easy charm? With studied equanimity? With a promise of better days to come? Nothing. When the question has been asked so often, and the possible replies to it exhausted, it can be answered with nothing that I know of. Does this mean, then, that I had fallen out of love with her? No, reader, I am almost tempted to say it means the opposite: that I had fallen *in* love with her, at last; but this has such an offensively occult sound that I shall simply say, as I have said to a far more indignant witness than yourself: I don't know what it means. We fell into our habitual silence.

I wish I dared to propose it as a universal truth that conversation is a substitute for understanding between persons—or, to put it a bit more agreeably, an expression of the desire to achieve that understanding—and that, conversely, silence is the expression of the consummation of that desire; but I am afraid the disingenuousness of such a proposition would be seen through immediately. Silence of such complexity, such profundity, such sublimity, that it contains within it all the redeemed actions and passions of its principals is not known upon this noisy earth, and therefore, to be sure, no earthly relationship can make claim to it. To this I agree. I will go further: I will agree that even such modest and imperfect degrees of silence as can be observed in human marital relationships do not necessarily represent a corresponding degree of understanding in the persons involved. Alas, silence between married mortals is a very curious thing. It *can* represent, of course, understanding of a very great degree; but on the other hand it can represent a passionate reserve, an armed truce, speechless perplexity, boredom, stealth, or the cunning noncommittal that precedes a coup d'état. Which of these figured most heavily in the silences that had grown habitual to Margaret and me I am not sure, but I am forced to admit by that smiling reader in the front row that there was perhaps an element of each.

There may be in this audience one or two unmarried persons, who will not find this confession consistent with my statement that I had not fallen out of love with Margaret. Young people, the only course I could recommend that would persuade you on the point is a long and hard one—perhaps as long as twelve years—and is more than can fairly be demanded of any reader. I must suffer your skepticism, therefore, and depend upon the sympathy of my fellow collectors for permission to say that I sat in armed, perplexed, bored, stealthy, supine silence, awaiting the arrival of veal cutlet, with the woman that I loved. After some time I turned my head from the ugly view of winter street, unlaced my fingers, examined my palms, and raised my eyes to hers.

"Was there any mail?"

"Yes, a card from Mitch. I've got it here." She turned to snap open her purse on the seat beside her, fished out a postcard, and dropped it on the table in front of me.

"What does he say?"

"He's sold the boat."

"The *Hyacinth*?"

"What other boat does he have?"

The postcard showed a colored view of the Dinner Key Marina in Miami: boats, docks, palm trees, coral sand, and blue water, all blazing in the Florida sunlight. On the back of it Mitch had written: *Eighteen days down on the Intra-Coastal. Great trip, but had trouble with the old girl. Hate to tell you guys this, but I'm going to sell her. Great deal going here on a second-hand Vanguard. But I'll bring you one of her sheet-winches for a souvenir. See you next month. Best, Mitch.*

"What's a Vanguard?" Margaret said.

"They're about thirty-five feet, I think," I said. "They're made out of fiber glass."

"Fiber glass."

"It's rot-proof," I said. "And worm-proof."

"I don't believe it," Margaret said. "Nothing is."

"Well, that's what they claim. The only sort of maintenance they're supposed to need is antifouling paint. With a wooden hull, like the *Hyacinth*'s, you've got to worry about teredo, dry rot, caulking—"

"What I'd like to know," Margaret said, "is do you really mind?"

"Of course I mind." I raised my eyes, and having held her gaze for a moment with a look of quiet indignation, tossed the postcard onto the table. She picked it up and began to tear it carefully into strips. As a gesture of exhausted forbearance, it far surpassed my own: deliberate, bitter, and clearly intended as an overture to something even worse. It made me cold with apprehension.

"Suppose we talk about something else for a while," she said.

"All right. What?"

"Us. I think it's time we had quite a long talk on that subject."

Readers, I don't know how many of you have lived for years, as I once did, in almost hourly dread of this Long Talk. I had thus far managed to defer it—only barely, and temporarily—by means of a magnified concern for such fortuitous confusions as the Cuban Revolution, race relations, or the Indonesian uproar, by sudden spurious enthusiasms for the latest play or novel or an Alec Guinness movie, providently playing at the local cinema. By claims of professional preoccupations, tax worries, anxieties about insurance matters, broken plumbing, or a misplaced receipt for carburetor repairs. By tragic imitations of the symptoms of indigestion, migraine, influenza. They were equally ignoble in their employment of such attitudes as indignation, anger, mockery, fatigue, or naked fear.

I do not think they deceived Margaret, but they propitiated her; they must, in their very crudeness, subterfuge, or savagery, sufficiently have revealed my terror in the face of the Long Talk, and the confessions, humiliations, and impossible resolutions with which it threatened me, to make her relent, and postpone that terrible occasion for my sake. Perhaps, too, even in those panic-stricken, extemporized, and shabbily transparent evasions of mine, there was discernible, to one of Margaret's intelligence, a principle of some kind. Threadbare and desperate, no doubt, but ancient; one to which generations of sufferers have clung when purer, less compromising ones have failed: the principle of Making The Best Of It. It is not attractive, of course, to anyone as idealistic as Margaret; and as a foundation for marriage, suffers from a certain lack of grandeur; yet women as a whole are wise enough, I think, at least to consider it in critical circumstances, and certainly to accord their sympathy—temporarily, at any rate—to anyone desperate enough to propose it, however indirectly. It has the advantage, they come to understand, of keeping things going, however ignominiously; and this is a compromise which many women are prepared to accept until life or imagination offers them a more satisfactory alternative.

And what more, after all, is accomplished by the Long Talk? The decision it must inevitably produce will be either to divorce or, on the part of the delinquent member, to improve his ardor to an acceptable degree. One was intolerable to me, the other a patent absurdity. I preferred the ancient, muddling, makeshift, but strangely poetic principle of Making The Best Of It. There was precedent for it; it was the way of my ancestors; it had kept society alive for two thousand years.

Therefore I procrastinated. I hemmed, I hawed, I was angry, coy, innocent, indignant, and insouciant by turns; I tried by every beggarly, importunate, and basically craven way I could devise to convince a woman for whom I no longer felt desire that I loved and needed her. But this, of course, will not do. To a wife, nothing will substitute, as assurance that she is still desirable, for desire. As long as he physically desires her, all else can be forgiven in a man: brutality, drunkenness, unpunctuality, uncleanliness, arrogance, anything at all. But let her feel that she no longer excites his desire, and even his noblest qualities will become for her contemptible—his wisdom, pedantry; his discretion, cowardice; his gentleness, docility; his chivalry, pomposity; his reverence, superstition; his morality, convention; and his love, a senile solicitude which she endures with the same disdain as does the high-spirited inmate of an almshouse the charity of that institution. It is flattering to be desired; it is humiliating to be pitied. And pity, evidently, is the prevalent feminine translation of love without sufficient and continuous desire. Margaret was not the kind of a woman to endure humiliation endlessly, I knew; nor to accept the charity of my hearth until better arrangements could be made. And so, although in my dogged, desperate way I held tight to the principle of Making The Best Of It for as long as possible, it was only a question of time, I realized, until the Long Talk became imperative. The time had come, apparently.

There was no way that I could any longer, with any semblance of dignity or veracity, postpone it. Her eyes were dark with determination. The frustration of the years had fulminated behind them and burned there, in a kind of purple incandescence. She was no longer to be denied a Reckoning. She would accept no more of my pusillanimous diversions. If they had ever had any power to deceive her, I had long ago exhausted them all: the whole range of current affairs, physical debilities, the arts, the antics of our friends, professional or personal anxieties. We had not been separated by as much as twenty-four hours since the day of our marriage; she knew every book I had read, every play or film I had seen, every concert I had heard, every infirmity to which I was vulnerable, every confusion or enthusiasm to which I had been subject for the past twelve years. That, I reflected, turning my eyes again toward the dismal stretch of Independence Avenue, was my chief dilemma. I could no longer beguile her. Through the soiled window I watched a sailor, holding a laughing brown-haired girl by the hand, go galloping through clouds of white steam that issued from the perforations of a manhole cover in the center of the windy street. There goes a fortunate man, I thought. Sailors have no such dilemmas as my own. Their desire, spaced out by years of intermittent voyages and stimulated by long absences and adventures in the far ports of the world, must be inexhaustible. What a blessing it would be to be a sailor. Or even a traveling salesman. Or one of those business executives whose work required constant flights to Rio, Rome, or San Francisco. If my own work had included some such requirement it might have made all the difference. Even an occasional convention, perhaps, for no longer than a week. A convention. The phrase had a delicious suavity. I repeated it. A week away from her. An unprecedented, revivifying, prospective-generating, life-giving week of liberty. I would come back full of stored-up energies, freshened vision, reanimated spirits, clothed in Ulyssean mystery. She would await me with the sweet impatience of Penelope. All past confusions would be swept into oblivion by the tide of our regenerated passion. I felt an extraordinary injection of vitality, a kind of ethereal levity which I would call inspiration if I were not embarrassed by the piece of cunning that was the source of it. A business trip! A convention! I was a fool not to have thought of it long ago.

"I don't know if you heard me—" Margaret said.

"What? I was looking at that manhole cover out there. You see it? All that steam coming out of it? You suppose it's going to blow up or something?"

"It's a strange thing you never notice the steam coming out of *me*," Margaret said. "I think I *am* going to blow up someday."

I turned upon her a round-eyed gaze of concern. "What's the matter?" I asked. "Have you got a headache?"

"A headache. I have a headache, yes. Also a stomach-ache. And a liver-ache, and a lung-ache. And especially a heart-ache.

Everything inside of me aches. Do you think you could tear your attention away from that manhole cover for just a minute and give a little of it to me?"

"I didn't think you felt very well," I said. "You seemed pretty crabby. Have you got a temperature or anything?"

"Yes. It's three hundred and sixty-five. It goes up one degree every day of the year."

"Listen," I said, "do you really want to wait for this awful veal cutlet? Why don't you come home and get in bed, and let me make you a bowl of hot soup? You'll feel a lot better, honest, Meg. I'll put the César Franck on, and you can just drift off to sleep."

"I don't want to drift off to sleep," Margaret said. "I want to talk. For quite a while."

"Well, you shouldn't sit here and talk all night, if you're feeling bad."

"Oh, yes, I should. I'll feel a hell of a lot worse if I don't. Stop being so damned patronizing, will you? It isn't hot soup that I need. And I don't want any nursemaid. I want a *husband*. Now are you going to listen to me, or not?"

"Sure, I'll listen to you. But you don't need to shout. I'm only about a foot away."

"And are you going to *talk*?"

"All right. If you really feel this is the best place in the world for an intimate discussion about family matters. And if you think you're in the best possible frame of mind for it."

"You're not, I suppose?"

"Well, no, not really. I've just put in ten solid hours of work, I'm sitting in the worst restaurant in America, attended by the ugliest waitress in the world, there's a draft around my ankles, there's some kind of a Hungarian or something sitting over there hanging on our every word, and in just a minute I've got to eat a veal cutlet, which I despise above all things in the universe. But if you really think it's the perfect opportunity, why, go ahead."

Margaret clenched her teeth so that her jaw muscles bulged.

"And when we get home," she said, "you'll bundle yourself into bed, and be asleep in five minutes, I suppose."

"No, not if you want to talk. Of course I've got to be at the office by seven in the morning, and get the Housmans finished up, so I can be ready to leave on Thursday—"

"Leave for where?" Margaret said.

"On this trip. I've got to be in Slagheap Thursday morning."

"*Slagheap?*"

"Yes. There's an A.L.A. meeting there I'm supposed to go to. Cornelius just told me this morning he'd like me to represent the division."

"He just told you this morning?"

"Yep."

"Well, why didn't you tell me, for God's sake?"

"If you think back over the last half-hour," I said, "you'll see I haven't had much opportunity."

"Oh, Lord, Mickey, do you have to?"

"It looks like it. There's going to be a lot of stuff on Aramaics and the Scrolls, and I guess Cornelius wants a report on it. Why? Do you mind?"

"Do I *mind?* Doesn't it occur to you that I ever get lonely? Just the *semblance* of a husband is better than no husband at all. How long are you going to be gone?"

"How long? Oh. I don't know, for sure." The idiocy of the whole idea, now that my panic had subsided somewhat, was becoming manifest; the inconvenience, expense, utter mendacity and cowardice of the thing—not to mention the very real danger of her eventually discovering its fraudulence—appalled me suddenly. The duration of my trip dwindled very swiftly. "Just a few days, I guess. Over the weekend. There may be a session on Monday that I'll have to get in on, I'm not sure."

Margaret dropped her chin onto her laced fingers and stared at a tomato stain on the tablecloth. She did not move for many minutes; not even her eyes blinked. Nor was it an idle stare, but one of burning inward activity, her eyes slightly narrowed with intensity, as if aching with the turmoil and complexity of the problems they enclosed. She was entirely remote. She had never been farther from me. She was almost, I realized with sudden fear, beyond the reach or need of my pity, charity, or love. She had the brave, lorn, solitary look of a fledgling animal about to fly or swim or stand, for the first time, alone.

Reader, do you know the meaning of remorse? Do you know what it is to realize that finally, after twelve years of the depredation you have fulsomely called love, you have reduced a human being to that state of terrible infantile solitude? I pray that you do not. Seeing this first of all her private agonies, one that I had created and therefore dared not ask to share or comfort, I felt remorse that was a nausea of the spirit.

The waitress came and set before us on that bleak, soiled cloth the two most monstrously unattractive meals I have ever seen. The reality of the act of eating is generally fairly successfully concealed for us by the proprietors of better-class restaurants by means of linen, floral arrangements, silverware, candlelight, music, tasteful furnishings, and the other ornaments, diversions, and ceremonies of their trade. Not in this case. I have never in my life been subjected to a more nakedly, obscenely revelatory event than the serving up of those two segments of the bodies of fellow-animals. Perhaps the remorse engendered, or at any rate enforced, the revelation; almost certainly, now that I think of it. In any case, I could not eat.

"Margaret, let's go home," I said. I did not dare to lay my hand on hers, as I longed to do. I did not even dare to call her "Meg," or "Maggie," or "Mickey." I scarcely dared to use the word "home." Yet it seemed the least presumptuous way in which I could express my yearning to preserve all of those prerogatives, to reclaim her from the solitude to which she had withdrawn, where I myself had banished her.

"Yes, let's," she said, not in a tone of warm affinity, but coldly, definitely, in a voice which asked no longer for consideration, whose tenderness threatened to be replaced forever by fortitude.

So much for the remorse I spoke of.

Remorse, theoretically, should be a very redemptive experience, because it breaks, temporarily, the terrible self-perpetuating cycle of marital discord; it makes one gentle. It suspends, for the moment at least, the habitual irascibility of the unhappily married man; it changes his tone of voice, the quality of his gaze, the inveterate irony and umbrage of his manner. He becomes courtly, solicitous, and for a time, determined to do more than Make The Best Of It. And if he has been sufficiently chastened, sufficiently shaken out of his truculence or despair by the experience, he may, in this period of humility, find the inspiration and resolve to set his course aright. He may, that is, if there are solutions which will yield to inspiration and resolve. I did not find any. I found that after this period of muted, mollified considerateness my remorse served only as a kind of subterranean fuel for future fires of misery. Remorse leads to guilt, guilt to further debility, debility to a more deeply indured, more dangerously offensive pattern of constant dudgeon and hostility. On this particular evening the whole wretched cycle seemed to become infernally accelerated: by the time I got her home, heated a can of vegetable soup and brought it to her in the bedroom, my remorse-begotten tenderness had already declined through guilt to a state of total romantic debility.

I sat on the edge of her chaise longue and stirred my portion of the can of soup that I was sharing with her. It was in a pretty blue bowl from her set of Johnson Brothers china that I had given her for Christmas. The room was warm and comfortable and saturated with her presence: the blue draperies, the toile coverlet, the Victorian writing desk, the dressing table with my photograph as a child in the silver frame, the Fragonard prints, the faint violet fragrance that perfumed the air. One or two of her books were scattered on the deep, lavender-dyed lambskin at my feet. Margaret sat before me at her dressing table in a dust-blue velvet dressing gown, brushing her loose and glowing hair in the soft light of a floor lamp that was held aloft by a pair of cherubim. May I be allowed one slightly Victorian sentiment, since it is in keeping with the furnishings? I loved this room, because it was where Margaret lived.

Now, this being the case, can anyone in the audience explain to me why, with so many of the requisites of romance at hand—art, velvet, soup, perfume, lamplight, and Margaret's ineffable presence itself—I was unable to profit by the occasion to the extent of making love to her? Especially considering the indispensability of such action on my part at this particular point in our affairs? To those of you whose discomfort, mirth, or indignation has been provoked by the question, my apology goes with it; to the more philosophical, the invitation to write out your reply (on a single sheet of paper, if possible) and drop it in the suggestion box at the entrance as you leave. The few of you remaining are asked to move down into the first few rows, so that I may use a somewhat less strenuous tone of voice while I describe the following abbreviated scene.

There was no sound for several moments but the whisper of the brush through her hair, the clink of china, and the crackle of a Saltine which I crumbled carefully into my soup; and, very occasionally, a thin, shrill whistle, where the winter wind drove at the windowsills. Margaret laid down her brush, lifted her spoon and touched her lips with it, but did not drink.

"Is it too hot?" I asked.

"A little. I can wait."

"Put a couple of Saltines in it."

"They get too mushy." She watched me darkly for a moment. "I am really dazed by all this attention. I wonder what it means?"

"Why does it have to mean anything?" I said.

"Everything means something."

"Not necessarily. It is sometimes better to accept life as a meaningless continuum, with only occasional moments of grace."

"Oh, for God's sake. Why do you have to talk such drivel?

It seems to me we're always talking drivel at each other, and never saying anything of the slightest importance." She raised the empty spoon and blew on it thoughtfully for a moment, her eyes wandering across the room. "When did we start doing that? Have we always done that? We can't have. It seems to me we used to understand each other. We used to say important things."

"The things I have to say haven't changed much," I said. "It's just that you regard them as less important. Maybe because they haven't changed."

She moved her eyes to mine and watched me studiously for a moment.

"Well, *that* makes a certain amount of sense," she said. She frowned with a sudden look of contrition. "Do I do that, honestly?"

"Do what?"

"Oh, get tired of what you say. Get bored. I suppose I do." Her frown deepened. "Which started first, I wonder?" She closed her eyes and shook her head with disgust. "Lord, we're all such monsters, aren't we?"

"I don't think so," I said.

"I do." She turned back to the mirror and studied her face in it in a lingering, scrupulous way. This mirror was the original Victorian one that had been manufactured with the dressing table, and Margaret had never had it refinished, on the grounds that such an act would have spoiled its look of authenticity. It was blotched and veined, its mercury backing eroded by the reflected images of half a century. A condition which produced in one's reflection, when visible at all, the rather desolate and ominous effect of being viewed through fathoms of murky water. I was accustomed to Margaret craning forward and peering closely into it under the very best conditions of light and leisure. She was doing so now, however, with a look of unusual attentiveness and alarm. She suddenly suspended her scrutiny entirely and clutched her head in agony, sitting frozen.

"Oh, my *God*," she said.

I was terrified. I thought she was suffering an untimely stroke or heart attack, or some other of those disorders to which an increasing number of our relatives and friends were yearly falling victim. I sprang from the chaise longue, spilling my bowl of soup across the lavender lambskin.

"What is it?" I cried.

"I've. Got. *Gray. Hair*," she said in a soft, stricken voice.

"My God. I thought you'd had a stroke."

"Look. Look at this." She turned toward me and bowed her head for my inspection.

"Where? What? I don't see anything." I was suddenly possessed by her own desperate disbelief. I saw them all too well, but I scrabbled my fingertips about in her hair in the idiotic hope of concealing them forever, or perhaps, mysteriously unknown to her, plucking them out of her head before their presence could be irredeemably confirmed.

"Well, don't mess it all up. I had them right *there*." She turned back to the mirror and peering into it sorted out the strands of her hair until she had discovered them again.

"Oh, they *are*! I *knew* it." She stared into the glass. "What in the name of God I've done to deserve this," she said in measured lifeless tones, "I wish someone would tell me." Then suddenly, astonishingly, her face crumbled in a piteous childish way which was the last thing in the world I would have expected of her. It made me ache, truly. Such a throe of pain and anger ran through me that I felt like raising my face to heaven and crying out with monstrous impertinence, "Why don't You leave Margaret *alone*! You had to twist her hand all up, and then You gave her a husband who can't love her properly, and now look what You're doing to her *hair*!"

"Well, Jesus *Christ*," I said, strangely turning my anger against Margaret herself in a bitter, churlish, scarcely less profane compromise with heaven. "Just look at that rug. Just look at my pants."

"Your *pants*? Just look at my *hair*."

"Well, my God, the way you yelled, I thought you'd had a stroke."

"You said that," Margaret said coldly, her voice and face now recomposed—upon the same foundation-stone of anger, apparently, as I had found. "About the only thing that seems to worry *you* is that you spilled a little soup on your pants. It's all right for you to be so self-contained about it; you're *five years older* than I am, and *you* don't *have* any gray hair."

"My gray is all inward," I said. "What I have is a gray soul."

"Oh, that's terribly funny. Maybe it's just as well you don't. The most incongruous thing in the world for you to have would be a gray beard; it's supposed to connote wisdom, isn't it?"

"Look, it's not as bad as all that. Maybe you're becoming interesting, at last. Look at Federico Fellini; you think he's fascinating *because* he's got gray hair."

"He's a *man*," Margaret said. "A certain amount of decay is irresistible in a man. In a woman it's just disgusting. Don't try to give me any of your cold comfort, anyway. Just let me die in dignified acceptance."

"Well, fine, if you can manage it," I said. "But if we could, we'd put the poets, stonemasons, ministers, psychiatrists, and a good part of the floral trade out of business."

"Oh, I guess that's why you say it isn't so *bad;* I never realized how much the national economy depends on despair."

"Got to keep things running," I said. "We all must do our part."

"Well, I'd a hell of a lot rather chip in with a couple of babies," Margaret said. "I think I'd rather keep a laundryman in business, anyway, than those poets and ministers and florists. Hanging their damned wreaths and garlands all over life. Who needs it?" She turned her head and stared desolately at the soup-stained rug. "And soup on my lambskin. I don't know. I just don't know how much more I can stand."

I knelt down and mopped at the blob of tomato-colored

soup with my napkin. "It'll be all right. We'll just throw it in the washer tomorrow and it'll be fine."

"You can't just throw them in the washer. Susie did that with hers and it came all to pieces."

"Well then, we'll get a new one."

"Yes, that's what people do these days, isn't it? When things wear out they just get a new one."

"Only if the thing is expendable," I said. "If it has no intrinsic value."

"Like the *Hyacinth*."

I dropped the sodden napkin into my empty bowl, came over to the dressing table and stood behind her, laying my hands on her shoulders.

"Poor Maggie," I said. "Everything happens to her at once." I saw in the mirror that she was crying.

"Some days," she said, "you just feel everything slipping away from you. And now I've got these awful gray hairs." She raised her hand and touched her temple with her fingertips. "I'm going to pull them out, that's what I'm going to do."

"You'd better not," I said. "Leave them alone. I love them."

"Why? Just tell me why?"

"Because they're yours, I guess." The wind whistled thinly around the sills. "Listen to that wind," I said. "God, what a night."

"You can say that again." She huddled her shoulders together in a shiver. I leaned down and kissed her hair.

"Mickey, I love being here with you," I said, "in our nice room, out of the cold. There's nowhere else I'd rather be. Don't you know that? I'm sorry about the rest of it." She leaned her head back and pressed it against my breast, lying quietly with her eyes closed. "Now have some nice warm soup," I said. "It'll be easy on your gums, poor old soul."

"Now listen, you," she said. "Don't you know when you're ahead? You'd better just keep quiet for a while!" But she grinned up at me very nicely, which soothed the cold fear that had developed in my breast that she might have forgotten how to form that quaint, complaisant, abused but wonderfully undaunted expression forever.

And so, for a time, there was peace. Not of any great order or permanence, but sufficient to keep me from getting out of bed at two o'clock in the morning, brewing coffee in the silent kitchen, and retiring to the study to translate the confusions of an eleventh-century satrap which, through many midnights, had served to ease my own.

Loyal reader, I don't know if you have ever spent three days in Slagheap, Pennsylvania, with absolutely nothing to occupy your time. If you have, the iron has entered into your soul sufficiently for you to bear with me while I describe to the uninitiated my quarters at the Hotel Thomas Edison. This establishment, to which I was driven by my own reckless stroke of virtuosity, is located In The Heart Of Downtown Slagheap, an advantage so equivocal that I am at a loss to understand the wanton advertising of the fact on its dinnerware, its stationery, its bedspreads, and its bathmats. There must have been at work, in my apparently extemporaneous selection of that particular city and that particular hotel as the site of my imaginary convention, some terrible, inscrutable principle of retribution. Nothing else could account for the horror of being incarcerated there for three entire days.

The lobby was full of white marble, a material which, even if it could be kept clean, would be suitable in my opinion only for tombstones. It was furnished with numberless brown leather sofas darkened by the hairdressing of generations of commercial travelers and deformed by their backs and buttocks into shapes of irredeemable agony. Along its length was laid a narrow Oriental carpet, frayed at all edges and worn to the warp at every point of commerce along the way—the revolving door, the registration desk, the elevator, and the cigarette-dispensing machine. There were at least twenty-five standing brass ashtrays of the receptacle type which, when a cigar butt is dropped into

97

them and a lever depressed, fail to operate. The ceiling was very high, very ornate, very dirty, and supported by six Corinthian pilasters which gave the improbable but very strong impression of being infested, in their upper regions, by bats. Everyone in the place, employee and guest alike, was full of understandable sadness.

I was escorted to the groaning and convulsive elevator, and thence to my room on the eleventh floor by a bellboy broken in spirit, mind, and body, and evidently mourning for his native Lithuania, for he mumbled ceaselessly in what could only have been the tongue of that land. He unlocked the door for me, carried in and deposited my suitcase, and then with an awful effort dragged up the window-frame and stared out, panting, at the wilderness of soot-darkened brick, chimneypots, and graveled rooftops, as if contemplating a plunge into infinity and blessed ease. I hastily offered him a dollar, which apparently barely turned the scales. He took it in trembling hands and staggered out into the hall, leaving me alone with my folly. This I sat down on the bed to consider for the next half-hour, watching the darkness fall mercifully over The Heart Of Downtown Slagheap. I have never in my life been so lonely, or felt so ridiculous. How in the name of God, I asked myself, am I going to stay in this place for three days? Or concoct a sufficiently detailed story about this "convention" to satisfy Margaret's questions when I return? And if I do, what shall I have achieved by the absurdity? Will my ardor really be restored to such a pitch that I shall fly into her arms and bear her ecstatically to the bed? I will much more likely be so demoralized by the experience that I will need a month of intensive therapy of some kind to rehabilitate myself. Look at this room. If ever there was a room calculated to lead more directly to a course in basket-weaving or ceramics, I have not seen it. I will go mad in this room.

In a vague search for comfort of some kind I removed my shoes, intending to stretch out on the bed, but the thought of yielding my body to that monstrous piece of furniture was so unpleasant that I must adjust to it, I realized, very gradually. I massaged my toes and hummed one or two Neapolitan melodies. Then I rose, opened my suitcase, took out my alternate suit and hung it up in a closet of unspeakable dinginess. While doing so I observed that someone had bored a hole with a knife-blade through the interior wall, affording a view, apparently, of the adjoining bedroom. I went back and sat down on the bed to prepare myself for my examination of the bathroom. Meanwhile the room had grown quite dark, as I had not yet dared to illuminate it fully. Outside the window the winter night had been pervaded with a hellish neon glare that bathed the whole of the dismal skyline visible to me in an infernal carmine haze. Beyond the chimneys of the adjoining warehouse a great blue and scarlet sign advised the world of the availability of HEAVENLIES—THE HAMBURGERS OF THE GODS. The room was becoming cold, and a strange sweetish smell of combusted fuel, like that of burnt caramel, invaded it from the open window. I rose and closed it, looking down through the carmine-flushed darkness into the bitter streets.

All this time some power or process was at work in me, so strongly that I was aware of it. I do not mean this in any mystic or spiritual sense, but in a psychological sense only: the acceleration into its fulminating stages of some psychological process that had been developing in me for a long time. It is very difficult to explain, and because of this difficulty is often misrepresented, I think, by careless or romantic writers, as possession. But I do not believe in possession; what it most closely resembles, I believe, is childbirth. A deed is about to be born. Out of past conflicts, torments, fears, insoluble dilemmas, a deed is being born. There is about the mind even some of the tenderness and pain associated with childbirth: it feels distended, great with its perplexity, like a woman's belly. It needs to be delivered. Something about the room had brought this process to fruition. About the situation, also: the long train ride in an ancient, nearly empty parlor car, the hideous town, the hotel, the loneliness, the subterfuge and undignified absurdity of the whole errand. But about the room, particularly. I hesitate to say that its ugliness was in some way familiar to me, yet I feel this to be true. I expected it, I welcomed it, perhaps I needed it. I do not mean to say that I was comfortable in it, that I felt toward it an affection or nostalgia of any kind—fortunately no room remotely resembling it had played any role whatever in my life. And yet the ugliness of this room extended from all its corners, from its very atmosphere, like palps, and pressed upon my mind, gently yet urgently, ministeringly, as the fingers of a midwife press upon the belly of a pregnant woman. I was in labor.

And what a place in which to be brought to labor! You should have seen the bathroom. Mercy forbids me to describe it to you at any length; I will only say that it had once been white, and now was largely brown. Everything was brown: the bathtub, the shower curtains, the toilet bowl, the walls, even the cracks between the tiles were being invaded by a creeping brownish stain, like mold. Some unexpected and impractical impulse led me to scrub one horizontal brown area for several minutes with a towel, hot water and soap, restoring it to a sort of lemon color, before setting down my toilet articles. I accomplished this in the murk of an unshaded forty-watt bulb, scrubbing away in my cell of cracked and tarnished tile like an abortionist.

I then came back into the bedroom, switched on the light, which emanated from the ceiling bowl like fog, and searched through the drawers of the night table beside the bed for the Gideon Bible. I opened it to the Song of Solomon and read the entire psalm through, whispering the words aloud. *O you who dwell in the gardens, my companions are listening for your voice; let me hear it. Make haste, my beloved, and be like a gazelle or a young stag upon the mountains of spices.* When I had finished reading I closed the Bible and lay back on the bed in a slow excruciated way, as of someone lowering himself into icy water. I lay staring up at the soiled ceiling bowl for perhaps half an hour, raising my arm periodically to look at my wristwatch. At six thirty exactly I rose, washed my face and hands, put on a fresh shirt and suit, and then picked up the telephone and called Margaret.

Her voice sounded gay and fresh, like sheets blowing out on a clothesline on a windy morning.

"Mickey! My goodness, you're so punctual! Where are you?"

"I'm in the Hotel Thomas Edison, In The Heart of Downtown Slagheap."

"Really? What's it like?"

"It's like hell," I said. "The Sixth Circle, at least. Maybe even the Seventh."

"Oh, dear. I told you it was foolish to try and economize like that. You ought to have stayed at the Ritz. What do you care, anyway—as long as they're paying the bills?"

"You were right," I said. "It was a mistaken scruple. Almost the only one I've had, and a total disaster."

"You poor darling. What are the towels like? Are there plenty of towels?"

"There are about three and a half," I said. "And some other nameless thing. I'm not sure; I don't go in there too often."

"Oh, dear; how awful. Mickey, will you promise to get a bottle of Lysol and sprinkle it all over the conveniences?"

"All right."

"Now promise."

"All right. What are you doing, Maggie?"

"I just put a chop on. Can you hear it sizzling?"

"No."

"You ought to see it: one solitary little chop, right in the middle of the frying pan. It looks so lonely."

"Put on another one," I said. "I might just fly back and have dinner with you."

"Oh, *darling*. Is it that bad? Haven't you eaten, then?"

"No, I'm just going out."

"Alone?"

"No, with Ed Casey. He's a hieroglyphist, from Denver. Seems like a very interesting guy."

"Well, that's good. Where are you going?"

"I don't know. Down to the Stygian Shores Café, I think. Some place where everybody goes, he says."

"Well, don't order any seafood, whatever you do. Have a steak or something."

"I was thinking of just a caraway seed and a glass of water, maybe."

"That's the safest thing. How long are you going to have to be there, Mickey, do you know?"

"Oh, I think I'll be back on Monday. Ed says they might move my talk up to Saturday afternoon, so I might even get back that night. I'll call and let you know."

"Oh, I hope so. It's awful here, without you." There was a pause. "Mickey."

"What?"

"I love you."

"I love you, too," I said, and added, for some reason, "No matter what anybody says."

"That's good. Don't forget about the Lysol."

"I won't."

"Good-bye, darling."

"Good-bye."

I hung up and sat with my hand resting on the cradled phone for several minutes, staring out at the bleak flushed silhouettes of the the rooftops. The silence in the room was suddenly appalling. I rose from the bed, went to the closet, and removed my overcoat from a wire hanger, discovering as I did so that through the hole bored in its inner wall a tiny circle of illumination now shone from the bedroom beyond. I closed the door, struggled into my overcoat, and went out to dinner.

I walked for an hour or more through the cold glare-ridden streets, entering and fleeing from half a dozen resturants, until

I discovered one with a carpeted floor, clean linen, soft lighting, and a general air of comfort and modest luxury. I bought a newspaper at the cashier's desk, took it to my table, and after ordering broiled brook trout with parsley potatoes and French beans and a bottle of Châteauneuf du Pape, began to read, with obsessive sedulousness, every item it contained, column by column and page by page. It had been a day, apparently, of almost unmitigated horror, domestic and foreign, a fact which confirmed my own experience entirely. After making my way through three pages of warfare, extortion, turnpike accidents, rapes, racial unrest, and an encephalitis epidemic, I turned to the amusement section, where I was confronted with a photograph of a woman named Astral Flame, who was performing at a local cabaret. Above the waist her only clothing was a pair of star-shaped sequins, one attached to the nipple of each breast; below, a complicated system of belts, garters, black-net panels, rosettes, and hip-length hosiery. I had never seen a more astonishingly intricate garment. It looked as if she had been fitted out for a scientific experiment of some kind, with various measuring devices attached to her anatomy to record the function of her liver, kidneys, digestion, and other abdominal processes. A very dangerous or painful experiment, apparently, or else some distracted lab assistant had got the wires crossed and inadvertently electrocuted her, for her half-closed eyes, gaping mouth, and tormented attitude of head reflected agony or apprehension of the extremest kind. Is this truly the face of Passion? I asked myself. Before I had time to compose a reply, the Châteauneuf du Pape arrived. I folded my newspaper guiltily to conceal the subject of my meditation and rapidly drank a glass of wine. Then I stealthily unfolded it and looked more closely at her features, almost expecting them to dissolve into a wink. But closer scrutiny did nothing to dispel the evident sincerity of her suffering. No one, I decided, unless motivated by the most invincible sincerity, could possibly find the fortitude to attire herself every evening in a costume of that design and get up on a stage to perform before a roomful of strangers. The thought had a certain nobility about it. Here was sincerity of a sacrificial degree, a degree to drive one, unyielding, through a lifetime of contumely, abuse, economic insecurity, and the gravest sort of respiratory problems. I drank another glass of wine to celebrate it. I became quite philosophical. What sort of a woman was this Astral Flame, I asked myself, to consecrate herself so sacrificially to Passion? No expeditious marriage for her. No Georgetown house for Astral, no poodle, no country club membership. No three-foot-long fold of credit cards. Naked she came into the world, and naked—save for her laboratory apparatus and her twinkling sequins—she made her way through it, with no credentials but her body and the fire in her heart. She was married to the World. Astral, the bride of Mankind. I turned my head aside as the waiter arrived with my broiled trout, to conceal the moisture in my eyes.

The trout proved to be the single blessing that that day afforded. "Margaret," I said to myself as I dislodged delicate flakes of the forbidden flesh, "this has an excellent taste."

"But you will suffer for it," said Someone.

"Perhaps," I answered proudly. "But Astral will understand."

Out of that meal I derived one piece of wisdom, slightly depraved: many indiscretions will serve to cancel one another out. Or so they did on this occasion, for by the time I had finished the trout it had so dissipated the influence of Astral and alcohol that my eyes were dry, my fingers steady, and my thoughts clear, if still somewhat lugubrious. What I need, I said to myself, is some wholesome family type of entertainment: a Walt Disney nature film, perhaps. I did not dare, however, to refer again to the amusement page; I would go out and seek my salvation in the streets.

It presented itself to me in the form of a Doris Day movie, a very curious form for salvation to take. Certainly not the family entertainment I had had in mind, unless, perhaps, the family in question were the Jukes. It concerned the ravishment, one after another, of the very voluptuous tenants of a luxurious apartment by its sybaritic landlord. The victims appeared in every state of seminudity imaginable: pajama-tops, bathtubs, underwear, bikinis, and bath towels. There were merry rompings in bedrooms, scenes of voyeurism from a garden trellis, bathing scenes, impishly detailed seductions, an atmosphere of mischievous depravity which found my thoughts turning respectfully to the far less frivolous, far less meretricious amusements of Astral Flame. The world apparently was dissolving in desire before my very eyes. I left the theater with a feeling of bitter privation, of exclusion, which no amount of sophistry could enable me to interpret as salvation.

As I walked home—what have I said!—as I walked back to the hotel this feeling was replaced by a gathering dullness of mind, a vacancy of sensation that was deliciously deathlike. A remission of my labor pains. The bellboy who had attended to me previously had died during my absence and been replaced by another, this one young, cunning, and with viciousness oozing out of every gland of his body. As he stopped the elevator at my floor he turned upon me the most feral smile I have ever seen.

"Well, how are you enjoying Slagheap?" he asked.

"Not too much," I confessed. This was a mistake.

"It takes a while to know the town. Of course, you can save a lot of time if you know the right people. If you happen to be looking for company by any chance—I mean you know real lively *company*—I might be able to help you out."

"Not by any chance whatever," I said, astonished by the Victorian indignation of my own voice.

I entered my cell, locked the door, and hung up my overcoat. As I did so I perceived that through the closet wall, in addition to its single piercing ray of tarnished light, there issued now the sound of subdued but merry conversation, hushed gigglings, grunts, and protestations. I stood listening for a moment and passed my hand through the thin shaft of light which fell across my palm like a stiletto blade. I closed the door quietly, went into the bedroom and pulled down the window shade to shut out the infernal glow of Downtown Hades, undressed, put on my pajamas, put out the light, and surrendered myself to the custody of the hideous bed.

In the morning I decided that everything was going to be different. I would put this day to use. My activities were to be purposeful, vigorous, instructive, and carefully planned. I would do calisthenics. I would buy a bottle of Lysol. I would take three nutritious meals. I sang in the shower, hummed while brushing my teeth, and whistled while tying my shoelaces. I put my resolution to an early test by breakfasting in the dining room of the Thomas Edison and remaining auspiciously undaunted by the condition of the linen, silverware, and orange juice. In the lobby I telephoned the chamber of commerce and compiled a list of the cultural opportunities available in the town: a municipal gallery, a zoo, a high-school production of *Ah, Wilderness* and a showing of *Henry V* at the Y.M.H.A. The gallery hours were from nine to five; I would spend the day there, have a leisurely meal in the vicinity—in the course of which I would invent a very different set of events for Margaret's benefit—telephone her to report them, and proceed to the Y.M.H.A. by seven thirty, in time for my fifth viewing of the film they were to show. I cannot tell you how reassured I was by these decisions; I even jotted down a little timetable on my memo pad, with the notation, *If gal. bad, sub. zoo for p.m., lunch there, etc.* It is the appointment book, not the Bible, that holds back the darkness for the human race. When we have defeated everything in this world which threatens us—warfare, poverty, ignorance, disease —we will have created the greatest enemy of all: leisure. Secure in my temporary solution of this terrible problem I briskly hailed a cab and made my way to the Municipal Gallery.

It was a horrendous red brick structure, rising incongruously in the midst of a clamorous commercial district, like a boulder in a stream. I was very much encouraged by my first view of it, for it seemed to have every characteristic of the exemplary institution: it was monolithic, archaic, ugly, very badly repaired, apparently in the way of everything going on around it, and patronized—on weekdays—almost exclusively by the indigent, whose chief purpose in attending was to get in out of the cold, rather than to gain enlightenment (on Sundays and holidays, of course, the clientele would be a good deal more distinguished). As an institution, it was admirable; and as a collection of painting, I found to my astonishment, almost equally satisfactory. There was a very good exhibit of Italian Renaissance works, of English landscapists, Early Flemish—including two excellent Brueghels—and, particularly, of French Impressionists. These remarks may give you the impression that I am a considerable connoisseur of art; it is not so. There are no more than a dozen painters whose work I can recognize at a glance, but before certain of the pictures of these I can report without embarrassment that I stand transfixed. Particularly those of Renoir, Caravaggio, and Cassatt.

The Slagheap Municipal Gallery was blessed by four of the latter, works of shimmering summery loveliness whose dappled colors swept across the canvas in a warm gust, like a stroke of massed cellos. I stood in front of them and let them blow against my senses, and lo, I was cleaned! All the ugliness winnowed away by those warm torrents of color that tossed my feelings like sheaves of tossed wheat in a bath of summer wind; so clean, so sweet, such laving winds of beauty; the very breath of innocence. Oh, no, I saw, *this* is the face of Passion. This purifying gust of exaltation that blows away the chaff of life, that bares the live and shining kernels, that breaks the seed out of the tarnished husk of man and spills it in the sun. Down that wonderful wind went flying into oblivion shreds of moldy carpeting, hamburger signs, uprooted lengths of plumbing pipe, bellboys, bathtubs, and the lobby of the Thomas Edison Hotel. I stood and smiled and sighed, and sat down, finally, on a backless bench provided for the purpose.

After half an hour of this kind of communion I was a new man. Outside of these dark walls lay not Downtown Slagheap, but fields of Normandy wheat with poppies blowing here and there like blood-drops, and Loire valleys, burnished by the sun, their châteaux sleeping in the shadows of enfolding cypress groves. How sweet the air seemed, perfumed by eucalyptus and the mallow of the river marshes. I heard the drone of bees and whisper of wind in grass and the creak of wooden cartwheels from a lane as I lay all through a drowsing sun-drenched afternoon in the Midi of France. God bless you, I said. I love you, Mary Cassatt.

And she heard me. She did. For she replied, in a voice as warm, as vibrant, as lambent with life as were her paintings, "I'm so glad." I closed my eyes for an instant in wonder-stricken gratitude at the miracle of this communication across the void, then opened them immediately as my reason took command and forced upon me the acknowledgment that there was in this voice, as well, a certain inharmonious hint of mockery and a certain touch of Boston dialect which were oddly incongruous. I turned in consummate embarrassment and found that immediately behind my bench a young lady had set up her easel and been for some time, apparently, engaged in copying the very painting that had inspired my profession.

"I love her, too," she said, and added, noting my confusion, "Did I scare you?"

"You almost evangelized me," I said.

"Not me," she said. "Mary did it. What I really thought I ought to tell you is that your wallet has just slipped out of your hip pocket." So it had, and fallen on the floor behind me.

"Oh, gosh, thank you." I rose to retrieve it and put it back into my pocket, whistling at the thought of what might have befallen me but for her observation. The only possible thing worse than to be in Slagheap at all was to be there penniless and without credentials. I did not think it tactful, however, to point this out to one of its residents, or inmates. I repeated my thanks and wished her luck with her painting.

"Don't let me drive you away," she said. "There's lot of room."

"Oh, no. I want to go and have a look at the Brueghels."

Now as a matter of fact, I had already seen the Brueghels, but something advised me urgently that I had better go and have another look at them. Something influenced greatly, I am afraid, by this girl's appearance; for she was about twenty-five, very pretty, and had a dark, elfish face of a type which has always appealed to me; one from which all conventional evidence of dignity has been evicted by a reckless and imaginative intelligence; sensitive enough to command one's interest, but not one's reverence; a puckish, perverse, willingly victimized face, which mysteriously assures one that After All, It Has All Happened Before, and which gives the general impression of being, like the work of its possessor, a very skillful copy of a masterpiece. It is a type of face to call forth both tender and predatory instincts in a man; in short, to bring out the very worst in him. In my present circumstances I did not think it wise to contend with such a face. Therefore, the Brueghels.

"Brueghel," she said. "Like ugh."

"You don't like him?"

"In my opinion some terrible infectious disease must have swept Holland about four hundred years ago. One characterized by nausea and high fever."

"They just don't speak to you," I said. "They have a very cool quality, really. The thing about Brueghel is that the internal experience is too intense for romantic imagery of any kind. So you get formality, austerity. They're a kind of visual epigram. The coolness is the coolness of geometry, a kind of frozen passion." The terrible thing about making a remark of this kind is that it requires the next twenty minutes of one's life to offset its effects on everyone in hearing distance. Perhaps I realized this subconsciously, for self-respect now obliged me to stay and acquit myself. "When I say 'cool,' " I said, "I don't mean it the way you would probably mean it."

Her eyes widened ironically. "How would I probably mean it, daddy?"

"Well, I mean in the existential sense that people of your age use the word today: self-composed, invulnerable, consciously uncommitted. *Dégagé*." I don't know what's the matter with me, I thought. My mind is absolutely disintegrating. She was the first person of her age, interest, and expertness with whom I had attempted to carry on a conversation for several years, and nothing is so calculated to reveal to man the state of his own decay.

"Well, when you get through telling me what I would have meant by something if I had happened to say it, I want to tell *you* something. Okay?"

"Okay," I said. "I'm through."

"Okay. There are three things you don't know anything about: art, existentialism, and me. Go look at your Brueghels."

"Forget you ever met me," I said.

"That'll be the easiest thing I ever did."

I have never in my life found it so difficult to get out of a room without breaking into a gallop. I fled into the Flemish room, which adjoined, and prowled about for some time in a state of nervous humiliation. This changed slowly, however, to one of growing indignation. I have strangely categorical concepts about certain types of faces which do not surrender easily; when the people in possession of them do not behave as their faces lead me to believe they should behave, it upsets me. Another evidence of natural order has been overthrown. I regard their behavior as false, cunning, designed, in some way, to discredit my perceptions. This makes me indignant. For some reason, however, such a misconception is less disturbing if a person whose face one interprets as basically ferocious turns out to be mild and conciliatory by nature. This I can generally accept as a pleasant surprise. But if someone whose face leads to the strong assumption of passive qualities in his nature—shyness, tenderness, stupidity—turns out to be very positive, aggressive, intelligent—and even rude—I am indignant. I look upon it as a presumption, a totally unlicensed display of qualities to which his countenance does not entitle him. This girl's face was an example of gross misrepresentation. It had led me to make a series of fatuous academic pronouncements. It had dismayed me by its unexpected pride and asperity. It had exposed an unsuspected callousness in my own nature. Somewhere along the line she had deliberately betrayed her own look of softness, of complaisance, of willing victimization, to my great disappointment and my grave discredit. I had emerged as pretentious, predatory, and capable of the shattered vanity of the aging cavalier. That look of hers—like her voice and her earlier remarks (not to mention her painting)—had been an imposture, a wanton forgery. How dare she lead a lonely distressed man of forty-one to believe, by her physiognomy, her forgedly tender voice, and such remarks as "Don't let me drive you away," that his attentions would be welcome; and then reject them on the grounds that they were academic, badly informed or—very properly—constrained? A vicious little creature. A snip of a girl. I started at my use of the phrase, for it was a type of epithet which I have often promised myself never to use, such complete demoralization does it represent. I stared disconsolately at the Brueghels, my discomfort increased by the discovery that there was, indeed, a febrile, even a nauseous, quality about them. I must get out of here, I thought. I'm going to pieces in this city.

It proved to be more difficult than I realized, for the only way out of the Flemish Room, I discovered, was through the French Impressionist Room from which I had just fled, and where she was still stationed with her easel, waiting to devastate more improvident middle-aged transients. I loitered about the Flemish Room for a length of time that was beginning to betray desperation, I feared, rather than transport. If I stay in here any longer, I thought, she will consider it even further evidence of my pretentiousness. Transport has its proper limits, which merge either into madness or into mummery; and I had exhausted them. I drew a deep breath, assumed a smile of moderate but unmistakable rejuvenation, restrained the nervous rapidity of my stride to a leisurely stroll, and made my exit. As I passed with composed goodwill behind her I even managed to pause for the barest, most judicious moment and cast an appreciative glance upon her work. I went so far as to murmur my approval. A piece of foolhardiness which undid me. Halfway to the door she challenged me.

"So, okay, Sainte-Beuve, how does it look?"

"You're very clever," I said.

"Clever schmever. Look at that green. That's a real rotten-egg green."

I turned to examine it more closely. "It does have a slightly decadent look."

"That's me," she said. "Slightly decadent. You can't hide it, can you?" She stared gloomily at her canvas. "Mary Cassatt would never have used a green like that in her life. She would have cut her arm off first."

"You're not Mary Cassatt," I said.

"You can say that again. I'm Hilda Hunzinger."

"I don't see how anybody can really criticize a copy," I said. "Either it looks like it or it doesn't. What is there to criticize?"

"There's that green," she said. "That goddam gangrene green." She plunged her brush into a jar of turpentine and began to squeeze the bristles moodily with a piece of toweling. "I don't know how I do it. I put together a few little innocent pigments and come up with all these filthy colors. It's mysterious."

"I think it's a very clever copy," I said.

"Would you mistake it for a Mary Cassatt?"

"No. Why are you asking me, though? I don't know anything about art."

"So what do you have to know about art? Would you mistake me for your wife?"

"No."

"No. The hell with it. I can type, anyway; I should worry." She flung down her brush and began to mop her fingers with the rag. "How about buying me some lunch? You owe me a reward or something. I could have kept the whole ten million dollars if I wanted it."

"All right."

"It'll take me a few minutes to clean up. You can go out on the steps and have a cigarette if you want."

"All right."

I went out through the enormous revolving door onto the cold portico, lit a cigarette, and stood smiling down at the clanging street. Mickey will be amused about this, I thought. I must remember all those funny things she says, to tell Mickey. She'll be very amused. In a moment the girl came out, wearing a green cloth coat with a dark pile collar that fitted closely under her chin. She had put on high heels, and looked much taller. I looked swiftly at her ankles and saw that they were very shapely. Her black hair had been combed forward into two curving crescents, one across either cheek. She had lined her eyes with green pencil, making them even more enormous. She looked trim and terribly young in her green coat.

"Hi."

"Hi."

She took my arm as we went down the steps.

"Where did you leave your things?" I asked.

"I have a locker in there. They let you leave stuff."

"Is that where you got the shoes?"

"Yep. What's your name?"

"Mike Pritchard. Is your name really Hilda Hunzinger?"

"Yep. You can fall down and scream if you want to."

"Why should I scream?"

"Oh, come on. Hilda Hunzinger. I still think my mother is kidding me sometimes. You can call me Hildy if you like. I don't really care what you call me."

"Do you come from Boston, Hildy?"

"Yep. Where do you come from?"

"Washington, D.C."

"What are you doing in Slagheap?"

"That's a very strange story," I said. "I'm not going to burden you with it at present. Where do you think we ought to eat?"

"How much can you spend?"

"Five dollars apiece."

"Wow. Really? Okay, we'll go to Bettino's. It's about three

blocks, okay? They have osso buco; I'm absolutely queer for it."
She squeezed my arm, like a child who has been told it can go
to the movies. "Can I have a cocktail, too?"

"I guess so."

"You mean *extra*? Or does that come out of the five dollars?"

I laughed at her, remembering suddenly my own student
days.

"Extra."

"Jesus, I'm going to have to do this more often. You know,
you're the first man who's been in that place for a week who
didn't ask *me* for a handout. We've got some real crazy art-lovers
in this town. Most of them walk around with their fly open.
It's a wonderful atmosphere for study."

She walked very rapidly, in a young vigorous stride which
I found myself delightedly matching. It was exhilarating to be
with her. She turned her face to me as she talked, and in the
bright noonday sunlight I saw the absolute clarity and tightness
of her white skin over the fine bones of her cheeks and jaw and
eye sockets. I had forgotten that breathtaking perfection of a
young girl's face, the dark eyes sparkling like chocolate-colored
quartz in their flawlessly molded hollows.

"What's the matter?" she said.

"Nothing."

"I'm sort of getting to you, huh?"

"How old are you?" I asked.

"Twenty-three."

"You've got pierced ears, haven't you?"

"Yep."

"But no earrings."

"Nope. I had a pair, but some guy stole them. Can you
imagine that? I take a guy to bed and he steals my earrings
while I'm asleep. What a world."

"You don't have much luck, do you?"

"Oh, I'm not bitching. I'm just lucky he didn't haul the
bureau out while he was at it. I sleep pretty sound." She pulled

me to a halt and I saw that we were standing in front of one of those Executive Luncheon-type restaurants whose pretensions are proclaimed by dark purple windows through which one cannot see. "Does it look all right?"

"Perfect."

"What do you mean, *perfect*? Don't get on that kick again."

"No, it looks fine, really."

"Well, it better. It's the only decent place in ten blocks, and I'm starved."

Inside it was quite crowded and full of the warm, dark, comfortable hum of a restaurant on a winter afternoon. We had to wait for a few minutes behind a brass rail with a hanging velvet gate. She pressed close against me and I could smell her hair. It was absolutely unperfumed by anything; it smelled simply like hair, which is one of the most intimate and powerful odors in the world. She turned her head to murmur into my ear in a restaurant voice. "I come here and get proposed to once a month. A guy named Herb Shoskers. Every payday he gets up the nerve to bring me in here and propose. It's a sort of ritual we have."

"Don't you like him?" I said.

"Once a month I like him fine. Here we go."

We were led gravely to a table, handed menu cards as if they were coronation invitations, and invited to order cocktails. She asked for a martini, as did I.

"Did you get that waiter?" she said. "Don't they bomb you? Holding together civilization like that? God." She laid her menu on the table, and moving her fingertip slowly down the tariff column began to do calculations, whispering the sums painfully. She looked up at me in a moment and frowned. "How much is two times two-seventy-five, plus sixty-five?"

"I haven't the faintest idea. What's the problem?"

"I've changed my mind. I want lobster instead of osso buco, but I think I'm going to need two of them. I eat quite a lot. And I'm afraid it's going to cost too much. I can't add. Wait a minute." She scrabbled about in her purse, found a mascara pencil and added up the figures on her napkin. "Oh, hell, it's six-fifteen. Listen, would you let me pay the difference? I've just got to have two lobsters."

"No," I said. "You can owe it to me. Till the next time I get to Slagheap."

"Oh, can I? Really? That would be wonderful, because actually I'm kind of hard up this month. But when are you going to leave?"

"Very soon," I said. "Maybe tomorrow."

"Hell. Well, anyway, here's to Now." She raised her glass and we both drank solemnly. I set mine down and tapped the stem with my fingers for a moment.

"What's the matter?" she asked.

"I was thinking how nice this is, and unexpected."

"I know. I think it's great, picking up people. It's the biggest kick there is, honest. I don't do it very ofen—*really*—because usually you can tell it wouldn't work out. Usually it's hell, like with that sailor. The one that lifted my earrings. But you never know. That's the kick."

"But this is working out?"

"I think so. Which is astonishing, because the way you started out with all that Brueghel crap, you were my number one choice for No Go. But I've decided I sort of like to talk to you. There aren't many people I can talk to."

"What about Herb?"

"Oh, Jesus, you can't talk with Herb. He stammers. I mean *awful*. The poor guy has never got out more than three consecutive words in his life. With Herb I mostly stick to basic stuff, like 'Pass the salt,' or 'Undo my brassiere.' But he has very nice hands. That's important to me."

The waiter had arrived, and stood at my elbow with poised pencil. I ordered three broiled lobsters and salad.

"Did you wish another place setting, sir?" he asked.

"No."

"I thought perhaps you were expecting someone else."

"No, we're just very hungry. And another pair of martinis, please."

"Certainly, sir."

I felt very pleased with myself. This sort of life suited me, I decided.

"You're a marvelous man," Hildy said. "I didn't dare ask you to order another one, but I admit I was hoping furiously. You see how important hands are? I always base my decisions on hands."

"And mine were all right?"

"Well, after that lecture they just barely tipped the scale. I had to have another look at them to make sure. But I was right. Have you ever noticed what women look at when they pass you on the street? It's very interesting."

"Not many of them look at me," I said.

"Oh, balls. Come on, haven't you, really?"

"No."

"You check on it some time. First the face, then the shoes, then the fly. Honest. It's almost invariable. Only I'm different; with me it's the face, then the *hands,* then the fly. Somehow a man's shoes don't interest me too much." She reached out to pry apart my folded hands on the table, take one of them in her own, and examine it delicately and thoroughly, in a connoisseur fashion, touching all the bones, knuckles, nails, and declivities between with her fingertips, frowning slightly with absorption. "Yes," she said, "that's what did it. That and the way you were looking at that Cassatt. When a woman sees a man looking at something that way—a dog, a shotgun, a painting, *any*thing—she gets jealous. You know that? She wants him to look at *her* that way. It's the truth."

I raised my eyes obligingly and looked into her own marvelous chocolate-colored ones. There was a considerable silence.

"Come on," she said. "Wait'll I eat, will you? Jesus."

The moment had done nothing to impair that faculty on her part. I have never seen a pair of lobsters destroyed more scientifically, thoroughly, or swiftly. It was wonderful, watching her eat. It gave me a feeling of great and gathering excitement to see the rhythmic bulging of her jaw muscles, the ripple of her throat as she swallowed, the sideways, tigerish tilt of her head, and delicate snarl of her lifted lips as she bit at a chunk of dripping, buttered lobster claw. There was a ferocious earnestness—nothing whatever to do with anger or sorrow—about everything she did.

"You haven't smiled once," I said.

"I know. I take things pretty straight."

She sucked the butter from each of her fingers in turn, wiggled them in her fingerbowl, dried them on her napkin, and sighed. "God, that was good. I love to eat. I could eat the whole world. I'm going to try it, too."

"You'll get an awful stomach-ache," I said.

"Boy, don't I know it. I've already had one or two. But it doesn't seem to have hurt my appetite."

We sipped hot black coffee luxuriously and smoked cigarettes.

"How long have you been painting, Hildy?" I asked.

"Oh, forever. I've only been studying, though, about nine months. I went to business college for a couple of years and had it up to here. Then I got on this painting kick, so I worked for a while and saved up enough to go to Constable. That's this local academy. They're giving me a partial scholarship, which helps. I guess it's all right, I don't know. But in my opinion, if you want to learn to paint you'd better stay away from anybody who thinks he knows how to teach you. Still, I've learned a lot of technical stuff—composition, perspective, all that crap." She stared at her cigarette, pushing distractedly at the black crescents of hair which lay against her cheeks. "I have this awful color problem. I don't know what the hell it is. I squeeze out a little dab of yellow for a buttercup or something, and what do I get? Vomit. It's awful."

"It'll come," I said.

"Yeah, like Christmas. Listen, I'd like to show you some

of my real stuff. Not copies, I mean. Maybe you can tell me something. None of that art gallery crap, though; I get plenty of that at school. You want to see them?"

"I'd love to."

"Okay. I'm just around the corner from here. Or have you got to go and see the mayor or something?"

I lifted my hand suddenly and clutched at the folded sheet of memo paper in my shirt pocket. My timetable, my gospel. It crackled gently from beneath my jacket.

"I had one or two appointments—"

"Okay, okay. Maybe the next time you get to town. If you do."

"They're not really that important," I said.

"You sure?"

"Yes." I took the slip of paper out of my pocket, studied it for a moment in a hectic, mournful, valedictory way, then lit a match, set fire to the edge of it, and dropped it into the ashtray, watching it writhe and blacken irredeemably. A solitary, well-balanced meal, *Henry V*, the Y.M.H.A., in favor of a Hunzinger Original. It was an exchange, some elfin voice advised me, that a man would be an idiot to forego.

"I mean I don't want to stop the march of American industry, or anything."

"Not industry," I said. "Government. Which as far as I'm concerned came to a dead halt about an hour ago."

"I'm glad you feel that way," Hildy said. "I really am."

She lived in a one-room walkup flat above a delicatessen, about three blocks from the gallery. One slice of the room was divided off by panel screens and furnished with a tiny refrigerator, stove, and sink, to form a kitchen the size of a boat galley. She had papered these screens with gallery reproductions of modern masters, and lacquered them. They were all gay, sherbert-colored, splashy paintings: Miró, Picasso, Dufy, Chagall, and Marin. On the wall above her studio bed was a large framed print of Velasquez' "Venus with a Mirror," the long ivory body of which lady was rather surprisingly covered with mouthprints in lipstick of various shades. All other vertical surfaces of the apartment were decorated with what were fairly obviously Hildy's own paintings. They were mostly portraits of young men and women, and perhaps the truest and briefest thing I can say about them is that they all looked as if they had been painted by someone who looked exactly like Hildy. They were bright, reckless, starved paintings. I loved them.

She sat down on the bed in her coat, lifted and clasped one knee, and watched me silently as I prowled about the room with my hands in my overcoat pockets, from one to another of her canvases. Her people did not so much have different characters as different flavors; some were strawberry, some chocolate, some raspberry, some vanilla, some pistachio, but all extremely edible-looking, and for the most part, delicious.

"They look good to eat," I said.

"Most of them look like they'd already been eaten, to me," she said. "And regurgitated. Jesus, those colors."

"I like the colors. I think probably you don't because you knew just what you wanted, and it didn't come out quite right. But most of us aren't that fastidious. They really have a terrific effect on me."

"Don't put me on."

"No, I mean it."

"You think they're sexy?"

"Well, I don't know about sexy, but they certainly stimulate the appetite. Which is pretty remarkable, considering the meal we just had."

"I want them to be sexy," she said. "I want people to want to kiss them. The way I do with that Venus. Just look at that doll. She gets me so wild I have to kiss her all the way from the back of her neck to her ankles. Sheesh." She stood up and took off her coat, dropping it onto the bed. "If you're going to stay, let me have your coat."

I struggled out of my coat and handed it to her. She carried it away behind the screen and said from there, "You want a drink?"

"Yes, please."

"What I've got is apricot liqueur. Herb gives it to me. I'm trying to find out why."

"That's fine," I said.

"You think it's cold in here?"

"Not terribly."

"I think it's colder than hell. I can't get them to give me any heat. I've tried everything; I even wink at the janitor every time I pass him on the stairs, but he doesn't catch on. He's sort of looney or something." She reappeared from behind the screen, clutching a pair of glasses in one hand and a bottle of apricot liqueur in the other. "Listen, I like what you said about my paintings. Thanks."

"Thanks for letting me see them." I looked about for a place to sit down; there were two chairs, but the seat of each was covered with a litter of paint tubes, brushes, linseed oil, palette knives, and other paraphernalia.

"Sit on the bed," she said.

I did so, and she came and sat beside me, pouring the two glasses full of liqueur and handing one to me. They were water glasses and she filled them to the brim. "It's a crazy thing about painting," she said. "When you're doing one you're absolutely queer for it. It absolutely bombs you. You can't wait to get home at night and work on it. You figure this is the great love of your life. Then when you get through with it, it appeals to you about like a stale cheese sandwich. Exactly like people. I mean absolutely. Did that ever occur to you?"

"I never did any painting," I said.

"Did you ever do any lovemaking?" The question made me blink. She watched me for a moment, then tapped the rim of my glass with her own. "Well, skip it. Here's to the poor, the ill, and the old." We raised our glasses and drank. It was terrible liqueur.

"That's a nice toast," I said.

"My dad used to say it." She shuddered, kicked off her shoes, set her glass on the floor, and moving far enough away from me to make room for the length of her body, put her head in my lap and curled up on the bed. I stroked her glittering black hair, following with my curved palm the shape of her small beautifully molded skull.

"You look Italian," I said.

"I know. I've even got hair on my stomach. It's wild." She turned over onto her back to look up at me. "What are you thinking about?"

"Herb."

"Balls. What?"

"Really."

"Well, forget him. Next to Barry Goldwater, he's the easiest man in America to forget."

I set my glass on the floor and clasped her face in my hands. I felt faint with a sudden scalding flood of tenderness that poured through me, devouring my faculties. Her dark, huge-eyed, soft-lipped face seemed to me the most beautiful thing that had ever been made in the universe. I lifted this face to me. She rose up, turning to meet me, and fastened her mouth to mine with a passionate, insatiable sweetness, breathing of apricots and sage and the odor of her own deep, scarlet mouth. I could not stop kissing her. I was blind with hunger for her. I kissed her eyes and ears and nostrils and the nape of her neck and her wonderful fluted throat and her collarbones, with their beautiful blunt modeling, and her lips and chin and shoulders and the shallow bowls of her temples and the firm, cool, bone vaults above her eyes.

"Oh, daddy," she said in a weak astonished whisper, "I didn't know if you were going to make it, but Holy God."

"Oh, God, you're beautiful," I said. "Oh, Hildy, you're so beautiful. Oh, you beautiful, strange wild child. I love you, I love you, I love you, I love you, I love you."

"Oh, God, wait'll I get these things off," she said. "Oh, I can't do it. Help me, will you? Oh, Jesus."

She had a magnificent body, whose thick, strong Mediterranean voluptuousness changed instantly my delicate tastes in women. Her hips were wide, her belly broad, boldly curved, and with an astonishing ridge of fine black hair that ran up its center to her deep succulent navel. Her breasts were huge and heavily round, with enormous copper-colored nipples that stood out like thumb-tips. Beneath them her great rib cage with its marvelous stippling tapered swiftly to a breathlessly narrow waist, then the vast woman-swell of hip and staunch hard thigh, narrowing again to knees that would be far too full and legs that would be far too thick, I thought, for anyone who worked in the Manuscript Division of the Library of Congress, but which I took as a sudden revelation of the capacities of the human mind to expand its vision. And the throne of all this beauty, her black-forested, lofty, Olympian Mount of Venus, with its tangled musky slopes falling down to the deep, enfolding, redolent, spring-sweetened valley of all life—where I planted myself with a passion and permanence unknown. Absolutely nothing was in doubt. I sowed her warm white acres two times consecutively, in the course of which she must have had ten crises of delight, increasing in frequency and abandon until they were finally indistinguishable; she was one long, quivering, unremitting spasm of felicity. I was awed by my own perform- ance. As I fell beatifically to sleep among her beauty I mused on what divine dispensation had granted me this burst of genius.

We must have slept for a long time, because when I woke and looked at my watch, it was half-past four. She was awake, too, fondling my face in an endless gentle way; and smiling.

"You're smiling," I said.

"You bet your sweet life I'm smiling. Holy God. How old are you, anyway?"

"Forty-one."

"Jesus, I'm going to have to find more old men. Listen, will you come back to Slagheap soon? Will you, Mike?"

"I'll try," I said monarchically.

"Please. Please do. Promise me, daddy, will you?"

"I'll see," I said. "I ought to be able to."

"Oh, please. I'll do anything for you, honestly. I'll beg, I'll keep house. I'll whore. I'll do anything you want. Please, daddy."

"You'd better stop that," I said.

"I can't help it. You wrecked me. Really." Her face had grown very solemn. "Oh, shit," she said, "I think I'm going to cry." I gathered her head against me and she cried, very softly and shamefully.

"Don't, sweetheart," I said gently, alarmed at what was happening to both of us, apparently. Very soon I would not be able to get out of it, I thought. I laid her head on the pillow and with a monstrous effort rose from the bed and went to the bathroom, which I found behind the screens. I switched on the light and stared at myself in the mirror. Who the hell are you, I wondered. I don't know you.

When I came out she had recomposed herself and was lying under a single sheet, staring up at the ceiling.

"Do you have to go?" she asked.

"Yes. I have a dinner appointment, and I have to make some phone calls."

"Oh."

I began to put my clothes on. She lay and watched me with her great eyes.

"Are you just going to stay there?" I said.

"Uh huh. Until I get hungry. Which probably won't be too long. Couldn't you let me fix you dinner?"

"I really couldn't, Hildy," I said. "I only wish I could."

"I'd love to cook for you."

I leaned across the bed and kissed her. She closed her eyes.

"Where's my overcoat?" I said.

"It's back there, on a hook. Behind a little curtain."

I went behind the screen and found it in a partitioned closet, hanging with her clothes: half a dozen supermarket-style dresses, and beneath them, on the floor, four pairs of cheap shoes, most of them with scuffed toes, lined up very neatly with balled-up nylon stockings tucked into them. I took one of her dresses in my hand and held it to my face, burying my nostrils in the folds of fabric and breathing in a long nourishing draft of her smell. Oh, a wonderful smell, of hot Tuscan meadows, sea-salt, poppies, apricots, and nard. I put on my overcoat and went out and stood looking down at her. I did not know what to say. Finally I kneeled down beside the bed, took her hand, and kissed all her fingers softly.

"I'll call you, Hildy," I said.

"Do you promise?"

"Yes."

"You won't, though."

I laid her hand back on the bed, rose, and went to the door, where there was a large unframed portrait of a peppermint-flavored blonde. I leaned forward and kissed her on the mouth.

"Thanks," Hildy said.

Downstairs, on the sidewalk, I paused long enough to take out my memo pad and write down the address.

I arrived at the hotel a little after six. It had already grown dark in the winter evening, and outside of my room the old carmine flush had once again flooded the sky. But do you know what had happened? The light had been transmuted. Truly. It was no longer the glare of infernal furnaces, but now the glorious warm flame of a Tuscan twilight, bathing the hushed and peaceful world, touching with little rags of carmine light the crooked rooftops of a retiring village where girls with olive eyes and black hair tangled on their pillows turned their heads toward the blazing windows and smiled to think of brown boys waiting for them in the shadows of the vineyards. A scent of oleander and ripe apricots blew up the terraced hillsides on the warm night air. I was in love with the world; and ashamed because I could not be ashamed.

I sat on the bed smiling, with the taste and smell of Hildy in my mouth and nostrils and the music of her profanity lingering in my mind like Mediterranean mist. But gradually I became aware that there were creatures in the room. One of them clung to my wrist, its little troll heart ticking gleefully. Another crouched on the table beside me like a gargoyle. In their presence my beautiful Italian world faded slowly. The olive groves and vineyards were replaced by an odorless monochrome vision of our apartment. Margaret was waiting patiently in the kitchen, humming Mozart as she tended her lonely chop, smiling with anticipation as she listened for the telephone. Sometimes she would raise her eyes to the kitchen clock above the stove and pause to turn her head attentively toward the kitchen door. How her eyes would light when it rang! How she would run into the living room, turn down the phonograph, and snatch it up, to hear her loyal, loving husband's voice. I closed my eyes and dropped my head. Thump, thump, thump, said the small demon clinging to my wrist; that's a heart-sound. Yes, I know, I said. He was a very primitive type of demon, apparently. The gargoyle was another matter entirely. Pick me up, he said. I am a magic gargoyle. Hold me to your ear like a seashell, and you will hear strange sounds. Stranger than mandolin music. Stranger than siren songs. You will hear the sounds of wind in ruined rigging, of torn sails flapping on a broken mast. You will hear the cries of starved comrades, and the scratch of their finger-nails on empty water casks. You will hear the roar of surf on terrible reefs, and the wail of drowning women, of women drowning in the unplumbed, salt, estranging sea.

A far more lyrical and learned fellow than his associate, whose persecutions never extended beyond a heartbeat (which I admit can be considerable). Not only did he appear to be familiar with Matthew Arnold, but I was pleased with his respect for the tradition which demands that with ruin there be associated a certain amount of rhapsody. He was monstrously cunning, this black, shiny creature; he knew me for what I am: a traditionalist. A piece of wisdom which, after the day's events, the reader no doubt shares. I accepted his invitation in a certain spirit of challenge; I will not go so far as to say of defiance— my position was far too weak for that—but, since you insist upon the term, of pragmatism. Let us see, I said in a properly professorial tone, very like that of my introductory lecture to Hildy, let us see just how far the claims of bourgeois life have laid hold of you; let us see if you cannot assimilate this perfectly normal "outlet experience"—a wonderful pragmatic touch, that!—with the equanimity it deserves; let us see whether you do not have a sufficiently comprehensive, sufficiently sophisticated understanding of human nature to be able to regard this event as neither evil, atavistic, treacherous, demented, nor particularly unusual. After all, a good half of the prime ministers of England were self-confessed adulterers. And that Voltaire, Napoleon, Shakespeare, Caravaggio—the list is infinite—could only very problematically have made their contributions to the world without the sustainment of their mistresses is too well known to require emphasis. You are in very distinguished company. Perhaps too distinguished. Well, then, if your comfort requires humbler instances, you have no more than to recall the three pages of newsprint through which you made your way at dinner no later than last night. Let us have less rhapsody, and more reason. *Tempora mutantur, nos et mutamur in illis.* Amen, I said, and picked up the gargoyle. Or telephone, I mean to say.

"Hello?" Margaret said. "Mickey?"

"Yes."

"Oh, it's so good to hear you! But you're *two minutes late!*"

"I'm sorry. My watch is doing strange things."

"Well, I'll get you a new one for your birthday."

"I wish you would," I said.

"What's the matter, darling? You sound tired."

"I am. It's been—well, a pretty busy day."

"Has it? How did your talk go?"

"I think it went pretty well. Part of it, anyway. I heard a couple of good comments."

"I'll bet it was the highlight of the convention. What did they say?"

"Oh, I don't know. The usual stuff. I don't really care. I just wish I was home."

"Oh, I do too. So much. You know what I even did?"

"What?"

"I even put on fresh lipstick and combed my hair, to be ready for your call." I was silent. "Well, aren't you flattered? Or do you think that's silly?"

"No, I think it's lovely."

"Thank you, darling. Well, what else did you do? Tell me."

"Oh, I looked over some of the exhibits, and then had lunch downtown."

"With Ed?"

"Who?"

"Ed. Isn't that who you were with last night?"

"Oh. Yes. No, he wasn't there. A fellow named Herb, a local fellow, and a couple of others. We went to this place called Bettino's. It was very good."

"I hope you didn't have any seafood."

"Well, I did, as a matter of fact. This place is supposed to specialize in lobster, so I though I'd try it. It was great."

"Oh, dear, I hope you don't come down with some awful disease."

"What disease?"

"I don't know, whatever it is you get in those places. Botulism, or whatever it is."

"I don't think there's much chance of that. I feel fine."

"But you said you were tired."

"Well, tired; but that's not a disease. How about if we get off this subject, anyway. I want to know what you've been doing all day."

"Yes, but first of all, when are you coming home? Tonight?"

"No, I think I'll wait till the morning, Mickey. I'm so dead beat I just can't deal with luggage and trains and everything right now. Do you mind?"

"Of course not, if you're tired. Have a hot shower and get right in bed. Are you sure you're all right, Mickey?"

"Sure. Just need a little sleep. Why?"

"You sound sort of funny. I don't like it when you go away. I worry."

"Well, cut it out. I'm fine. You still haven't told me what you did today."

"Well, I had the Baptist Home this morning, you know. Oh, there's the dearest little boy there now. I played Scrabble with him for *hours*."

"You win?"

"No! And that was *your* fault! I was thinking about you so much I couldn't concentrate properly. But he's so smart, honestly; he could probably beat me anyway. And then I went and bought some new placemats at Woodie's. Oh, and listen; some bill came that I don't understand at all. Did you get the transmission fixed or something?"

"Yes. From Mack's?"

"Yes. It's absolutely *awful*. I'm not even going to tell you about it."

"Well, stick it in the desk. I'll take care of it. Listen, Mickey."

"What?"

"I miss you. I missed you all day."

"Are you sure?"

"Yes."

"I'm so glad. I did, too. Mickey, will you have to go to the Library tomorrow, or are you coming straight home, or what?"

"Well, I'll come by and leave my things off, but I may go down to the office in the afternoon. And then again, I may not. It depends."

"On what?"

"On how pretty you are. And how persuasive. Stuff like that."

"I'll bet you stay."

"I'll bet I do, too."

"Well, we better hang up, darling. I've got a lot to do tonight."

"Like what?"

"Well, I've got to practice a French accent, and learn to

play the dulcimer, and get my hair dyed raven-black. Lots of things."

"No, don't do that," I said. "Just be you."

"I've been me for so long."

"Well, try it a little longer," I said. "I think it's going to work."

"All right. Good night, darling."

"Good night."

I hung up, and sat staring. Before going to bed I took a scalding shower and brushed my teeth for half an hour, but the taste of apricots is a very difficult one to eradicate. I take it that there was a storm during the night, for throughout my restless sleep I was aware of the turbulent, derelict sounds of a ship adrift; the snap and lash of flying halyards, the lurch of rolling cargo in the hold, the jarring thud of an untended, swinging boom.

In the morning I was up before it was light, and left the hotel before even the dining room was open. I posted myself in front of the first jewelry store I came to in the silent street, and the moment it had opened, went in, bought a pair of gold hoop earrings and paid to have them gift-wrapped and mailed to Hildy's address. I enclosed a card that said: *Here are your earrings back. I learned a lot about art, and many other things. Thanks. Mike.*

And if I have never been to Slagheap again, Hildy, I hope this will help to explain why.

I have recently acquired a cat. A grandiose remark, for the self-possession of these animals is proof against acquisition in anything like the ordinary sense. It would be better to say that I have been introduced into the mysteries of his companionship, a circumstance which provides me both with comfort and a certain amount of apprehension. Living as I do a very solitary life, my vulnerability to the charms of these creatures was perhaps predictable. It is interesting to note how Destiny, even in such an overcrowded world, manages to keep abreast of our fortunes and dispense accordingly. A cat, apparently, was the very thing I needed.

I live, as I say, a very solitary existence. It is relieved only by an infrequent invitation to dinner by one or another of my colleagues, an occasional play or concert in the company of acquaintances who have an out-of-town guest or relative in need of an escort, or, very much less frequently, a visit from, or to, one of my and Margaret's friends of better days. None of these occasions is an unmixed blessing. The domestic felicity of others, the atmosphere of a concert hall, and the company of people who knew Margaret and me of old are things composed for me almost equally of grace and pain. There was a time, shortly after my return from Europe, when I kept in nearly constant contact with the more intimate of our friends, in the hope that they would be able to give me news of Margaret—perhaps even a message from her—or be willing to intercede on my behalf, at least to the extent of persuading her to write to me. It took many months for me to be convinced of the fatuity of such hopes. If she wrote to them, or spoke to them by telephone, it must have been very rarely, and on those few occasions she must have made them swear so solemnly not to relay to me her conversation, whereabouts, activities, or intentions that she overrode successfully any ambitions they may have had to reconcile us.

In Susannah's case this must have required a very stern injunction indeed; one which included, perhaps, a full account of everything that had happened at Cap Ferrat. I could conceive of nothing less that would deter her from the attempt to bring us back together. The thought paralyzed me. It did, reader, although the present manuscript may seem to belie the fact. I had not yet decided, you see, upon the expedient—to which you find yourself so beleaguered a witness—of writing what amounts to an open letter to my wife. This stratagem—whether it constitutes an act of contrition, a confession, or a final moribund attempt to restore what I have desecrated—was still as far from my mind as it is presently, I am afraid, from my capacities, and I was far from enthusiastic about anyone (particularly Susannah) being in possession of the facts which I am so recklessly about to set down here.

Eventually I was able to dismiss the possibility, because I believed endlessly, and in spite of everything I had done to her, in Margaret's taste, tact, and mercy. She would never have told Susannah—or anyone—facts which would have exposed me to such shame and pain. How then, account for Susannah's silence about her present circumstances? The only explanation was that she was ignorant of them, as she insisted; that Margaret, in her determination to begin a totally new life, had broken off their friendship, as she had relinquished everyone and everything that would ever again remind her of me and of our marriage. It was a very believable conclusion; entirely consistent with this houseful of her abandoned possessions, to the custody of which my final years are dedicated: her books, her clothing, her photographs, her paintings, her box of garnets, her ticket stubs, her purple china ducks—every emblem of our life together. It is consistent, too, with three years of total silence.

Silence, of course, is the most equivocal factor in all human affairs. It can mean yes or no; it can signify outrage or consent; impregnability, fading resolution, surrender, or a hundred points between. It does not in itself dispose; it simply holds things in a fearful abeyance until they ripen or decay, until a principle matures, until a word or action has been found to match the disposition of the heart. Ladies understand the concept very well—almost as well as God, I think, on Whose enthusiasm for it they may well have modeled their own. Margaret understood it, always, and used it far more effectively and imaginatively than most people are able to use speech to heal, nourish, or sustain us in other times of tribulation. It is the memory of this fact that enables me to find comfort as well as condemnation in the silence which enfolds her now.

For example, she has never, through a lawyer or any other intermediary, requested a divorce. This is very strange. Our relationship, legally, stands exactly as it did three years ago. The titles to our house and automobile are still in both our names. She continues as beneficiary to my life insurance policy and as sole inheritrix of our estate. We are both, I take it, still mutually responsible for one another's debts. I continue to carry a joint checking account for which she still presumably has a checkbook, but on which she has never drawn a penny. A fact which led me to the inescapable conclusion, later confirmed by Susannah, that she was working; but where or at what I still have no idea. Not at the welfare agency, I know, because I called there shortly after my return and learned that she had submitted her resignation. She had asked permission to use them as a reference, but they had no knowledge of her present occupation. Had she expressed an intention to continue in the same sort of work? They had no idea. Would they let me know if they received a request for a testimonial from a prospective employer? If it were consistent with her wishes.

When she left Cap Ferrat she had, as nearly as I can calculate, three hundred dollars in the form of cash and traveler's checks, a return ticket on Air France, and a private savings account of her own—the fruit of her labor at the welfare agency —of about two thousand dollars. This was the foundation of her new life. To someone of Margaret's intelligence, education, and determination it would have served, but it did not add to my joy to consider how comfortably.

A week after my return I called the bank and asked for the balance on her account. The information, I was told, could not be given over the telephone, and in any case to no one other than the holder of the account.

"She's my wife, damn it," I said.

"I'm sorry, sir. A personal bank account is a strictly confidential matter."

"Can you let me know if the account is closed?"

"It has not been closed."

For a time I made a really desperate attempt to find her. I suspect that she went to visit her father in Kansas almost as soon as she returned. Certainly she had called him immediately, because I spoke to him myself within six hours of my own arrival (which followed hers by a day), and he admitted that she had telephoned him the evening before, but he would tell me nothing of her plans or whereabouts.

"Is she with you now?" I asked.

"No. Oh, no."

"Is she coming there to see you?"

"I can't . . . Michael, I can't . . ." (In his shock, confusion, and grief, the old man's sentences ended frequently in a gasp for self-control. It was a conversation I do not like to remember.)

"Will you let me know her address?"

"I can't tell you anything, Michael. She made me promise. She was very firm about it. She hasn't even told me what it was that happened between you. I can't understand it. My little girl has always seemed so happy."

"I want to speak to her. You've got to tell me where she is."

"You'll have to give her time, Michael. You'll have to give her time."

I called him again, periodically, but he would tell me nothing. Only that she was "getting along quite well, considering." His confusion grew into irascibility, then an old man's implacable hatred. Eventually he would not speak to me at all. "You must let her alone," he said. "You've got to stop bothering us this way." I wrote several letters, to him and to Margaret in care of him, but they went unanswered. The last few times I called he hung up the telephone the moment he recognized my voice.

My conversations with Susannah, as I have said, were no more fruitful. The first of these, like that with Margaret's father, was on the evening of my return from France. It seemed very probable to me that in her shame and humiliation, Margaret would have fled to her for refuge. But Susannah had heard nothing. There was no doubting her word, on that occasion at least; no one could have simulated such dismay. "I don't believe it," she kept saying. "I just don't believe it, Mickey. It's too awful."

"Well, I don't quite believe it myself," I said. "But it's true. It's been coming on for a long time, as I say. It had to happen sooner or later, I guess."

"But I thought. Well, we *all* thought. Well, you know what we thought."

"Are you sure she isn't there, Susie?"

"No. Oh, Lord, I wish she *was*. Oh, Mickey, do you think she's all right?"

"I hope so. I know she spoke to her father last night, because I just called him. But he wouldn't tell me anything."

"Maybe she's gone *there*."

"Maybe. But he says not. Will you let me know if you hear from her?"

"Yes."

"You promise?"

"Yes. Well, if she says it's all right. I can't if she doesn't want me to."

"No. Well, thank you, Susie."

"I wish there was something I could do."

"Yes, so do I."

I called her again regularly, once a week, but she continued to deny having heard anything from Margaret. I could not believe it at first, as I have said; it was not reasonable to suppose that, as lonely, as desperate, as she must be, Margaret would not have written or spoken to her dearest friend. And yet, if she had, it was not consistent with Susannah's character to conceal the fact, to refrain from making some sort of attempt, however contraband, at reconciling us. I could only suppose that Margaret had told her everything and that, inspired by this ugly knowledge, Susannah was dedicated to keeping her friend out of my clutches forever. Yet this conviction, too, passed in time. She was not sufficiently hostile, not sufficiently guarded or devious in her manner, to warrant Margaret's having confided any such facts to her. Nor could I truly believe that Margaret, in her mercy, would have done so. The only eventual conclusion was that Susannah, like everything and everyone else associated with me, had been cut out of her life forever. Discouraged by this growing conviction, my calls became less frequent, less animated.

Then, in October, three months after my return, Susannah called me one day at my office.

"I'm in Washington," she said. "I've come down to do some shopping, and I thought we might have lunch together."

"Have you heard from Mickey?"

"Yes. Just yesterday."

"What did she say?"

"She wrote. Why don't we have lunch, and I'll let you read her letter."

"Fine. I'll meet you at the Methodist Club on the Hill, at two. The cabby will know where it is. Is two all right?"

"Yes, fine."

I was filled with a wild anticipation which I had to suppress very carefully. Whether her news would demand celebration or mourning I was in awful doubt; I felt, in either case, it would incapacitate me for the remainder of the day, and instructed my secretary accordingly. By two o'clock the thundering midday patronage of Capitol Hill employees had decently subsided and we were able to speak quietly in the restaurant. It was a year since I had seen Susannah, and the first time ever, I realized suddenly, that I had seen her alone and apart from Margaret. Perhaps it was this fact that was subtly subversive to her beauty, for although she was as elegant, as darkly dramatic, as perfectly appointed as ever, she seemed, in the absence of Margaret's patronage, to have suffered some elemental diminution of her charm (as had, indeed, the world). She gave the impression of being rendered in a pastel-colored blancmange from some extremely ingenious mold for an exquisite but ephemeral occasion, a wedding, a garden party, or the centenary of a ladies' musical society. I drank a martini rapidly, considering this phenomenon, while we exchanged civilities. Poor Susannah, I thought; you need her as much as me.

"I don't know if you remember or not," she said, "but next

week is little Maggie's birthday. *My* Maggie's, I mean." I had forgotten. "Well, there's no reason why you shouldn't, with what you've got to think about. Anyway, I got a package yesterday from Margaret, with a present for Mag. It was a beautiful Algerian doll. I don't know if you know anything about it— it seemed to come from France."

I was not likely to forget. We had bought it at a market-stall in Nice, from a rolling-eyed, gelatinous Gypsy woman who had assured us that it was *"absolument exact, en tout respect."* I had lifted its skirts to verify the fact, at which the Gypsy woman had shrieked with brown-toothed laughter, and Margaret had slapped my fingers, calling me *"un monstre, n'est-ce pas, Madame?"* The Gypsy, with the cunning of her race, had confirmed the accusation.

"Yes," I said. "I remember. We bought it in Nice."

"Well, it's absolutely beautiful, and Mag is thrilled with it. She has a collection of them, you know."

"Where was it mailed from?" I asked.

"From her father's. But she isn't there. It's in the letter. I guess you want to see it right away."

"Yes."

She unsnapped her purse and took the letter out. It was in an unstamped envelope, written in Margaret's sprawling hand, but with unusal care, it seemed to me, as if it had been copied from a draft:

Dearest Susie:
   This is for Maggie for her birthday, with love from Mickey and me. What a big girl she must be now. Give her a kiss for me.
   I'm sure Mickey has been in touch with you by this time, and that you know about our separation. I'm not going into a long explanation of what happened; Mickey has already told you what happened—the facts, *anyway—and that's probably as much as either of us knows about it. How do we know how these things happen? Anyway, it can't be too much of a surprise to you, after that letter I wrote you from Cap Ferrat. Forgive me if I don't say any more about it just now.*

I'm all right now, and working at something I like very much. I work hard, and believe in what I'm doing, and have some interesting friends, for which I thank God.

I do hope you and Nick and the children are happy and well. Give them all my love.

I'm leaving this package with my dad to mail. I'm sure he'll forget it, so I'll have to call him a couple of weeks before Maggie's birthday and jog his memory.

I may be near Philadelphia this winter, and if I am I'll call you, if it seems the thing to do at that time. Be happy, dear.

Love, Maggie

I read it three times, while Susannah sipped her martini and sighed audibly. I searched every line for meaning, for some sort of cryptic message which she might have concealed behind the confoundingly bland and noncommittal tenor of the words, but I was forced to the conclusion that it was deliberately laconic, designed to yield nothing whatever in the very likely case that Susannah would show it to me. I put it in the envelope and gave it back to her.

"I'm afraid she doesn't have very much to say," Susannah said.

"No."

She plucked the olive out of her martini and nibbled at it. "I don't understand what she says about the letter. I didn't get any letter from her."

"Maybe she forgot to mail it," I said.

"I guess so. I wonder what she said in it?"

I shook my head.

"She sounds so sort of—gray, or something, I don't know. Oh, it's awful. It's just awful." She bit her lip and stared across the dining room. "You know, Mickey, I love Meg more than anybody else I ever knew."

"I know," I said. "I do too."

Her eyes swung back to mine with a startled look of incredulity.

"Well, then, why in heaven's name—? Then, why—"

"What she discovered in France," I said. "What we both discovered, is that I just don't deserve her. Or anything else, very much. She's a hell of a lot better off by herself. Believe me."

"Oh, for God's sake, Mickey."

"No, it's true. Really."

She stared at me with a look of bewilderment and disbelief which I did not at all enjoy. "Have you heard from Mitch lately?" I asked.

"Oh, Christmas cards. He's in Florida, you know. Mitch is not exactly a literary type. Do you?"

"Once in a while. He's written a couple of times, but I don't answer. He asked me once if I'd like to come down and spend a couple of months cruising the Keys with him. He has a new boat."

"Why don't you? It would be good for you."

"I might, if he stays." There was a considerable silence. My state of wild anticipation had withered into a gray deathlike composure. I was now very tired. "What are you doing in Washington, anyway?" I asked.

"Oh, just shopping. And I wanted you to see the letter, of course. There's a woman here who fits me better than anybody in the world, so I come down every fall and buy a suit from her. Do you remember Ima? I saw her last night."

"Oh? How is she?"

"She's fine. She's going to New York, I guess, with Wanamaker's. I didn't know whether to tell her about you two or not, but apparently you'd already talked to her."

"Yes, I called her a couple of times. She hadn't heard anything, either, I guess?"

"No. Mickey, do you mean to tell me you haven't heard a word from her, ever? Not since you came back?"

"No." I drained my martini and rapped the stem of the glass with my fingernails. "That's one thing that keeps me going, actually. She hasn't asked for a divorce. Of course, she probably will, any day. I almost dread hearing the phone ring, anymore. I don't know whether to pick it up or not."

"Oh, it's awful," Susannah said. She looked as if she might cry. "I wish sometimes that I'd never allowed one of those parties of mine to end. Stationed a gunman at the door, or something, and refused to let anyone go home. Then we'd all still be sitting there on the living-room rug drinking martinis and eating canapés and talking about love. And I'd just keep turning the clock back, every hour. That's the way it was best. I think that's all we're really good for, any of us: just to talk about love, not to really make it."

"You may be right."

"I wish there was something I could do."

"You can let me know if you hear from Meg."

"I will if she lets me, but you know I can't otherwise."

"Yes, I know."

"Why don't you come up to Philadelphia, Mickey, and spend a week with us? It would do you good."

"I don't know whether it would or not," I said. "But thanks."

It was a dreadful luncheon, and Susannah did not deserve to be subjected to it, but I was simply incapable of any effort at charm. That was the last time I have seen her, although I called her again several times that winter and spring, to learn if she had heard from Margaret. She had not. Mitch, as you have learned, had gone to Florida, and Ima to New York. Such other of our close friends as remain in Washington I studiously avoid.

Now this makes—as I began this chapter by telling you—for a rather reclusive life; excessively so, to be candid. One from which, for the simple sake of sanity, I have had occasionally to seek relief.

I would propose, as one of the most pernicious of all possible states of mind, that engendered by arriving home weary, with wet feet and aching eyes, after a forty-five-minute bus ride through the city of Washington, to a silent, dark house where still—although the mad hope reigns eternally that there may one day be—there is to be seen no woman's coat thrown across a chair, no seated figure rising with a tremulously spoken greeting, no scent of verbena freshly diffused in the air, as subtly as if the blossoms of that flower had been bruised by a shower of rain. The state of mind is one all too well known to me, but recently and with mysterious providence it was relieved by the advent of the cat, a creature whom I brought to your attention in the opening paragraph of this chapter. Let me very briefly describe this advent to you, since I have a feeling that the influence of the animal may make itself felt in the pages of this book which follow.

I arrived home one evening about a month ago in much the condition I have described above, hung my overcoat over the radiator to dry, and went into the bathroom, where I removed my wet shoes and stood my umbrella in the tub. Carrying the shoes in my hand I climbed the stairs to our bedroom door, where I stood for a moment with my hand grasping the cool French porcelain knob, feeling a ridiculous but irrepressible quickening of the heart before I thrust it open to stare into the dark still room. (It contained shadowy tumuli, portraits of night on the pale walls, and sudden parched, maniacal tickings from the huddled cabinetry.) I went in, took off my suit and hung it up, put on a pair of slacks, a pair of slippers, and a sweater, and carrying to Margaret's bed the pair of china ducks, dumped out upon her counterpane the contents of their abdomen: a shower of frayed, gradually disintegrating theater and concert ticket-stubs, bearing each the date of a magical evening in the span of fourteen years. (There are five hundred and twelve of them; which, divided by two, equals two hundred and fifty-six nights of winter brilliance, of dark seas of symphony, of taxicabs with windows illuminated by cold, streaming fireflies, and afterward, of late suppers of turkey breast, pickles, and Zinfandel wine by firelight, in the course of which one might sometimes fall asleep before the embers in a litter of crumpled paper napkins and bread- and cork- and turkey-crumbs, until the Sunday paper thumped against the door.) Having completed this little ritual, I restored the ticket-stubs to the ducks, went out of the bedroom and down the hall toward the kitchen, where I prepared a meal consisting of a lamb chop, powdered mashed potatoes, and half a package of frozen succotash. After eating it in a very methodical way (twelve bites to the mouthful), I stacked the dishes in the sink, ran hot water over them, and went back down the hall to the living room, where I sat down in front of a coffee table on which, on a playing board, there were chess pieces set up for a game in progress.

This game had become one of the chief stratagems in my struggle against the elves of silence. About a year ago, while sitting in the dentist's office, I came upon a magazine called, with splendid simplicity, *Chess*; and leafing through its pages I discovered the announcement of an international correspondence tournament. I submitted my entry fee of ten dollars and within a week was rewarded with the name and address of my first opponent, Senor Esparolini, a milliner, of Santander, Spain. His chess, like his correspondence, proved to be florid, impassioned, and fascinatingly undisciplined. He attacked very much as had his forebears of the Armada fleet the isle of Britain, and with much the same results. Within a month his forces lay in ruin around me, the result much less of my cunning than of his own abandon. He wrote me a tragic, animated letter of capitulation which contained eleven exclamation points. My second opponent, a Herr Zimmerman, and the Obermeister of an Austrian town named Glug, was a very different matter. Here was a man concerned with power, not millinery, and his letters, like his play, reflected the fact in a stern, ferociously formal, and intractably unimaginative style whose chief characteristics were Wagnerian capital G's and great epic sweeps of his rooks and bishops across whatever open spaces were unimpeded.

This diversion, as I say, was very beneficial to me. It reawakened both my intellectual and my competitive instincts, and afforded what was virtually my only constant contact, in a recreational way, with other human souls—however remote or mysterious they might be. I was in the eighth week of my contest with Herr Zimmerman, and much stirred by it. But not sufficiently, I must confess, to prevent my looking up occasionally in the midst of my cogitations—with a pawn, perhaps, dangling between my thumb and forefingers—to catch what I imagined was the sudden, spine-chilling rattle of a latchkey in the door, the creak of a certain loose board beneath the Oriental carpet in the foyer, or perhaps the first faint chiming note of the merry tinkling of her keys against the throat of a cloisonné vase on the hall table with which she used to announce her arrival home. These sudden startings-up, with parted lips and suspended fingers, characterized, as a matter of fact, all of my domestic activities: reading, listening to records, paring turnips, ironing my handkerchiefs. And on this occasion I had just succumbed again to such an illusion, raising my head with sudden scalded attentiveness to what was almost certainly the nervously ineffectual efforts of fingertips about the brass key-plate of the front door. But in this miraculous instance the sound did not dissipate, as usual, or transpose into the chirping of an insect, the tick of woodwork, or a mechanical flurry of some kind from the street or the plumbing. It continued for a moment, paused, then resumed unmistakably—a gentle persistent scrabbling, quite undoubtedly issuing from the entrance door. I set down my pawn with a stealthy, transfixed movement, and after listening for another excruciating moment, rose swiftly and plunged toward the foyer, upsetting Herr Zimmerman's machinations almost as operatically as he had conceived them. I steadied myself, opened the door unhurriedly with an agonizing composure, and murmured, "Mickey?" But Margaret, of course, was not there. There was this cat, black as satin, looking up at me with amber, oceanic eyes. I could see in them the glint of northern sun on silent floes of ice.

He entered immediately, loped down the corridor ahead of me toward the living room, leapt onto a copy of *Sartor Sartoris* on the bookshelf, and after blinking for a moment with royal indolence, began to burnish his black breast with a scarlet tongue.

That was very nearly a month ago. Since that time he has been almost constantly in my presence when I am at home, an arrangement from which I derive considerable satisfaction, although I am at a loss to explain it. It is a less than usual occurrence to find a cat of such obvious pedigree and value wandering at liberty in the neighborhood. I posted a notice of his whereabouts on the mail-box panel, I advertised the circumstances of his arrival in the lost-and-found columns of both the morning and evening newspapers. No owner materialized. I was delighted. I purchased a large supply of cat food, a toy called Hap-E-Kat in the form of an extremely realistic rubber mouse, a small sachet of catnip, and a publication entitled *Keeping Kitty Kozy*. All very mistaken provisions, for this creature, I have discovered after a month of fascinating introduction to his ways, eats nothing but milk and honey, puts to scorn all conventional efforts at animal husbandry, is far above petty amusements or the use of intoxicants of any kind, and apparently requires, for the satisfaction of his predatory instincts, something of infinitely greater consequence than mice. Although he appears to enjoy my company to the extent of submitting himself to it for hours, he is certainly not affectionate, intimate, or even domestic in any ordinary sense. He dislikes being held, groomed, caressed, or even touched. He is, in fact, markedly aloof. He will not even suffer himself to occupy the same altitude as I; he stations himself invariably upon the bookshelf, sideboard, mantelpiece, or some other elevation superior to my own and stares down at me for hours with intent almond eyes in which I see glimpses of a cool, illimitable, sauterne-colored sea where amber icebergs glint and snap and floating faces sometimes touch the surface to thaw unnameably in the sun. This might well be thought to unnerve one, but its effect, in fact, is quite the opposite: a strange, enfolding sense of comfort, of profound companionship, perhaps even of patronage on his part. A remark which may appear absurd to all but the confirmed cat-fanciers among you. These few will be aware of the deep sense of communion, of luxury, largess, even license, that is bestowed by the illimitable arctic light of such an animal's eyes.

· · ·

In my enthusiasm about the cat I have neglected to tell you the outcome of my trip to Slagheap. As a matter of fact, I would very much prefer to say nothing at all on the subject, but since it is necessary to account for our decision to spend a holiday in France I feel obliged to record the episode, in the name of logic. So many outrages have been committed in that name that it can't do very much harm to add another.

Very well. I am standing in the blue bedroom, my suitcase in my hand. It is very close to noon, and the sunlight streams strongly through the blue veils of the curtains and falls across the bed, which is freshly made and turned down. I hear a bird singing, muted, through the windowpanes. I look about, bemused. Margaret, who is standing behind me, speaks.

MARGARET: Does it look nice?

MYSELF: You have no idea. You have no idea how dreadful a bedroom can be.

MARGARET: You're never to go away again. You've suffered.

MYSELF: I have indeed. (I set my suitcase down and stare at it in dismay. Someone has fixed to it a huge circular orange sticker bearing the arms and title of the Thomas Edison Hotel and the legend: In The Heart of Downtown Slagheap.) That's got to come off. I never want to see it again.

MARGARET: Isn't it awful the way they do that to your luggage without even asking? It's an especially horrid one, isn't it? (She kneels down and scratches at the sticker with her fingernail.) Gosh, I don't know; it's going to be pretty hard. These new glues they use are awful.

MYSELF: I don't care if it takes nitroglycerin; it's got to come off, or it gets thrown out. It's like advertising that you've spent a season in hell.

MARGARET: My poor Orpheus. What season was it?

MYSELF: It was winter. It's always winter there. Don't let anyone fool you: hell is cold. (I sit down on the bed and reaching toward her, take two thick strands of her hair in my hands.) What made you say you were going to dye it black? That's an awful thing to say.

MARGARET: I thought you might be tired of it this color. I wanted to be strange and wonderful for you. Wicked.

MYSELF: Wicked Mickey.

MARGARET: Wicked Mickey. Sticky wicket. Shall I unpack you?

MYSELF: Yes, please. (I lie back on the bed, lace my fingers on my chest, and stare up at the ceiling.) There's a bird singing. A cardinal. I used to be able to identify thirty-two birdcalls. I astonished my scoutmaster. Am I really forty-one years old?

MARGARET: Yes, you have to be, because I'm thirty-six. Why?

MYSELF: I think we ought to start lying about it. Shall we?

MARGARET: All right.

MYSELF: Have you ever lied to me, Maggie?

MARGARET: Yes, once.

MYSELF: Have you really? When?

MARGARET: I'm not going to tell you. I'm wicked.

MYSELF: No, really, have you?

MARGARET: *Yes!* Listen, did you ever change your socks?

MYSELF: Certainly I changed my socks.

MARGARET: You did *not*. I gave you four pair, and there are still three here that haven't even been touched. Honestly.

MYSELF: I don't know; maybe I forgot. The whole thing was such a nightmare.

MARGARET: Well, tell me about it. What actually happened? Did you distinguish yourself?

MYSELF: Distinguish myself. I suppose I did, yes. In a sense.

MARGARET: Well, how? What did you talk about?

MYSELF: Talk about?

MARGARET: Yes. Your famous lecture. What was it about?

MYSELF: My famous lecture was about art, mostly. And love. There was a little bit in it about death, too. It was pretty comprehensive.

MARGARET: It sounds like it. Isn't that all a little out of your line?

MYSELF: Yes, but I thought I'd have a fling at it, anyway. They were all pretty drunk, and it was my big chance. I did pretty well, too. Of course, it took a while to warm them up, but then I really got going. I really think they were quite impressed. It was very surprising.

MARGARET: Mickey, stop being *arch*. I want to know. What did you talk about?

MYSELF: Egyptology. The Hanes Index System. Triple Reference.

MARGARET: Oh. Well—did they like it?

MYSELF: They loved it. *Loved* it. Listen to that cardinal. Listen, Meg!

MARGARET: Isn't he sweet? He does that all day. I put raisins on the windowsill, and when they run out he gets so *mad*. He pecks right at the window pane. I think he's going to break it some day. Where is your blue necktie? I bet you've left it.

MYSELF: I don't know. I love it in this room.

MARGARET: It's a nice room, isn't it? I love it, too. But I don't know what's happened to our scarlet tanager. We had a scarlet tanager last year; remember?

MYSELF: We always have red birds. Why is that?

MARGARET: For me, of course. (She sings, to the tune of "Red Roses for a Blue Lady," Red *bird*-ies, for a blue *la*-dy—.)

MYSELF: That's lovely. Sad and lovely. Listen, Meg, did you really lie to me?

MARGARET: Certainly. Do you think I'd lie about it?

MYSELF: I don't believe you. When? What was it about?

MARGARET: I'm not going to tell you. Ever. You can scream, or languish, or do whatever you like. You'll just never know. Who did you like most in Slagheap?

MYSELF: I'm not going to tell you. Not until you tell me what you lied to me about.

MARGARET: Oh, *ho!*

MYSELF: Oh, ho, *ho!*

MARGARET: I can see it's going to be horrible, being married to greatness. You've come back all pompous and mystic. I'm never going to let you go to Slagheap again.

MYSELF: Do you promise?

MARGARET: *Promise?* That's a *threat.* There, now. You're all unpacked. Now all we've got to do is get that sticker off and you'll be as good as new.

MYSELF: Do you think so? Won't it leave a big blotch, or something?

MARGARET: Well, if it does, we can paste another one right on top of it. A lovely romantic one of some kind. Susie has some wonderful ones she got at Nice last year.

MYSELF: That would be nice.

MARGARET: They say IMPERIAL—NICE. CÔTE D'AZUR. With a big sunburst and a blue sea.

MYSELF: Wouldn't that be lovely. It must be very clean there. All sun and water.

MARGARET: (Now rises and comes to sit beside me on the bed. She sits looking down at me for a moment, shakes free a Kleenex from the pocket of her skirt and wipes my lips with it.) Lipstick. You didn't shave this morning.

MYSELF: No, I couldn't wait to get out of there. If I had spent another moment of my life in that bathroom I would have gone mad. I would have come home gibbering and squealing.

MARGARET: You might never have got here.

MYSELF: Very likely.

MARGARET: I would have had to advertise for a pompous, mystic, gibbering, squealing husband. It was pretty bad here, too. I've never really been lonely before, do you know that? I got terribly sentimental. Do you know what I used to do?

MYSELF: No.

MARGARET: I used to put your picture under my pillow at night. And I graduated from college. Think of that.

MYSELF: What picture?

MARGARET: That one, on my table.

MYSELF: Bring it over here, will you? (Margaret rises and brings from her dressing table the silver-framed photograph of myself as a child. She hands it to me. I study it for a moment.) I used to know thirty-two birdcalls. The summer that picture was taken I made a sewing basket for my mother out of raffia. I learned how to do that at camp in Maine. You know the camp I showed you, near the cottage? There was a craft shop where we went on rainy days. It was so nice in there, with the rain on the roof, and the smell of sawdust and leather. I can remember so well, working on that basket, all day long. It was for her birthday. I can even remember printing on the card, very carefully, with a red crayon, "I'm not sure when your birthday is, but happy birthday when it comes. Sincerely, Michael."

MARGARET: Oh, that's sweet.

MYSELF: I was a very nice little boy. Do you know that, Mick? I miss me.

MARGARET: (She lies beside me on the bed, resting her head on my breast.) Never mind, darling. You're still somewhere.

MYSELF: No. I'm gone. You look around one day and can't find yourself anywhere. It's very depressing. (Margaret's head rests immediately beneath my chin, and I become aware of a very curious fact: her hair is perfumed. Perhaps only with lacquer or shampoo, but at any rate it has a definite artificial scent. I ponder upon what a curious thing it is that my wife's hair should be perfumed while that of that poor reckless vagabond should be as pure and scentless as a child's. I am in a strangely sensitive frame of mind which lends an enormous, rather morbid significance to everything.) Why don't you give me a drink, so I'll stop gibbering and squealing so much?

MARGARET: No, I'm not going to move.

MYSELF: Suppose somebody hit you on the head with a framed photograph; would you move then?

MARGARET: No. I want to hear more about your buried life. Right up through the Slagheap chapter.

MYSELF: I'll go to work unless I get a drink.

MARGARET: You better *not*!

MYSELF: All right, then. (Margaret sighs theatrically, rises from the bed, takes the photograph to the dressing table, and replaces it. She lifts her arm to look at her wristwatch, then turns to face me.)

MARGARET: Do you know what time it is? A quarter past twelve. You can't start drinking at a quarter past twelve.

MYSELF: I can start drinking any time I like, because of the beauty and sensitivity of my nature.

MARGARET: A very beautiful nature you have. You wear dirty socks, you drink from morning to night, you gibber and squeal. You've gone absolutely to pieces in that town.

MYSELF: Roll up a barrel of Scotch, woman, and hush. (She goes out of the bedroom with a sneer. I rise from the bed, undress, take a pair of pajamas out of the dresser drawer, and put them on. I hang up my clothing in a meditative way, then get into the bed and pull the sheet up to my chin, staring out of

the window. An undulant, pale shadow of a sycamore tree falls across the blue gauze of the curtains.
My thoughts bend slowly into elegant deformities,
like the shadow. They rise and spiral slowly, like
smoke from an autumn bonfire one believed safely
out, but which has gone on smoldering through
the night. Can you guess what they are, reader?
Can you imagine what I am thinking of while I
stare at the pale, smokelike shadows of the sycamore on the bedroom curtains? Ah, one of you can,
I see. That one—that reader, there, with the somewhat heavy eyes and gently smiling mouth—has
guessed it perfectly. A woman's body. You are very
clever, sir. And what woman, smiling reader? Hildy
Hunzinger. Exactly. And now may I rely further
on your perception to exonerate me from the
charge of perfidy? Dare I call on you to explain
to your fellow readers that these thoughts of mine
do not represent wanton treachery, but something
—if it is conceivable—very nearly the opposite?
That they are in fact a willed, deliberate technique
on the part of a desperate man to accommodate his
wife? That the slumbering fire has been stirred,
as it were, by an artful toe? Would you undertake
that, sir, on my behalf? No? I do not blame you.
A most unpleasant premise of which to serve as
advocate, and one which you might find some difficulty in convincing your fellow readers of. I appreciate your understanding, however. Let us hope
it is infectious, for I see I have no more time to
illuminate the point. Margaret has returned, bearing an iced-tea glass filled to the very brim with
what I sincerely hope is whisky. She pauses in the
doorway with a smile whose satisfaction she does
nothing to disguise.)

MARGARET: Well, look at you.

MYSELF: I'm in bed.

MARGARET: I see you are. Do you think this will put you back together?

MYSELF: What is it? It had better not be tea.

MARGARET: It's the very best Jack Daniels, saved to celebrate your return. I didn't think it would be quite so precipitate, however.

MYSELF: If there is one thing in the world that should never be put off, it is the mood for revelry. It is the most sovereign of all impulses; did you know that?

MARGARET: I've always suspected it. Is this the Creed of the Conventioneer? (She brings the glass to me and sits down on the bed.)

MYSELF: Oh, absolutely. (I sit up to take the glass from her, drink deeply, shudder, and lower the glass to clasp it between my knees. I have had no breakfast; I am drunk almost immediately.) The oldest institution, and the only one that will endure, is the carnival. Do you know why?

MARGARET: Why?

MYSELF: Because along with the knowledge of death goes the necessity, and the capacity, to laugh at it. Both are peculiar to mankind. Now. You know what? We're going to have a carnival.

MARGARET: How lovely! Will there be a clown?

MYSELF: There will certainly be a clown. Also a *jongleur,* and a fortune-teller, and a tattooed lady. Would you care to bring me three small objects of roughly the same size and weight from somewhere in the room?

MARGARET: Oh, yes! (She rises and goes with gay consent to the dressing table, where, after a moment of searching about, she selects a cigarette lighter made of blue-and-white Wedgewood bisque, a small cut-glass pin-tray, and a perfume bottle.) Will these do?

MYSELF: Perfectly.

MARGARET: You'd better not break them.

MYSELF: Well, I might. Something always gets broken at a carnival, but that's the nature of the institution. The thing to do is to put yourself in the proper carnival spirit of abandon, and then it doesn't really matter. Now, will you just hold my glass for a moment? (She does so. I take the three objects she has placed on the bedsheet and begin to juggle them expertly. This is a trick I learned as a boy, with tennis balls, while awaiting the turn of my brother and myself to use the court. Margaret is astonished.)

MARGARET: Mickey! That's wonderful! I had no idea you could do anything so clever. How in the world did you learn it?

MYSELF: You mustn't ask. The mysteries of the *jongleur*'s art die with him. This is nothing. Before the show is over I will do you a piece of magic that will leave you gasping. (I set down the objects, raise my glass, and drink deeply again. The whisky has a lovely earthen, elemental taste: sunlight, Italian earth, a wet wind blowing off the sea through acres of rustling vineyards where clusters of blue grapes hang glowing.) Now, another little sample of what it is that makes a man doggedly swing his feet onto the floor at six o'clock in the morning, or into bed, at ten o'clock at night. Bring me a shining silver coin.

MARGARET: A coin?

MYSELF: You'll find one on the bureau, with my keys.

MARGARET: (She goes to look, plucks up a coin, and returns with it.) Will a quarter do?

MYSELF: Nicely. Observe that I hold it in my right hand. Now I lean forward and place my left elbow on my knee. And now you're going to see me rub the coin into my arm. Into the living flesh. Silver, transmuted into hungering tissue, into uproarious blood. (This is a parlor trick a school friend taught me, and with which I used to hold my campmates spellbound at the mess table. I open my fingers quickly to show my hand is empty.)

MARGARET: Oh, my goodness. It's gone!

MYSELF: Gone. Into the greedy flesh. Into the ravening flesh that gathers all into itself. Gone with all the treasure of the earth, to feed the avid heart of man.

MARGARET: Where is it? Where? It isn't in your avid heart, at all. It's in your sleeve. (She seizes my arm, twists, prods, and peers at it, shakes my sleeve.) Well, that's fantastic. You're a very mysterious man. My heavens, I didn't know I was married to a magician.

MYSELF: You are indeed. It is what no woman knows. (I raise the glass and drink again.)

MARGARET: Listen, I'm supposed to get *some* of that, you know.

MYSELF: You?

MARGARET: Yes, me. It was supposed to be a loving cup. I thought you said this was a carnival.

MYSELF: That's true. Drink. Fortify yourself. You're going to see strange sights. Feats of necromancy that will chill your blood, or possibly boil it.

MARGARET: Do you know *more*?

MYSELF: I've only just begun. In a moment I'm going to perform the supreme act of sorcery. The ultimate spell.

MARGARET: My goodness. It's exciting.

MYSELF: We'll begin with a minor piece of witchcraft. Close your eyes, please. (She does so. I lean toward her and kiss her on the mouth. Our lips are wet with whisky. A wild Italian girl laughs darkly in the shadow of an orchard.)

MARGARET: (Opening her eyes slowly) My goodness. How did you do *that*? That was a wonderful one. It made me go all shivery.

MYSELF: Necromancy, daughter. You've got to stop asking how I do things. Accept the enchantment without questioning. To understand the wizard is to slay him. And yourself.

MARGARET: Oh, dear. Don't tell me, then.

MYSELF: Don't worry. Now you have to go and get me a lipstick and one of your eyebrow pencils. A green one, I think.

MARGARET: What for?

MYSELF: We're going to have the second act. The Tattooed Lady. This is your chance to participate. I think you'll enjoy it.

MARGARET: I think I'd better have another drink.

MYSELF: I think I'll join you. (We drink in turn. The glass is very nearly empty. Margaret raises her eyebrows very high and blinks.)

MARGARET: My. (She lays her hand against her throat.) What was it you wanted? An eyebrow pencil?

MYSELF: And a lipstick. But maybe you'd better fill this up again first. We can't let the carnival spirit lag.

MARGARET: I don't think it's lagging a bit. (She takes the empty glass from me, sniffs at it, and smiles.) Jack Daniels, that old necromancer. I'll be right back. Don't go away.

MYSELF: There is not the smallest chance. (Margaret rises from the bed and with only the barest hint of instability makes her way to the door and out of the bedroom, bearing the empty glass. I watch her, squinting to maintain focus. I am appalled equally by my own vulgarity and by what I consider to be its absolute inevitability. I am sworn to the success of this carnival. As against the disaster of its failure this present loss of dignity is nothing. I smile with drunken determination. There is a huge, comic desolation about everything. I get out of bed with slow, elaborate precision and wander to the dressing table, where, after considerable poking about in the center drawer, I find a lipstick and two eyebrow pencils, one black and one green. I place them in the breast pocket of my pajamas and am wandering about the bedroom in search of cigarettes when Margaret returns.)

MARGARET: What are you doing now?

MYSELF: Looking for cigarettes. There's a kind of counter-magician or something at work around here. Cigarettes weren't supposed to disappear.

MARGARET: They're right in front of you.

MYSELF: I'll be damned. Have you got the stuff?

MARGARET: I've got it, but I'm not sure you ought to have it. I think you're getting a tiny bit drunkie.

MYSELF: I'm not surprised. I didn't have any breakfast.

MARGARET: Oh, Mickey! Honestly. You know that's the very worst thing you can do, not have any breakfast? That's how you get ulcers.

MYSELF: I don't believe it. I've heard it all my life, and I just don't believe it. Do you know the ancient Greeks never ate anything until noon? Think of that. Think of all those rumbling stomachs in the Acropolis in the morning. Must have sounded like a thunderstorm around there. That's the kind of atmosphere that breeds philosophy. (I light a cigarette and get back into bed. Margaret sits beside me. I take the glass from her hand and drink from it.) Oh, that's very good. Did you put garlic in it?

MARGARET: No, does it taste like it?

MYSELF: Something does. Definite taste of garlic. Now, will you put that on the table for me, please, and turn around?

MARGARET: Why do I have to turn around?

MYSELF: Because I want to unbutton your blouse. And the buttons all seem to be in the back.

MARGARET: (Sets the glass on the night table for me and obediently turns her back, sitting patiently with bowed head. I unfasten the buttons of her blouse, very inexpertly, with poorly coordinated fingers. The buttons are pale pink mother-of-pearl. They glow softly. Her blouse, which is of pink silk, parts slowly, in a widening V, from her neck to the small of her back, revealing a white slice of her spine and the crosswise strap of her brassiere. I now search for the snap of her skirt-band, unfasten it, and run the zipper down the length of her hip, freeing the skirt of her blouse.) Lift your arms, madame. (She does so. I lift the loosened blouse from her shoulders, draw it over her arms, and lay it on the bed. She sits patiently, in her brassiere and loosened skirt. I unfasten the metal snaps of the brassiere and slipping the backs of my hands under its two straps, lift it also from her shoulders and lay it beside her blouse.) Now stand up, please, for a minute. (She stands, the loosened skirt slipping to the floor about her feet. She wears a white half-slip. I spread its elastic waistband with my fingers and draw it down over her hips, letting it fall to the floor upon her skirt. All of these acts are performed with what I imagine to be the deliberate, scrupulous skill of the experienced seducer. She stands now only in her white nylon panties. I extend their elastic band with my spread fingers and pull them down over her hips and thighs. She is nude, her back to me, bowed slightly, her body in its delicate and slender length as familiar to me as my own hands, whose palms I place now upon the slightly protruding bones of her narrow hips. Their conformity defies in some mysterious way the thing I seek to create: a composition, a newness. I feel within myself the flare of an emotion with which I am unfamiliar. I am going to call this feeling, because I do not understand it any better, an aesthetic one. It is characterized by a curiosity as bright, intense, and delicate as the white pencil-tip of flame from an acetylene torch. What has begun as a parody, a desperate game, has begun to fascinate me. I want to make a composition. Of what? Something that has been born I want to redesign. I want to disarrange an ordained integrity. Her skin is very white. Oh, as white as milk, and with the same bluish bloom within it. It cries out to me like virgin canvas to an artist. I know, as a child knows the number of his fingers without being able to speak the numerals which represent it, the number of vertebrae in her spine. I could, blindfolded, ladle into the hollows of her hips the exact amount of water they could contain. I could place upon the opposite arm of a scale the exact weight, in silver, of each of her breasts. And because of this, the disgusting things about her body offend me, as do those of my own. She is too familiar to me to offer me the salvation of her strangeness. She has given it to me, long ago, and often. She has fed me with her strangeness, I have drunk her strangeness. She has given me her greatest gift: her mystery. I have drunk the mystery out of her breasts. I have made them barren with my thirst. She has allowed me to unwind the white skein of her body until I have unbound its dark burden, its corruption. Now she stands silently, patiently, before me in almost total nudity, with this last gift. We are both suddenly fearful. We are terribly shy. I feel her tremble. But I am bold. The tiny pencil of white flame in my mind scalds me. From the pocket of my pajama jacket I take the green stick of eyeshadow and remove its plastic sheath. I press the point to the white flesh of her buttocks. She shivers and cringes from its sharpness. With the green crayon I encircle carefully the dimple at each side of her spine, just above the buttocks. The effect delights me.)

MARGARET: Mickey, what are you *doing*?

MYSELF: I'm drawing. You're going to be the Tattooed Lady. I'm making wonderful magic designs upon your marble body.

MARGARET: Well, it hurts.

MYSELF: It's a very painful process, as any sailor can tell you. But you must bear with it. You're going to be a great *artiste*. The chief attraction of the carnival. Stand still. And be transformed.

MARGARET: You know you're very, very drunk? I don't think you've ever been any drunker.

MYSELF: Never, never, never. Stand still. (I remove the lipstick from my pocket and in green and red pigment I draw, on each of her buttocks, a design, a portal-like affair, a sort of totem: fantastic animal heads, compiled into a pair of pillars. Then, down the length of her spine, I inscribe a flaming serpent whose forked tongue licks with delicate avidity at the cleft of her buttocks. I am very pleased with this work. I fill in the empty areas with garlanded leaves and fruit of various kinds: apples, oranges, and pears.) Now you have to turn around.

MARGARET: Are you going to do it in *front*, too?

MYSELF: Oh, everywhere. The true carnival artist gives himself completely to his art.

MARGARET: The true sideshow freak, I think you mean. I'm not sure I want to be a Tattooed Lady.

MYSELF: You do, believe me. It's the experience of a lifetime. Really, Meg. Just watch what I'm going to do I'm getting quite good at this. (I turn her body gently, insistently, my hands upon her hips. She yields in a shy, somber way, turning to face me with the timidity and fearful fascination of a virgin. Her body is tense, compacted with energy, excitement, fear, and something more: some inspired ether which gives it a living, quivering, resilient plasticity, which restores to it the firmness, the fullness of contour, of a girl's. Her breasts are freshened with this essence; they seem newly or originally hard and crescent, the areolas darkly flushed, the nipples swollen bitterly. They are filling newly with the milk of mystery. They are restored springs. We have drilled deeper into colder, paler waters. We have touched secret reservoirs. A flow is beginning; cold, pale waters that chill her nipples as they well. She is chilled by the gravity of this sensation. She shivers. She does not understand. If she speaks she will say only, I am cold. Let me come now into bed. Comfort me. But I am not a comforter. I am an inspirer. My hands are trembling with design. I raise the green stick and outline carefully the areola of each breast. She cringes with sensitivity, recoiling.)

MARGARET: *Mickey!* That's *sharp!*

MYSELF: I'm sorry. I'll be gentler. (I turn the pencil sideways and with the flat length of its point I paint her breasts the pale glowing green of apple rind. She giggles suddenly, a little stricken sound of strange revelry.)

MARGARET: Color me green. Honestly. (Her voice catches slightly as she speaks. I finish my work upon her breasts. They are little hard fruit: persimmons or green apples that wring the tongue with their tartness. She looks down at them with startled eyes. I put my hands on her hips and draw her closer to me. Her belly tightens and quivers at my touch, drawing inward quickly. I hear the swift soft gasp of air through her nostrils. Holding her with one hand on her hips I paint the whole length of her thorax, from her breasts to the swell of her belly, in Harlequin diamond patches of red and green and black. She trembles constantly.) No, Mickey. I'll never get it off. Please. (Her voice is rather hushed and hoarse.) Well, let me have a drink, at least. (She takes the glass from the night table, and while I cover the white flesh of her torso in bright panes of motley she sips from it convulsively. She is unable to swallow properly; she twitches and gasps at my pencil strokes, holding the whisky in her mouth. It trickles from between her pursed lips. She wipes her chin with a fingertip.) You're going to get me hysterical in a minute. Honestly, this is weird.

MYSELF: Be patient, now. Just one more bit to do, and then you'll be the queen of the carnival. You'll reign supreme. (Her belly I have left bare of ornament. It swells, startlingly white and nude, from the jumbled panes of motley. That it resembles a face —a bearded cavern-pale face with one blind sunken Polyphemus eye—is a fact which I artfully enhance with rapid strokes of the lipstick and eye-shadow. I describe an eyebrow, arched in horror or hauteur, a Grecian nose, a dire mouth. It is, in its way, a work of considerable skill: an an-guished, blinded god or ogre, swathed in Harle-quin rags, has been born out of her tenderness. Margaret sets down her glass and bends forward to what I have done. It is no doubt difficult for her to obtain the full effect, since she views my chef-d'œuvre from upside down. When she does, the spell is broken. My magic has failed. The pa-tience, the amusement, the uncertain enchant-ment drain out of her face. She bends down quickly

to gather up her fallen skirt and cover herself.)
No, you mustn't get dressed. We've just gotten to
the interesting part—the whole point of the carnival. Where the Magician takes the Tattooed Lady
into bed.

MARGARET: I don't think I want to go to bed. Please, Mickey.

MYSELF: You don't? Not with the Great Magician? But it's
the whole point of the thing. The Main Act. You
don't want to make love with the Great Magician?

MARGARET: (She snaps her skirt-band fastened and takes her
blouse from the bed.) No. Not like this. It isn't
fun. It isn't flattering.

MYSELF: Flattering? Is that what you make love for? To be
flattered?

MARGARET: Oh, don't be silly. You know what I mean. (Her
face is solemn with disenchantment. She holds the
silk blouse spread against herself, covering her
painted breasts.) I'm going to take a shower and
wash this stuff off. Then I'm going to make you a
sandwich or something. You're going to be sick,
without any lunch.

MYSELF: I don't want any lunch. I want you to come to bed.

MARGARET: No, you don't. You have some lunch and a nap
first. Then we'll see what you want. And you've
had enough of this, too. (She takes up the glass
from the night table and carries it toward the bathroom, pausing at the door.) Do you want me to pull
the blinds?

MYSELF: No. I want you to stop being Clara Barton, and
come back here. I want the lovely Tattooed Lady
to come and stroke my hair. I want to do more
magic.

MARGARET: You've done enough magic for one day. It was a
real tour de force. You'd better conserve your
powers for a while. (She goes into the bathroom.
I hear the splash of the whisky in the sink.)

MYSELF: You have a great sense of humor, you do. You really know how to enter into the spirit of things, don't you?

MARGARET: The spirit of things, or things of the spirit?

MYSELF: Oh, for Christ's sake. Things of the spirit. Is that what you're worried about? Your spirit? Honest to God. Talk about a pompous remark.

MARGARET: Go to sleep.

MYSELF: Go to hell.

MARGARET: I think maybe you mean that. (I do not reply. In a moment I hear the rustle of the shower curtains and then the spray of water in the tub. I sit starkly in the bed, staring at the sunlit windows. Many centuries later Margaret emerges from the bathroom, wearing a pair of faded denim jeans and a blue calico blouse. The skin of her face and throat is flushed from the warm shower and the tips of her hair are damp and hang in open curls. She brings into the room the clean fresh fragrance of steam and soap and lavender-scented talcum powder. She carries over one arm her discarded skirt and blouse and underclothing, all evidently spotted with lipstick and eyeshadow stains.) Well, those have got to go to the cleaners. (She comes to the bed and gathers up the objects I have juggled, the pencils, and the photograph.) Mickey.

MYSELF: What?

MARGARET: Will you promise to eat a sandwich if I make it for you? And a glass of milk?

MYSELF: All right.

MARGARET: And then just lie down and have a nap? You're worn out and starved.

MYSELF: I don't know.

MARGARET: Well, try. I'll be back in a minute. There's a new *New Yorker*; do you want me to bring it up?

MYSELF: No, thanks. (Margaret goes out of the bedroom. I

lie back in the bed and watch the sunlight through the pale blue curtains. The bird is singing far away, sadly. There is a rumor of traffic. I remember other still, sunlit hours of agony. My mother is somewhere far above me, in the forbidden upper regions of the house, smiling over her antiquarian literature. I come into the hall from the garden, where, sitting in the boxwood tree in the warm September sunlight, I have gone to sleep, and fallen down through the branches onto the slate path of the garden. A terrible blinding rebirth, in pain and shock and dazzling sunlight. I lie on the slate squares for a moment, uncomprehending, smitten into consciousness by the savagely possessive earth, reading, in bewildered obedience, the words of an apocalypse that has been set before my very eyes: *The Witch in the Wood*: the title, I realize slowly, of the book I had been reading, which has fallen with me and lies before me on the path, tilted slightly, in an oracular way, upon a boundary stone. I run screaming into the hall, and stand now, clutching in one hand the other, from which a broken finger, already plump and blue and cold, curls upward in excruciating, terrifying deformity. I want to run to her, up the million stairs, to the attic where she smiles away her loveless life, peering through her lorgnette at gravures of ormolu commodes; but she will not understand, she will not take away the pain, she will not even fully recognize me. I stand clutching my hand in pain and terror in the silent, sunlit hall, surrounded by frayed and fading virtues: PITY, LOVE, CHARITY. In a soft, hopeless voice I sob, almost to myself: Oh, Momma, I'm hurt. Momma, please.

Margaret returns, bringing me a sandwich and

a glass of milk. We say studiously inconsequential things. I eat cautiously. I promise her to sleep. She lets down the venetian blinds and closes them, making an artificial twilight in the room. She bears away the empty glass and plate, closing the door softly behind her. I stretch out on the bed in weary luxury, now softly ravished by the cool dusk of this dark chamber we have founded in the heart of the noon sunlight. I sleep.

I sleep through the afternoon, through dinner, apparently; for when I wake the room is full of the true dark of night. It is very quiet; the rumors of traffic have died and the faint light through the blinds is pale and of a different order: moonlight. The electric clock purrs tinily and blushes in the dark. Margaret lies in the twin bed beside me. I know she is awake; I feel her consciousness, and her breath is not the breath of sleep; it is too soft, too controlled. I lie and look up at the ceiling, which is mottled with formless pallors. In a moment I speak softly.)

MYSELF: Mickey. Are you awake?

MARGARET: Yes.

MYSELF: Let's go somewhere.

MARGARET: Where?

MYSELF: I don't know. Some nice place. Some warm, bright place. Somewhere by the sea.

MARGARET: We'll be going to Maine in August.

MYSELF: No, I don't mean that. It's too cold. And it's not far enough away. That's not what I mean.

MARGARET: What do you mean?

MYSELF: I mean abroad somewhere. Greece, or Italy, or France. Where they speak a foreign language. Where we can lie in the sun all day and dance all night. Where you can put on a different dress and wonderful new earrings and we can go out to dinner three or four times a week. Would you like that?

MARGARET: Would I like it?

MYSELF: Well, why don't we?

MARGARET: Well, how can we? Are you expecting an inheritance or something?

MYSELF: No. But you can't wait for that. You have to do it, if you want to. I think we ought to have a last chance to be young, before we get old.

MARGARET: (After a considerable pause) It's sweet of you to suggest it.

MYSELF: You know, if you put things off too long, all of a sudden you find somebody trying to shove you into a coffin some day.

MARGARET: (Reaching out in the darkness to lay her hand on mine) Are you kidding about this, Mickey?

MYSELF: No. I was just thinking how much fun it would be to go and buy steamship tickets together, and pick out a stateroom on a chart. And to watch you buy a whole batch of new dresses and evening shoes and earrings. And to stand by a rail together and watch the stars in the sea. I was thinking about those hotel stickers that Susie has, from Nice.

MARGARET: Well. You've been doing some pretty fancy thinking.

MYSELF: I think we ought to do something like that, before it's too late. We really ought to, you know, Meg.

MARGARET: (She moves her hand from mine and lies still for some time.) Do you think it would help us, really?

MYSELF: Yes. (There is another considerable silence.) Something must.

MARGARET: Yes, I know.

MYSELF: If we were both happy again; do you know what I mean? Unhappiness is a habit as much as anything, I think. I want to see you happy again.

MARGARET: I know.

MYSELF: I'd love to see you tanned, in a white evening gown, with a camellia in your hair.

MARGARET: Could I really have a white gown?

MYSELF: You can have three.

MARGARET: I saw a wonderful one at Lord and Taylor's, but it costs a fortune. Oh, Mickey, it's a mad idea. What are you getting me all worked up like this for, anyway?

MYSELF: I mean it. You'll see.

MARGARET: How could we possibly do it? What about the boat? I thought we were saving up for a boat.

MYSELF: That boat costs twelve thousand dollars. It'll take us another five years. And in five years God knows what will have happened. This is something we have to do now. If we took two thousand out of the boat money and another two thousand out of this year's savings, we could live on that for three months in Europe if we're careful.

MARGARET: Three *months*? How in the world could you get away for three months?

MYSELF: I have a month of annual, and almost that much of sick leave that I've been saving up for two years. I could take some leave without pay, if I had to. We could do it easily.

MARGARET: My gosh. You really have thought about it, haven't you? Three months on the Mediterranean. Heavens.

(We lie in silence for a while, lost in our respective fantasies. Mine are of water: shoreless expanses of ocean, pitching under blue, empty skies. I sink into these waters slowly, deeper and deeper into their bottomless chill depths, at last beyond all memory of the sun.)

Part Two

The Chemin du Roy is a sinuous and undulant road which winds upward across the approximate center of Cap Ferrat to the summit of that flowered, sun-drenched peninsula and then drops downward with equal Gallic deviousness through clusters of bursting roses, bougainvillea, and breezy, scented pine to the dusty fishing village of St. Jean-Cap Ferrat. This and the tiny artificial beach called the Plage Passable on the opposite side of the peninsula are its termini; between them, scattered on both sides of that fragrant lane, are twenty or more pastel-colored villas, coral, salmon, and pale blue, with vine-clad loggias and geranium-sprinkled terraces that look out across the hot blue sea. It is very still. Only, sometimes, the sea-wind in the pines and the occasional drift of fallen needles on the striped canvas of a canopy. The perpetual silence is one of the chief beauties of the place; a hot, sweet, perfumed silence, into which the little languid sounds of early afternoon drop and melt and fuse, like coins into a cauldron of melted gold: a phrase: ". . . met Adrian in Nice . . ." the silver chirp of a siskin in the pines, the chiming of ice cubes in a lifted glass, Gwynyth laughing softly, the shuffle of a sandal on the stone. But sometimes a living thing is tossed into that boiling gold; we hear its scalded shriek through the pines; a sudden, jeweled scream, rising intolerably, then curving downward into death. One morning of the first week of our stay it wakens me in terror; Margaret is gone; I rise and go swiftly through the French doors to the terrace where she stands leaning against the parapet, her hair fallen about her shoulders, her dressing gown clutched loosely to her throat, staring through the morning mist that rolls among the pines.

"Did you hear it?"

"Yes. What is it?"

"I don't know. Listen."

We stand stricken by the long brilliant, bitter carol that wells and dies among the distant bowers.

"Lord. How weird. How beautiful."

"It's terrible. What is it?"

"Come in. You're cold. We'll find out later."

They are peacocks, Adrian tells us, his narrow face refreshed by the opportunity. There is a zoo, a little farther up, on the Route de la Mer; a small private zoo, with apes and peacocks and a marvelous collection of European adders, all very spoiled, although the apes have learned to perform, somewhat unpredictably, on bicycles, in Louis XV costumes. For ten francs one can witness this performance. He will take us one afternoon.

"You will not take me," Gwynth says.

"Peacocks," says Margaret, staring into the silence which has folded over its anguished jeweled victims.

Our villa has a faded blue sign above its door, on which is written in vanishing ornate script: LA FLEURELLE. One approaches it along a path of brightly speckled artificial stone sunken between billows of massed oleander, where great clumsy black-and-yellow bees hum and stumble among the coral-colored blossoms. At every window there is a whitewashed stone flower-box, blazing with flung blood-drops of geranium. The villa is very cool. It has stone floors and walls with blunt corners, washed with aquatint. It smells of stone, bread, copper, and geraniums. In the narrow entrance hall there is a tiny Oriental rug on the stone floor, a copper urn, an Algerian tapestry on the wall, and, opposite, a portrait of a nude girl standing on a sand dune, holding her breasts and dreaming. In the living room there is a fireplace with a huge stone mantel, on which hangs a tar-nished ornamental halberd, bound with loops of crimson velvet cord. On either side of it, along the stuccoed walls, are book-shelves of richly polished mahogany which hold, along with a collection of African ebony carvings, an incongruous assortment of books: the works of Darwin, Erasmus, and Montaigne, bound in plum-colored leather, and a few ragged French-language copies of the detective stories of Simenon. Under a pair of nar-row Mediterranean windows with curved wrought-iron grill-work there is a baby grand piano, across which is flung a tasseled flamenco shawl of brilliant scarlet, black, and green embroidery. Margaret sets here every morning a bowl of fresh bougainvillea blossoms. The huge Oriental carpet of this room glows with rich wine-colored radiance in the slanted squares of light from the French doors to the terrace. They face south, so that there is sunlight all day long upon the rug, the long bright rectangles tilting gradually, and thinning, from the doorsills. Yvonne, the most feline of our friends, likes to lie there in her bikini on the hot, plum-colored pile, so that she has constantly to be stepped over by people bearing drinks onto the terrace. When I am forced to do so I dip my fingertips into the icy gin and sprinkle her bare brown torso, at which she shivers and murmurs in her resiny voice, "Beast. Oh, that's delicious."

The terrace, too, has stone floors, and a parapet, against which are set a pair of gigantic stone urns that pour out of their mouths fountains of columbine. The tangled leaves and frail blue blossoms spill onto the floor, and must periodically be tied up with bits of twine. The walls of the parapet are mottled with vaguely animal-shaped stains of something (wine, one hopes) that has dried and deepened to the dark ox-blood red of liver. Margaret has scrubbed these stains for hours with a brush and soapy water, but they remain unaltered. Above the terrace is a raftered loggia, roofed with a tangled, blazing canopy of bougainvillea. All day the sunlight pours down through the leaves and purple tissue-paper blossoms, casting a weirdly tinted light upon the terrace that stains the white bodies of the girls like a wash of wine. On a very hot day the dim ruby-tinted shadow is delicious; one bathes in it. Far below the parapet lies the limitless, blue, burning sea. Sometimes a tiny white triangular sail inches across it from cape to cape through the mirrored sunglaze on the water. The warm wind that blows across it, rustling the bougainvillea blossoms, comes out of Africa, out of the still white desert, out of beaches where the lions come down to the surf to shake their great manes in the foam.

Far above the villa, to the right, the mainland rises in a huge barren promontory, girdled by the terraced highways of the Corniches, along which crawl tiny automobiles, their glass and chromework glittering in the sun. At its summit stands a crumbling castle, like a chess-piece, its broken ramparts limned very clearly against the vast blue heights of sky about it, its fallen stonework tumbling down the slopes toward the great blue basin of the sea, almost a mile below. At the foot of that gigantic promontory and the center of the tiny bay it shelters lies the ancient sun-bleached village of Villefranche, with tottering tall stone houses and faded tile roofs and scraps of clothing strung like ragged pennants across the narrow streets. There is a granite quay with stone steps leading down to a strip of pebbled beach which the tide erases, and dark red fishing dories moored motionless in the blue jelly of the water. On the cobbled quayside we can see the parasols of the cafés, like paint-drops, and bicycles standing against the yellow plaster walls, and dogs sleeping on the cool stone in the shadow of the buildings. In the day, Villefranche lies washed by rain and sun and centuries, a pile of faded blue-gray silent stone; at night it sparkles far below us in the Mediterranean darkness with wicked brilliance, its clustered lights quivering in the water, its stone streets tinkling with laughter from the cafés. It is at exactly the right distance to encourage romance, philosophy, and spells of startling volatility in the tenants of the villa, which may account in part for the volumes of Erasmus, the halberd, and the wine-stains on the stone.

On this coast the mountains come almost to the sea. They rise behind it steeply, barren at their heights—great blunt, towering, treeless promontories, like that on which the ancient castle stands—and yield, as they descend, to the wild, hot, luxuriant verdure of the coast. From Villefranche to the tip of the peninsula on which our villa lies the shores curve softly in their cape of green velour: pine and eucalyptus and plane and poplar, splashed with blazing blotches of tangerine and purple and scarlet-colored blossoms and the blue walls of villas and sloping red tile roofs that burn with a soft matte luster in the sun. Here and there a wrought-iron balcony breaks out of the greenery, trailing flowered vines that clutch at it from the ravening foliage below. On one of them a man in white flannel trousers and an open shirt stands every afternoon with his hands spread on the railing and stares for hours at the sea. I have watched him through the binoculars; his face, burnished by the low evening light, is like the face of Zeus on a Corinthian coin: weary, delicate, and avid. Sometimes he lifts a fine dark hand to smooth dreamily his crisp and silvering hair.

Margaret has begun a garden. Every morning she rises early to tend it, setting her coffee cup on the parapet while she freshens her flowers with a little zinc watering can I bought her at the Prix Unique in Nice. She has brought an envelope of moonflower seeds from our garden in Washington and planted them at the foot of a little latticework trellis against the stone wall of the villa. They grow almost overnight, yielding delicate white-flowered vines. I love to see her bending over them with her grave look of absorption, frail as a child in her blue nylon dressing gown.

We shop in St. Jean-Cap Ferrat; I have rented a tiny Citroën from an agency in Nice, because the roads are too steep to climb with our bundles of groceries. We walk from shop to shop along the single narrow stone street of the village, filling our string bags slowly with slabs of cheese, eggs, and bottled milk from the *crémerie,* moist packages of meat from the *charcuterie,* where the great quarters of freshly slaughtered animals hang dripping onto the sawdust of the floor, beets and cabbages and dusty green beans wrapped in newspaper, and gaping, glass-eyed, bitter-faced scarlet snapper from the reeking stalls of the *poissonnerie,* where trays of whelks and flounder and silver slabs of sole glisten under the slowly turning wooden-bladed fans. At the top of the village street there is a bench under a *flamboyant* tree where we sit sometimes with our packages beside us in the shade of the flame-colored blossoms and fernlike foliage to watch the sunburnt harbor, the old men fishing on the sea wall, the cats gnawing scraps of offal on the wharves, and the slender white yachts, their strings of pennants drooping in the hot still air. Sometimes, when it is in, we go to visit Ian on his, a stately 1922 Dawn cruiser, upright, monolithic and glowing with devotion, like a Sunday school piano. Ian is exactly like his boat, almost to the Union Jack flying from the stern staff, with which imagination unconsciously supplies him. But he is a wise and wounded man, who makes no effort to dispel the parody which shields his sadness from examination. We have met him one day while walking on the wharf; hearing us admire his boat in English, he has invited us aboard. He is always pleased to see us; he is lonely. He lives aboard her with a crew of two sullen Algerians, a steward and an engineer, who abuse him in benighted French and are generally drunk. He wears, on the very warmest days, a flannel blazer with metal buttons on which are engraved the arms of Magdalen College, white linen trousers, and a pair of chuplee sandals on his otherwise bare feet. He serves us martinis under the canopy of his afterdeck, stirring them cautiously in a silver canister on which cool beads of moisture break out deliciously. He is very fond of Margaret, and she of him. He looks at her for long moments in perfectly candid admiration, about which there is not the least offense, as if he were examining a rose. He is perhaps sixty-five, a quiet man, beyond all further injury. A chunk of his left earlobe is missing, as cleanly as if it had been clipped away with scissors. He talks to us, for our respective benefits, I understand, about boats and poetry, and very occasionally asks delicate questions about ourselves, and America, which he has visited once, in 1932. He has the air about him of a retired, cultured pugilist; of a man who has earned his fortune by some form of professional brutality, and is very anxious to avoid it in his retirement. His boat is named *Victorious*. We enjoy very much our visits with him, and marketing afterward in a haze of conviviality from two or three martinis and the glow of teak and polished brass and the tinkle of Noel Coward records from the Gramophone inside the cool saloon. We walk back up the village street, past a stucco schoolhouse from whose open windows we hear the chant of children reciting chorally, under palms whose broad leaves clatter softly in a stir of wind, to where we have parked the Citroën in a field above the harbor. There are white doves perched on the telegraph wires along the road. Margaret leans her head out of the window and coos to them. We seem to be always a little drunk.

Sometimes we take day-long excursions in the Citroën, driving west along the coast to Fréjus, Antibes, Juan-les-Pins, and St. Tropez, prowling among the marketplaces and waterside cafés and stopping along the road to picnic in the shade of gnarled humming pines on rocky headlands above the sea, where, while I lie staring into one or the other of those two illimitable blues which drench all life on this coast, Margaret wanders among the boulders, picking violets. We spend evenings at the roulette tables of the casinos in Cannes and Nice, and afterward, thrilled with our own reckless urbanity, emerge with a single pair of souvenir *plaquettes* to rattle in our pockets as we stroll through the glittering chiming darkness of the Croisette or the Promenade des Anglais. There, in a shop window one evening, Margaret spies the only object I have ever known her truly to covet: an Italian glass figurine of Harlequin with exquisitely fashioned, haughty, impudent features, a tunic of spangled blue and scarlet panes, and a pair of ragged peppermint-striped pantaloons. It costs three hundred francs, a figure at whose absurdity she rejoices. ("If it cost any less," she says, "if it were even *faintly* reasonable, I might do something awful.") On occasional afternoons we wander through the Old City, musing over the market stalls and eating lunch in a cavernous, whitewashed pizzeria where the spicy fragrant pies are baked in stone ovens, fished out on wooden paddle-blades, and served up on trestle tables with dark green bottles of cool, bitter wine.

Our days begin to fall into a pattern. In the morning we have coffee and croissants on the terrace in our bathing suits and beach robes and then walk down the Chemin du Roy through pines and hedgerows of honeysuckle to the Plage Passable. It is an artificial beach whose caramel-colored sand has been carted here in trucks and dumped on the stony shore to form a soft brown crescent no longer than a football field. There is a pavilion where one may rent beach chairs, umbrellas, and *pédalos,* pontoon boats which seat three very slender people and are lazily propelled by pedaling a revolving waterwheel. In the mornings there are always boys with rakes smoothing out the moist cool sand and stabbing scraps of paper with a rubbish fork. We walk past them to the far end of the beach to a rocky cove where great monolithic boulders stand in the gentle blue pellucid water. Here we spread our beach towels on the sand and rub each other's backs and shoulders with suntan oil; there is a lovely smell of scented oil on hot skin, of freshly laundered owels, sand, salt, warm hair, and the hot rubber of Margaret's bathing cap, which is leafed with little quivering white scales. In the beach bag we have brought a French conversation text, two apples, a chunk of Gruyère cheese, postcards, fountain pens, a copy of *Paris Match,* and a thermos full of iced Cinzano. We instruct each other indolently and recklessly in French. It has been humiliating to discover that when this language—which I read fluently, and of which I believe myself to have a thorough academic grasp—is spoken by a Frenchman I can scarcely understand a word of it. Life and Theory, it grows evident, are farther apart than ever on the Mediterranean.

"Dun mwah een pum," Margaret says. I do so, ceremoniously, as a reward for her accent, which is really excellent.

"Vwahlah oon pom." I make dreadful sounds. I cannot understand it. Margaret, who has never studied the language, speaks far better in a week than I shall ever do. "Why is it?" I ask, "that I can recite Baudelaire, but I can't order a lamb chop?"

"It's a matter of dignity," says Margaret. "You have too much dignity. People with a great deal of dignity can't learn languages. Or arts. Ask Adrian."

"I don't have any more dignity than you do. What are you talking about? Adrian has dignity."

"Yes, but he knows how to turn it off. You have to do that. Really. You have to make yourself innocent."

"Then I'm sunk."

"Oh, yes. Evil you. That's not what I mean, anyway. I mean innocent, not un-wicked."

"You don't make any sense at all. The sun's affecting you. You need Cinzano. Too ah bayswahn day sanzano."

"Oh, that's awful," Margaret says. "You make awful sounds."

The sea flames. The blue sky pours upon us. We munch apples and cheese and sip cold Cinzano. A girl and young man come down to the water and splash each other, standing to their calves. He chases her, laughing, through the shallows, her long hair flying. They wear bikinis and have beautiful, hard, slender bodies. The girls wear jewelry in the water, earrings and bracelets and necklaces that sparkle against their wet brown skin.

And the boys, medallions on silver chains, which fly and dangle against their brown chests. They are lovely to watch, nimble, glittering, nearly naked, lacquered with sunlight and water; and yet they are quite formal in their behavior. They do not kiss in public, or lie with their bodies twined, or stroke each other, as couples do on American beaches, although they laugh and chatter happily. And they have a charming way of shaking hands, boy and girl, when they meet or part, formally, almost gravely. There is a kind of sexual contentment about them which I have become aware of very quickly. It is a subtle yet immediate sensation, like fresh air. I am beginning to enjoy a very new concept of etiquette.

In front of us *pédalos* languidly navigate the bay, blue and red and yellow, bearing spellbound couples who sit upright in the slatted chairs and vanish slowly on the blue horizon, like people in a dream, adrift on park benches. A child in rubber bathing sandals and a white sunbonnet totters along the rim of the shallow water, his arms raised for balance, crooning merrily. Behind him his naiad mother prowls, with shining ankles, through the shoals.

To our left, beyond the jumbled cairns at this end of the beach, there is a wide flat concrete quay which forms the anchorage of a private villa; into it are incorporated several of the huge gray boulders of the shore; the wall is part concrete, part stone; from the smooth, troweled stretches of cement the boulders bulge out randomly, like the great gray bodies of mired elephants. It reaches fifty yards into the bay, and above its flat ramparts the varnished tips of the two masts of a sailing yacht rise sparkling in the sun. From the taller of them flies a small triangular owner's flag of white silk on which is inscribed a single scarlet poppy. Later we shall swim out to the wall and climb the boulders to its top and sit there swinging our white legs in the sun, our bodies chilled by the cold of the deep water, looking down at the heaving bowers of green sea grass, swaying silently in the surge and lapse of gin-clear water. Through the restless swaying grasses schools of tiny brilliant fishes slip, striped with burning strips of cobalt and vermilion. They blow like streams of petals on a wind over the dark rocks. The sunken rocks are metal-colored: rusted iron, pewter, steel, corroded bronze; and pocked and gnarled like gigantic cinders.

"Now, where is the countess' villa? Adrian said you could see it from here."

"Yes. Up there, see? Among those tall Lombardy poplars. It's the only white roof on the Cape." ("White is for purity, child. I never miss an opportunity to acquaint myself with it. And then, it's so much more comfortable, you know, in this climate.")

"Then is that where we played badminton, on that lawn?"

"Yes. There are the Chinese lanterns, still up. Do you see them?"

"Yes. Oh, what a lovely place to live. Can I be a countess someday?"

"If you can find a count, and some way to get rid of me."

Adrian, David, and Yvonne have arrived. They wave to us from the shore. Adrian plunges into the water and swims toward us swiftly. He swims beautifully; he is an Australian, from Sydney, and has grown up at Rose Bay and Bondi Beach. We watch him from the wall, both smiling; it is an expression which Adrian's arrival invariably creates. He reaches the wall and raises his head to us, panting, his yellow hair soaked to his skull, his face crinkling gaily about his pale blue eyes.

"Hullo, you two. You're up jolly early."

"Too lovely to stay in bed," Margaret says. " 'There'll be time enough to sleep.' "

"Yes, I know." His smile broadens immediately with appreciation of Margaret's quotation, in a look which is mischievous, shy, cynical, sensitive, and prepared for anything. Adrian's eyes tilt steeply upward at their inner corners, almost triangularly, as do those of many Englishmen, creating a fundamental expression of anxiety which can be modulated infinitely by the gradual rising of their outer corners and the broadening of his smile, through confusion, moderate concern, studiousness, relief, dawning insouciance, mischief, gaiety, and lubricity to candid depravity. It is the sentiments in the upper half of this register which predominate, although one is never unaware of the basic one of lonely perplexity upon which they are founded, nor of the intelligence and equanimity which permit them to prevail. From this face, in the span of a single instant, one gains an impression of reckless generosity and irredeemable self-interest, of cunning and artlessness, of dignity and the willed dismissal of that virtue that Margaret has suggested. I conclude it is an artist's face.

He climbs up onto the sea wall beside us, sits down, and contemplates his knees, which are rather oddly formed. His knees are a great source of satisfaction to him. An expensive and cunning tailor, who claims to have outfitted Augustus John, Ralph Richardson, and H. G. Wells, has once assured him that all of these distinguished men had sharply pointed knees, and that this phenomenon, which he shares, is a certain sign of genius.

"Just have a look at those knees," he says. "Do you see that? Like absolute poignards. You can feel, if you like."

"No, thank you."

"I'd like to feel them," Margaret says. "My goodness, they are sharp, aren't they? You must be very careful when you pray."

"I am, very." He chuckles happily. "I say, have you seen Gwynyth?"

"No. Did she come?"

"Don't know where she is. I went round to her room, but she'd gone. I think perhaps she took the bus to Nice. She likes to do that, you know: get up early and prowl around the old part."

"I do, too," Margaret says. "I did that one morning last week."

"Did you really? It's lovely, isn't it? Much nicer than Cannes. Cannes has no character, at all. But a better beach, of course."

On the shore, Yvonne has taken a towel and is flapping it in front of David, who is galloping at her on his hands and knees.

"What's Yvonne doing?" I ask. "Bullfighting?"

"Yes. We went to Spain last year, and she's been doing it ever since. I don't think she should, really."

"Why?"

"I don't know. Some women simply shouldn't fight bulls. It's a thing you sort of sense about them. Others ought to do nothing else; the countess, for example. But I don't think you'd find a bull who'd fight with her." He stares down into the water at the surging grasses. "I say, it's lovely down there, isn't it? I've brought the snorkel, Mickey. Shall we have a go at it later?"

"Yes. Wonderful."

"God, isn't it lovely? Look at those rocks. It's like that Blake painting, isn't it? Isaac Newton. Do you know it? Those rocks he's sitting on."

"I don't think I've seen it."

"Haven't you really? Oh, I must get you that, Mickey. You'd love that picture. There's a place in Tottenham Court Road where you can get the most marvelous reproductions, dirt cheap. Five shillings, or something. You've really got to come over to London, you two."

"You'll have a hard time getting us away from here," Margaret says.

"I know. Still, you can't just sit here and decay forever in all this sunshine, you know. Got to get a bit of soot and fog into your lungs now and then, to keep the motor running."

"I'm just going to let my motor idle for a while," Margaret says.

"I know. It's extraordinary, isn't it, the way people react to places? In lovely places like this they just go all to pot, and in filthy spots like London they get all orderly and ambitious. I don't know what to make of that." He does, of course, but one of his minor graces is to arrange so carefully for you all the introductory steps to a conclusion of some merit that you are left with the delightful sensation of having discovered it your-self. He then congratulates you with a smile. I am not sure that this is an entirely generous stratagem on his part, for some of the conclusions he manages to propagate in this manner are so forbidding, or even sinister, that he is much better off letting someone else pronounce them.

"In filthy places like London," Margaret says, "they get all orderly and ambitious so they can make enough money to go away to lovely places like this and decay."

"Yes, exactly." He chuckles merrily, showing his fine teeth. "I've always been rather suspicious of ambition. And of order, Lord knows. I studied medicine for a while, you know, and I've never seen a more orderly, ambitious, or rapacious set of fellows in my life. Really incredible."

"Did you really?" Margaret asks. "I'd never have guessed that. How did you happen to study medicine?"

"Well, my father was a doctor, you see; and it was his prin-ciple that all decent fellows ought to be doctors, so he made jolly sure that I was going to be. It was the only principle he had, really, so he was rather keen on it."

"Well, how did you happen to give it up? How did you get to be an actor?"

"Oh, I simply flunked out. Couldn't make it out, at all. You see, my father had got on to the idea that the answer to most of life's problems was just a bit of bandage and a dab of iodine. He was of the Band-Aid School, you might say. But I didn't see it that way, at all. I thought for a while of taking up the ministry—the Bible School, you know—but of course I've got the wrong sort of knees, entirely, for prayer. So that left just the theater, really. I mean for someone like me."

"What school do you call that?" I ask.

"Well, I suppose you could call it the Velvet Codpiece School. I do mostly Shakespeare, you know."

"And you find that more effective?"

"Oh, absolutely. It's astonishing how many of life's prob-lems can be solved by way of the codpiece. You've no idea. It leaves the Band-Aid nowhere at all." He stands up on the sea wall. He is very thin, which gives him an illusion of height much greater than his actual six feet. "Shall we race?"

"Oh, you'll beat us."

"Yes, I know. That's why I suggested it."

"Oh, it is! Well, come on, Mickey; we'll just show him."

We plunge into the chilled purple depths and splash toward the shore. Adrian teases us by swimming only a yard or two ahead and pretending to flounder. Close to the shore he cries out in a strangulated voice, "I'm afraid I've had it!" and disappears beneath the surface, letting Margaret win. We stagger up the moist brown sand to our beach towels, where David sits grinning at us with a copy of *The Tempest* on his knees and Yvonne lies on her back, dozing, in the sun. David has a dark Irish face with very black thick eyebrows and hair, a fine nose and mouth, a sharply cleft chin, and a ruddy complexion which will grow florid as he ages. He is stocky and muscular, and perhaps a year or two younger than Adrian. Yvonne is like a warm, slightly overripened fruit. She is delectable, and gives the impression of being constantly surrounded by a cloud of tiny, buzzing fruit flies of the kind that hover about a bowl of pears or peaches. Her face and throat have the bloom and slightly sticky patina of plums and her cloyed voice drips out of her bursting lips almost like the juice of nectarines. I imagine her playing an endless succession of tavern wenches and Restoration parlormaids, being flung, shrieking with enthusiasm, across the knees of Shakespearean roustabouts or satin-clad profligates in powdered wigs. She cannot be older than twenty-five or twenty-six. All of these people are actors who have finished a winter season at the Old Vic and come on holiday together to the South of France. There are five of them, altogether; but Gwynyth and Tessa are missing this morning, having gone in to Nice, according to Adrian's guess. They are staying in a *pension* in Villefranche; for how long seems not to concern them. Until their money runs out, apparently, for none of them, except David, has an engagement to perform until the fall. They have become our great friends. Our vacation friends, in every case but two, for we are bound together really only by the English language and our common holiday mood. In Adrian's case, however, I feel that we should be friends in any circumstances, and in Gwynyth's, not truly in any.

We dry ourselves with towels, panting from our swim, and Margaret strips off her Ondine bathing cap.

"I think you'd have let me drown, the lot of you," says Adrian.

"*I* certainly should," says David. "I've got words to learn. And there can't be too many actors drowning, as far as I'm concerned. All the more work for me."

"Good old David. You should have come in, you know. It's lovely."

"I will, in a bit. Water is something I have to adjust to very, very slowly. You two look jolly well today."

"We went to bed very early," Margaret says. "Oh, how I sleep here! I wake up absolutely bursting with life every morning. It's glorious." She looks down at Yvonne, who has not stirred. "What's the matter with Yvonne? Is she asleep?"

"I've been gored," Yvonne murmurs.

"Yes, and not for the first time," says David. "Sit up, old girl. We've got company."

I lift the thermos bottle and shake it gently, tinkling the ice. Yvonne's eyes open immediately with the mechanical swiftness of a tilted doll's, which they resemble startlingly.

"What a lovely sound," she says. "Heavenly bells. I've died and gone to Paradise."

Adrian chuckles, accepting the cup I have offered him. "Absolutely. The Eternal Cocktail Hour. With the Old Boy Himself shaking the martinis. Cheers." He takes a long swallow of Cinzano and hands the cup down to Yvonne who holds it in her cupped hands and buries her nose in it.

"Oh, that's lovely," she says. "Things taste different here, don't they? They really do." She passes the cup to Margaret and sits with her blue eyes basking in the sun. "We used to have

Cinzano in Spain. We'd sit in the cafés on the Avenida de Espana after the bullfights and drink Cinzano until midnight. Do you remember, Adrian?"

"Oh, yes."

"God, those men. With their little leather vests and lovely tight trousers and Cordobés hats. What beautiful men there are in Spain. So shy, and arrogant. That's a lovely combination. I don't like French men much."

"Why not?" asks David.

"I don't know. They're *mañé*. Do you know, I haven't seen a single one I'd really like to go to bed with. Can you believe it?"

"I cannot," says David, draining the cup. "What about this Jean-Vincent who's always hanging about?"

"There's absolutely nothing about him, that's the point. Do you know what he wants more than anything else in the world? A pair of cowboy boots. I can't think why." She looks at me meditatively for a moment. "What are men like in America, Michael? Are they like you?"

"Only one of them," says Margaret.

"Really? What a shame. We had a good many Americans at RADA, but they were nothing like you. Of course, actors aren't like anything anyway."

"What the devil do you mean by that?" says David.

"I mean they're clods, who never understand what anyone means by anything."

"Oh. Now I understand you. Somehow I can always expect to be upset when I understand you. Women should learn either to be utterly inscrutable, or pleasant."

Adrian leans back on the sand, bracing himself on his elbows, and stares out at the sea. "'That dolphin-torn, that gong-tormented sea,'" he says softly. "What a lovely phrase. Do you know what's down under that water? Etruscan bowls, and bits of Greek statues, and the hulks of triremes. Phoenician coins and Roman goblets. It's truly haunted, you know. A bit different from what you see off Margate."

He has hypnotized Yvonne. Her blue eyes well with mystery. "Do you know what Gwynyth said to me the other day? She said, 'Yvie, put some of that water in a wine bottle, will you, and take it back to London. And give it to Peter for me.' I said, 'Why don't you do it yourself?' And she said, 'I don't know. I might not go.' What do you think she meant?"

Adrian lifts a handful of sand and lets it drift between his fingers. "Did she say that?"

"Yes. What do you think she meant?"

"I don't know."

I pour out a fresh cup of Cinzano and sip it slowly. It is sweet and cold and bitter, like lemons and honey. I hold the cup closely, breathing the dark fumes, and think of Gwynyth's face.

"You're being selfish," Margaret says.

"Sorry. Here." She takes the cup, dips her finger in, and sucks the tip of it.

"I'll never forget her as Ophelia," Yvonne says. "Absolutely never. Tearing that little handkerchief with her fingers while she sang. When she said to me, 'You must wear your rue with a difference,' I burst out crying. I actually did. It's the only time I've ever cried on stage."

"Were you Gertrude?" Margaret asks.

"Yes. Can you imagine? Oh, I was glorious. I filled my brassiere with Kleenex and let it go at that."

"Jolly sound approach to the part," says David. "I wish you could have seen Adrian do Bosola, when *we* were at RADA. I think he had the whole of the Sunday *Times* stuffed in his codpiece. Got fifteen luncheon invitations from agents the very next day."

Adrian rises, smiling. "It's a frightful canard," he says. "You're not to listen to him. What do you say we have a go at those rocks, Mickey?"

"Yes, I'd like to."

We put on the masks, snorkels, and flippers he has brought and wade out into the cool blue water. For an hour or more we float above the gnarled grottoes, our hair drifting, our out-stretched arms and bodies lighted with the rippling chiaroscuro of the sunlight through the water. Sometimes we kick down into the cold violet depths to pursue a darting rainbow-colored fish or sidle through the softly billowing grasses, whose ribbons slither lingeringly over us, coated with cool, burnished slime. Adrian's reverie has furnished the ocean with imaginary relics: I search among the grasses and the crevices of boulders for the gleam of a gold goblet or a broken sword. I should love to find something that I could give to Margaret: an ancient ring or brooch or silver comb, something that no one has seen or touched since a Roman lady plucked it from her hair, or breast, or trembling fingers and flung it into the sea from the terrace of her villa, one midnight, two thousand years ago. But the Mediterranean is not ready to yield her tarnished jewels to us; not on this day.

We kick back to the shore and sit in the darkening after-noon sunlight among the cries of wading children, the reeling shadows of doves about the flowered cliffs behind us and the endless gentle wash of the sea's rim. David reads to us from *The Tempest*:

> *"All the infections that the sun sucks up*
> *From bogs, fens, flats, on Prosper fall, and make him*
> *By inch-meal a disease! His spirits hear me,*
> *And yet I needs must curse. But they'll nor pinch,*
> *Fright me with urchin-shows, pitch me i' the mire,*
> *Nor lead me, like a fire-brand, in the dark*
> *Out of my way, unless he'll bid 'em; but*
> *For every trifle are they set upon me:*
> *Sometimes like apes, that mew and chatter at me*
> *And after bite me; then like hedge-hogs, which*
> *Lie tumbling in my bare-foot way and mount*
> *Their pricks at my foot-fall; sometimes am I*
> *All wound with adders, who with cloven tongues*
> *Do hiss me into madness."*

He is transformed. The old, golden words are formed like ingots in the dark forge of his mouth and fall, bluntly glowing, terrible with weight, before us. He is no longer an agreeable, good-looking, pleasantly profane young Londoner, but a snarling, tormented monster with foaming lips and twisted animal hands, howling his anguished hatred to the heavens. We sit hushed, staring at the hot sand. It is very strange to see this metamorphosis of a man by talent. When he has finished the passage he turns it off as neatly as a water tap, raising his face to us with a smile of innocent achievement. "Lovely stuff, isn't it?"

"You're going to do jolly well, David," says Yvonne. "It's so good for you, getting this part. The only trouble is, if you're all that good I may have to come back to Stratford for your opening."

"Bloody likely, that is. When did you ever prefer to nourish your spirit to your body?"

"Don't be beastly. I was flattering you."

"It's just as well you don't, actually. You've done a jolly good job." He casts an appreciative eye over her bare sunburned body.

"It's absolutely astonishing to me the way you do that," Margaret says. "Change yourself so utterly. How do you feel when that happens to you? Do you feel different?"

"Oh, I don't know. Not a lot different, really. Just another part of one takes over. There're such a lot of people inside of one, you know, that never get a chance, ordinarily."

"I'd be terrified. Do you ever get stage fright?"

"Oh, no."

"Do you, Adrian?"

"No." He turns to her, smiling. "As a matter of fact, it's the only place I really feel safe, you know. I don't so much have stage fright as what you might call World Fright: I get frightened the moment I step *off* the stage."

"That's jolly well put," says Yvonne.

The shadows of the boulders lengthen on the sand. The sea darkens to purple. The *pédalos* shimmer in a sheet of heat above the water. Yvonne shakes the last drops of Cinzano from the thermos and mourns.

"Come up to the villa," Margaret says. "We'll have a decent drink, and something to nibble at."

"You'll get jolly tired of us, you know; drinking all your booze and laying about."

"Don't be silly, we love it."

We walk slowly up the steep road between the pines to the villa, trailing towels and beach bags. There are yellow finches fluttering among the hedges, and everywhere the scent of jasmine in the warm air. We sit on the terrace under the wine-colored shadow of the bougainvillea and look down at the beaten silver of the evening sea. All of us but David, who is playing Ivor Novello tunes on the piano inside the living room. The sentimental notes come tinkling out through the bead curtains that swing softly in the breeze.

"They're having a fête in Villefranche on Friday," Adrian says. "St. Jerome's Day. He's the patron saint of fishermen, or something. Will you come down?"

"Oh, lovely," Margaret says. "Of course we will."

"I think it'll be rather interesting. They have fireworks at night, and dance on the quayside under the lanterns. And then they set fire to a dory and drift it out to sea, as a sacrifice. I believe it's a pretty gay business, altogether. Goes on all hours."

"Oh, what fun. What time shall we come?"

"Why don't you meet us at the Provençale about seven? We'll have dinner there, and get properly in the mood. They have wonderful bouillabaisse."

"Is that the one right on the quay?"

"Yes. Just there, you see. With the canopy. I thought of asking the countess to join us, but I don't know that these rustic entertainments are her sort of thing. Do you think I should?"

"Oh, yes, do, Adrian. I think she'd love it. And it's always wonderful to hear her commentaries."

Yvonne sucks the rim of her glass and stares at the sea. "I think she's frightful," she says. "She smells of blood, that woman."

"Rubbish. She's just a bit corroded, that's all. Have you noticed her flesh? Rather green, like Greco's nobles. But very different eyes. And a mind like flint; when you strike it, it gives off fire. I think she knows everything indecent that has happened in Europe for the last fifty years."

"I'm sure of it," says Yvonne. "I think she instigated most of it."

David has begun to sing, very loudly and passionately, *I Left my Heart in an English Garden.*

"Oh, isn't he awful," says Yvonne.

Someone has arrived at the front door of the villa; we hear the little iron bell in the foyer ringing. Margaret rises and goes in to answer it. In a moment we hear their voices, Gwynyth's and Tessa's and that of a young man with a strong French accent, who has paused in the living room to express his delight at meeting David. They come through onto the terrace, Gwynyth standing a bit behind them in the doorway, as she loves to do, tangled in burning strings of blue and green and scarlet sunlit beads. The young man, it develops, is their acquaintance of half an hour. He has given them a ride from Nice, having been thumbed down by Gwynyth at a bus stop and cajoled into delivering them to the villa. He is evidently beginning to doubt the wisdom of his impulse but is being determinedly civilized about it. He is handsome in a knifelike way, and has the over-scrupulous tailoring and manners of a certain type of very ambitious young bourgeois. He shakes hands all around and bows deeply.

"Maggie, forgive us for bursting in like this," says Tessa. "We just came to gather up these types, really. We rather thought they'd be here." She is older than her fellow-actors; a woman in her early forties, with graying black hair, a thin, fine face, and sorrowful brown eyes. There is an air of tension about her, of continual concern; although sometimes she will laugh

suddenly and brilliantly, and one has an image of a graceful girl who must have existed before many disappoint-
ments.

"But we won't let you have them," Margaret says. "Not
until you've had a drink, anyway."

The young man lifts his hand and tucks his chin in protest.
"No, I must not stay, thank you. I only came to deliver these
delightful beings."

Gwynyth murmurs from her tinkling drapery, "Oh, you've
got to stay, Philippe, if we do. You promised to drive us back
to Villefranche."

"Ah. In that case, of course. If I can serve you."

"We simply can't get along without you." She clutches a
handful of the glass beads and presses them against her cheek,
then moves them to her throat and folds them beneath her chin,
peering at him with a look which could be interpreted either
as innocence or insolence, according to the state of mind of its
witness. She is small and exquisite, with a startling combination
of bright gold hair and black eyebrows and lashes. Her eyes are
enormous, and the color of very deep, cold water. About her
lips and nostrils there is the faint expression of bitterness that
many Italian women have, as if half-sensing a disagreeable odor,
or some barely perceptible rumor of corruption at the heart of
things. This fades, when she is dreaming—as she often does—
to a sweetly petulant look of interrupted suffering, like that of
a child who has been unjustly scolded or abused and is distracted in the midst of its self-pity by the sudden flittering passage of a lovely butterfly. Beneath all of her sudden, great-eyed,
virginal absorptions in the unexpected splendors of the world,
one feels always the constant threat of a resurgent wail or sob.
Only her hands are not physically beautiful. They are ugly old
woman's hands, wrinkled, short-fingered, strangely gnarled-
looking. She almost always wears skirts with pockets in them,
so that she can hide them.

"We're having gin and bitter lemon. But there's whisky,
if you'd rather have it. Or Cinzano."

"Oh, gin would be ideal," murmurs Philippe. "Thank you so much."

"Tessa?"

"Gin, lovely. But you must promise to give us only one. It's awful of us to do this."

"It couldn't be nicer, stop fussing. Gwynyth?"

"Can I have mine neat?"

"Yes."

I move past her in the doorway, parting the bead curtains with my hand and closing my eyes as I do so with an exaggerated expression of disgust, for she reeks of garlic. She has a ridiculous habit of carrying a handful of garlic cloves around in her pocket, and occasionally munching one. Her upper lip lifts in a silly, guilty smile from the tips of her white teeth.

"You hate me, don't you?"

"No, I just hate garlic."

She breaks into a startling peal of robust, boyish laughter. As I move across the living room I hear her say to Margaret, "That man hates me because I smell. He's very fastidious, your husband."

When I return she is sitting on the parapet with a handful of potato chips in her skirt, listening smilingly to Philippe, who is discussing the English cinema, and maintaining a studious obliviousness to Tessa's gaze, which is bent broodingly upon her. When I present her with a glass of gin she murmurs, "Ta, love," and hugs it to her breast.

"Of course, what I love most are your comedies. Your Alec Guinness films, for example. This, to me, is the real English genius. The ability to laugh at yourself. Oh, I admire him very much. Do you share this?"

"Do you mean the admiration or the genius?" Gwynyth asks.

"Oh, no; I mean the admiration. The genius I am sure of."

"Adrian doesn't," says Yvonne. "You ought to hear him on the subject."

"You do not, Mr. Blackmon?"

"Well, not actually, no. I think they're very funny, of course; but there's something terribly sad to me about the way we celebrate eccentricity in our films. There's a sort of admission in it that our form of life is apt to produce a frightening number of casualties; so we're pretty well bound to be nice to these people. Smile at them, you know, and say, 'That's all right. You're a lovely old English eccentric, and we're proud of you. Have some of that camomile tea you're so fond of.' I speak, you understand, as one of the oddest of the lot."

Gwynyth's eyes grow lustrous. She has seen another butterfly go by.

"You're going to get grease all over your skirt," Tessa says. Gwynyth looks insolently toward her.

"And then do you know what people will say when I go downtown? 'There goes a girl with grease all over her skirt.'"

"Well, of course, if you don't mind."

"No, I don't, really."

"Well, I shall watch your films with a very different point of view," Philippe says. "Have you made films yourselves, any of you?"

"Tessa has," says Adrian.

"Have you really? Did you like it, Miss Blanchard?"

"No, not at all," says Tessa. "It appeals to the two very worst elements of the artistic temperament: vanity and felicity. It is much too easy."

"Ah. And you disapprove of ease?"

"Yes. Ease in one's work. I don't think anything can be of value unless it has some quality of ordeal, of pain, about it."

"That is what is meant by dedication in an artist, I suppose."

"I don't know what is meant by that. I only know that some performances—which I have heard very highly praised—are distasteful to me, because they are so felicitous. Felicity is not very far removed from frivolity. I dislike it in everything. In style of dress, in manners, in conversation, in relationships." The categories seem to be very deliberately chosen.

"How do you mean, in relationships?" asks David, with a kind of indolent alertness.

"I mean those which are too comfortably formed, too full of ease, of self-congratulation. It is a very easy thing to form a friendship with someone who flatters you, or who offers many opportunities to your virtuosity; but it will do you very little good. A relationship, like a work of art, to be of value should have a very different basis."

"Of pain, I suppose," says David.

"That would be preferable."

"What a bloody idea. That's what Catholicism did to Europe. I'll take compatibility and simpleminded pleasure as the basis of my relationships, thank you."

"I'm sure of it," says Tessa.

Yvonne suddenly drops her glass; drops it and shatters it on the stone floor of the terrace. The cold liquid splashes everyone about the ankles.

"Oh, I say!" she cries. She is terribly embarrassed. Apparently she has quietly become quite drunk. "I've broken your glass. How stupid of me."

"That's all right," says David. "You're just a lovely quaint old English eccentric, and we're proud of you."

"Yes, I know, but that's getting a bit too quaint, I'm afraid. I'm awfully sorry, Maggie."

"Oh, it doesn't matter at all," says Margaret. "We got them at the Prix Unique, anyway, for parties. I wouldn't dare use those Venetian goblets Madame What's-Her-Name has got in there. Mickey, get Yvonne another drink, will you?"

"What were you having?" I ask, rising. "Gin and bitters, wasn't it?"

"Yes. Oh, dear, do you think I should have another one? Well, make it a very small one, won't you, Michael, or I'll disgrace myself."

I go in through the bead curtain and across the living room to the kitchen, where I stand for a moment before the sunlit sink, listening to the murmur of their voices from the terrace.

In a moment, while I am dislodging ice cubes from a tray, Gwynyth enters.

"I've been sent to tell you to bring the broom and dustpan," she says.

"Oh. All right."

"Perhaps I'd better take them. You'll have your hands full. Where are they?"

"Just in that cupboard there. Thank you."

She finds them and stands for a moment, watching me, with the dustpan upside down on her head, like a helmet. "Are you making that for Yvonne? You'll kill her. She's very vulnerable to alcohol."

"Then you can finish it for her."

"I'm not sure that's very flattering."

"A relationship should not be based on flattery, from what Tessa says."

"You're not to listen to Tessa: she's too bloody keen on suffering to suit me. I'm like David."

"You mean just compatibility and simpleminded pleasure."

"Absolutely. What more could one ask for from a shipmate? After all, we've been to Africa together, or very nearly; and we got along quite well, I thought. Didn't you?"

She goes out of the kitchen, balancing the dustpan on her head, and in a moment I hear a great clatter as she drops it on the stone floor of the terrace, apparently in negotiating the curtain. When I return Margaret is sweeping up the bits of broken glass and Gwynyth is crouching before her with the dustpan to receive the debris. Yvonne blinks in apologetic incapacity.

"Michael, you mustn't give that to her, really," says Tessa. "She'll have the most dreadful headache in the morning."

"Don't be such a bloody mother duck," says Yvonne. "I shall have as many headaches as I jolly well like. I thought you believed in pain, and all that rot." Tessa looks bitterly aside.

"What I love about the theater," says Adrian, "is that there's such a wonderful sense of community. You know: teapot bubbling away in the dressing room, and all that. Is that a thing you enjoy in your profession, Philippe?"

"Well, not exactly in that sense. I am connected with a hotel."

"Oh."

There is a polite but remorseless silence.

"Yes. I do what you call, I believe, public relations work. Promotional banquets, securing celebrated guests to stay with us. Things of that sort."

"Oh, yes. It sounds very interesting. What hotel?"

"The Continentale, in Nice."

"Do you mean to say these celebrated guests stay with you for nothing?" asks Gwynyth.

"Yes. Of course, they must be agreeable to our advertising the fact. It has a certain publicity value."

"My God. And here we are staying in that bloody *pension* in Villefranche. Why don't you have *us* come?"

"I'm sure there will come a day when the management will be delighted with that suggestion," says Philippe with a somewhat disconcerted but very ready smile.

"But look here, we're all frightfully celebrated. They talk of nothing else but us, in London."

"Unfortunately my countrymen are slower to perceive greatness. But I have every confidence that they will soon be awakened to it." He is not at all sure that Gwynyth is jesting, and smiles at Adrian for reassurance.

"I'll tell you what. We'll do recitations in the lobby, if you like. 'Boots' and 'Recessional'; that sort of thing."

Philippe now dares to laugh. "I will suggest it to the management," he says. "I'm sure they will be very pleased with the arrangement."

"Of course if you can't work out the free lodging," David says, "you might get us booked into the cocktail lounge for a week or two. I juggle, you know; and Gwynyth does a very daring turn with an Alsatian. I think it'll go over very well in your place."

"You don't think I'd do it, do you?" she cries. "By God, I would. Anything to get out of that wretched barrack we're in." The two of them break into peals of laughter, David doubling over in his chair and Gwynyth collapsing limply over her dust-pan, her yellow hair hanging.

"You'll cut yourself, you silly creature," Tessa says. She rises, blushing, and sets her glass on the parapet. "Do come along, the lot of you. Philippe's waiting for us like an angel, and we're holding him up dreadfully."

As they leave, at last, Gwynyth pauses in the doorway of the villa and turns to us. "Has Adrian told you about the fête?"

"Yes. On Friday?" Margaret says.

"Oh, good. You're coming, are you?"

"We are indeed."

"I'm so glad. You're sweet to us. I mean you're so nice, to understand, when we're naughty. Most people don't, you know." She looks shyly at the ground for a moment, then leans toward Margaret and kisses her on the cheek. "Good night."

"Good night, dear."

In a moment we hear her marching down the stone path to the roadway, crying out into the warm dark summer air, " 'Boots, *boots*, boots, *boots*. *Mar*ching over *A*frica!' "

We sit on the darkening terrace among the empty glasses and the snack bowls, watching the stars come out above the bay. The air is sweet with gardenia and jasmine. Villefranche begins to glitter far below us at the rim of the ancient, sighing sea. A bird rustles in the dark bougainvillea vines above us, settling for the night. Margaret laughs softly.

"They're mad. But wonderful. What lovely people."

"Do you like them, really?"

"I love them. I don't think I'll ever get used to ordinary people again."

"I know."

We sit listening to the hot silence of the summer night. Far above us on the Grande Corniche the tiny headlights of an automobile crawl slowly across the darkness of the mountain.

"I got burned today. My shoulders are sore. Are yours?"

"A little. You ought to use more cream. It's hot, in that sun."

"I know. I love our little beach. I can't wait to get there, in the mornings. What a life we lead."

"It's pretty strenuous, isn't it? Do you really like it here, Mickey?"

"Oh, my. You've ruined me forever, bringing me here."

I light cigarettes for us and carry one to her, then sit down on the parapet and watch the red ember glowing in the dark. When she inhales her face is illuminated by a soft scarlet flare.

"Are you hungry?" I ask.

"A little."

"Have your cigarette and then we'll dress and go down to Beaulieu for dinner. I have a new place for us."

She sighs. "Oh, every day is like a dream. You won't be able to do anything with me for the rest of my life."

"Well, it isn't the time to worry about that."

"No."

She rises and comes to the parapet, standing beside me and laying her hand on my shoulder. "I hate to go in and bathe off this lovely feeling. The Mediterranean makes you feel so wonderful, doesn't it? It's not as sticky as the Atlantic; it just leaves a soft hot glow on your skin, like a fine old patina. It makes me feel sort of Roman."

"You're beginning to look sort of Roman, even."

"Am I? I feel it, too. Do you know, just at first—just for a day or two—I wasn't really sure I'd like it. I wasn't. I was sort of scared or something, I suppose."

"Scared of what?"

"Well, it *is* very different from Kansas, you know. And after all, I've always been taught to have a very great suspicion of luxury and idleness. But I'm beginning to think I could develop a very great tolerance for them."

"To understand all is to forgive all."

"Oh, exactly. As long as you're allowed to get in on the

fun, yourself, of course." She laughs in a soft, excited way. "On that basis, I think I could forgive almost anything."

"You can't have gotten to that stage already."

"Well, very nearly. As long as she keeps getting nice surprises, it's astonishing how philosophical a woman can be."

"That's a very Roman point of view. You'd better go in and have a bath."

"All right." She leans down and kisses me on the temple. "I love you, Mickey."

Having dressed for dinner, we drive down through the fragrant darkness, past the lights of villas sprinkled on the hills, to the little harbor town of Beaulieu, where we dine by candlelight at a very old stone restaurant at the edge of the warm, black, glittering sea.

Yvonne's remark that the countess "smelled of blood" was extravagant, of course, but not out of the question; because she certainly smelled of a great many things: of cornstarch, which I am almost certain she used as talcum powder; of some ancient, unidentifiable perfume, vaguely animal in origin; of cologne of an entirely different brand and vintage; of pomade, which she used to smooth back the stray hair about her temples; of dusty lace; of tobacco, bay, and Sen-Sen; and, generally, of vermouth. She was the most aromatic human being I have ever known, and her nature was just as pungent as her person and just as much of a potpourri. It was composed of a heady assortment of opinions, enthusiasms, and prejudices whose chief common quality was their intensity, and which, like her perfume, was vaguely redolent of some departed form of life which had been sacrificed to help her formulate them. If she expressed the belief that early marriage was bound to be disastrous, one felt that somewhere in the past some unhappy pair of young lovers of her acquaintance had met with tragedy. If she said that she considered the taking of hot baths a deadly habit, one felt assured that someone had died to furnish her with the belief. She sometimes managed to convey the impression that the whole of human history had been conducted expressly to supply her with a set of precepts. They didn't all concern death or disaster, however; she had an enormous range of interests and sentiments, from the barbarous to the exquisite, and a communicating mechanism to match. Sometimes she spoke loudly and majestically (or at the worst, militarily), and sometimes very softly indeed; sometimes her old lavender-colored eyes would blaze like amethyst, and sometimes grow as mysteriously soft as opals.

Although she must have been very nearly eighty, she was astonishingly nimble, and played a very creditable game of badminton. She had an equal passion for cigars, vermouth, and marinated herring, of which she required an almost constant supply; and yet she managed to exercise it without the least impression of comedy or of that type of demoralized eccentricity of which you have heard Adrian complain; for everything that she did, she did with such authority that one automatically regarded it as a criterion, and the very different behavior of the world at large as vulgar or anomalous. If she had worn a burlap dressing gown to the opera at Nice, one would have been inclined to wonder what lapse of taste on the part of Princess Grace of Monaco had been responsible for the appearance of that lady there without one. She drove about in a gigantic black Bugatti which must have been manufactured at almost the same time as herself, and which had acquired over the years almost the same degree of intractability. To this, and to my offer of assistance in the face of it, we owed our acquaintance with her.

One day during the first week of our stay at La Fleurelle we took the bus to Nice to hire an automobile, and drove back in the product of our expedition, a tiny tremulous Citroën put together out of what looked like sheets of corrugated iron and painted a miasmal battleship gray. Like almost everything in the world, it was infinitely less magnificent than anything the countess owned, and much more practical. Halfway up the first, and steepest, of the hills which the Nice road climbs on entering the Cape we discovered her and Nicolas, her chauffeur, at the mercy of one of those Gargantuan indispositions to which her Bugatti periodically yielded. She was sitting on a collapsible canvas chair with the shaft of a lavender-colored parasol resting on one shoulder, reading a paperbacked edition of *Lolita* which she held at arm's length, as if afraid that it might ignite the soft dove-colored silk of her high-throated blouse. The Bugatti, with its huge, leather-strapped bonnet upreared in agony, was parked on a dusty verge at a bend of the road, while Nicolas, in his shirt sleeves and murmuring Catalonian obscenities, was passionately disemboweling it. Until we had stopped the car and backed it onto the verge beside the countess, neither she nor Nicolas so much as glanced at us.

"Can we help you?" I asked. *"Est-ce que nous pouvons vous aider, Madame?"*

She raised her eyes from the page and smiled.

"Thank you very much. I'm afraid no one understands the machine except Nicolas."

"I'd be glad to run him down to the garage at St. Jean."

"I think he has everything he needs in the way of equipment. It's very much a matter of time."

"Well, perhaps we could take you somewhere where you'd be more comfortable," Margaret said. "Are you staying on the Cape?"

"Oh, that would be a great convenience. Yes, I am. On the Passage Vietor. Would that be a trouble to you?"

"No, of course not."

"How very kind you are." She spoke to Nicolas in Spanish, rose, and let down her parasol. I got out of the Citroën and went around to escort her back to it, while Margaret clambered into the back seat.

"Shall I fold up your chair?" I asked.

"Thank you. Nicolas will attend to it."

Despite the fact that she was nearing eighty and inclining toward stoutness, she maneuvered herself into the front seat of the tiny car with surprising grace. She adjusted herself in a swift over-all way with several comprehensive shakes and flaps, like a large ornate bird which has just alighted on a limb.

"You are Americans," she said as I started up.

"Yes."

"Then that accounts for your generosity. I have never been to America, but I have been a very enthusiastic observer of your country, from afar, for many years, and I have formed a good many agreeable impressions."

"Well, I'm pleased to hear it," I said. "Perhaps that's the best way to judge a country; from afar."

She smiled and inclined her head slightly in approval. "I am at present reading a book about America, however"— with a little tap of her fingertips on the cover of *Lolita,* in her lap— "which I feel will demand a certain amount of reconsideration on my part. Can such occurrences be common in your country?"

"Oh, I don't suppose it's any more common than what goes on in *Les Liaisons Dangereuses,* say, is common in France."

"Ah. Of course that isn't very reassuring." Her smile broadened, and she turned to make a closer examination of Margaret, who, cramped in the back seat of the tiny car, had up to now been obscured from her full view. Her look was long and thoughtful. "You're very pretty, my dear," she said. "I hope you're not suffering, back there."

"No, not at all," Margaret said. "Thank you."

The countess returned her attention to me. "You're mistaken in assuming that I am French," she said. "Or that I'm capable of chauvinistic sentiments of any kind."

"I beg your pardon."

"I'm not offended. Such few allegiances as I've ever found it to my advantage to cultivate have long since been dissolved. With the exception of that wretched machine back there, which I don't seem able to dispose of. It suits me so well, you know; as nothing else in this world has ever done."

"It's very handsome," Margaret said.

"And like most handsome things, completely unreliable.

Mind you, I shouldn't object to being French, if I could do the thing well. But it requires a devotion to so many things that I find tiresome, or inscrutable, that I could never manage it. This Cape, however, is a notable exception." She nodded through the window at the passing foliage. "I've spent over fifty summers of my life here, and each one I find more enchanting than the last."

"I can understand that," Margaret said. "We've only been here a few days, and we never want to leave."

"That is a very proper reaction. I hope you will be able to satisfy it."

"I wish we could, but we only have three months. I don't even like to think about going back."

"Where are you staying?"

"We've taken a villa on the Chemin du Roy. La Fleurelle."

"Oh, yes. The Auriol place. It's charming."

"It is," Margaret said. "We absolutely adore it."

"Do you know Madame Auriol, then?"

"Oh, no. We rented it through the agency in Villefranche."

"Oh, that's a pity. You will no doubt be paying three times what you should. You would have done far better to let it directly from Madame Auriol."

"I wish we could have," Margaret said. "But of course we didn't know anything about her. Still, it was fun, discovering it for ourselves."

"Yes. You will pay more, but you will get far more out of it in the long run. One should ideally arrive at any place—including this earth—with no connections or credentials of any kind. It makes life much more difficult, of course, and one is apt to be abused, as you have been; but one's achievements are so much more genuine. I have always regretted that I couldn't take full credit for my own few, very modest ones."

"Still, the way a person uses his circumstances—whatever they are—is as much a credit to him as anything, don't you think?" said Margaret.

"Thank you, my dear. No, I am just naïve enough to doubt

the fact. Now we must turn right at this next corner. My villa is just below us, on the shore."

"Does it have a name?" I asked.

"Yes. I call it Quelques Saisons." She smiled at me delicately. "That is one of the few, very modest achievements I speak of. It is as near to poetry as I can ever hope to reach."

"It's a lovely name," said Margaret sadly.

"Well, it will do. It deserves far better, like so much that I have attempted to classify. Now, do you see the gatehouse, there? That Moorish affair? You must turn right, just beyond it."

I did so, turning the Citroën into a gravel driveway lined with gigantic eucalyptus trees that cast a broken shadow across the pale blue stone. At the end of it we saw the front of the villa, a long cloister of Moorish columns supporting an entablature of trefoiled arches, in the style of the Alcázar at Córdoba. In front of it the driveway made a circle around a blazing bed of poinsettias set in a wide lawn of faultless green which yielded to the tangled trellises and purple shadow of a grape arbor. Beyond the arbor we could see the scattered stones and boulders of the shore, a little crescent of brown sand, and the flat, blue, shimmering sea.

"Oh, this is a heavenly place," Margaret said.

"I think, rather, that it's an earthly place," the countess said. "Which is why I am so fond of it. I do hope you have the time to stay and have a drink with me. I should enjoy showing you about."

"We'd love to," Margaret said.

"I'm so glad. I'm afraid I don't know how to operate this handle."

"Oh, let me do it." I got out quickly, circled the car, and opened the door for her. As I did so a maid in a black uniform came out of the central arched doorway of the villa and down the stone steps from the cloistered gallery to the lawn.

"*Oh, la la! Madame a eu encore une panne?*" she asked with a great show of compassion.

"Bien sûr," said the countess. *"Monsieur et Madame ont eu la bonté de m'amener chez moi. Veuillez m'assister, Amélie."*

"Oui, ma Comtesse." She took her mistress' arm and we followed the two of them up the steps and into the villa. Inside it was cool and dim; the arched windows all were shuttered and let through only thin strips of light onto the marble floors.

"Veuillez ouvrir les jalousies, Amélie," the countess said.

"Oui, ma Comtesse." She unlatched and pushed open one by one the shutters of the windows which fronted on the sea, and as the light spilled in, the full magnificence of the room was revealed. The ceiling was cross-vaulted, of blue mosaic tile, and supported by Moorish columns with spiral fluting, set on the polished black marble floors. All the furnishings were Spanish: massive paneled chests of glowing olive-wood with hand-forged iron clasps and hinges, cabinets with delicate barred windows, huge dark Castilian chairs with leather-padded backs and seats, antique wall tapestries figured with faded scenes of conquistadores in casques and breastplates, enormous black iron candelabra and massive framed portraits of what could only have been her ancestors, proud, passionate, austere, and occasionally retarded-looking people in Toledo armor, chasubles, farthingales, or satin breeches, painted in the style of Velasquez. In the center of the room stood a huge baronial table whose top was formed of a single slab of ebony-dark wood, three inches thick, on which was placed a giant silver bowl with a single scarlet camellia blossom floating in clear water. There was a cool, ancient odor, like a tomb.

"As you see," the countess said, "I have been forever deprived of the right to establish my own identity, or my own achievements. At any rate, this serves me very well as an alibi. What would you like to drink?"

"Well, I don't really like anything stronger than Cinzano before five o'clock," Margaret said. "If you have it."

"I have. And for you, sir?"

"That would be fine, thank you."

"C'est entendu?" asked the countess, turning to her maid.

"*Oui, Madame. Et pour Madame, un Campari?*"

"*S'il vous plaît, Amélie.*"

"*Merci, ma Comtesse.*" The maid departed through an arched portal with a hollow tapping of her heels on the marble floor.

"Perhaps I had better introduce myself," said the countess. "I am Elena Delgado, Marquesa de Puertavallone, La Contesa de Baroja."

"How do you do," I said. "We're the Pritchards. Michael and Margaret."

"I'm very pleased to know you."

"Do you mind if I'm terribly provincial and ask you to explain your title to us?" Margaret said. "We don't know anything about titles."

"It is a Spanish—or rather, *they* are Spanish titles, very old and insignificant. Their only meaning, any longer, is that roughly five hundred years ago that man there"—she raised her hand indolently in the direction of a thin, darkly bearded, lonely-looking man in a scarlet doublet—"was sufficiently cunning with his tongue and with his dagger to be awarded sovereignty over two hundred acres of dust and stone and approximately the same number of human souls. A distinction to which the rest of these people clung as rapaciously as he had earned it." She let her eyes roam along the row of portraits for a moment. "Some of them were idiots. I mean literally; which it may not surprise you very much to learn. Others were artists of near-genius; which it may. In any case, they are all long dead, and I do not intend to say another word about them." She took our arms and led us into an alcove under a large grilled window which was furnished, as the rest of the room was not, in a manner to induce a certain amount of ease and informality. There was a chintz-covered sofa, a coffee table, one or two upholstered chairs, and some flowering plants in wrought-iron stands. She deposited us on the sofa and sat facing us in a damask-covered chair.

"You are to be here for three months," she said. "Do you play badminton?"

"Mickey's very good at it," Margaret said.

"Then I shall require your competition," the countess said. "It's something which I understand Americans are well able to provide."

"We'll be very pleased," I said.

"Good. I shall expect neither mercy, charity, nor pity, and I shall give none. Badminton is a thing which I take very seriously. Do you see my lawn there?"

"Yes," I said, turning to admire it through the iron bars of the window. "It's very elegant. Almost like a putting green."

"It is. I've had it specially installed and very carefully maintained. It is my chief extravagance. Badminton is my *métier*, you see. It's my way of getting at life, and at people. Nowhere in the world are people so ruthlessly revealed as on a badminton court, except possibly in bed or on a battlefield. And I am much too old to perform to advantage on either. But at badminton you will find me a formidable antagonist." She picked up a black quartz humidor from the table beside her and selected a cigar, from which she began to peel a wrapper of gold foil. "Would you care for a cigar?"

"No thank you."

"Mrs. Pritchard?"

"Oh, no thank you," Margaret said, turning quickly to decline the offer. She had been looking at a statue in a far corner of the salon behind the countess, a representation of Actaeon, apparently, in a dramatic transitional stage between man and stag, being set upon by a pair of ravening marble hounds, all done in the florid romantic detail of Victorian art and very much out of keeping with the rest of the room.

"Do you like that statue?" the countess asked.

"It's very interesting, isn't it?" Margaret said. "Is it Victorian?"

"Yes." She smiled in acknowledgment of Margaret's tact.

"It was done by an idiotic but adorable friend of mine, whom I subsidized in a small way, until she developed this unhealthy passion for stags. Are either of you artists?"

"No," Margaret said.

"What is your profession, may I ask, Mr. Pritchard?"

"I'm a curator of manuscripts," I said, "at the Library of Congress, which is our Bibliothèque Nationale, or British Museum."

"How very interesting. What sort of manuscripts?"

"Literary and liturgical, mostly. I'm a specialist in Eastern languages." I rose and snapped my cigarette lighter to ignite her cigar. She leaned toward me, puffing out clouds of gentle violet smoke.

"Literature and liturgy," she said. "Surely those are wayward preoccupations for a twentieth-century man. For an American, particularly. I was prepared to discover that you were a business executive, or a sociologist, or a dentist."

"No. There are a certain number of other professions in America."

"Well, you see how innocent we are about it all. Still, I'm delighted to find that you are not what I regard as typical. In my experience typical people seldom have any insight whatever into their own condition, and I expect to learn a great deal about America from you."

"I'm afraid you'll be disappointed," I said.

"I believe not. If I wish to understand a country I don't ask to be shown its typical inhabitants, but its revolutionaries, its renegades, its unregenerates."

"I don't think Michael would qualify as any of those things," Margaret said smilingly.

"Really? He has never wished to overthrow an institution? Or fly into obscurity? Or commit a sin?"

"Not that I know of," Margaret said.

"Then he's even less typical than I thought. He is phenomenal, in fact. Mr. Pritchard, you astonish me. Or your wife does. Can this be true?"

"I suppose it's as true as any wife's conception of her husband," I said.

"Ah. Then there may be room for doubt." She drew a great draft of smoke and blew it out slowly in a thin blue stream.

"Don't you think wives understand their husbands?" Margaret asked.

"My dear, I found it my greatest misfortune that *I* did not. I'm afraid we regard them, and judge them, essentially as husbands; whereas they are essentially men, and husbands only very incidentally. It limits both our understanding and their own capacities. A prophet is not without honor, save in his own country and his own house."

"My husband isn't a prophet, either," Margaret said.

"But, you see, already you've disqualified him from the fields of revolution, of prophecy, of apostasy, and of sin. Which I think you'll agree limits his opportunities considerably. It leaves him little to practice but husbandry—that nameless, that demoralizing thing. Now I intend to regard your husband as a prophet. It is much more flattering; and I find that when a man is made aware of his potentialities to that degree he will almost invariably produce at least one revelation in the course of his acquaintance, out of common courtesy. I shall expect it of you, Mr. Pritchard."

"I'll try to oblige you," I said.

"See that you do. I must have at least one revelation per season, or I wither. It is all that postpones the Final One for me. You see what a great responsibility I've placed upon you."

"It's awesome," I said. "I think I should be allowed to demand something in return."

"Indeed? What would that be?"

"Well, I'll have to decide," I said. "A handicap at badminton, maybe."

"Ah. You should have been a businessman, after all. You have an eye for a bargain. Well, it will have to be a virtual apocalypse to earn you a concession such as that."

The maid arrived out of the marble vastness of the villa

with a tray of drinks, which the countess checked her from distributing.

"Shall we have our refreshment *en plein air*?" she asked. "I have a little pavilion in the arbor, where one can see the water. I think you'll find it very pleasant there."

"That would be lovely," Margaret said, and I agreed. We rose and offered the countess each an arm, following Amélie down the stone steps and across the wide lawn to the arbor, where, under the broad cool leaves, we discovered a stone-paved circular patio furnished with white cast-iron chairs, which looked out through a cluster of gnarled pines and gigantic boulders to the sea. It was cool in the shadow of the vines, and the heavy bunches of blue grapes glowed through the frost of their bloom. Amélie set down our drinks before us on a glass-topped table and departed.

"When I was a girl," the countess said, "this slope was all gorse and rock. I used to play here for hours as a child. It was beautiful, but treacherous. I still bear the scars of thorns." She turned back her sleeve and bared her wrist, which was crossed with several fine white scars, like the rays of frost on a window-pane. "Each of those is a memento of a beautiful afternoon, and a testament to my energy and adventurousness. I was a dauntless child. As in many places on this earth, I bled, and gave thanks, here daily. I think I love it even more than my native land, or quite as much."

"Do you spend any time at all in Spain?" Margaret asked.

"Oh, yes. I spend alternate winters in Madrid; but all of my summers here. Most of our acquaintances summered in San Sebastian, but my father always preferred the South of France. He built this villa, some of it with his own hands, for he loved to work with stone. He entertained Dostoevski here, and Georges Sand, and Nijinsky." She raised her glass and looked through the dark garnet-colored liquor at the sea. "My young friends, I give you the Mediterranean." In the shadow of grapes we drank to that old beauty.

"Now you have been very kind to me," the countess said.

"And I must do something for you in return. As this is your first trip to the Côte, you will want companionship. Young people your own age, with whom you can share far more exhilarating pastimes than badminton, and far more advanced opinions than my own. Fortunately, I am able to supply them. Last winter I was in London, where I saw an extraordinary production of *The Changeling*, a Jacobean tragedy with which you may be familiar. It was extraordinary chiefly for its performance of Beatrice by a young girl named Gwynyth Rees. I was so moved by her acting that I sent her round a note, asking if she would do me the honor of having dinner with me. She came with her young man, who is also an actor, and equally delightful. We had a thoroughly enchanting evening—or at any rate, I did—and I learned, among many things, that they intended to visit the Cap this summer. I made them promise to come and see me here at Quelques Saisons, and I'm delighted to find that they have not forgotten me. They have come with three other friends— all of them on the stage—and have been to see me twice since June. They're staying at Villefranche, and it occurs to me that you would enjoy knowing one another very much."

"I think we may have seen them on the beach," Margaret said. "Is there an older woman, and two young men?"

"Yes, exactly."

"Yes, we heard them speaking English one afternoon. We almost introduced ourselves."

"You should have done so. You would have found them very interesting. Well, I shall give you a chance to correct your lack of initiative. They're coming to a little soiree that I've planned for Friday evening. You must come and meet them, by all means."

"Oh, that would be lovely," Margaret said. "We don't know anyone here at all. And we've *never* known any actors."

"Then you'll enjoy them enormously," the countess said. She sipped from her Campari and set the glass down cautiously, studying Margaret's face. "What a lovely smile you have, my dear."

"Thank you," Margaret said.

"It is a type of smile that has become almost unknown in Europe. It has no function whatever. It appears as spontaneously and ingenuously as a daisy. It is quite alarming."

"Alarming?" Margaret said.

"Yes. I accept it as evidence of the fact that you are a very dangerous nation."

"Because we smile?"

"Because you smile so innocently. Have you ever known innocence to make its appearance in this world without introducing danger, as its handmaid? It encourages the most reckless pretensions and ambitions in us fallen folk. I'm not sure that I approve of innocence, or beauty, or anything of that sort. They upset our world. They are *provocateurs*."

"Oh, you don't mean that," Margaret said.

The countess laughed and lifted her glass, swirling the stained cubes of ice about in it. "Of course I don't. As a matter of fact, I once smiled, myself, in just that very way, if you can conceive of such a thing. I have one or two photographs which will support that very unlikely claim, that I may show you one day."

"I'd love to see them," Margaret said.

"But it isn't your smile only. I don't know if you'll believe me when I say that I've been sitting here in gathering astonishment at the way you recall myself to me, when I was a young woman of your age. It's really quite uncanny. Your style, your bearing, your features, your voice, the color of your hair. I see myself reincarnated, as it were, in you."

"That's astonishing," Margaret said.

"It is indeed. Not entirely reassuring, perhaps, to you; but astonishing. Even your physique I find almost identical to my own, at your age." She swung her wrist, studying for a moment the spinning cubes of ice. "Mrs. Pritchard, I am old and infirm, and full of odd and sentimental ideas; and this leads me to press a request upon you which you may find offensive or eccentric. If so, you mustn't hesitate to say so, for the last thing I would wish to do is to begin our acquaintance by offending you. Do I have your assurance that you won't allow me to do so?"

"I can't imagine it being possible," Margaret said. "I'd be happy to oblige you, if I can."

"You mustn't be rash. However, I'm touched by your generosity. Let me tell you, then, that this soiree I have planned for Friday evening is to be a masquerade. Oh, nothing at all elaborate—there are to be no rented costumes. People are simply to improvise, out of hand, impersonations of characters from history, literature, or art which interest them. Such things are often very ingenious and amusing."

"Oh, it sounds like fun," Margaret said.

"I do hope it will be. We had an affair of that kind last season, and got a great deal of entertainment out of it. But now I have a further confession to make: I am a junkwoman. I have, stuffed into the bowels of that villa, absolute railway cars full of souvenirs, mementos, memorabilia of my past, from my Confirmation Bible to a stuffed Pomeranian, with whose departure from this earth I was never able to reconcile myself. I find it impossible to part with anything which has the slightest emotional significance for me. Some of the most interesting of these relics are costumes which I have saved from almost every era of my life; and of these, there is one of which I am particularly fond. One which I wore at the very prime of my life, on the happiest and most triumphant night of my most glorious year. It was a gift to me. It is the most beautiful dress I have ever had." She set down her glass and studied it for a moment, still clasped between her fingers, before asking, "I wonder if you would wear it on Friday evening, for my sake?"

"I'd be honored," Margaret said.

"It is I who would be honored. It would give me the opportunity of seeing myself, as I have said, virtually reincarnated, at a time of life which was supremely beautiful to me. I don't think I could ever express my gratitude to you."

"But you mustn't try," Margaret said. "I'll have the double pleasure of wearing your lovely gown, and of pleasing you."

"You're very gracious to indulge an old woman so."

"I'm not at all," Margaret said. "It's a privilege."

"Perhaps you would care to come and look at it now; then you could take it with you."

"I'd love to."

"Mr. Pritchard, I don't know that you have any interest in these matters, but you're perfectly welcome to accompany us, if you have."

"I'd like to see it very much," I said.

We left the arbor and walked back across the lawn to the villa, the countess bearing her still smoldering cigar between the frail forefingers of the hand she laid upon my arm. She conducted us across the marble-floored salon, pausing to crush out her cigar in an ashtray of the same material, and down a corridor to the great oak door of a room which might once have been a study, but whose original purpose had been entirely obscured by its conversion into something resembling a warehouse or antique dealer's shop. The jumbled attics of my childhood home in Georgetown, amongst which my mother had once roamed lost and spiritless, came immediately to my mind. There were bits of statuary, pictures, and containers everywhere—antique leather hatboxes, hair trunks, Jacobean presses, Gladstone bags, and steamer trunks of every vintage, with scratched and faded railway stickers, cargo tags, and customs clearance forms. A large commercial clothing rack, of the kind used in department stores, was extended across one end of the room and filled to capacity with feminine costumes from almost every decade of the century and of great magnificence. They were perfectly preserved and had obviously seen very little use; none of them was visibly worn, soiled, crushed, or faded. They were encased in transparent plastic bags which must have been manufactured especially to enclose the voluminous bustled skirts and petticoats of those of Victorian design, of which they mostly were. They were all of them museum pieces, but the dress of which the countess spoke was apparent the moment we approached the wardrobe. It was set apart from the others at one end of the rack, and furnished with a pomander which dangled on a velvet ribbon inside of its protective bag and which issued, as the countess ran down the zipper and shook the garment free, a sudden paralyzingly nostalgic fragrance of old rose. She dropped the plastic bag to the floor and taking the hem of the skirt in her hands, spread out the dress for our examination. It was really dazzlingly beautiful: an Edwardian evening gown of crushed-strawberry satin with a great regal, cream-colored train of the same glowing fabric swelling out from the sash of its tiny waist. The skirt and bodice were decorated with delicate embroidery of silver and mauve, and the consummate grace and femininity of this artistry were completed by the short shimmering sleeves of pleated strawberry-colored chiffon with ribboned edges which must have fallen once like veils over the cool white shoulders of its bewitching mistress. It was the kind of dress that only a man who adores and understands women to a perilous degree could design, or purchase, for one of them; and only for one.

"Oh, my goodness," Margaret said. "Oh, my goodness, how beautiful." She put out her hand and brushed timidly, almost fearfully, the cool cream-colored satin of the train with her fingertips. As she did so there was a tiny audible snap, the exchange of a spark of static electricity between the fabric and her fingertip. She recoiled and gave a little gasp: "Oh." Then, staring at the gown with growing fascination, she murmured, "Oh, I wouldn't dare wear that dress. It would make me feel so—I don't know—*desirable*. Oh, I wouldn't dare wear it."

"Nonsense," said the countess. "You are the only person who could, and whom I would permit to do so; and who would do it justice. You shall wear it. You've given me your word."

"Well, I know, but I didn't know it would be *this* beautiful," Margaret said. "I feel absolutely wanton, just *looking* at it." She turned to me in a shy, subject way. "Do you think I should?"

"Of course you should. It'll make the whole trip worthwhile."

"Then I will," Margaret said. "But I can't be responsible for my actions."

The countess laughed. "I've already explained to you," she said, "that to be beautiful is to be beyond responsibility. You'll have to be contented with the role of *provocateur*. It is we who will suffer." She slid the plastic bag over the gown as she spoke and sealed it with the zipper. "Will you take it with you now?"

"Oh, I don't think we should," Margaret said. "It'll get so crumpled, in that tiny car, and then riding here again, in the evening. May I put it on here, after we arrive?"

"Perhaps that would be best. But you must come a bit early, in that case, so that you can make your entrance. It will give me time, as well, to dress your hair, if you'll allow me to. I should like it just as I used to wear my own."

"I wish you would," Margaret said. "I'd have no idea how to do it."

"Splendid. I have all the accessories for this dress, as well: bracelets, an aigrette for your hair, a little pearl bag, a pair of long silk gloves—the very ones I wore with it. But I won't trouble you with showing them to you now. We must save some few delights for the masquerade." She adjusted the gown on the rack and for a moment regarded it and Margaret alternately with a look of great content. As we walked back down the corridor to the salon she said to me, "And what guise do you intend to assume at our masquerade, Mr. Pritchard?"

"I haven't thought about it," I said. "But I should think a slave would be the most appropriate thing."

"Just so," she murmured.

We stood on the steps of her villa under the trefoiled arch of its entrance and looked for a moment at the sea. Its blue was darkening to violet in the afternoon light. The countess took Margaret's hand and pressed it against her cheek.

"You have accommodated me more than I deserve," she said. "I shall look forward very much to seeing you again."

"So shall we," Margaret said. "It's been a lovely afternoon."

"Mr. Pritchard." She offered me her fragile porcelain hand

and I bent and kissed it. It was the first time in my life I had ever done such a thing, but I was surprised at how naturally the gesture came to me. She stood on the steps and lifted her hand to us delicately as we drove away.

"Oh, dear, what a wonderful woman," Margaret said.

"Well, why do you say, 'Oh, dear'?"

"I don't know. I feel rather sad about it all, too. Sort of a delicious sadness." She hunched her shoulders together in an artless, exclamatory way. "Oh, that dress! It's done something to me. *She's* done something to me."

"I can just see you in it," I said.

"I can see *her* in it. I can see the whole evening. I can almost feel it. I almost know the things she said. It's really eerie." She frowned at me suddenly. "Didn't you like her, Mickey?"

"Oh, I liked her all right. But she seemed pretty patronizing part of the time."

"I don't think so; that's just her way. She's much too well-bred to deliberately insult anyone. She was very sweet. You didn't understand her."

"I don't have the advantage of being her reincarnated self," I said.

"You sound jealous."

"I'd just like to be able to buy you dresses like that."

"That's very nice to hear," she said, and sat thoughtfully for a moment. "Never mind. You give me lots of wonderful things. This glorious trip. This glorious automobile."

"The trip lasts three months," I said. "And the automobile is rented."

"No, the trip lasts forever. And I'm sort of glad the automobile *is* rented. It's really quite an ugly automobile, isn't it?"

"It's not like a Bugatti."

"No. It looks sort of homemade, or something. Out of washtubs." She laughed and drew a great contented breath.

"Are you having a good time?" I said.

"Yes, I am."

We went to dinner that night at a restaurant called Da Bottau in the Old City of Nice. It was a provincial-type restaurant with sawdust on the floor, great trestle tables of hewn planks, and torches flaring on the whitewashed walls. There was a legend on the menu which explained the meaning of the name (which I have forgotten) in the ancient Niçoise dialect, and something of the history of the city and the district. The Niçoise, it appeared, were a sturdy, independent, and unassimilable people who had resisted all foreign domination from Roman times until the present. They served their food with a rough red local wine which no doubt had greatly aided them in this resolve, but which produced in Margaret and me almost the opposite effect; by the time we had drunk two bottles of it we had yielded to foreign influence to the extent of being eternal champions of all things Niçoise, of all places warm and blue, of cobbled streets, siestas, bouillabaisse, and, in my case, of torchlight especially. For what was this that had happened to my wife's face in the flickering, caressing crimson-and-yellow light of those soft flames? Her eyes had darkened and deepened and filled with fluctuating shadows and sudden hectic glints of fire. Her face was smoothed and tinted with a soft carmine flush and rabidly, continually remodeled by the flames, like warm wax stroked by the burning fingertips of some inflamed artist. It had no exact delineation; it appeared to be in a state of feverish metamorphosis. One which affected her throat and arms as well, for they were bathed in the same transforming glow. It got into her voice, too, in some way, this torchlight; for it had —although this may sound comical, perhaps—a definitely hot quality. Her words came out with a burnt sound, and her lips, wet with the red Niçoise wine, had a lacquered, resinous look, like nearly kindled wood. Well, this is not a usual sight, of course: one's wife, after twelve years of married life, on the virtual point of combustion. Perhaps, I thought, I ascribe too much to the wine, or the torchlight. Perhaps some of this transforming fire lies in my own beholding eyes. I was ravished by the possibility. The trip, then, was "working," was it? It had "paid off," this reckless, extravagant adventure? The old Mother Mediterranean had perhaps requited our homage. I had one of those lyrical, tingling sensations in the blood and along the nerves, like the chiming of a carillon, which men of little imagination and much good fortune are perpetually mistaking for religious experience, and on the basis of which they plan deeds, empires, and reforms of insupportable ostentation.

"You look absolutely beautiful," I said.

"Do I really? I feel beautiful, too. I feel sort of coated with something. Gilded."

"We ought to move here, you know. We ought to spend the rest of our lives here."

"I know. Maybe you could start a Division of Middle Eastern Liturgical Studies in Nice."

"It would fill a great need."

"Yes. It would give those poor people who lounge about on the beach all day and while away their evenings in the casino something to do. Something really exciting to occupy them. You've no idea how thrilled they would be."

"I could make a real contribution."

"You could, Mickey." She laughed and lifted her glass, peering through it at the flames of the brazier on the wall beside us. "Oh, that's lovely. Dancing crimson flames. My heart feels like that. I want you to call me Flame, or Blaze, or Torch, or something. Will, you, just for tonight?"

"Yes."

"And then tomorrow I'll make you an omelette."

"Two months from tomorrow make me an omelette. Tomorrow *Volaille de la Mer aux Champignons*." This was the tuna fish concoction she had made for us on the *Hyacinth* on her maiden voyage. She smiled at me with her glittering flame-lit eyes.

"I thought you hated that."

"No. As I remember, it was delicious."

"I'm afraid I may have forgotten the recipe."

"There wasn't any recipe," I said. "That was its charm. It was made out of imagination, and whatever was at hand."

"Mostly tuna fish," she said. "I'm afraid you have a much finer palate now. You'd never be satisfied with tuna fish." She looked suddenly a bit downcast. I refilled her glass and rested my hand on hers.

"Blaze, honey, I wouldn't care if you couldn't boil water. You're my dish." Margaret grinned at me.

"Well, I'll put some of *this* in it," she said. "Anything would taste good with this in it."

We finished our second bottle of wine and then went out and wandered about the ancient narrow streets for an hour before we drove home. The shops were closed, and there were groups of people sitting on chairs on the sidewalks or lounging in doorways or leaning from windowsills in the summer darkness, chattering sharply to each other in that tone of indignation which seems to characterize all of French civil life. There was a fine white quarter-moon hung above the city in the clear sky, and many stars, and the warm soft air smelled both of the village —stone and bread and onions—and of the sea—salt and space and silence.

We drove home along the Moyen Corniche, and it was incredibly beautiful. Behind us, among the dark palms and minarets of the casino and the *grands hôtels* lay all the scattered diamonds of the Promenade des Anglais, and far beneath, at every bend of the road, the great lambent, moonlit sea.

I made gin and tonics and brought them to the terrace where Margaret lay on a padded chaise longue in the moonlight. She was dressed in white and looked luminous and impermanent. I came and sat beside her, bending down to kiss her throat and lips and shoulders. Nude, she was like a pool of quicksilver. We made love wildly, shattering glasses, splashed with cold gin, tearing her filmy summer dress, a peacock screaming in the darkness. Then she lay panting, holding my head against her breast, calling in a soft, desperate voice, "Oh, love. Oh, love."

. . .

Margaret rose early and, as she always did, wandered about the garden with her coffee cup, a pair of gardening shears, and a wicker basket, which after half an hour or so she brought and set down at my feet—I had sat all the while on the terrace steps sipping coffee and watching her—filled with the booty of her excursion: a glowing tumble of allamanda, oleander, hibiscus, and bougainvillea blossoms. I picked out a yellow trumpet of allamanda and put it between my teeth.

"Those are poisonous," Margaret said.

"I don't believe it."

"Still, you mustn't tempt fate. The countess will be very disappointed if you die, or go into convulsions or something at her party."

"Don't you believe it. Nothing would please her more."

"Now why do you say that? She's just a sentimental old lady. You're not kind to her."

I put the tip of the blossom between my lips and pretended to blow a bugle call on it, making, with a trumpet sound in my throat, the tune of "Parade."

"What was that?" Margaret said.

"A flourish. For the festivities."

"In the mornings you have spells," Margaret said. "Why is that? Most people get visionary in the evening."

"I'm different. I see better by morning light, like mathematicians and lyric poets."

"I think it's because I make the coffee too strong. You get overstimulated or something."

"Nothing to do with the coffee. It's the morning light. It flays the shadows off things, washes everything to awful cleanliness."

"Oh, pot." She sat down on the step beside me and nudged me with her hip. I could feel the excitement in her, a restlessness that was very different from the wan morning anxiety we were accustomed to.

"Don't you believe it?"

"What?"

"About the light."

"No, it's nonsense."

"It isn't. Now look closely." I turned my face full into the morning light, raising it for her inspection. "What do you see?"

"Michael Pritchard. Unshaven and prophetic."

"No, but look closely at my skin. At my nose, and ears, and eyes. Do you see anything new? Anything you never noticed?"

She studied my face for a moment, turning it from side to side with the tips of her fingers on my chin. Dismay grew slowly in her eyes. "Oh, my goodness, I *do*. You're starting to have hair grow in your ears. Oh, Mickey, how awful!"

"Aha. And what else?"

"How long have you had that? Do you mean to say I never noticed?"

"Years and years."

"Oh, you haven't either. It must have just happened last night. It must have been all that wine we drank."

"Now, what else?"

Her eyes grew seriously studious. She pored over my face with a look of faint anxiety. "Well, for heaven's sake. You've got a lot of little tiny broken blood vessels in your cheeks, and on the sides of your nose. A little fine network you can barely see. Mickey, have you got thrombosis or something?"

"Nope. Keep looking."

"Oh, this is awful. You're falling to pieces right in front of me. And what's that mole thing? Right there by your ear." She touched it with her fingertip. "You certainly didn't have that when I married you. What's the matter with you, anyway?"

"I have a dread affliction. Mortality."

"How awful. Is it dangerous?"

"It's mortal."

"And I never noticed. And you've been suffering so, all these years. Oh, my poor Mickey. How did you ever get it?"

"I contracted it in the womb."

"But why didn't I *notice*? I mean if you've had it all that time?"

"The symptoms are delayed," I said. "But the course of the disease is irreversible. All it takes is a good clear morning to reveal it."

She laid her palm against my cheek and closed her eyes compassionately. "I'm never going to get up again in my life until three thirty in the afternoon," she said. "Or maybe five. Just in time for cocktails."

"That's a very good idea. And the other thing to remember in dealing with victims of this malady is to be gentle with them. Try to exercise understanding at all times. You mustn't expect too much of them. You must respect their frailty."

She bent down and laid her forehead on my knee, from which position she murmured contritely, "I will."

"Shall we go swimming, then?"

"I can't, because the countess is going to fix my hair this evening, and it mustn't be wet. But you swim, and I'll just bake."

We had croissants and raspberry confiture for breakfast, and Margaret had, as well, a poinsettia blossom, which she dipped in the preserves and munched happily.

"You said they were poison," I said.

"Oh, not these. These are like lotus blossoms."

"That's a pretty exquisite taste you're developing."

"No more than yours."

In the middle of our breakfast the countess telephoned and asked if we would join her at six for a light supper before the party.

We walked down to the beach through the hot late-morning sunlight, almost falling down the steep incline of the Chemin du Roy, stopping sometimes to stand and look out at the blue of the sea between the pines. I swam in the cool violet water and Margaret dozed in the sun. We came back early to the villa and sat on the terrace in our bathing robes and drank iced Cinzano, I reading Erasmus in a very irreverent frame of mind, and Margaret, with a card table set up in front of her, writing a letter to Susannah. She gave it to me to mail a little later when I drove down to St. Jean to pick up my costume for the party, but I forgot to do so. I found it two months ago, in the hip pocket of the trousers I was wearing at the time, and opened and read it with considerable astonishment:

Dearest Susie:

This morning I had a poinsettia blossom for breakfast, and last night, for dinner, a red Niçoise wine. I am turning very brown, even below the navel, and my hair is three shades lighter. And this sun has gotten to my brain, too, I think. Oh, Susie, Susie. I'm too old for transfiguration. Some morning soon, I'm sure, I'll wake up and have a brand-new hand—a strange, perfect, waxlike thing, full of foreign impulses and gestures which I won't know how to manage or restrain. Sometimes I'm almost afraid to take the glove off—when we've finished bathing, or when I take a shower or change for the evening—I'm so afraid of seeing it, this white, straight-fingered, flawless, terrible hand. With a ring on it, perhaps—a gift from some unknown prince or pirate that I don't even remember, for some favor, some nameless liberty, that I've forgotten ever giving or promising. Oh, darling, why don't we understand in time what we do to men's souls, and our own, when we make them promise to be divine? If there's nothing more than vanity or fear at the root of this terrible deed, then women are cursed indeed, as the Bible says, and as people have been whispering for centuries. Now, of course, it's too late, because one simply has to know.

Well, now you will have gathered that there is something wrong between Mickey and me. I'm sure you have suspected it before now, and you must forgive me, dear, for not confiding in you sooner, but I couldn't. I'm not sure, you see, what it is. Oh, Susie, how I wish I could tell you! Do you know? If it happens to everyone who is married, then you should know, because you've been married almost as long as me. But perhaps it doesn't; and that's what I'm afraid of, and why I feel ashamed so often. But it has something to do with familiarity, *I'm sure of that. Some essential privacy of our spirits has been violated somehow—I don't know how—and we're angry.*

And so we resent and resist each other in those awful little devious, demoralized, pretty ways that can't really be challenged. We sort of bombard each other with bonbons, with scraps of icing from our wedding cake. This morning, for example, we were talking on the terrace (and we should have been talking seriously and straightforwardly, because it was a strange and rather solemn morning, really) and we fell into that awful, impish tone of voice which is a sort of shadow of the way we used to talk when we first knew each other. I didn't decide to do it—it's just a terrible desperate habit. The most distressing habit we have, the saddest, the most servile. But it's just a tone of voice, an accent, carefully imitated or preserved. It's like hearing dead people talking; like listening to records of Caruso or Galli-Curci. And then when we hear these old records of our love being played, it gives us a sort of ghostly comfort, I suppose; and that's the saddest thing of all. Mickey and Margaret in their high-school play. Oh, I could weep when I hear myself doing it. But I don't weep, of course. I just grin and listen to these awful little frozen frivolities come tinkling out of my mouth like confectionery, like sugar rosebuds. And I mustn't weep, anyway, because I came to Europe on a bet with myself that I could stop that sort of thing.

But why do we do it, darling? What is it that we've injured or violated in each other? Have we found out things about each other that even the other doesn't know, or want to know, or to have known? Or are we full of fear and trembling before the final, entire, terrible nudity that real marriage requires of us? This morning I fell asleep on the beach in the sun while Mickey was swimming, and I dreamt that I had killed him. With a blade of ice that melted in his heart and so could never be found. I stood over his corpse and said to it, "Now you know me for what I am, a murderess. A catamount, a venereal nun. Well, you wanted to know. You made me promise to show you." That's the sort of dreams I have. But good ones, too, sometimes. Of blowing up balloons before a party —the most marvelous party—I don't know whose or where; or of you and I sewing before my wedding. Do you remember how we did that—sitting there sewing and smiling for hours, without saying a word, all one afternoon, in that sunny little sewing room you had on Massachusetts Avenue? Well, now you understand why we really came to Europe, don't you—

and why I haven't written sooner and asked you to come and visit us. It has to be worked out here, alone. Maybe it will be, soon.

You said that when the baby was born you would name her after me and make me her godmother if she was a girl. Mickey and I have bought her a lovely little doll in Nice, in anticipation of that disaster; but here is my real present to her —a piece of mumbo jumbo which you must whisper into her ear every night before she goes to sleep until her sixteenth year: I promise to ask no promises of anyone. I promise to be brave enough for one, not two. I promise never to judge anything in the name of love.

The worst thing is not that we impose this terrible burden of idealism—which is almost certain to deform them or destroy them—on men we love, but that we rejoice unconscionably at having done so. This was pointed out to me the other afternoon by a remarkable woman we've met. She's a countess who lives all alone in a vast villa on the Cape. She's about a hundred years old, and even wiser than a woman should be at that age. She understood immediately what was the matter between Mickey and me, and chided me terribly. But she's so lovely that I couldn't be angry, and I decided, anyway, that I'd better listen. She told me that if I insisted on forbidding him the right to revolt, or prophesy, or renege, or commit sins, I really didn't want to be married to a man at all, but to a god—which she implied was a very unsatisfactory arrangement. And then she did the wildest thing, Susie; you won't believe it. She gave me the chance to go back and change everything. To go back and relive the night in her life when something went wrong, and to be able to see it clearly, through her eyes, as another person. At least that's what I think is happening, because she wants me to wear the evening gown —oh, it's so beautiful!—that she wore on that night, and her jewels and fan, and to dress my hair as she wore it; to impersonate her exactly. I don't really understand it terribly well, because she's a pretty mysterious woman, but she seems to be saying to me: live this night out of my life, as I lived it, and learn from it, as I did not. I'm not at all sure what she has arranged, and I feel a little frightened, but sort of hypnotized; as if it were something I absolutely must submit to before I can go any further. The party is tonight, and I've been getting more excited about it all week, and even more now, as I write to you about it. Whether it will be the night of my redemption or damnation I'm not entirely sure, but I'll let you know next week. I'll send you a postcard that says either "Hallelujah!" or "Yipes!" so you'll know how things stand. Maybe all this air of apocalypse is just the result of wine and sunshine, because I've been lying on the beach all morning sipping Cinzano.

There is the nicest man at St. Jean, who lives on a lovely old boat and who would marry me instantly if anything went terribly wrong. I know that sounds awful, but it's nice to know, isn't it?

Now, Susie, I'm going to tell you something that isn't very nice, and that might hurt you, darling; but you must forgive your broken-winged dove and remember that it's your love for me that gives me the right to say it. I've seen in you and Nick the kind of marriage, the kind of relationship, that I might have had with Mickey, but it isn't the kind that I want. I know it's a perfectly good, perfectly respectable, perfectly fine, American marriage. But I don't want an American marriage. I want a marriage with nothing in front of it—no qualifying adjective of any kind. I renounced my right to an American marriage when we came to France, and my right to American womanhood, and all the privileges and penalties that both of them imply. I don't mean that I came to seek a European marriage, either; or European womanhood; because they are just as provincial, just as categorical—although in very different ways. I mean that I wanted to stand in a foreign land, surrounded by foreign tongues and foreign gods and declare my marriage, and seek my womanhood, before this strange bright ancient sea. The piece of mumbo jumbo that I have written down for little Margaret is for her to say—in the perfect world which I hope that kind of creed may help her make—but not for me. It's too late for me, as I've said already. I've made too many promises. I must be satisfied with the resolution to trace my womanhood to its first, true springs, and whether I find mud or crystal water, or a god dreaming or a demon gibbering, I'm determined to be content. It's the only way I can be married to Mickey truly, or to anyone. Sometimes I'm afraid that marrying him may have been the most selfish and dishonest thing that anyone ever did, and I need to know. I need to correct that wrong I did him, if it exists.

229

*Now say "hooray!" because your little schoolmate is going
to make her debut!*

*I sent you a basket of purple grapes from Beaulieu by air-
mail the other day, so you could have a taste of this country
in your mouth. Let me know if they arrive all right. Grape
pudding is what you'll get, most likely. Give Nick a kiss for
me, and be very careful with my little Margaret. She's got to
reform the world for us.*

Love from your wild dove,
Meg

Carrying this unknown, forgotten, never-to-be-delivered
letter in my pocket, I drove to St. Jean-Cap Ferrat, bought a
packet of hairpins for Margaret and a black mask for myself in
the *épicerie,* and then strolled along the sea wall where the
pleasure yachts were berthed to the *Victorious* to borrow a skipper's uniform from Ian as my costume for the masquerade. It
was to be a surprise for Margaret, as much as anyone; I had
decided upon it the afternoon before, watching a sailboat tack
across the immense blue distances beyond the arms of Villefranche Bay, and I had driven down to St. Jean while Margaret
was cooking dinner to ask Ian if he would accommodate me.
He would be delighted, he said. I had arranged to pick up the
uniform the following afternoon.

He was sitting on his afterdeck reading a very old copy of
the *National Geographic* magazine.

"Ah, you're here. Come aboard."

"Thank you."

" 've you got time for a drink?"

"Yes, thanks."

"I'm having Scotch. Will that do?"

"Fine. Shall I fix it?"

"Yes, do. Chap next berth but one lent me a stack of these
things. Absolutely fascinating. D'you look at it, at all?"

"Once in a while."

"Absolutely splendid. Just look at this." He held the magazine toward me, its pages open to a pair of beautifully colored

photographs of lonely purple buttes and silent, towering, scarlet-and-yellow canyons.

"Oh, yes. The Grand Canyon. Beautiful, isn't it?"

"Absolutely. 've you seen it?"

"No."

"Pity. One ought to see that."

He went on reading while I made myself a drink. I raised it toward him and said, "Cheers."

"Yes, cheers."

We sat silently, Ian occasionally murmuring with pleasure and turning a page with a slight lisping sound of the heavy, shiny paper. "Oh, bloody strange," he said once.

"What?"

"Why, to have that great empty, desolate, silent hole, right in the middle of your country. And then all around it, all that roar and glitter—New York, Chicago, Dallas, San Francisco. And right in the middle, this vast barren hole, with wind howling through the canyons day and night. Bloody strange country you've got, altogether." He set the magazine down and lifted his glass from the wickerwork table beside him. "What time is your do, then?"

"Six."

"Oh, yes. Baroja, you said. Lovely name, that. Is it the Moorish-looking place, on Vietor?"

"Yes."

"Yes, I've been there. Years ago. Queer old duck."

"Yes, but bright."

"Oh, very. What made you decide to go as a sailor, then?"

"Well, I like boats, you know."

"Yes."

He sat staring out at the sunlight on the harbor water, his eyes narrowed against the glare, plucking at the ruined lobe of his ear. He had huge but very gentle-looking hands with almost square tips to the fingers.

"Light bother you? Catches you in the eye a bit, I know, but I hate to let the screens down. See the gulls, and what not."

"Not for me."

"Good. You're sure?"

"Yes. Ian, how long have you been sailing?" I asked.

"All my life, off and on. But I've only lived aboard for the last ten years."

"You're a real sailor, then."

"Oh, no. Damned sight I don't know about motors or electricity, or I wouldn't have those two buggers about."

"But you do the navigating?"

"Oh, yes, I do the navigating. I do know a bit about that."

"Have you ever tried sail?"

"Oh, yes, a bit. But it makes me nervous, you know, all that flapping about. I hate flap, of any kind." He lifted his hands and examined the tips of his fingers. "I'm what you'd call a harbor sailor now. Mind you, there's a few places I'll get to yet. But I don't go on about it. That's the great thing about the sea, isn't it? There's always time. You don't get that, ashore."

"No."

He made himself another drink and held the bottle toward me.

"I'm all right, thanks."

"Right. Just speak up, you know."

"I will. What would you call the most interesting place you've been?"

"Most interesting place? Oh, I d'know. I like it round this part of the world, you know. Africa, Italy, France. Spanish Morocco's an interesting spot. Barbarous, of course, but interesting. That's where I got these two chaps—Tangier. Dead sure they bugger each other at night, but I can't catch 'em at it. You get that sort of thing over there. Get anything you like."

"I suppose."

"I knew a chap once bought a girl in Tangier. Child, twelve-year-old girl. Bought her outright, from one of those flesh merchants or something. Kept her aboard for a week, and then he'd had it, apparently. Turned her loose. Absolute beast of a chap, and if you'd met him in Scott's you'd have thought he played for the Gentlemen. You learn something about people, on the water."

"I should think so."

"Of course Greece is lovely. You get the loveliest mornings on the Aegean. Something about the light there; very hard, bitter sort of light, but beautiful. Shadows like steel." He leaned forward in his chair with his forearms resting across his thighs and stared at the deck, frowning mildly.

"I envy you, Ian," I said.

"What? Skippering this tub? Don't be daft. If I'd anything sensible to do, I'd be doing it, don't you worry."

"Why do you do it, then?"

"Well, I reckon I'm a bit better off than holed up in a club in St. James, or some bloody cottage in Devon. Mind you, I did a job of work before I packed it up. Twenty years and a bit in the City. I still have these voyages, you know. It's just that the best of them is over."

I had had just enough to drink, and was curious enough, to say, "Which was the best of them?"

He turned his head to smile at me charmingly. He had very fine teeth for a man of his age. "You're a cheeky beggar, aren't you? Still, I'll tell you, because I like your wife. It was to a place called Providencia, in the southwestern Caribbean. I don't suppose you've heard of that. It's not fashionable or anything. Tiny little place, way below the Virgins. Belongs to Colombia, actually, although it's off the Nicaraguan coast. No landing strip or anything. Really a primitive place, even today, and this was fifteen years ago. Nothing there at all, really, except a few shanty villages, coco palms, valleys with lovely rivers running through them, water so clear you can see every pebble on the bottom, and mountains that touch the clouds. Two mountains, as green as Hertfordshire. Oh, greener. And a regular muddle of Caribbean people, you know—Spanish, Negro, Carib—the whole lot, all mixed together. Beautiful people, really. Spanish-speaking. And oddly enough, some English; because some of your chaps—or ours, I suppose they were then—are supposed to have migrated down there from the colonies, very early on, after the first bad winters. Really enchanting place. You've no idea. I heard about it from a Colombian chap who was a coffee merchant in London. I hadn't bought the *Victorious* then. I was chartering in those days—sail. I was a young man, you know. Forty-five. That doesn't sound young to you, does it? You'd be surprised.

"Well, I went over to the Bahamas and chartered this ketch. Forty-five feet. Native-built. Not very beautiful, but rugged. They make seaworthy boats in the Bahamas. Well, do you know what I had in mind? I was going to single-hand down to Providencia. Yes, actually. Mad as a hatter. I had her all fitted out, you know, ready to go—food, water, charts, parts, the lot. Then I met this girl wandering about the quay at Hope Town. Tiny little thing, I don't think she weighed over seven stone. Cardboard suitcase in one hand and a shabby little blue velvet hat on her head. D'you know what she was? A schoolteacher. From Devon. Come over as private tutor for some millionaire's kids, and got fed up. Old boy used to chase her about the nursery all night. 'Are you going to leave shortly?' she said to me. 'Yes,' I said. 'Which way are you going?' 'I'm going to Providencia,' I said. 'Wretched little jungle island, down in the south Caribbean.' 'How much would it cost for my passage?' she said. 'I'm not taking any passengers,' I said. 'And it's the last place you'd want to go, if I were. You'd better wait for the next Matson, and get yourself back to London.' 'I'm not going to London,' she said. 'I want to go to Providencia with you. I have twenty-eight pounds and a Swiss watch, and I'm very strong. I know a bit about sailing. I can work out the rest of my passage.' Well, of course, the upshot was she talked me into it.

"I don't know if you've ever sailed a forty-five-foot ketch in the South Caribbean, but if you have you'll know that trip wasn't all moonlight and roses. We ran into a gale the first night out. I've never seen seas like that. Forty-footers, breaking like surf. Eleven days we had that sort of thing, and you should have seen her. Strapped to a lifeline, soaked to her bones, wind blowing her teeth out, bloody near, hauling sheets like a madwoman.

God. Absolute miracle we ever got out of it. Four-hour tricks, on and off. Vomited up her kidneys the first day out. Never saw such a woman. Then after the storm we had doldrums. Thirty-eight days it took us, altogether. Of course there was moonlight and roses, too, some of those nights. It doesn't really do to talk about it. I don't know if you've ever been far out on a tropical sea at midnight. Well. That was it, of course. I'd found what I wanted. Some people don't until they're forty-five, you know. Even older.

"Well, we made Providencia, and it was everything I've said about it. *And* more. Don't think there'd been another boat in there all year. They treated us like gods, or something. Absolute paradise. We lived in a hut on a riverbank in a little valley that opened right out to the sea between two hills. Just a brook, really. Water clear as gin. It got salt water on the tide, and there were these carp or something that used to come in and get caught in the pools. Beautiful things. Scales on them like gold sovereigns and went three or four pounds. I could catch them by hand, you know. Actually. Just reach my arms down and flip them out. She'd stand there in the water with her skirt spread out, and I'd flip them into it. Lovely sight. Great shiny gold fish flopping and bouncing in her skirt and she standing there laughing like a kid. She could cook, too.

"Well, we were there two weeks; or rather *I* was. It had taken us over a month to get there, and I had to get back to London. 'Come on,' I said to her one day. 'We've got to push off.' 'I'm not going,' she said. 'What do you mean, you're not going?' 'I can't go. I belong here. I can't go back.' Never heard such rubbish. 'I thought you loved me,' I said. 'I do,' she said, 'but I can't go back. Stay here with me. Let them do whatever they like out there. Stay here with me.' 'Absolute rubbish,' I told her. 'Look, I've got a job. I've got work to do. I've got sailing to do. I've got to be back in London next month or there'll be the devil to pay. Now stop being a bloody ass, and come back to London and marry me properly.' 'No,' she said. 'Then I'll jolly well drag you back,' I said. 'If you do, I'll jump overboard the first night out. Or the second; or the third. You can't stay awake forever.' And she meant it, you know. Absolutely flat refused to go. So I left. Nothing I could do. I left her there."

He took a drink of whisky and let one wrist droop, rubbing it thoughtfully with the expression of a man adding up sums in his head. He ground the coarse gray hairs of his wrist with his fingers, making a rasping sound.

"So she wouldn't come?" I said.

"Absolutely flat refused. Extraordinary, isn't it? Still, that's a woman for you. That's a woman for you."

"That's *one* woman," I said.

"Yes, well I only knew the one, you know. Just the one."

We sat silently for a moment, Ian rubbing his wrist, I looking into my whisky glass. "And you've never heard from her since?" I asked.

"How the devil should I hear from her? She wouldn't have known where to write. Nor I. Done no good, anyway—she was probably living with one of those Carib beggars by that time. Hut in the mountains somewhere, with a passel of brats. Wouldn't know her if I saw her now, most likely; and she bloody well wouldn't know me."

"It's a pity," I said.

"Yes. Still, I got her there safely, you know—where she wanted to be. I suppose that's all I was meant to do for her, really."

I drained my glass and set it on the table. "I guess that's the way to look at it."

"Yes. Well, look here, the suit's in there in the saloon, if you're in a hurry. Bit of grease or something on the jacket, but I don't suppose that'll put you off. I d'know that it'll fit."

"No, I don't either," I said. "But it's just a masquerade."

"Well, have a good time. Jolly amusing, those things can be."

"Can I put it on here?" I asked, rising.

"Yes, if you like. Hanging on the locker door in there."

I went in through the slatted teak doors to the saloon and

stood in admiration for a moment before I put on the uniform. It was really a beautiful boat. There wasn't a piece of wood on it that wasn't solid Burma teak, edge-grained and hand-rubbed to a soft chocolate luster. Everything that might have been cheap, cast bronze or galvanized iron was stainless steel and everything that might have been cotton twill was wine-colored glove-tanned leather. Up three steps through a narrow companionway was the wheelhouse. I went up and stood for a moment with my hand on the wheel. Ian's own, on the course of his many voyages, had worn the wooden spokes to a satin finish, and they gave to my hands an elegant and royal feeling, like a scepter.

I changed clothes and came out in the uniform, which as I had anticipated was considerably too big. Ian smiled merrily.

"Oh, wizard," he said. "The jolly tar. Never mind; few safety pins and a bit of tissue paper in the hat band and you'll be all right."

"I don't think I'll fool anyone," I said.

"Oh, well, it's a bit of fun, isn't it? You're not to worry about them at all. They've very near had it, as it is."

"OK. Thanks, Ian."

"Glad to help out. Well, cheer-o, then."

"Good-bye."

I turned to wave to him as I left the wharf, but he was back in the *National Geographic*.

I drove back to La Fleurelle, parked the Citroën in the shelter of the oleander hedge so that Margaret would not see it, went up to the front door of the villa, and rang the bell. Margaret opened the door and her eyes went through two rapid and unfathomable transformations.

"*Mickey!*" she cried. "I saw you through the window and I thought it was Ian! Oh, what a wonderful idea. You look marvelous!"

She pressed her hands together in a prayerful gesture of admiration and let her jaw sag open.

"Needs a pin or two," I said. "And a certain amount of

authority, wisdom, courage, tenacity, honor, experience, reliability, and strength. Otherwise it's a pretty good imitation."

She shook her head in a generous and fervent way. "No, just the pins. Come in and let me do them."

She managed, through some uncanny and disturbing gift that women have with safety pins, to make the uniform look as if it had been made for me; and very much encouraged by this piece of fraudulence, I drove her down to Quelques Saisons for dinner.

Before we arrive at the countess' villa, I think it might be a good idea for me to pause for a moment to issue a word of warning to the ladies in the audience. Ladies, this party holds a particular delight in store for you in the person of Andrea d'Agostino, and I am going to let you have just a peek at him, in his dressing room, as it were, so that you will be prepared for your first encounter with him on the stage; otherwise it is possible that you may behave foolishly.

He is wearing for your inspection the costume of Razullo, a roguish minstrel character from the commedia dell'arte (there is a charming candor in this choice), and is perched on an enamel stool, peering into the unwholesome-looking mirror of the bathroom of a cheap flat in Cannes, plucking his eyebrows with a pair of tweezers. I think you will forgive the vanity of this behavior, ladies, when you have a closer look at its results; for if ever there was a pair of eyebrows deserving of such cultivation it is Andrea's. The perfection of his features is the only undertaking, I am sure, in which God and Andrea will ever be known to have collaborated; which seems a very great pity, for what a job they do together when devoted to the same ideal! Through their united efforts these fine, black, gleaming, tragi-poetic brows curve upward in an inspirational arc, then drop in a dying fall over eyes as black and huge as olives, as luminous as quartz, as liquid, deep, and full of lyrical mystery as well-water in moonlight. The nose which separates them is as fine as that on an Augustinian coin, a supremely classical nose, in which is combined hauteur and sensitivity of a royal order. And his mouth, ladies—here is a Mediterranean fruit to whet your appetite! A succulent, exquisite Italian mouth, full of disdain and, at the same time, boyish, Pan-like impudence and abandon. He has a cleft chin, very square, the color of steel. His ears are small, close-set, delicately whorled, and almost buried in banks of black bright curls, like threads of onyx. It is an infinitely expressive face, a perfect instrument for the registration of every known mortal feeling, and Andrea has mastered them all, from rapture through beatitude to digestive satisfaction; from metaphysical terror through physical disgust to a kind of winsome pique. He can, with equal virtuosity, reflect appreciation of a resurrection, a sonnet or a good meringue; or distress appropriate to the fall of man, of Troy, or of a sparrow. And all without the slightest experience of the emotions which are ordinarily responsible for these expressions. It is the appearance which concerns Andrea, not the feeling which inspires it. He has observed that in civilized society certain expressions occur in certain contexts, and produce certain results; and he has learned to put them on with the skill and promiscuity of a politician quoting scripture. I'm not sure that there is anything terribly wrong in this, or even very extraordinary; all human sentiments are after all to some extent impostures. But what is extraordinary is the degree of his accomplishment, which reaches almost to aesthetic heights; and what is wrong is the amount of havoc which it leaves behind. For Andrea—or someone very much like him—is to wreak a great deal of havoc in these remaining pages.

When he rises, as he is about to do, you may find—particularly the American ladies—that he is not quite as tall as you would wish, for he stands an inch under six feet; but there is a proportion to his physique and a nobility in his bearing which more than compensate for the relative modesty of his stature. If you should develop an acquaintance with him sufficiently intimate to make the discovery—which, if you are either modestly wealthy or pleasant-looking, is far from improbable—you would find that a Grand Prix accident in 1957, in which he demolished a ton of steel and the southeast corner of the Banque de l'Orient at Monaco, has—unlike most of the devastations he has wrought—left a scar upon the man: a broad, flat, livid welt across his belly. One would think that the actual origin of such a fascinating stigma, with all that it implies in the way of courage, verve, and reckless sportsmanship, was picturesque enough, but Andrea, driven by the same instinct which leads him to improve upon his eyebrows, is often led to improve upon his history. He sometimes finds it useful to adjust the circumstances of his injury to include an element of sacrifice: a bloody skirmish in Algeria, a heroic stand upon the battlements of Dien Bien Phu, impalement on the palisades of an Eastern prison camp while valiantly escorting captured comrades to the West, or—as on one reckless occasion, when he had drunk more wine than he was used to—a Resistance action in the cellars of Montparnasse, in which he was brought low by German hand grenades. By the time it had occurred to the lady who was the distraught beneficiary of this version that his age could not possibly correspond with his participation in such an action, he had converted into cash the diamond cuff links she had brokenly pressed upon him, and fled to Biarritz.

You may ask what accounts for the effectiveness of such a transparent rogue in his depredations upon womankind. Well, first of all, the type of woman who is his natural prey—the type who would chiefly qualify, in terms of profit, for his attentions —while no doubt sophisticated, educated, and articulate, is also generally rich enough, idle enough, and by reason of inhabiting the Riviera at all, sufficiently preoccupied with Beauty, Adventure, and Romance to be more than ordinarily vulnerable to his talents. Secondly, he is not, perhaps, quite so transparent as I have made him out. He may have more dimension than I have granted him thus far. I will admit that there is a certain amount of prejudice at work in my description of him, which will be made more understandable, I am sure, as you proceed in your acquaintance with the man. That he has style, and of a considerable order, I think I have made clear; but it may be time to confess that he has something more, as well—some genuine and partially redeeming qualities of humanity, some affecting flashes of insight, some wit, some sort of groping, desolate tenderness which might make justifiable—even moving—his selection, for example, of the Razullo costume for the countess' masquerade, and which at times reveal him for what he once was and still may be in part: a desperate Neapolitan *ragazzo* with empty pockets and an overflowing heart. I should like to think so. For though it costs me a considerable effort to grant him any merit, any excellence, whatever, a certain amount of the dignity of everyone involved depends upon it.

I think you should be told, for example, that he believes humbly and unquestioningly in both God and Hell, and that consequently the thought of the eventual retribution of some of his transgressions causes him moments of very real concern. This, of course, is just another way of saying that he is concerned with his own welfare, present or prospective; but at least it puts the concern in metaphysical terms, which makes it seem more stately. More to the point is the fact that he manages by some miraculous prudence to send home every month to his mother in Naples ten thousand lire. (That this money is the prize of his beauty and cunning concerns her no more than does the origin of the equivalent remittance which is sent home by his sister in Milan, a girl of equal beauty, who is married to a vulgar, crafty, and rapacious lawyer.) I am also able to report in his defense that he has been seen to perform little spontaneous, anonymous acts of charity, such as sharing a slice of pizza with a beggar or tossing a coin to an urchin on the Spanish Steps. And of course he loves opera; predictably, to be sure, but with an absolute and unforged passion, in the name of which a great percentage of his sins are committed. There is something very illustrative in this fact. Perhaps the strongest thing that can be said in Andrea's favor is that he loves life as he loves a performance of *Aïda,* and that he would, in either case and without a moment's hesitation, steal or prostitute himself in order to enjoy it from the best seat in the house.

His ultimate ambition, of course, is a wife, indispensably wealthy, and preferably young and beautiful; failing either of these, he will be satisfied with a mistress provident enough to pay his tailor and his restaurateur, to provide him with an automobile, and to meet his tennis dues. In fact the latter arrangement, being basically more liberal and informal, would probably suit him better, but its impermanence, and the increasing difficulty of finding successive benefactresses (he is thirty-four and working against time) make him regard it only as an alternative. Meanwhile he requires diversion. There is a certain daily quota of Beauty, Adventure, and Excitement to be met, and it is here that even members of the middle and lower classes are pressed into his service. As a matter of fact, the number of deflorations he has wrought amongst the ranks of laundresses, milliners, stenographers, and *tutti fatto's* may exceed those amongst the ranks of heiresses and debutantes.

Well, ladies, I think I have given you sufficient warning to insure your discretion when you are introduced to him. Let me just sum up briefly: you will not find him at all a common type of Riviera predator. He will disarm you with his attentiveness and courtesy. He will give you a beguiling impression of mingled masculinity and frailty and an even more illusory one of culture. You will find that he spends sufficient time in public libraries and museums to be able to discuss with you—briefly perhaps, but stylishly and fluently—the main types of classic architecture, a representative literary or artistic figure from each of several principal eras, the more dramatic historical motifs and the elements of existentialism, and that he has given particular attention to certain exotic, recurrent themes which he has discovered are characteristically dear to the hearts of several very eligible types of women: equitation, bridge, Kahlil Gibran, dog-breeding, and Rosicrucianism. Let us hope that none of these is of special interest to you. He will hum or sing you operatic airs in a very respectable tenor voice, and he will almost certainly quote you one of the five poems he has memorized (they are chosen from widely separated areas of the emotional spectrum so that he will have one ready for almost any contingency). He has the whitest teeth and the blackest hair you will ever see, and you will discover that at his center there is an absolute, a total, a consuming void, which sucks into itself every scrap of unanchored matter that touches its periphery. So, ladies, look to your moorings.

Now it may occur to you to ask how, if the man is not entirely transparent, and since I am excluded by my gender from his confidence, I come to possess such very private knowledge about him; or to have gained such unbecoming access to his bathroom. Aha. That must remain my secret for a while. I should like to remain clothed in at least the shreds of respectability for as long as I am able. The more observant of you, however, will already be provided with a clue. You may have noticed, reflected in the mirror of his medicine cabinet, the open door of the adjoining bedroom, and beyond it, athwart the small area of disordered sheets visible between the brass bars of the Edwardian bed, a pair of nude brown legs. If you care to stay around for a moment you will see these legs kick briskly up and down, then a flash of naked torso as their owner springs from the bed, then, at the very edge of the reflecting mirror, a flutter of flapping paisley-patterned yellow silk as she apparently dons a dressing gown. In another moment this lady appears in the bathroom door; or rather, that portion of her does which can be contained in the surface of the mirror. This is an area extending roughly from her shoulders to the center of her thighs, and includes one of her hands, which holds in its fingers the stem of a martini glass, brimming with colorless icy liquid. The glass is drawn back slowly and deliberately, and its contents flung, with great accuracy, at Andrea, splashing against the back of his head with a sound of molten impact which I must confess I find delightful. He stands for a moment with bowed and dripping head, plucks an olive from the ruff of his costume and plops it in the toilet bowl. Then he takes a towel from the rack, lays it across his hair, and presses it gently against his sodden curls.

"*Ebbene*," he says in a sad but firm and veteran tone of voice. "*È finito.*"

"No, it isn't finished," the lady says. "It never began."

"As you say."

"I hope you enjoy yourself tonight."

"Thank you. I will try very hard."

There is a rustle of silk, which he turns to investigate. The lady has withdrawn into the bedroom, and we see the dressing gown fly through the air and land on the edge of the bed, from where it slides down slowly to the floor.

"Is there any particular reason—" Andrea says.

"Yes. You'll find it in the newspaper there, on the bed. I was just reading a story about the death of fourteen schoolchildren. They were killed in a school bus that was crushed by an avalanche in the Savoy mountains yesterday afternoon. That's the reason."

Andrea smiles. "I understand," he says. There is no reply.

In a moment (she must dress very rapidly) we hear a door close quietly, with neither care nor emphasis. Andrea sighs. He turns back to the mirror, removes the towel from his head, and touches his damp curls tentatively with his fingertips, making a wincing expression of distaste as they encounter the sticky film upon his hair.

The countess was very pleased to see us and more than ever elliptical, elegant, and redolent. She had spilled a great dollop of cologne on the front of her dress, which dried slowly as we ate, emitting a suffocating odor, pungent and earthy, like a compound of tangerines and mushrooms. She served us a supper of cold delicacies on the pillared verandah of her villa: pâté de campagne, smoked oysters, brawn, marinated herring, two wonderful cheeses, and a bottle of chilled Alsatian wine that cooled our tingling palates.

"Mr. Pritchard, your costume intrigues me very much," she said. "Whom do you represent, may I ask."

"No one but himself," Margaret said. "Captain Michael Pritchard. It isn't an impersonation at all."

"Ah. You are a sailor, then?"

"I used to be something less than a weekender," I said. "And a very indifferent one, at that. But I love it."

"So do I. We had boating parties here, at one time, years ago. Moonlight cruises up to Cannes, or down to San Remo, with a little calypso band on the deck. They were a great success. Unfortunately we have had to give them up."

"Why?" asked Margaret.

"There was a misfortune. A young man drowned one evening."

"Oh, dear," Margaret said.

"Yes. It was unfortunate. There was a great deal of confusion and unpleasantness about it, as you can imagine. It cast a pall over the entire season."

"What an awful thing," Margaret said. "Was it someone you knew well?"

"Yes, very well indeed."

There was a dreadful pause.

"Oh, forgive me," Margaret murmured. "I shouldn't have asked."

"You were perfectly correct to ask. I have survived it. My chief regret is that another form of amusement has been cut off to me."

"Oh."

"You're not eating any herring. I'm surprised at you. You are constantly ignoring opportunities."

"It's delicious," Margaret said. "It's just that I'm not very hungry, I'm afraid."

"You are excited."

"I suppose I am, a little. Parties always make me excited."

"Then you may be forgiven. In the name of excitement it's forgivable to neglect almost anything in the world, even herring such as this." She sat back in her chair, took a cigar from the humidor which Amélie had set beside her, and began to peel the foil from it with a look of great content. In front of us, on the badminton lawn, Nicolas was standing on a stepladder, hanging paper lanterns to a system of electric wires that was strung across the grass. There were fifty or more round-topped wickerwork tables with chairs to match them set out on the lawn, and five very solemn men in maroon jackets and tuxedo trousers—from a catering agency, apparently—were gravely polishing glasses at a portable rattan bar. A very early moon, almost full, had risen, and stood in the clear sky above the bay. It was a calm warm evening of velvet air and subdued sounds.

"We have a moon," Margaret said.

"We have indeed." I lit her cigar. "Thank you. What a lovely evening." She blew out a soft cloud of violet smoke. "I shall die soon."

"Oh, nonsense," Margaret said.

"No, no. On evenings such as this death comes and kisses one—just here—behind the ear." She raised her hand to touch the spot gently with her fingertips. "It takes a very virtuous woman indeed to resist that sort of kiss."

"Then I know what you must wear to the masquerade," Margaret said.

"What is that, my dear?"

"The mask of virtue."

The countess laughed quickly in a manner that was both delicate and ribald. "Oh, you're very shrewd. You've seen through me, haven't you? But, no, I'm afraid it won't do. I've found that there was literally nothing in the world that I could not purchase with my virtue—or my money—except time. Mind you, I don't complain. We're very fortunate that the most interesting things in life can be purchased in that way, since, to a really clever woman, virtue is practically inexhaustible. I have one acquaintance in Milan who has lost hers, at a very conservative estimate, no less than fifteen times." She tapped the ash from her cigar with a frail, translucent finger and turned to pick up from the table beside her a small parcel wrapped in blue tissue which had stood all the while beside her humidor. "I want to show you a little purchase I made this very morning, in Nice. Will you open it?"

"Oh, it's tied so prettily," Margaret said.

"Still, it must be opened."

"All right." Margaret slipped off the satin ribbon and parted the paper carefully, so as not to tear it. Inside there was a small white box which she opened, revealing, on a nest of absorbent cotton, a heart-shaped garnet pendant, the size of a damson plum, suspended from a very fine-linked golden chain.

"Oh, it's exquisite," Margaret murmured. "What a lovely stone. Look, Mickey, isn't it beautiful?" She lifted it, letting the gold chain drip from her fingers, the crimson-colored stone swinging and glittering.

"It certainly is," I said.

"It will look well on you," the countess said. "Try it on, my dear."

"On *me*?" said Margaret. "Surely it isn't for *me*? Oh, countess, you can't have bought me anything so lovely. Why, for heaven's sake?"

"You must call me Elena," the countess said. "Of course it's for you. Do try it on."

Margaret unclasped the chain and lifted it to her throat, her lips parted in astonishment. "But *why*? You really mustn't. I don't deserve it."

"I saw it in a shop window this morning and knew immediately that you would adore it. I felt that I owed you, or would very shortly owe you, a very great deal; so I determined to adjust the matter immediately."

"But you don't owe me anything. How ridiculous."

"But I shall, you see, when our charade is over. Ah. Yes, that's lovely on you. One of the most endearing of the French attitudes to life is embodied in their little social epigram, *Payé d'avance*. I think we should all be a great deal better off if we paid in advance for life. For whatever we may find here of beauty, pleasure, amusement; and for the occasional privilege of interfering with another life. It's a very great comfort, when one feels the impulse to enlighten a fellow creature, to be quite sure that one can afford it. Yes, you wear it beautifully."

"But you're a very silly woman," Margaret said. "How can I ever thank you?"

"You really mustn't try. It's a very small token of my appreciation. You'll make me very happy by accepting it."

Margaret pressed the stone against her bosom with her fingertips, evidently much moved.

"And now, Mr. Pritchard, I'm going to take Margaret away from you for an hour and transform her. I'm afraid you'll have to shift for yourself."

"Will you need an hour?" I asked.

"Unfortunately. My fingers are not as nimble as they were. However, since you've come so beautifully prepared for the role, perhaps you'd enjoy rowing for an hour on the bay. Down there on the shore, where we had our drink the other afternoon, you'll find a skiff moored, with oars in it. It should be lovely on the water, this time of evening."

"Thank you. Maybe I will. On the other hand, I've drunk a good deal of wine, and I wouldn't want to add to the casualty list at Quelques Saisons."

It took her a moment to formulate her smile, but it was dazzling when it came. "Ah. How very thoughtful of you. And how prudent. Then perhaps you can persuade Nicolas to furnish you with a racquet, and practice your badminton shots. Or you might just sit here quietly and compose a litany, since that is your particular enthusiasm."

"Thank you. I'll find something useful to do."

"I'm sure of it. For a man of your resources I have no real concern. We shall see you very shortly."

I rose to draw back her chair and watched them walk arm-in-arm down the tiled portico. In a moment Amélie appeared out of the villa and asked if I would like a liqueur. I said that I would, and she brought me a glass of Drambuie which I sat sipping while I smoked a cigarette and watched the sun descend into the sea. Then I walked down across the lawn, pausing to speak to Nicolas, who was so startled at my textbook Spanish that he nearly fell down off his ladder. I strolled through the darkening arbor to the shore, where I found the skiff drawn up on the stony beach of a little cove. I sat in it for a while on the sand, listening to the cries of curlews and the lake-like lapping of the gentle water. The sun had set and the vivid summer twilight had begun. On a promontory of land to my left there was an ancient grove of rotting olive trees, and their black branches against the crimson sky was wonderful to see. I sat in the boat until it was dusk, and across the bay the lights of Beaulieu had begun to twinkle in the water. I saw that Nicolas had lit the paper lanterns, for they burst suddenly into glowing blossom above the tops of the olive trees, great soft orange, blue, red, and yellow globes, swinging gently in the dark air. Beyond the ruined orchard a stretch of the distant driveway was visible, and there was the occasional quick glitter of a European sedan, moving swiftly between the eucalyptus trees. The guests were arriving. There was a growing surf-like swell of sound blowing down through the vineyard from the terrace. After a while I strolled back through the arbor toward the villa. The lawn had been transfigured. Now it was populated by dream-creatures, elves and pharaohs and hunchbacks, two-legged donkeys and bird-men with beaks and dangling coxcombs, milling about the bar and buffet and between the wicker chairs and tables, spilling out onto the edges of the lawn in capering festive groups, like the ragged monsters in a Brueghel painting. From flood-lamps on the lawn a violet light fell over them. It stained their eyeballs like porcelain and flushed their hands and faces in a luminous purple glow. They swarmed in a sea of zoo-sounds: nickering, chattering, howling, peals of neighing laughter, the clatter of glass and china, and sudden senseless parrot-shrieks of gaiety. When I was halfway up the slope a girl clad only in a fishnet ran down the lawn toward me from the tables, her hair a tangle of seashells, anemones, and streaming seaweed, her narrow face masked with huge overlapping sequins, like silver scales. Through the knotted cord of the seine her naked body, painted a livid green, glowed like phosphorus. She stopped to take my head in her hands and bestow a flurry of cold kisses on my cheeks and eyes.

"Ah, *mon marin*," she murmured. "My beautiful sailor. Ave you drown for me? Ave you come down to my kingdom to make love?"

Down the lawn a Benedictine monk came running in pursuit of her, his cowl flapping, his white ankles, in their sandal-straps, gleaming like fish-skin under the hem of his flying habit.

"I have to go," she said. "But I wait for you, *mon marin*, in my cavern, in the sea." She turned and fled toward the darkness of the vineyard.

I went on up the lawn and made my way through the crowd of derelicts, beasts, and madmen toward the bar. Inside the villa a progressive jazz quintet had begun to play; the cool elegant notes came tinkling out through the open doors and windows into the darkness. I took the paper mask I had bought in St. Jean out of my pocket and put it on as I approached the bar. I ordered a vodka and tonic and leaned back against the slatted rattan, looking out across the tinkling din of the party. A tall young man beside me set a pair of empty glasses on the bar and asked to have them refilled with Scotch and water. He turned to smile at me, the intelligence and good humor of his face not at all concealed by the narrow black mask he wore across his eyes or the flowing white beard that fell almost to his waist. This was Adrian. He was wearing a tattered but somehow regal-looking robe, a broken diadem-like headpiece on his white hair, and carried clutched in one hand the shaft of a huge gnarled staff.

"Are you English?" he asked.

"No."

"Oh. I thought you were. You've got the Magdalen College arms on your blazer."

"Oh. No, I borrowed it."

"Oh, I see."

"You pronounce it 'Maudlin'?"

"Yes. Silly way of saying it. Something about foreign names and places that brings out British perversity as nothing else can."

"*You're* English, then?"

"No, Australian, actually. But I've been living in London for some time." He let his eyes roam about the lawn and the lantern-lit tables for a moment. "Really quite a do, isn't it? I'd no idea it was going to be so elaborate when the old girl asked us."

"No, I didn't either."

"At a thing like this a man can go either of two ways: either toward total, undiscriminating tolerance, or Pauline abnegation. I must say I generally find myself leaning toward the tolerance end of it."

I laughed. "Well, I guess it's better not to make a disturbance at the time."

"Oh, absolutely. No good being boorish." He joined in my laughter in a merry, perceptive way that I found very appealing and suddenly familiar.

"Haven't we seen you on the beach here?" I asked. "I wonder if you're one of the actors the countess was telling us about?"

"I'm an actor, yes. What was she telling you?"

"Well, she said she'd met you in London. She wanted us to meet you."

"Did she really? Yes, I suppose we're the ones. Well, what a good thing we've met, then. I'm Adrian Blackmon." He held out his hand.

"How do you do. I'm Michael Pritchard."

"Look here, why don't you come over and meet the rest of us? Are you alone?"

"No, my wife's inside, getting herself disguised. She'll be out in a minute, I think."

"Oh. Will she be able to find you?"

"As well one place as another, I guess."

"Oh, good. Well, come along, then. We've got a table just over here." He guided me, moving cautiously with his brimming glasses, through the jostling groups of celebrants toward a table at the center of the lawn where Gwynyth, Tessa, Yvonne, and David sat, masked and, like Adrian, as I discovered, all wearing the costumes of characters in *The Tempest*. David rose and shook hands when we were introduced.

"Awfully good to know you. Do sit down," he said with a smile whose earnest affability managed to penetrate even the monstrous depths of his makeup, for he was gotten up horrifically and, considering his nature, altogether incongruously as Caliban. He wore a very large suit of long gray-flannel underwear, painted with scales and stuffed lumpily to give him a potbelly and a rash of terrible tumorous protrusions all over his body. At the groin and armpits there had been sewed on long, ragged, verminous-looking tufts of hair which had apparently been cut out of a fright-wig. He wore a similar wig on his head with a pair of horns, one broken, projecting out of it, artificial wolf-like rubber ears, and a set of plastic fangs which reached almost to his lower jaw. He was also furnished with a very long thick tail, made out of stuffed stockings tied together like link sausages and carried up and draped over his left shoulder. On the tip of it was tied a tiny delicate blue bow.

"Now you've got to guess us, before you do anything at all," said Yvonne, beaming at me as a lush, vine-ripened Miranda. "Who is David?"

I considered him for a moment, and then the rest of them alternately. "Well, I'll say Caliban. Although it's a toss-up, really, between Shakespeare and Dr. Seuss."

"Oh, that's wonderful," she said. "Or else we're very transparent. I'll bet you won't get the rest of us, though."

"I'll bet I will," I said, having discovered the motif.

"Oh, aren't you conceited! You jolly well won't. How much will you bet?"

"A hundred francs," I said.

"How much is that, Adrian?"

"Just on a pound," Adrian said.

"All right, you're on. Who am I, then?"

"Miranda, of course."

"And we thought we were being so clever. And Adrian?"

"Prospero."

"Oh, it's too easy. Once you've got one of us, you see the whole thing. Well, who is Gwynyth?"

"Gwynyth is Ariel."

Gwynyth is Ariel. It is extraordinary how the echo of one's own voice will haunt one, sometimes, for years: ringing in an unpredictable and apparently interminable reverberation in one's mind. At the strangest, the most incalculable, most unexpected times I will hear my own voice speaking that phrase: walking along a crowded street, at a concert, undressing for bed, making a move at chess, stirring a cup of coffee, suddenly I hear myself speak the words in just that tone, in just that categorical, psalm-like way: *Gwynyth is Ariel.* As far as I can determine it has nothing to do with neighboring events or preoccupations; I need not have been thinking of her; I need not have engaged in any analogous circumstances or series of events; there need have occurred nothing to remind me, however indirectly, of the girl. It is simply a mindless, irresponsible echo of one moment in the life of one human imagination reflected endlessly through time. And what makes it doubly inscrutable is that Gwynyth, of course, was not Ariel; then or ever. She had tricked me. She had done me out of a hundred francs with her duplicity. Something more than a hundred francs, actually. And now, for the first time, I heard the harsh boyish laughter that generally accompanied such achievements.

"Oh, no, I'm *not* Ariel! You see, I told you it'd work, Yvonne. Oh, they're so ruddy sure of themselves, aren't they? It's delicious. I'm not Ariel at all, and I've written down here on a piece of paper who I am, so that I can prove I haven't changed it just to make a bit of money. And now I'll have that hundred francs if you don't mind. Unless, of course, you want to bet and guess again."

"I'm no match for you," I said, taking out my wallet. I removed a hundred-franc note and dropped it in front of her on the table.

"I think I ought to get half," Yvonne said. "I do all the work."

"You get five bob and not a penny more. You do nothing but the labor. It's my marvelous ambiguity that takes the money."

"Who are you, then?" I asked, "if you're not Ariel?" She might very well have been Ariel, judging by her costume, which was a vague, filmy, fairy-like concoction, featuring a pair of drooping gossamer wings made out of clothing-hanger wire and surgical gauze.

"You've got to guess."

"Puck?"

"No. I'll give you a clue, since you've taken it so well." She flung out her arms and cried in a voice of woeful supplication, " 'Do you believe in fairies?' "

"Be jolly hard not to," David said. "Many of them as there are around here."

"Peter Pan," I said. "All right, I lose. But I think I'll have a look at that piece of paper, just the same."

"Do you mean to say you don't trust me?"

"Oh, yes. But I paid a hundred francs to see it, and I think I have a right to."

"Well, I suppose you have." She reached deep into the folds of her costume and from some buried pocket produced a folded sheet of paper which she tossed onto the table in front of me. I unfolded it, and as I read the first few lines (there were several more, but I didn't have the time to absorb them), I took a long drink of vodka to conceal any very possible incongruity in my expression:

I don't know how long you think I can endure this. Do you have to see him *every* day? Perhaps you didn't realize that I knew, or perhaps you don't care. I may not

"Well, are you satisfied?" Gwynyth said.

"I suppose I'll have to be." I refolded the paper and tossed it back to her across the table, hoping to heaven she would restore it to its resting place without inspecting it.

"Oh, you can't outwit her," said Adrian cheerfully. "Not when there's a hundred francs involved."

I looked at him with considerable awe. The British, I thought, are a truly remarkable people. I was not yet clear, of course, whether it was he or David who was paired with Gwynyth; but even from our few minutes' acquaintance, it seemed to me that the former was much more likely. Whichever of them it was, he was a living example of the legend of British equanimity. One would never have known what the man was going through.

"Now it's time to unriddle Mr. Pritchard," said Tessa. She had not spoken before.

"He's a sailor," said Yvonne.

"Of course he's a sailor; but what sailor? Is he Captain Ahab? Is he Francis Drake? Is he John Paul Jones?"

"No, he'd need a sword," said David. "He's a modern sailor of some sort. Sir Thomas Lipton, or something."

"Is he right?" asked Yvonne.

"Not exactly," I said.

"Perhaps he's the chap who made that one-man voyage 'round the world," Adrian said. "What was his name? Slocum, I think."

"Oh, yes, Slocum, of course! He's Slocum!" cried Yvonne.

Their speculations were ended by the appearance of Andrea, clad as Razullo and strumming a mandolin. The impact of his first appearance was as physical, as bitter, as disruptive as a blow. From his tattered brindled mass of rags and bells and ribbons an easy, arrant, inexhaustible sensuality, an air of physical luxury and wisdom as palpable and intense as the scent of his cologne emanated in waves. This may have been responsible for the ease with which my companions recognized him; none of them seemed to have the slightest doubt whatever as to his identity.

"Oh, Andrea," cried Yvonne. "How absolutely lovely you look! Isn't he lovely?"

He took off the ragged minstrel's coxcomb he was wearing, swept it grandly so that its little bells jingled, and bowed very low.

"You have found me out very easily," he said. "I have never been able to deceive ladies. It is my great misfortune."

It was disconcerting to discover that after hearing him speak these twenty words I disliked him as much as anyone I had ever met.

"It's because you're inimitable, Andrea," said Yvonne. "Now sing us a song. We must have a lovely tragic song."

"Not too tragic, please," said Tessa. "There should be a decent limit to counterfeit." She evidently shared my feelings.

"Very well," said Andrea, apparently undisturbed by the irony of her remark. "A moderately tragic song, only. Which I dedicate to the most enigmatic creature at the ball." Leaving this creature in cunning anonymity he strummed a lyrically mournful introduction and began to sing in a fine clear tenor voice the Italian popular song "Ciao, Ciao, Bambino."

"Oh, I do love Italian music," said Yvonne, when he had put a finish to it with a wilting arpeggio. "It's so wonderfully vulgar. All slop and spice, like canneloni."

"I say, that's a bit hard," said David. "Here he's sung you this marvelous song, and you go on like that."

"Oh, but he knows it," said Yvonne. "They do it on purpose, the Italians. You're not offended, are you, Andrea?"

"Indignation is a luxury I have never been able to afford," said Andrea. "In Italy we are used to the cruelty of Anglo-

Saxon ladies. We take our revenge by serving them these can-nelonis and ruining their figures."

"Yes, and not only by means of canneloni," said Yvonne. "Italy, in general, seems to be very bad for the figure."

"But very good for the appetite," said Tessa.

"Andrea, you've not met Michael," Adrian said. "Michael Pritchard, Andrea d'Agostino."

"How do you do," I said.

"Ah, you have an American accent." He bowed, jingling his bells.

"Yes."

"We are countrymen," he said. "In Detroit I have six cousins. Also an aunt and uncle, a brother-in-law, and two nieces. And in Brooklyn, another uncle and two nephews."

"I think you have more relatives in America than I have," I said.

"Really? How extraordinary. It is something that never occurred to me. Then, in a sense, my family is more influential in America than your own?"

"I'm sure of it," I said. "They must put together twice the voting power of mine."

"How extraordinary. It must give me privileges of some kind, I should think. How shall I claim them?"

"It would be very difficult unless you paid taxes."

"How does it happen you got left behind, anyway, when there was this mass exodus of D'Agostinos to America?" Gwynyth asked.

"I should have gone as well, I suppose. Perhaps I will yet. But, foolishly—up to now, at any rate—I have preferred Italy. There is less opportunity there, of course, but perhaps a bit more poetry, if Mr. Pritchard will forgive the opinion."

"But you're not *in* Italy," said Tessa.

"No, not now. Unfortunately I engaged in a certain amount of rather reckless idealism which has made my residence there embarrassing. But still, I am beside our sea, which comforts me. There are points here, on the Cap, where one can see the lights of San Remo in the water at night. I cannot tell you the number of hours I have stood and looked at them."

"Oh, dear. What on earth did you do?" asked Yvonne.

"I supported certain causes which were not popular in my country," said Andrea with the diffidence of a saint alluding to his martyrdom. "Certain political causes which I am afraid it would not be very wise to discuss in any great detail."

"Do you mean to say you're in exile?" said David.

"Not exactly, no," said Andrea. He smiled and lifted his eyes to the sky, as if seeking counsel on how to explain a status as delicate as his. "I am in what you might call—limbo. I am waiting—as we all are, in a sense"—here he dropped his eyes gravely—"to learn if I am going to be understood, or forgiven, or condemned." He tossed his hand bravely and drew himself up with a jest. "Of course, I don't complain. A limbo which is furnished with music and paper lanterns and beautiful young ladies makes a very pleasant place to wait."

"Still, the suspense must be agonizing," said Tessa.

"There are difficult moments," he admitted. He raised the instrument he carried with a little flourish. "That, of course, is when the mandolin is useful."

Inside the villa the quintet had begun to play a Bossa Nova number, "Recuerdos." Gwynyth tapped out the rhythm on the tabletop with her fingertips, then folded her hands suddenly into fists when she became aware of my watching her.

"What a marvelous beat," she said. "It's just come over from America, hasn't it? What do you call it?"

"Bossa Nova," I said.

"It's absolutely ravishing. Come and show me how to dance it."

"I'd be delighted," I said, rising. "Will you excuse us?"

"Oh, that bloody man," she muttered as we walked across the lawn.

"Andrea?"

"Yes. Did you ever see such a blazing awful humbug?"

"Well, you've certainly found him out very quickly," I said. "I thought he was rather charming."

"Oh, we've met him before. He's always about if there's free liquor going, or girls, or Opportunity." She laughed suddenly in her coarsely merry way. "I must say I loved that bit about poetry versus opportunity. God!"

"Well, he's apparently underprivileged," I said. "Or dispossessed, or something. That's apt to make a person awkward."

"You'll look a long way to find someone more underprivileged than me, but I don't spin those bloody awful yarns about myself."

"But you have talent," I said.

"So I have talent. Some people have warts."

"You don't make any distinction between them?"

"Not in their effect on character. How do you know I have talent, anyway?"

"The countess says you were an inspiring Beatrice."

"Oh. Yes, I was good in that. But I did the suicide bit all wrong. I'll know next time."

"Well, I think you're wrong," I said. "Talent makes you feel secure, it's bound to. Knowing you can do something very well. You know that you're unusual."

"Don't you believe it. I'm bloody ordinary, and I know it. My father was a butcher and my mother was a seamstress."

"Which of them are you more like?" I asked.

"Oh, my father, much. I'm a great deal better at hacking things to bits than I am at sewing them together."

"You sound as if you rejoiced in the fact."

"I do. I want to do a great deal of damage in this world."

We walked up the villa steps in the pale violet glare. "Oh, how lovely," said Gwynyth, turning toward me with bruised purple lips and great drowned eyes. "I feel like a Windmill Girl."

"What's a Windmill Girl?"

"Oh, there's this girly theater in London called the Windmill, where they all stand about nude in violet light. I wanted to work there last year, but my agent nearly had convulsions."

"Why on earth did you want to work there?"

"I like standing about nude. It's a marvelous feeling."

Inside the villa the great salon was crowded with dancers. The heavy Spanish furniture had been removed or pushed to the walls to make room for them, and in one corner the quintet —a guitar, a bass viol, a clarinet, drums, and a baby grand piano—were placed on a carpeted dais, their hands flying, jigging and jouncing like clockwork as they stared out impassively at the furore they presided over. Over the horde of prancing, spangled gargoyles a great wrought-iron chandelier cast the spoked shadow of a star.

"I may as well warn you, I'm an awful dancer," she said.

"So am I."

"Really? Why did you come, then?"

"Because you asked me. Why did you ask me?"

"Out of spite," she said.

"Toward me, you mean? Or Adrian?"

"No, neither. Come on, let's get on with it, then."

I put my hands on her waist and in the strangely solemn, panic-stricken way in which I dance, drew her in amongst the mummers.

"My God, you *are* awful, aren't you?" she said in a moment.

"Yes. Shall we stop?"

"No, it's sort of fascinating, actually. Like dancing with a gnu or something."

We ploughed through the throng, drawing looks of indignation on all sides.

"Everyone hates us," Gwynyth said. "Have you noticed?"

"I don't blame them. As far as doing damage goes, this ought to be a red-letter night for both of us."

"I know. Lots of opportunity for havoc, out here."

A man wearing a straw sombrero and a red beach towel as a serape waved to Gwynyth languidly across the shoulders of his partner. "You look absolutely shattering, Gwyn," he called.

"I shall have you on the pantomimes at Christmas." She put out her tongue at him.

"Who was that?" I asked.

"Preston Mansfield. He's a famous agent and bore."

"You stick out your tongue at famous agents?"

"At the ones who are bores."

"How do you suppose he happens to be here?"

"I've no idea. Everyone seems to be here. How do *you* happen to be here, by the way? Is she an old friend of yours, the countess?"

"No. We only met her last week. On the road. Her car had broken down, and we gave her a lift."

"Who's we?"

"My wife and I."

"What, you've got a wife? Where is she?"

"She's here, somewhere, putting her costume on; but she seems to be taking quite a while about it."

"Putting her costume on? How did she happen to get out of it?"

"No, you see she didn't wear it here. She's borrowed it, from the countess."

"Oh. Well, what are you doing here at all, though? Are you a sort of wandering millionaire or something?"

"No. I'm a librarian, on holiday."

"A librarian? Really? And you've come to the Riviera?"

"Yes. Is that unusual?"

"Well, I should think you'd be in Constantinople, or somewhere; poking about in the ruins."

"No. The nearer I approach a state of ruin myself, the less exciting I seem to find them."

"What do you find exciting now? This?"

"Yes. Music. Mummery. Cunning young actresses to lose fortunes to. Life."

"Oh. You're having fun, then?"

"Don't I look as if I were?"

261

"Well, it's rather hard to judge. You look just a bit agonized at the moment."

"That's only because I'm dancing; I have to carry on a conversation and count at the same time."

She smiled at me and said, "You're a jolly nice man. I'm sorry about your hundred francs."

"That's all right. It was very well spent, really."

"Perhaps I'll give you a chance to win it back. We can't have you losing everything over here, when you're worried about having so little to lose."

"Oh, it isn't that. I have a great deal to lose, actually."

"Have you? What?"

"Oh, all the things that people lose. Money, keys, identity cards, self-composure, wives and husbands."

"How awful," she said. "You must go about all day long patting your pockets and frowning with anxiety."

I laughed. "I'm afraid most of us do. Don't you?"

"Lord, no. There's never anything in them except a few garlic cloves."

"Garlic?"

"Yes, I love garlic. Do you mean to say you hadn't noticed?"

"I guess I'd better admit it," I said. "I can't lie very well."

"Really? You find it difficult to lie?"

"I find it difficult to deceive people when I do."

"I think I'll just put that to the test," Gwynyth said. "There's something I've been wondering about."

"What's that?"

"Did I by any chance give you the wrong piece of paper, back there at the table?"

"The wrong piece of paper?"

"Yes. What did it say?"

"Well, it said, 'Peter Pan'—in a roundabout sort of way."

"Oh, really? That's the impression you got? Not Catherine the Great, by any chance?"

I smiled rather shamefully. "Well, I guess I'd better admit that, too."

"Well, I'll be blowed," she said. "D'you know, it occurred to me that that's what I might have done, when I put the thing back in my pocket. What a bleeding idiot I am. I must say you carried it off very well."

"I'm sorry," I said. "It looks as if you'd better start doing a little pocket-patting, too."

"No bloody fear. Do you think I mind?"

"Don't you?"

"Not really. I'd rather people *didn't* have any illusions about me."

"You *do* have a passion for nudity, don't you?"

"I do, yes. I think most actors do. It's the only way anyone will ever know what we really look like, you know; we do so bloody much pretending." She turned her head to look at me and chuckled in a guttural, gnomish way. "You'd make a jolly good actor yourself, you know. Well, what are you going to do, now that you find you've got this awful, odorous courtesan on your hands?"

"I thought we might just go on dancing."

She chuckled again. We barged into an elderly emperor who turned to scowl at us. "It's really quite exciting, isn't it? I'd no idea dancing could be so dangerous."

"I didn't either," I said.

Amongst the surge of dancers Andrea appeared, very close at hand, in a jingling swirl of rags and silver bells, bearing with him a loudly laughing blond Daphne, all leaves and paper laurel blossoms, through whose aging, loose-fleshed face several valedictory gleams of vitality still shone fiercely, principally in her splendid eyes and teeth. He sighted us and tossed his cap into the air in greeting, catching it nimbly behind his lady's back.

"That awful wop," Gwynyth said.

"Is he drunk?"

"Not bloody likely. He's never drunk at parties. He's very careful to keep his head clear, that one."

"You sound as if you hated him," I said.

"I bloody well do. He makes me sad."

"Why?"

"I don't know. I suppose he's one of the very few people I've ever had to pity."

"You don't pity Adrian?"

"Adrian? Why should I pity Adrian?" She frowned at me for a moment. "Oh, I see. No, you've got that wrong."

At this moment the music stopped and there was a shower of laughter, chatter, and handclapping from the suspended dancers. The clarinet player set down his instrument, took up a trumpet and, advancing to the edge of the dais, blew an elaborate flourish, after which he raised his hands for silence and called out alternately in French, Italian, and English, "Ladies and gentlemen. Pray silence for your hostess, Her Grace the Marchioness of Puertavallone, the Countess of Baroja."

A beam of light was directed upon the arched entrance portal of the salon, and with a voluminous rustling and whispering the crowd of dancers fell away to form a circle in front of it. In a moment the countess appeared and advanced into the surrounding circle, her soft white hair astray and the amoebic blotch of cologne on the front of her blouse stained darkly by the soft lavender light. I saw that Margaret, in the Edwardian ball gown, stood behind her in the shadows of the corridor. The countess raised a fragile hand in welcome and began to speak in her gentle, penetrating voice:

"You are all of you very welcome to this entertainment, and I appreciate the honor of your attendance here. How very gay you all look. It does me a great deal of good. As some of you are aware, this little festival has become an annual occasion of mine, by means of which I seek to commemorate some of the events of my own existence. I hope you'll forgive me this pretension, as I am very old, and as you appear to be done no harm by it." There were cries of protest which she stilled with her raised hand, smiling. "Now, those of you who've celebrated the occasion with me before will know that it's our custom to award a prize for the most effective costume. This is not ordinarily done until midnight, at the unmasking, and after a thorough study of all of your disguises. Tonight, however, I'm going to give delight to those of you who have for years considered me a wicked and prejudiced old woman by violating that custom, for what I'm afraid will be quite transparent reasons. I've found among you a young woman who is so much the living image of myself as I was on the night I've chosen to perpetuate with this masquerade that she might well bear my name. So I'm afraid there's no doubt whatever about who shall win the prize."

She turned and extended her hand toward the shadows of the corridor, from which Margaret emerged with shy obedience, holding out her hand to take the countess' own. I had never seen her more beautiful. The tight clasp of the narrow bodice and the mauve-colored sash about her waist made her body appear girlishly slender, and her naked arms and shoulders and nude and elegant neck, given an exquisite length and grace by her upswept hair, flowed out of the great rustling, tinted cloud of satin about her hips like a nymph ascending from a sunset. Her skin was stained by the floodlight to an opalescent luster and her eyes shone like blue jewels sunken in pale wine. She wore long white silk gloves to her elbows and carried clasped against her thigh a delicate little fan of chantilly lace with polished ivory spines. On her hair the countess had performed a genuine work of art; it was swept up from her neck and brow and temples and sculptured in three queenly, ascending tiers that were miracles of softness and proportion, ornamented with a white camellia blossom and a trembling aigrette. It left bare her ears, as small and fine as alabaster cameos, in whose lobes a pair of miniature diamonds flashed softly. There was a moment of silence from the encircling crowd, then a gathering murmur of admiration which broke into applause. Margaret curtsied to them, spreading her fan and lowering her face behind it in a charming parody of the manners of the times she represented; then she rose, snapping her fan closed and laughing with candid delight at the success of her appearance. She turned to embrace her hostess lightly and receive that lady's affectionate kiss on her cheek. The countess raised her arm again to quiet the admiration of her guests.

"This is Mrs. Michael Pritchard, who has come to us from the capital city of America, and who brings with her, to grace our festival, the freshness, the vitality, and the unspoiled charm of her great country." There was a renewed burst of applause and cries of greetings and felicitations in several languages.

"Do you mean to say that's your wife?" Gwynyth said. "She's absolutely lovely."

"Thank you."

The countess now held up into the violet light the small white box which she had given Margaret at dinner, opening it and removing the jeweled pendant as she spoke. "I have here the Grand Prix de la Fête. It is, as you see, a heart, which symbolizes my own, as well as the world's. I'm afraid it is not an adequate reward, yet, such as it is, I present it as tribute to the youth, the beauty, and the innocence we have known, and as an amulet against all that would despoil it." She unfastened the clasp and laid the golden chain about Margaret's neck, standing behind her to secure it. The purple jewel glowed like a great drop of frozen blood on Margaret's breast. She lifted her hand and touched it with her fingertips, her face full of a sweet solemnity.

"Take this lawful prize," the countess said, "and rule over us as queen of this festival."

There was a flourish from the trumpet player, which was drowned midway by an unrestrained burst of celebration from the dancers who now surged forward, showering Margaret and the countess with handfuls of confetti, handkerchiefs, paper horns and rocketing, dying, falling bright-colored streamers.

"Lord, she's won the prize," Gwynyth said. "Isn't that marvelous!"

"Come and meet her."

"Yes, but it doesn't seem quite the moment. Why don't you bring her to the table? And the countess, too, if she'll come."

"All right," I said. "Thank you." Gwynyth slipped away among the crowd and I pushed forward toward Margaret. She stretched out her hand to me through the throng of her admirers and clutched my fingers happily.

"Mickey!" she said. "I'm the queen! Isn't it wonderful?"

"It certainly is." I kissed her on the cheek and she laughed delightedly.

There was a Coronation Waltz in her honor, which the countess commanded us to dance together, and alone, until the first reprise. I swept her out onto the marble floor with a brave attempt at gallantry. The vast circle of silent mummers, in their ragged motley, surrounded us like goblins. I had the distinct sensation of a nightmare.

"This is terrible luck for you," I said. "You get the worst dancer in the world for your Coronation Waltz."

"Oh, don't be silly. Try to feel a little arrogant, and you'll have it perfectly."

She looked wonderfully stately and contented, the rustling satin of her train sweeping regally about us.

"You look marvelous in that dress," I said.

"Do I?" She laughed. "I *feel* marvelous. I love being a queen."

"I must say you're getting the hang of it very quickly."

"Do you know what I've just decided? Something really tremendous. I never realized it before."

"What's that?"

"That what people appear to be is much more important than what they are. It really is."

"Well, which is the real you, then?" I said. "This queen, or that girl from Elk Falls?"

"I wish I knew."

The music completed itself, subsided rhapsodically, then swelled into a reprise. The throng of maskers paired themselves into couples and came billowing and swirling in their rags and ribbons to surround us on the floor. The Benedictine father whom I had seen earlier on the lawn plunged toward us, a bottle of champagne in one hand, and cast himself at Margaret's feet, begging for her slipper.

"For one drink only!" He cried. "I must drink from the slipper of the queen!"

Margaret shook her head at him, laughing. We swirled away and left him on his knees, his arms outstretched beseechingly.

"Oh, what a lovely feeling," she said. "Here I am destroying the pillars of society, and I feel such a lovely warm glow." She settled her head against my shoulder and asked in a moment, "Who was the girl you were talking to?"

"Gwynyth Rees. She's the actress the countess was telling us about. I met them out on the lawn. She's asked us to join them."

"Is she nice?"

"Well, she's got a sort of tough, urchin quality, but she's nice, yes. They all seem to be."

Out of the press of dancers the mermaid swept toward us in the arms of a bearded Cossack. Her nude green body glittered through the netted cord of her seine. She swung her head toward us, smiling, her wild hair tinkling with seashells. As they spun by she took one corner of her seine, lifted and tossed it over us, scattering a cloud of luminous silver dust from the gilded cord. I raised my hand to protect Margaret's coiffure, and the net brushed over our heads and shoulders as they swung away, leaving a faint glowing powder, like phosphorous, where it touched our skin and costumes.

"Well, who was *that*!" Margaret said.

"That's a mermaid of my acquaintance. We sailors get familiar with all the creatures of the deep, you know."

"Well, I wouldn't get too familiar with that one. She looks ravenous."

"I think she is, a little."

"She's also stark naked. Did you notice?"

"Yes, I noticed that. Mermaids are inclined to be naked."

"Well, all right. I've got my monk. Monks are more fun than mermaids."

"But much more limited," I said. "With a mermaid you can experience the real sea change. But you get a monk under water, and what have you got? Just a soggy monk."

The music came to a rippling ornamental finish. I released Margaret and bowed to her. The dancers parted to make a lane for us, applauding as I led her from the floor.

"You were a very impressive couple," the countess said as we rejoined her. "You were both quite aglow."

"Mickey, especially," Margaret said. " 'These are pearls that were his eyes.' "

"Why do you say that, my dear?"

"There was a mermaid out there casting her net for him."

"And did she sing his knell?"

"She wasn't a particularly lyrical type of mermaid," Margaret said. "But I'm sure the idea would have pleased her."

"Well, you must remember," said the countess, laying her hand on Margaret's wrist, "that if there is any irregular behavior amongst our mermaids, or monks, or anyone at all, it will be your duty to correct or punish it. You are the queen of this carnival."

"I'll remember that," Margaret said. "Everyone had better be very nice to me."

"It will be the easiest thing in the world," the countess said.

We made our way across the lawn to Adrian's table where Margaret was introduced by the countess to all but David and Yvonne, who had gone to dance.

"We've been trying to decide whether you wore a wig," Tessa said. "But I see that you didn't."

"No. That was the countess' work," Margaret said. "It's *all* the countess' work. I was nothing but clay in her hands."

"She should have been in the theater," Tessa said. "She's a master of illusion."

"As a matter of fact, there was a time when I was tempted to it," the countess said. "But then I married, and discovered that the opportunities for that particular talent were even greater in ordinary domestic life." She removed a coffee-colored lace handkerchief from her sleeve and pressed it to her brow. "I am very warm. Mr. Blackmon, perhaps you would see to our drinks. I think we should have a toast to our queen."

"Yes, of course," Adrian said. He took our orders and relayed them to a waiter who had followed in the countess' wake like a hound. Our hostess had meanwhile examined each of their costumes in turn.

"You are all very impressive," she said. "You are *The Tempest*, aren't you? All but this errant creature, who appears to be Peter Pan." She clasped Gwynyth's wrist, smiling approvingly.

"I shall win no money from *you*," Gwynyth said.

"No money?"

"I won a hundred francs from Michael, because he thought I was Ariel. But you're another matter."

"I am indeed. You must not expect to deceive me in any matter of identity."

"Still, you didn't get Michael," Margaret said.

"I can be forgiven for that," the countess said, turning her eyes upon me, "since he comes to us in the most mysterious disguise of all."

"But we got him right away," said Tessa. "He's a sailor. What's so mysterious about that?"

"So he claims," the countess said. "But I'm not convinced of his entire candor in the matter. If you notice, he's wearing the arms of Magdalen College. It's my opinion that his true impersonation is of a gentleman."

"Still, I don't see anything so mysterious in that," Gwynyth said.

"Then you have never known one. I have known bull-fighters, thieves, procurers, poets; and yet the older I grow the more certain I become that there is nothing in this world quite so mysterious as a gentleman."

Our drinks had now arrived. The countess raised her vermouth to Margaret and pronounced ceremonially, "To Queen Margaret. To the gaiety of her reign, the frivolity of her subjects, the folly of her realm."

"Hear, hear," Adrian murmured. We all drank solemnly. Margaret then raised her glass and toasted us in turn: "To my Subjects, to whom I promise every liberty but sadness."

"Hear, hear," cried Adrian, more enthusiastically than ever.

"You're going to make a jolly fine queen," Gwynyth said. "We could use you in England."

David and Yvonne now appeared, weaving their way among the tables in a state of staggering hilarity.

"David's gone mad!" Yvonne cried happily. "His costume's got the better of him. He's become an absolute beast!"

"What's he done?" Adrian asked.

"He's bitten an empress! Sank his fangs into her. Right to the bone, I should think."

"Broke one of them off," David said, tapping a shattered fang with his forefinger. "My word, she was tough. You can't tell about these empresses. I would have thought she was succulent as a grape."

"I won't have you savaging my guests," the countess said. "That is my exclusive privilege." She turned to Margaret. "Your Majesty, I think this monster must be tried."

Everyone agreed with great enthusiasm, and there was a mock trial of David which lasted half an hour. He was flamingly indicted by Tessa, whom Margaret appointed as prosecutor, and eloquently defended by Adrian, the counsel for the defense, who maintained that his behavior was a heroic example of eccentricity, and British to the core. Margaret seemed to agree. Her costume, the champagne, the party, and the triumph of having been chosen as sovereign of it all combined to produce a kind of hectic audacity in her that I had never known before. Her verdict delighted everyone.

"This is a charming monster," she said. "He has great sincerity. He behaves according to his nature, which is more than most of us can claim. As far as nibbling the empress goes, *someone*'s got to take a bite out of the mighty occasionally, or we'll be in a very bad way. I think we need more like him in this world. His sentence, therefore, is to produce more of his kind."

"What a splendid idea," David said. "I'll get right to it."

"Whether you produce them by procreation or conversion is up to you," Margaret said solemnly in a happy parody of judicial rhetoric and tone-of-voice. "I'd recommend procreation as the more enjoyable method, although of course, much slower. A fully fledged, practicing monster can be produced almost instantly by conversion, whereas to breed and rear one requires years of patient nurture. You might try both."

"I will," David said. "You can be sure of it. I must say, Your Majesty, I hadn't expected such a grasp of jurisprudence on your part. I'm really quite moved."

"I think we will all agree," said the countess, "that we've witnessed a very stirring example of justice at work. Our queen is as wise as she is beautiful. She deserves another toast."

The belief was unanimous and resulted in empty glasses all around. As we set them down, Andrea appeared out of the glitter and murk and tintinnabulation that surrounded us, announced by a rippling chord on his mandolin and a flourish, voluptuous, tawdry, spice-scented, of his tattered cape. He swept off his cap, its bells jingling brazenly, and bowed very low to Margaret.

"I have come to pay my respects to the queen," he said. "Permit me to offer you the loyalty of a poor minstrel forever."

She regarded him stilly for a moment; then, turning to the countess, she asked, "Who is this rogue?"

"He calls himself Razullo. A minstrel. I should beware of him, Your Majesty."

"Of me?" protested Andrea. "A poor *paisano,* whose only wish is to amuse?"

"We'll have to test your loyalty," said Margaret, turning to him.

"Name the test, Your Majesty. I will be equal to it."

"It will take time to consider," she said.

"I await." He bowed again, replaced his tinkling cap, and addressed the countess. "Your Grace, it is a magnificent *ridotto.* How can I express my appreciation?"

"You've just missed the opportunity," the countess said. "We've been considering the proper punishment for an outrage, and your opinion would no doubt have been valuable. However, that has all been settled now."

"An outrage?"

"Mr. Conley, here, was overstimulated by his costume and bit an empress. He has been tried and sentenced."

"I have never known a lady to complain about being bitten," said Andrea. "Not if the proper introductory steps were taken. Mr. Conley's fault must have been one of execution. The concept is sound."

"That's very possible," the countess said, extending her arm smilingly toward him. "Why don't you demonstrate, for his benefit, the proper way to bite a titled lady, so as to avoid complaint on her part?"

"Ah, that would require more time, and privacy, than we have available at the moment," said Andrea, raising an admonitory finger.

"I daresay there are many ladies here—titled and otherwise—who would be willing to place both at your disposal," the countess said.

"You may be sure of that," said Tessa softly.

"Of course it would require a philosophical spirit, which I am afraid is sadly in decline in our society."

"On the contrary," Tessa murmured. "I'd say that it was rampant."

The countess turned upon her a look of amused astonishment. "Would you? And do you yourself feel moved by this spirit of philosophy?"

Gwynyth laughed coarsely and merrily, covering her lips with her fingertips.

"Not to that extent," said Tessa, her face flaming. "I make no mistake about my appetites."

"I don't understand you," said the countess with gentle insistence.

"I don't confuse an appetite for sensation with one for understanding."

Andrea tossed his hand aloft in a gesture of dismay. "I don't understand this disgust of sensation," he said. "Forgive me. I am a simple Italian."

"And you imply that I'm an even simpler Englishwoman," said Tessa. "But I'm not simple enough to deny that we all of us live for sensation. What needs to be pointed out to you, apparently, is that some sensations are of a considerably higher order than others."

"Of what sort would these be?" asked Andrea, crouching down and cradling his mandolin across his thighs.

"Aesthetic sensations. Intellectual and moral ones. Any involving sacrifice."

"But any sensation involves sacrifice," he said, his smile undiminished. "I, for example, am addicted to the sensation of speed. It is natural to me. I revel in it, I live in it. I enjoy it as a bird enjoys the sensation of flight. Or I did. For I have sacrificed much to it: my health, my career, my future. Even my capacity to enjoy it any longer. Do you see?"

"He's quite right, you know," said Adrian. "I think it was Hemingway who pointed out that the position prescribed for procreation was extremely undignified. To which I should like to add that it is also uncomfortable, unreasonable, and sometimes even injurious to the health. But the sensations incidental to it are usually more than adequate to compensate for this sacrifice of dignity, comfort, and good health. Not always, of course."

"It's quite true, Tessa," said Gwynyth with an infernal smile. "Really, it is."

Either Tessa's eyes darkened or her face paled dramatically. She stared into Gwynyth's eyes, looking quite ill.

"You're interested in speed, Mr. Razullo?" Margaret asked, turning to Andrea with a casual promptness that was as graceful as it was merciful. "What sort of speed?"

"D'Agostino," said Andrea, flinging out his open hand in humble admission of his identity. "I am, yes. Any sort of speed. Of bullets, birds, arrows, airplanes, light. But principally, of automobiles. I was a Grand Prix driver."

"Oh, how fascinating," Margaret said. "And when you said you sacrificed your capacity to enjoy it, did you mean by an accident?"

"Yes. At Monaco, in 1957. Do you know Monaco?"

"No."

"You must go there. It is very beautiful, and very close, of course. An hour away. The race is run through the main street, you know—the Boulevard de Monte Carlo—along the sea. It is a very dangerous course. There is one corner which is particularly difficult, at the Banque de l'Orient. I struck it at perhaps sixty miles an hour. My gears failed. Poof!" He clapped his hands together, smiling ruefully. "So. No more racing."

"How awful," Margaret said. "You must miss it terribly."

"Yes. Very much. I have tried again, but it is no good." He spread his hands before him with a look of sorrowful resignation. "I flew over one hundred feet through the air, striking a lamp post. My right arm was shattered like glass. It was operated on at the American Hospital in Nice for eight hours by a team of three surgeons. Fortunately, they were excellent men, so that now I am able to use it very well for ordinary social purposes—for strumming a mandolin, for example." He allowed himself a wan look of irony. "But for racing, it is destroyed. There is damage to the nerve. And at one hundred forty miles an hour, one must be very sure of his reflexes."

"I should think so," Margaret said. "What a tragic thing to happen. I suppose you've had therapy and everything."

"Of every kind, yes. Water, heat, massage. There is great improvement; but nervous tissue, you know, cannot be regenerated." He extended his hand, waggling his fingers with a philosophical frown. "And so a certain amount of sensation is lost to me forever."

"I should think you still enjoy well above the average amount," said Tessa.

"Oh, I don't complain," said Andrea. " 'Though much is taken, much abides,' as your Lord Tennyson says. Nothing teaches one contentment so well as to lose a part of it." Margaret's attention to him seemed to be magnified by this observation.

"Tennyson's a very old-fashioned poet," she said. "I'm surprised that a racing driver should admire him."

"I admire much that is old-fashioned," Andrea said, permitting his great black eyes to linger upon her costume and the soft Pompadour styling of her hair. "Clothing, jewels, wine, books, and of course, virtue; which I think Miss Blanchard will agree is the most old-fashioned thing of all."

Margaret seemed confused by this confession. "Does your arm ever pain you?" she asked unexpectedly.

"No," replied Andrea, just as unexpectedly. "Not at all."

"It's as easy to praise virtue," said Tessa, who had meanwhile apparently been composing a reply, "as it is to praise the monarch of a foreign country. She demands nothing of us."

"That is true," said Andrea soberly. "And it is no doubt the reason I am able to praise it. As you are able to praise sacrifice because you have not picked grapes for twelve hours a day in the sunlight of Campania so that one of your six brothers might learn to read." He rose from his crouching position, setting his mandolin against the table's edge. "They are playing a waltz again. This is another of the old-fashioned things which I admire. Mrs. Pritchard, perhaps you would share my enjoyment of it?"

"I'd like to very much," said Margaret. "Thank you." Andrea drew back her chair and she rose.

"Will you excuse us?" he asked. There was a general murmur of consent, and David, Adrian, and I stood up as they walked away together across the lawn.

"Damned interesting chap," David said. "And clever. You'll get nowhere, crossing swords with him, Tessa."

"My very last intention," said Tessa, "is to cross anything with him."

"You're jolly rude to him, all the same," said Yvonne. "After all, it *is* a party, you know. You're in a foul mood altogether, Tess."

"You are," said David. "What you need is a good brisk waltz with a beast. Come along, old girl."

She sat for a moment staring at her spread fingers on the tablecloth, then rose suddenly, saying, "Perhaps I do," and went off with David toward the villa.

"Miss Blanchard appears to be upset," said the countess.

"She's a bloody bore," said Gwynyth. "I can't stand these sensitive, suffering types. Is there anything on earth more boring than a human being who thinks he's been badly treated?"

"And yet you portrayed one with great sympathy in *The Changeling*," said the countess.

"So you did," said Yvonne. "That sort of thing is your forte, and you know it."

"Oh, well, it's so ruddy easy. Just stand about looking statuesque, and use your low register, and you can bloody well bet there'll be phrases like 'the white light of human agony' or 'the burning dignity of her sin' in the *Observer* next morning. They love it. It's all such a bloody fraud. If there's one thing in this world that strikes me as being really undignified it's sending up a long eternal howl about human dignity. I won't do any more of them, I can tell you."

"You prefer the role of Peter Pan?" asked the countess.

"I bloody well do. Thumb your nose at the whole show and fly out the bedroom window."

Adrian chuckled at her, the corners of his eyes dissolving into a fretwork of merry, ancient-looking crinkles. "Oh, that won't do at all," he said. "I've heard you read Isabella, in *Measure,* you know."

"Oh, don't be so bloody clever," Gwynyth said, breaking into an even merrier chuckle than his own. She thumbed her nose at him, then leaned back in her chair, tilting her face toward the dark sky and howling with laughter. *"Dignity!"* she shrieked,

> *"Dignity, dignity, dignity, dignity!*
> *Dignity, dignity,* dignity!"

Heads were twisted toward her at surrounding tables. Adrian joined in the chant with her, dropping his head back and adding his thundering baritone to her piercing soprano. Together they howled up into the dark sky:

> *"Dignity! Dignity! Human Dignity!*
> *Dignity! Dignity! Human Dignity!"*

"Oh, shut up," Yvonne said. "You're crackers, both of you."

"But we have great dignity," said Gwynyth.

"We have indeed," said Adrian. "I am by all odds the most dignified Australian actor of my day. Of any day, very likely."

"Well, you've certainly managed to conceal the fact," said Yvonne. "One would never have known."

"Naturally one doesn't make a parade of one's virtues," Adrian said. "As the truly generous man is careful to conceal his charities, so the truly dignified man is careful to behave outrageously at all times. To do anything else would be vulgar."

The countess leaned back in her chair, breaking into a ripple of amusement. "I'm afraid you're a rogue," she said. But not a vulgar one, at any rate. Suppose I give you the chance to add mercy to your list of virtues, Mr. Blackmon? I'm going to challenge you to a game of badminton."

"Perhaps you'd better have a handicap instead," Adrian said. "My mercy isn't entirely reliable."

When the others had returned, the countess took my arm and led us down among the tables to the badminton court which had been set up on a lower stretch of lawn, bathed in the soft confectionary glare of colored floodlights. As a handicap, Adrian was required to carry a brimming glass of champagne in his free hand, which, if he spilled it, would automatically disqualify him. It soon became evident, however, that neither this handicap nor his mercy were necessary to the countess' victory. She stationed herself expertly in the center of the court and lashed the shuttlecock back across the net with a ferocity which confounded him. She beat him 21 to 7 and retired to the uproarious acclaim of the gallery which had gathered about the court to watch her play. Seated magisterially in a wicker chair and refreshed with a glass of vermouth, she issued clouds of fragrant and voluminous tobacco smoke and watched the doubles matches which followed. Margaret presided over these, awarding points and regulating play with an air of royal caprice which matched the countess' own.

Gwynyth and I played David and Yvonne in the first match, a very antic and contentious one. Gwynyth, who had decided that champagne, rather than being a handicap, would add a certain amount of zest to her performance, carried a full bottle onto the court with her, paused occasionally to refresh herself, and at critical moments, stoppering the bottle with her thumb-tip and shaking it vigorously, doused our opponents with a stream of hissing froth. I was by now fairly thoroughly intoxicated, no more by the wine I had drunk than by the evening's chimerical air of fantasy. I played in a haze of luxurious impressions which flowed about me with the nonsensical elegance of a dream: the shuttlecock soaring like a hectic lavender-feathered swallow against the black sky; the net stretched out before us and stained by the violet light, like a seine spread deep in Mediterranean water; the capering trio of my comrades—a horned, cavorting monster, a distracted princess, and

an exquisite barefooted elf with wings of trembling tinted gauze
—the surrounding gallery of motley gargoyle creatures, sometimes ominously silent, sometimes maniacally enthusiastic; an
occasional burst of sequins exploding over us and drifting downward like a ruptured star; the splash and tingle of champagne
on my skin; the twinkling cries of girls; the soft, scented darkness and the white moon sailing over us.

We were very predictably defeated, and surrendered our
racquets to a bedouin and a Polynesian lady, whose terrible
determination to win Margaret obviously disapproved of, and
penalized with a series of outrageous judgments. (She deducted
points from their score for "unbecoming zeal," for removing
their shoes without proper authorization, for challenging the
authority of the umpire and for "malignant intentions," each
of which verdicts brought forth a roar of approval from the
gallery and a smile of admiration from the countess. "Your
wife," said Adrian, "has a talent for the arcane." A thought
which had absolutely never occurred to me.) I watched until
they were defeated, applauding Margaret's decisions vigorously,
and in the midst of the next match—in which Yvonne and
David, still undefeated, were pitted against a caveman and a
ballerina—wandered back to the bar where I ordered a vodka
and tonic, drank it in one long, leisurely, continuous swallow,
then ordered another and, in a sudden quest for solitude, carried it away with me among the teeming tables, past scattered
groups of revelers at the outskirts of the lawn, and down through
the dark vineyard toward the sea. In the pavilion at the arbor's
edge Gwynyth was sitting alone at the marble-topped table in
the moonlight. On a tray in front of her there were three bottles
of stout and a bottle of champagne.

"Well, you're having quite a party," I said. "What happened, did you get fed up?"

"No, I was just exploring."

"You do quite a bit of that, don't you?"

"Oh, not properly. I don't stake out any claims, or bring
home any trophies or anything. I just like variety."

"I see." I looked about at the moonlight in the little clearing, the purple shadows in the vineyard, and the silver sea beyond. "It's beautiful here, isn't it?"

"It's jolly nice. Why don't you sit down?"

"You sure I won't spoil it? You look very complete, just the way you are."

"Oh, I'm not that complete."

"All right. Thanks." I sat down and looked out at the sea.

"I'm having Black Velvet," she said. "They don't do them right at the bar, so I brought my own ingredients."

"Champagne and stout?"

"Yes. Of course it's the proportion that's everything."

We sat in silence for a moment.

"Have you got any cigarettes?" she asked.

"Yes."

"Oh, good. Can I have one? I've run out."

"Yes." I found the pack and lit one for each of us. Gwynyth took the cigarette from my fingers, murmuring appreciatively, tilted her chair back, and put her feet on the table. From among the vines there came the sound of distant music and laughter.

"It's sort of nice to be on the edges of things sometimes," she said.

"How do you mean?"

"Well, I mean sitting on the stairs in your nightdress and peeking down between the banisters. Everything seems so much more mysterious and wonderful, that way."

"It seemed pretty mysterious to me right from the front row," I said.

"Did you think so? God, I don't call that mystery. Just a lot of shabby social intrigue."

"Well, I guess you had a better idea of what was going on than I did."

"Yes, perhaps I did. Still, it wasn't all that hard to figure out, was it? God, that Tessa. What a bore she can be. Do you mean to say it wasn't totally transparent? About that note, I mean?"

"Do you mean *she* wrote it?"

"Yes. Does that shock you? I suppose it does."

I had a very strange, chilly feeling of acceleration and breathlessness, as if I were coasting down a steep hill on a bicycle without brakes.

"Is she in love with you?" I asked in a carefully controlled tone of voice.

"Oh, she thinks she is. There's nothing sillier than a love-struck human being. God, I hate love."

"Well," I said, "there's a lot of it around."

"Don't I know it. Like mud. You're up to your knees in it, most of the time. Spend half your life trying to wash it off." She drew a great draft on her cigarette and shuddered. "Bloody awful cigarettes you've got. What are they: American?"

"Yes."

"Aren't they awful." She filled up her empty glass with two alternate reckless splashes of liquid from the stout and the champagne bottles, then sipped at it with a delicate, experimental air. "Absolutely perfect. I don't know how I manage that. I think God guides my hand, or something." She separated a strand of her long yellow hair, dipped it into her drink, and sucked at it meditatively for a moment. "No, I had a disastrous experience with Tessa. I'm such a bloody fool. We were playing in this dreary little rep down in Bournemouth, and I got drunk after a party on closing night and let her take me home. Of course I told myself that I didn't *really* know what she was up to; but I did, you know. And then I got so drunk that it didn't seem to matter a great deal. And it wouldn't have mattered, except that she got so bloody soppy about it. I mean a thing like that doesn't do anyone any harm, as long as they don't go on a steady diet of it. Actually, I don't think I'd mind going to bed with everyone in the world—one at a time, of course, and only just the once. Be bloody interesting. But I don't *love* them all, for God's sake. I don't know why they don't understand that. Well, the minute we got over here she started up again. Absolutely frantic with jealousy every time I go out of the *pension* for ten minutes. It's too much to put up with. I really think I'm going to have to pack it up."

"Do you mean go back to London?" I said.

"No bloody fear. Not till I'm ready. Just get away from her, I mean. You can be jolly sure *she's* not going, as long as I'm about." She looked suddenly at me, sidelong, as if she had been almost unaware of my presence. "I don't know why I'm telling *you* all this. Give you a bit of a thrill, I expect."

"Do you like doing that?" I asked.

"What? Giving people a thrill? I suppose I do, yes. It's really the whole point of things, isn't it? In a civilized world, I mean. Be jolly dull if whoever you were busy with couldn't care less." She plunged the strand of her hair back into the glass and began sucking at it again, her face growing thoughtful. "Yes, that's what it is, really, isn't it? Exciting people. It's what you really want to do: create excitement in the world. It's the same in acting. You want to stand out there and get them so bloody excited they'll start masturbating all over the theater." She broke into a sudden bark of coarse gay laughter. "What a performance that would be! Everyone sitting there going at it like mad, holding his program over his lap." She took a deep drink of her Black Velvet, chuckling into the glass. The sentiment sounded very familiar to me, but I could not remember where I had heard it.

"Do you think that's a pretty common idea?" I asked. "Among artists, I mean?"

"I d'know. I can't speak for the rest of them. Of course there's a bloody lot of them don't admit it. Tessa, for example. She's got all these theories about aesthetic experience, and sacrifice, and all the rest of it. God, they're all such flaming humbugs. And the worse the actor is, the more he talks about aesthetics and dignity and that sort of rubbish."

"I take it, then, that you're a very good one," I said.

She turned upon me a sustained, smiling look of concentration. "I could take that either way," she said. "But I'll take it as a compliment."

"That's how it was meant."

"Good. Have you got another of those filthy cigarettes?"

"Yes." I produced and lit it for her.

"Jolly sexy, the way you do that: light a cigarette and hand it to one. Do you do that for everyone?"

"No bloody fear," I said. She laughed delightedly.

"You do that very well. You rather surprise me, you know. I've never known anyone like you before. It's jolly interesting."

"What do you find unusual about me?"

"Oh, it's not that you're *un*usual; It's that you're *usual*. And I've just never known any usual people. I mean respectable, middle-aged civil servants. I'm enjoying it no end." I winced in an exaggerated way, as if I had been shot or stabbed. "Well, you are middle-aged, you know. Or you look it, anyway."

"That wasn't the part I minded most," I said.

"Oh. Well, what was it, then? The respectable bit?"

"No, not that either. It's just that the whole thing adds up to such a totally depressing picture. I can't believe that's what I am."

"Well, there's nothing wrong with it, of course. As a matter of fact, you're a damn sight more interesting than a lot of professional romantics. That race-driving wop, for example."

"Whom you see every day," I said.

"*Saw*. No more."

"Oh. I wouldn't have expected his charms to wear thin quite so soon."

"He's a bloody awful humbug," Gwynyth said. "But we've been through all that, haven't we? Oh, he might do for some women; someone frightfully innocent and romantic, but not for me. I've seen too many like him."

I finished my vodka and tonic and studied the empty glass for a moment. "What I don't understand," I said, "is why a woman would do that, then. I mean if she had no respect for a man at all."

"Well, there was nothing else going at the time, you know. And he *is* rather beautiful. And really quite good, in bed."

"Oh. I see."

"And of course I *am* on holiday."

"Yes."

She finished her cigarette and flung it away, making a swift red arc across the darkness. "Of course you know it's a pretty dreary question to ask anyone."

"I suppose so. Sorry."

"It's got that awful melancholy, moralistic sound of somebody who's getting just a bit moonstruck. That's something I really can't bear."

"Sorry," I said. "I must have picked it up from Tessa."

"That's one thing about Andrea, anyway. He doesn't go on about love and morality and all the rest of it. I never in my life knew a moralist who wasn't either too old for sex, or too incapacitated, or just bloody well not getting his fair share of it. Morality is envy, as far as I'm concerned."

"I guess it very often is," I said. "But there must be a young and beautiful moralist somewhere."

"Oh, there are," Gwynyth said. "The convents are full of them. It's the ghastliest form of perversion in the world." She took my empty glass and set it in front of her, lifting the champagne bottle. "Look, I'm going to make you one of these Black Velvet things. Would you like that?"

"I guess so. It's a long way back to the bar."

"You'll like it, you know. You'll see things much more clearly, and then I won't have to do so much explaining."

"Oh, I don't want to discourage that," I said. "I'm enjoying it very much."

"Oh, God. Now you're going to patronize me. That's what older men do, you know. They give you that bloody *smile*. 'That's all right, dear; just go on and natter away. Some day you'll understand.' That and morality. The two great patented substitutes for energy and intelligence. If you smile at me just once I'll split your bloody skull with this bottle."

"It's the last thing I'll ever do," I said.

"Yes, and it *will* be, too. I don't mind you screwing me, if you like; but please don't smile at me that way. There, now taste that." I did, and found it very refreshing.

"That's good," I said. "I could drink quite a lot of it."

"So could I. God, I love to drink beer. Do you know where they have the most marvelous beer? Australia. I went to Sydney on a tour two years ago with Adrian and we drank absolute gallons of it. There's the most wonderful beach there called Bondi, with some pine trees on a sort of bluff above the sea; and we used to lie there in the shade—it was hot, you know; beastly hot—and drink this marvelous beer out of huge quart bottles. Melbourne Bitter. It had a tiger's head on the label and a sort of stone stopper in the top. God, that was marvelous beer. And the breeze was so lovely in the pines. We'd lie there and drink beer until we were bursting and then run down into the ocean to have a pee. I loved Australia. Adrian hated it, though. He was born there, you know; but he hadn't been back for years."

"What did he find wrong with it?" I asked.

"Oh, I d'know. Too many automobiles or something. Adrian's very allergic to progress."

"I like him very much," I said.

"Yes. *I* do."

"I had the idea that you and he were here together."

"We are. We go quite a lot of places together." She stood up and walked across the grass to stamp out her cigarette butt, which was still smoldering redly. Then she stood for a moment and stared out at the sea which lay shimmering and heaving gently in the moonlight. "I say, there's a boat down there on the shore. What do you say we go and have a cruise? You've got the right clothes for it."

"All right. Shall I bring a bottle?"

"Oh, absolutely. Bring them all. We've got to have survival rations." I took the bottles from the table, cradling them in my arms, and followed her down to the beach. She climbed into the skiff and sat down in the stern, taking up an oar and fitting it into the lock.

"Lord, that's heavy. I've only ever used a paddle."

"Wait a minute," I said. "Let's shove off first, or they'll go adrift." I set the bottles against a gunwale and then went back to unfasten the painter line from an iron ring in a block of concrete to which it was hitched. I tossed the line into the boat, set my knee on the bow, and shoved off. The bottom came clear with a grating sound on the coarse sand and we drifted out idly for a moment with a gentle lilting motion on the dark water. Gwynyth sat smiling at me happily.

"Oh, that feels so lovely, doesn't it? That breaking free. That moment when you feel yourself adrift. Shall I set the oars in now?"

"All right. You'd better let me handle one of them." I climbed back and sat beside her on the stern seat, taking the portside oar and setting it in the lock. "Are you ready?"

"Yes."

"Heave."

We started out across the Mediterranean. The water was very gentle; there were no waves at all, only great slow swells that mounted and fell hugely, with shadowed valleys between their silver crests. We rode across them, rising and sinking in a long majestic rhythm, watching the colored lanterns rise above the tops of the vineyard trellises as we moved out into the bay, and then the candlelight and the sudden flaring of matches, like fireflies, among the lawn tables, and the lighted windows of the villa with the silhouettes of dancers blowing across the curtains.

"God, it looks beautiful, doesn't it? You'd think it was an absolute fairyland, if you'd just happened to pop in from Mars or somewhere."

"Yes."

She let her oar drift for a moment, staring at the distant twinkling lawn, then raised her hand and waved happily. "Well, cheer-o, chaps. It's been a lovely party."

"Where are we going?" I asked.

"Oh, Lord, who cares? That's the last thing one should want to know. Come on, heave."

She handled the heavy oar very well, learning quickly to set the blade in the water without splashing. I rowed only one stroke to two of hers to prevent our circling. We moved out beyond the arm of the little cape on which the countess' villa stood, and into sight of the lights of Beaulieu across the bay.

"Great fun this, isn't it? Sometimes I take a rowboat out on the Serpentine all by myself. It's lovely in the rain. But you've got the bloody swans to contend with. They hiss at you, you know, when you go by; and sometimes charge right at you. One of them actually bit me once: took a great nip out of my finger. Awful things, swans."

"What's the Serpentine?" I asked.

"Oh, it's this wretched little pond in Hyde Park. You can swim there in the summertime. They've got what they call a Lido." She burst out laughing. "God, the English! You've no idea what a potty lot we are. The Lido: can you imagine it?"

"What's the matter with the Lido?" I said.

"Well, it's so bloody *festive,* isn't it? Or grandiloquent, or euphemistic, or something. That's what we do, you know: scatter about a few bathboards and parasols and put up a tea stand, and we call it a spa. Or a church and a barracks, and call it a civilization. In Torquay, for example, they've got *palm* trees. Can you believe it? And the water's so bloody cold you freeze your kidneys. And the wretched little warrens they've got up aren't *houses,* of course; they're villas. Oh my word, yes: *villas.*"

"Well, I suppose you could consider that ambition, or imagination, or aspiration, if you wanted to," I said.

"I suppose you could, yes. It's rather sweet, actually. A certain amount of humbug, when it's on a modest and absolutely transparent basis, is rather charming. Your type, for example."

"What is my type?" I said.

"You know very well what it is. Do you mean to say you've been getting away with it all this time?"

"I guess I must have; nobody's ever charged me with humbug before."

"Oh, come off it. She can't be all that gormless." She let her oar drift again and plunged her hand into the water. "God, it feels lovely. I'd love to go for a swim, only I'd get my hair wet and they'd all start screaming at me."

"What does gormless mean?" I asked.

"Oh, I don't know what it means. Dense. Not very clever about people. No gorms." She raised her hand from the water and pressed her wet palm against her brow. "I'm not saying she is, mind you. Perhaps she's a jolly sight cleverer than you think, not to let on that she knows you better."

I felt both mildly angry at her impertinence and excited —somewhat beyond proportion—at the air of intimacy she managed to establish between us with her insinuation. The nameless subterfuge of which she accused me seemed to imply a strange confidence between us, some sort of renegade fraternity, like that of fellow-adventurers or fellow-pariahs. It was a rather disturbing sort of fellowship to consider, and one that had been very seditiously and skillfully proposed, I decided— or else supremely ingenuously and candidly. She dipped her hand back into the sea and flipped water into my face with her fingertips.

"Are you angry?"

"Angry? No, why should I get angry?"

"I d'know. Men do, I find. I find they're inclined to hate me the way fat women hate chocolate cake. Groaning about the calories all the time they're sinking their teeth into me. It's bloody depressing."

"I thought you didn't know any respectable men," I said. She laughed in her harsh bright way.

"Right. You score one. But he's not a middle-aged civil servant, so it wasn't an absolute lie."

"What sort of man is he?"

"He's an archaeologist who spends his life in the British Museum. I met him when I was going to RADA, because it's just down the street, and we both used to have lunch every day in a little place called Olivelli's."

"Are you in love with him?" I said.

"No bloody fear. I just keep him in the back of my mind as a possible solution."

"Solution to what?"

"To my particular problem."

"What is your particular problem?"

"Life. Hand me the bottles, will you? Did you bring a glass?"

"No."

"Bloody lot of help you are. I'll just have to mix them inside of me, then." She lifted the champagne bottle, took a long glugging drink out of it, set it down and followed with an equal portion of stout, after which she issued a great whistling sigh.

"How did it work out?" I asked.

"I think I did them the wrong way round. I'll have another go." She reversed the procedure, winding up by blowing out an unswallowed mouthful of champagne in a fine spray that sprinkled our hair and faces.

"Oh, lovely. Champagne rain. God, it's marvelous out here, isn't it? Are we getting close to Africa?"

"We can't be far away."

"I thought not. I keep thinking I hear drums. Or perhaps it's just the blood in my ears. It does that when I get drunk. Sounds like a bloody water closet." She turned her face toward the open sea. We had rowed almost to the tip of Cap Ferrat, and in the open water beyond the arm of the little bay we could see now the periodic rotation of a great beam of light sweeping over the black swells. It cast a broad slanting plane downward through the dense sky from some point at the extremity of the Cape, circling out to be buried in the Mediterranean darkness, then reappearing, momentarily, above our heads. Gwynyth watched it gravely.

"It's a lighthouse, I suppose. At the tip of the Cape, it looks like. I didn't know there was one, did you?"

"No."

"Do you suppose they've turned it on for us?"

"Possibly," I said. "They may have given us up for lost."

"I say, do you think they have? Would your wife mind about this?"

"She might be just a little annoyed."

"Well, perhaps we'd better not mention it. Go back separately, or something. I don't want to go smashing up your marriage. How long has it been, anyway?"

"Twelve years," I said.

"Twelve years? Really? God, is it possible to live twelve years with one human being? I wouldn't have believed it." She set her elbows on her knees and her chin on her fists, staring down at the darkly gleaming water. "What was I doing twelve years ago? Galloping down Church Street, I suppose; in pigtails, with a parcel of books under my arm. And here you were out in the back garden in the moonlight, proposing to Margaret."

"Not in the back garden," I said. "On a boat."

"Really? Like this, you mean?"

"Not like this, no. A sailboat."

"How extraordinary. Are you going to propose to me, then?"

"That's not what I had in mind."

"Oh, blast. Nobody ever proposes to me. It's because I smell, I suppose."

"Do you mean to say no one ever has?"

"Lord, no. Not that I mind, you know. As a matter of fact, if anyone came up to me and said, 'Look here, how would you like to spend the next fifty-odd years of your life with me?' I'd say, 'You're out of your bloody mind.' Men sense that about one, I suppose." She took up her oar and set it back in the lock. "Shall I start rowing again?"

"It would be a help," I said.

"Right. Are we still going to Africa, or what?"

"No, we're going back. I'm afraid they'll have a search party out for us soon."

"You're really rather nervous about it, aren't you? Still, I suppose it's just as well, because I've got to pee most awfully. Are we nearly there?" She turned to look back across the stern toward the shore. "Lord, I don't know if I'll make it. That's the awful thing about beer, isn't it?"

"It's a great disadvantage," I said. I turned to smile at her. Her hair was a wild tangle and her costume was in tatters; her wings were now badly bent and wilted by salt water, champagne, and labor, and drooped comically. "You're a very funny girl," I said. I took my hand from the oar and laid it on her head, cupping her skull in my palm. It felt small and cool, like a melon. She pressed her head back against my palm, rubbing it gently.

"You've nice hands. Awfully gentle hands. You're a jolly nice man."

"Do you think so?"

"Yes. I thought so before, of course, but I wasn't sure. I never really know about men till they touch me."

I took hold of the oar again and we recommenced rowing. We sat side by side, bending forward and leaning back rhythmically against the handles, looking out at the moonlit sea.

"It's peaceful, isn't it?" Gwynyth said.

"Yes."

In a few minutes we ran aground with a sandy rasp. She dropped her oar and bounded out of the boat instantly, fleeing up the beach to the shelter of a boulder. "You'll have to excuse me," she called. "Sorry. I won't be a moment."

I climbed out of the boat, hauled it up onto the sand with the painter line, and moored it to the block of concrete.

"Oh, blast!" Gwynyth cried from behind her boulder. "I've wet my pants!"

I stowed the oars under the seats, gathered up the bottles, and stood waiting for her, staring at my shadow on the moonlit sand. In a moment she reappeared and came toward me along the beach, a luminous, bedraggled fairy, her underpants dangling from her hand.

"I couldn't get the ruddy things off in time," she said. "What on earth shall I do with them? You can't just leave underpants lying about. And I'm jolly well not going to put them back on."

"Throw them in the water," I said.

"But they'll wash up. The old girl'll have fits. I'd better put them under a rock or something." She hunted about the shore for a rock of the proper size, lifted it, shoved the scrap of underclothing beneath, and set it down again. "There. I've buried my shame. Perhaps I ought to erect a little cairn or something." She stood up and grinned at me. "I'll have another go at that stout, now. I've made room for a bit more."

I handed her the bottle and watched her tilt her head back and take a tremendous drink, draining the bottle, her throat rippling in the moonlight as she swallowed. She blew out her cheeks and chuckled.

"I'm a bit squiffy, you know. I suppose you'll write home now, and tell everyone that English women are beasts."

"No."

"I don't mind if you do, actually, because I'm Welsh. Did you know that?"

"No."

"Well, I am. I'm rotten black bloody Welsh, and my ancestors came from these shores, so I'm entitled to pee on them if I like. Do you see?"

Holding the bottles in the bend of one arm I put the other about her shoulders and drew her against me in a very light embrace, feeling miraculously nourished, enriched, and rejuvenated by the fragile touch of her body against my own. We stood together silently.

"Do I feel good to you?" she said.

"Yes. Very."

"You feel bloody good to me, I can tell you." She turned her face up to look at me with the same harsh and candid intensity in her eyes as that which filled her voice. "Do you think we've got time?"

"Not now."

"I suppose not. Still, I might change my mind, you know, when I'm not so squiffy."

"What does that mean? Drunk?"

"Well, not drunk, really. Just a bit squiffed."

"Maybe we ought to wait and see." I kissed her lips very lightly with a deliberate, almost professional, restraint. "I'd sort of like to know."

"Know what?"

"How you feel about it when you're sober."

"Oh, I see. Well, you'd better go along, then. I'll come up after a bit. That might be better, I think."

"Yes."

"Just leave me my bottles."

"All right." She took them from me one at a time and stooped down to set them on the sand.

"When will I see you again?" I asked.

"Oh, I d'know. We come over to the beach here almost every day. Perhaps we'll see you there."

"I meant alone." She lowered her head and nibbled with her lips at the neck of the champagne bottle for a moment.

"Lord, I don't know. I can't think just now. Let's just leave it that I'll see you on the beach one day soon. Perhaps I'll think of something in the meantime."

"All right. You're going to stay here for a while, then?"

"Yes, I'm going to wade a bit. You go along."

"All right." I walked up the beach to the grassy bluff beyond the boulders and turned to look back at her. With the champagne bottle clutched to her bosom like a baby she was wading through the shallow water at the sea's edge, kicking up silver sprays of foam with her toes, her broken wings flopping about her shoulders. I walked up past the pavilion and through the vineyard, hearing, as I approached the lower slopes of the lawn, the shrieking of a girl, a chorus of masculine voices chanting, "Heave!" and bursts of cheers and laughter. As I came out from the shadows of the trellises I saw, outlined against the light of lanterns on the lawn beyond, a group of ten or twelve revelers in their disheveled mummery staggering, chanting, and cheering in a curious explosive rhythm while a naked girl catapulted upward from, and then plunged down amongst, them recurrently. They had stripped the net from the mermaid and were tossing her in it, like a blanket. One of them, squealing wildly, sprayed her with soda water from a siphon as she soared and fell. I walked past them toward the glow and glitter of the tables on the upper lawn. Halfway up the slope a girl in a pageboy's costume lay face down in the grass, crying quietly. I stooped to touch her on the shoulder and she shook my hand away, saying, *"Allez, allez."*

The badminton games were over. Margaret and the actors had returned to the table and sat clustered about Adrian, their heads bent down to watch while he drew cartoons on a napkin with a ball-point pen. I came and stood behind Margaret, laying my hand on her shoulder. She looked up at me and clasped my hand with her own.

"Who won the tournament?" I asked.

"An octopus and a bearded lady. I had to disqualify David, finally. He was awful. He made a scene."

"It was rigged," David said. "I far outplayed them all."

"You did nothing of the sort," said Yvonne. "You were beastly. He did improper things with his tail."

"Adrian's making a drawing about it," Margaret said. "Look. He does the most wonderful cartoons."

The sketch showed David, in his monster-suit and with a fiendish grin, evidently pausing in the act of tickling Tessa's behind with the tuft of his lumpy tail while she, clutching her buttocks and wearing a look of astonished delight, was at the zenith of a stratospheric leap, her head among the stars. In a balloon above David's head was written the admonition, "Dignity! Mind your dignity!"

"I think it's absolutely astonishing the way he does that," said Yvonne. "Gets right at people's character, I mean, with half a dozen lines."

"If human nature could be portrayed in half a dozen lines," Tessa said, "you'd be out of work. There'd be no need for drama, at all."

"Oh, I know; but the essence, I mean. The way he puts his thumb right on it. Oh, you know what I mean. God, you're so bloody pompous about everything, Tessa."

"I despise deftness," Tessa said, her face darkening. "I despise adroitness, and waggery, and facility. And everything that threatens the art you're supposed to be devoted to." She clenched her hands and jaws and stood up suddenly, her voice growing quite shrill. "I despise the whole bloody lot of you, if you want to know. I think you're a lot of ragged little vandabonds and vaggles."

"Vaggles?" said David. "What the devil is a vaggle?"

"Oh, don't be so bloody clever!" She snatched up Adrian's cartoon, crumpled it in her hand, flung it to the ground, and made off in an angry, unsteady half-run toward the villa.

"Oh, now, see what you've done," said Yvonne remorsefully. "You've not got to mock her, David; you know that."

"Well, I won't be called a vaggle, not by anyone," said David. "Anyway, you were at her just as much as I was."

"Well, I know, but it's too bad, really. Oh, Lord, she's so difficult when she's potted. Still, it is funny, of course, being called a vaggle. What was the other thing? Vandabonds." She burst into a pealing giggle and rocked forward across the table. "Oh, dear! Poor Tessa. She's no luck at all, you know. Just when she gets all full of righteous indignation she starts talking about vaggles."

"I suppose I'd better go and try to comfort her," David said. "Give her an affectionate little nip in the neck or something."

"Oh, no, David; leave her alone. She'll be much better off, honestly."

"Do you think if I went and chatted with her for a little—?" Margaret said.

"No, she'll come round in a moment. But we must all be very casual, when she does. And Adrian, you're not to draw any more beastly pictures of her. It's really your fault, you know."

Yvonne had guessed correctly. When she returned, after half an hour or more, she was in very much better spirits; perhaps because she came back to the table arm in arm with Gwynyth, who carried leashed in one hand half a dozen bright-colored helium-filled balloons.

"Do you know where I found this creature?" Tessa cried. "Sitting on the wet sand sucking a bottle of champagne, all by herself. She'll have pneumonia, I'm sure of it."

"I shall have chilblains on me bum," said Gwynyth, "and stars in me eyes, forever. There are ten million and fifty of them over that sea. I counted them. God, it was beautiful."

"I'm afraid we shall have to give up trying to reform her altogether," Tessa said, touching her cheek with an air of tender indulgence. "Still, she's rather nice, just as she is. When she means to be."

Gwynyth turned to smile at me. "I love stars," she said. "I really do."

"Well, they're very easy to love," I said. "Unlike people."

"Oh, *dear*," Tessa murmured, turning her head to smile into her shoulder.

We played a game of puncturing the balloons, which Gwynyth released one at a time, by flinging lighted cigarettes at them. All but three of them escaped, however, and went fleeing up into the black sky like frightened, fugitive moons.

On the stroke of midnight the countess came back to our table, escorted by a sheik clad in a bedsheet and a pair of Turkish slippers, who rapidly bowed himself away into the enfolding tumult.

"I have just come to say good night to you all," she said. "I shall have one more glass of vermouth and then I shall go to bed."

"Oh, not already," Yvonne cried.

"I must, my dear. The hour of truth is upon us, and I should be at a great disadvantage if I were to remain abroad."

She had barely made this announcement when the clanging of a bell rang out above the soft clamor of the lawn. We looked toward the villa and saw Nicolas coming down the front steps, swinging a huge old wooden-handled refectory bell as he descended. He moved down among the tables, pealing this instrument and calling out like a town crier: "It is midnight, *Mesdames et Messieurs*. It is time to unmask. Ladies and gentlemen, it is the hour of truth. You must make yourselves known."

"This is Nicolas' supreme pleasure in life," the countess said. "He loves being the herald of Truth. I think he lives for this moment every year."

"Who is he?" David said. "He must be bloody wealthy if he can enjoy a luxury like the truth."

"On the contrary. He is my chauffeur. It is generally those with only a very small investment in the world who can afford to be enthusiastic about the truth."

Nicolas' announcement seemed to refute this point of view to a degree, for it created a great deal of excitement among the revelers. This was largely spurious, however; for in fact, most of the masks had by this time either been discarded or dilapidated to an extent that rendered them, as disguises, frivolous or tattered formalities; many had been no more to begin with. There was nevertheless much screaming, laughter, applause, and perhaps a few genuine expostulations of astonishment.

"We have drunk to frivolity, to folly, to deceit," the countess said. "Now it is twelve o'clock, and we must drink to candor, to the lowering of disguises, to sincerity in all things. My young friends, I give you Truth." We raised our glasses and drank with a solemnity that was subverted somewhat by Gwynyth winking at me over the rim of her glass. Then, with equal solemnity, we all removed our masks—David removed his horns and fangs, as well, and Adrian, his beard—and sat regarding one another for a moment with a curious shy air of circumspection that was difficult to account for. Margaret's eyes were a very deep blue; a grotto-blue—the effect, I assured myself, of the violet light which flooded everything.

"Hello," she said to me.

"Hello."

The countess rose, gathering up her humidor. "Thank you so much for coming to my little entertainment. I've enjoyed your company enormously. Margaret will accompany me to the villa. Good night to you all." We rose, murmuring a chorus of combined appreciations and farewells, and watched them stroll away together across the lawn.

I don't know that the remainder of the evening, so promisingly dedicated to Truth, yielded any more of it than that part of it devoted to Folly had produced. Certainly no more of the candor or sincerity that the countess had invoked. (That these may be an even greater Folly to which to dedicate an evening she may have implied by her retirement.) Perhaps it is true enough to say that we danced, we drank, we smoked cigarettes, we talked, we observed the stars, the paper lanterns, the grotesqueries of our fellow-revelers—in much the same manner as before her invocation—until three o'clock in the morning. It is true that I removed my shoes and socks and danced barefooted on the lawn with Margaret, and that when, in the course of this experience, she raised her face to me with the spellbound delight of a child and said, "Oh, Mickey, aren't we having fun?" I felt positively golden-hearted with gratitude. This would have been evident, I think, to any sensitive observer; whereas nothing that occurred would have betrayed the fact that not ten minutes later, seated at the table in the center of a spirited discussion about the role of craft in art, my thoughts had nothing to do with the principles of Ruskin, Coquelin, or Hazlitt, nothing to do with aesthetics or divinity or the aspirations of the spirit, but with the burning realization only that Gwynyth, who sat chuckling and chewing alternately on a clove of garlic and a champagne cork, was wearing no underpants. That is the truth. Yet far from complying with the countess' injunction to publish this preoccupation in deeds or words, I continued in what I consider my very sensible efforts to keep it decently inconspicuous. A decision of a type with which some of you may be familiar, and all, I hope, in sympathy; it being the one upon which civilization is founded. After all, we are not responsible for our feelings, only for our behavior. In my case, these were still tolerably, if not eminently, distinct; Lack of Opportunity, that great expediter of virtue, had thus far kept them so.

That is the reason that I—again, like yourself, perhaps, on many an occasion—was able to go home from a party feeling powerful, refreshed, delighted with my own success and sufficiently uncompromised to be able to dismiss my imprudence as a forgivable and rather engaging dalliance which required no more in the way of expiation than a couple of aspirins and a good night's sleep. After all, what harm had there been done? No more than a party-kiss on a beach, given under the influence of champagne, moonlight, and paper lanterns; and if one were to judge humanity by the number of indiscretions of that magnitude committed annually one would have had to abandon all hope for it long ago. As for the future—that very remote and unlikely future when Opportunity should smile fully upon me—well, its very improbability dismissed it as a source of serious anxiety. The desire I had expressed to see her privately and the partial willingness she had indicated to accommodate me would, neither of them, withstand the harsh morning light of the Plage Passable on that indefinite and very casual occasion when, as she had "left it," we might see one another again. No; we would chuckle over a salami sandwich about our Midnight Cruise to Africa and the Incident of the Underpants, and dismiss them, as such carnival improprieties are regularly dismissed, by mutual consent and in the best of humor. All was well; and in the meantime I had made, for a middle-aged civil servant, a rather good showing. The fact gave me quite a glow. Far from guilt or apprehension, I found myself entitled to a certain amount of self-congratulation. It was not every man of my age and very modest status who could enjoy the attentions of a brilliant and beautiful actress of half his years. And quite unscathed. With dignity intact, all around. With Margaret unharmed.

We were gaily retrospective about our new friends, driving home through the moonlight.

"I think they're marvelous," she said. "I don't know if they're quite sane, of course; or quite respectable. But my goodness, how exciting they are! They're so interested in life, and so full of it. And so ingenious and articulate. I just wonder how long they can keep it up."

"Keep what up?"

"The way they live. I don't know quite what it is, but I'm sure it's very bizarre. Have you figured out their relationships yet?"

There was a moment of silence, dedicated to the expiration of my misbegotten sense of prosperity. Then I said, "No. I think they need a good bit more study than I've had time to give them yet. I have the feeling that they're pretty complicated."

"So do I. David and Yvonne seem to be pretty straightforward, but is Adrian with Gwynyth, or what? And who is Tessa?"

"I don't know. But I'll bet *she* does. She gives me the impression of being very careful about where she leaves her fingerprints."

"She does, doesn't she? I don't really care, of course. It's just a sort of luscious mystery, like everything else tonight."

"Everything but Andrea. He was luscious all right, but not much of a mystery."

"Oh, I don't know. He's poor, and proud; and poverty and pride have a great mystique about them."

"He isn't poor and proud. He's penniless and vain."

"Well, what's the difference?"

"I don't know; it just sounds a bit shabbier. There isn't any mystique about it."

"Oh, poor Andrea. Leave him something."

"I think he's had more than he deserves, already," I said.

"I wonder if he has," said Margaret.

In the villa, having removed the countess' gown, she hung it on the wardrobe door and stood staring at it.

"Now I'm a pumpkin," she said. "A common Kansas pumpkin."

"You're some pumpkin," I said. I came and stood behind her, circling her with my arms. She stood humbly, with the shy, almost penitent attentiveness of a woman who feels homage descending upon her with its warm diaphanous fall, like a fine mantle. I lowered my hands slowly, barely brushing her breasts, and clasped them lightly about her waist, feeling the flood and ebb of her breath under the cool white nylon of her slip. She stood patiently and humbly. I dropped my head against the bare flesh of her shoulder. After a moment she turned her head and pressed her cheek against my hair and said, "Why don't you go and make us some coffee, dear, while I'm getting undressed? I think we ought to have some before we go to sleep."

When we had drunk the coffee, in bed, by moonlight that fell through the open window, still chattering about the party, I reached out to take her hand and after lying for a long while in silence, felt her fingers loosen gradually, as she escaped me.

We sat drinking brandy after dinner on the quay at Villefranche, watching fireworks explode above the bay. A clown on a bicycle was riding around the stone-paved square, synchronizing his antics to the pyrotechnic bursts above him. There were crowds of people staring up into the sky, issuing soft multitudinous cries of awe as the showers of scarlet, blue, and silver sparks drifted down idly through the warm darkness. Each burst lighted the quay, the standing crowds, and the fishing boats riding gently at their moorings in the black water with a soft hectic glare; and because we had folded our umbrella to give us a better view of the display, it cast a strangely pulsing, weird illumination also on the littered table around which we sat: the scarlet shard of shattered lobster claws, the wine-stained tablecloth, the empty bottles, the crumbs of breadcrust, the pannikins of congealing liquid butter, the wilting, oil-drenched remnants of salad bowls. They took on, in that light, an extraordinary, accidental, devastated sort of beauty; a quality which, as a matter of fact, seemed to pervade the entire evening, and to which I yielded myself, with a kind of quiet drunken joy, as another of its picturesque, partially consumed, rapidly deteriorating elements. We had drunk Cinzano all afternoon on the beach, a Campari aperitif, several bottles of Châteauneuf du Pape with dinner, and now, brandy.

Gwynyth sat directly across the table from me. I tried to avoid letting my eyes linger upon her, but it was not easy to do. She had made herself exquisite for the evening in a clinging champagne-colored knitted dress, a pair of white bone earrings and a necklace of the same material which matched the porcelain gleam of her eyes in her tanned face, and a pair of straw-colored linen pumps out of which flowered her slender sunburned ankles. Nor was it made any easier by the memory of her wading through the sparkling shallows that morning at the Plage Passable, clad in a white bikini which barely concealed her small sharp breasts and not at all the swell of her brown belly, dusted with the faintest pollen of incandescent down.

"They're going to burn the boat now," Adrian said. We turned in our chairs to watch. At the right extremity of the harbor a group of shadowy figures carrying torches made their way along the stony beach to a point of rocks where a fishing dory tilted idly at her tether in the oil-dark calm water. One of the figures climbed into the boat and apparently doused her with kerosene, for we heard the clunking of a heavy can thumping against timber. There was a small ceremony; a priest in a white chasuble performed a consecration, holding up in the torchlight an ornate Gothic cross. Then a torch was flung into the dory; it burst instantly into clambering scarlet flames, was cut loose from its moorings, and set adrift. It must have been equipped with a small outboard motor of some sort, for it made slowly and steadily to sea, casting all across the harbor a wallowing carmine glare that stained the shining water and the faces of the watchers and the white plaster walls of the village houses. A chorus of cheers went up from the quayside, confetti was thrown, and paper horns honked stridently. We watched the floating pyre drift out into the dark sea, dwindling to a tiny scarlet flicker in the vast obscurity. Yvonne began to cry, pressing her napkin against her mouth. David pinched her on the ear.

"I can't help it" she said. "It's jolly moving. They're such simple people and they have such wonderful simple faith. It makes one go all soppy."

"Faith enough to put their money into jewelry and Swiss currency," said David. "Go into the *poisonnerie* tomorrow morning and buy a pound of haddock from that chap over there with the Turkish mustache; it's an even more moving experience, I can tell you."

"Oh, shut up, David. You're always making fun of my finer feelings. What does it matter, anyway, if one is mistaken about what he feels sentiment for? The important thing is to feel it."

"It's exactly that idea that makes it possible for there to be an organized church, at all. Also wars and pogroms and National Socialism. If one can't feel sympathy for the proper things it's a damn sight better not to feel at all."

"Oh, what rubbish. Suppose a woman refused to feel sentimental about a man until she was absolutely certain he was pure and noble and deserving. You'd be in a jolly bad way, wouldn't you?"

"By Jove, I never thought of it that way," said David. He seemed genuinely impressed. "Look here, you don't get more than one idea a year; why does it have to be some bloody upsetting thing like this?"

"It's gone out," Gwynyth said, staring out at the darkness which had engulfed the distant ember of the burning boat. "Has it sunk, do you suppose?"

"I should think so," Adrian said. "Someone used to bury their dead that way. The Vikings, wasn't it?"

"Yes," Margaret said. "I think that's a lovely way to be buried."

"There's no such thing as a lovely way to be buried," Adrian said.

"Well, I know, but you've *got* to," Yvonne said. "And you might as well do it in a fine poetic way like that. Margaret's right."

"Worms or fishes, something's going to eat us in the end," Gwynyth said. "It makes no odds to me."

"Of course some people get eaten by tigers," David said. "That's neater, I think."

Adrian leaned back in his chair and stared up at the sky. He was wearing a white linen suit and looked very elegant. "I shall never get used to these stars," he said. "They're quite different, you know, in Australia. Every time I look up at the sky here I get the feeling that something's gone terribly wrong. Everything been yanked awry up there, or something. Keeps one feeling a bit nervous."

Everyone turned his face upward involuntarily and studied the heavens in silence for a moment. Everyone but myself, who took the opportunity to study Gwynyth's own.

"It must," Margaret said. "How strange. It never occurred to me that you could miss stars."

Gwynyth lowered her eyes to mine and held them there in a steady expressionless gaze that scalded me.

"We have a cross, you know," Adrian said. "Blazing great cross hanging up there."

"Make you even more nervous, I should think," David said.

A warm night breeze blew lightly over us from the sea.

Gwynyth turned her face into it, drowsing her eyes. The crowd had dispersed from the quayside and was drifting about a low wooden platform covered with a mat of artificial grass, on which the members of a five-man band were removing their instruments from black cardboard cases in the light of a string of yellow paper lanterns. They were all workingmen, dressed in blue trousers, shirt sleeves, and berets, with red silk scarves knotted about their throats. One of them was already tuning his violin, seated on a folding chair with a bottle of wine between his feet. A girl at the edge of the platform flung a paper rose at him. He caught it and tucked it behind his ear, calling out coarsely and gaily to her. A group of young men and girls with their arms about one another's waists were prancing in a side-stepping circular dance, chanting the words of a folk tune as they swung recklessly across the stone paving of the quay. In the arched entranceways of the narrow cobbled streets that opened into the square there were couples and small groups leaning against the pale plaster walls of buildings, laughing and roistering in the shadows. There was a thrilling compound odor of damp stone, fish, wine, onion soup, and a hundred brands of cheap cologne.

Margaret wanted to walk through the town.

We wandered through the old streets in the darkness. They were lighted only by the glow through the louvered wooden blinds of deep-set narrow windows, and occasionally, a naked light bulb hung above a weathered wooden door. The town was built almost perpendicularly up the hillside and the streets were not really streets at all, but passageways, or alleys, too steep for any vehicle, paved with cobbles and mounting by successive flights of stone stairs that were hollowed smoothly at their centers by centuries of footfalls. The passages were so narrow in some places that one could touch the walls of both opposing buildings. We climbed them up the hillside, pausing sometimes to stand panting and look down over the tiled roofs to the dim starlit sea and the festive quay where throngs of dancers milled rhythmically in the soft light of the paper lanterns and the candles on the café tables. Far out on the water the tiny cluster of cabin-lights of a liner twinkled, in solitary passage toward Italy. While we watched, a star fell.

"Oh, look!" cried Yvonne; and we saw the sudden vermilion brush-stroke across the darkness.

"We must all wish," Margaret said. We stood in silence for a moment.

"Well, that'll take care of Mum," David said. "She can't say I haven't done my best for her, now."

"Oh, you've spoiled it," Yvonne said. "It'll never work, now you've told."

"Poor old soul. And just when I'd got her nicely fixed with a pension."

"I can't walk in these bloody shoes," Gwynyth said. She sat down on the steps to remove them, then went prancing ahead of us over the cobbles, yelping with delight. "Oh, that's wonderful! They're so marvelously smooth and cold, these stones." She turned to call back to us at a bend of the passageway, "I say, let's go and knock up Tessa."

"Don't you bloody well dare," said David. "Let's have one evening unmarred by thoughts of God and Duty."

"You're all beastly to her," Yvonne said. "That's the reason she wouldn't come tonight. She didn't have a headache, at all."

Margaret walked with me, our hands clasped loosely.

"Are you glad?" I asked.

"That we came? Yes." After several minutes she added, "I'll remember these nights."

"What did you wish?"

"That it would go on forever."

We ran down over the cobbles and dark stairs to the quay. Gwynyth stubbed her toe and collapsed, cursing, on the stone. We knelt about her to offer aid and comfort, but she would have neither.

"I'll carry you," David said.

"You'll not. Don't make such a bloody fuss. Just leave me alone."

She came hobbling behind us, carrying her shoes. We had another round of brandy, tossing back paper flowers that were flung onto our table by the dancers. The air was filled with them: blue and red and yellow puffs of rustling crepe paper, splashing everywhere.

"I should like to dance," said Adrian. He led Margaret to the square.

"Well, Gwyn's had it, so that leaves me only you," said David to Yvonne. "Come on, old girl."

"You have such charm," said Yvonne. "It's no wonder you're always cast as a fiend of some sort." They rose and disappeared into the swaying throng.

I sat staring recklessly at Gwynyth across the littered table. She stretched out her leg and set her foot on Margaret's vacant chair, bending forward to examine her toe. It was swollen and blue.

"What a bloody bore *this* is. I suppose I've broken it."

"Does it hurt?" I asked.

"It does, you know."

"You'd better soak it in Epsom salts and hot water when you get home. That takes a lot of the soreness out."

"I've not got any Epsom salts. *Or* hot water. There's not been any hot water in that hole since the day we arrived."

"Then I don't see any hope," I said.

She looked up at me and grinned. "So you've given up hope for me already. Are you like that about everything?"

"Not everything."

"I should hope not. I thought Americans were the eternal optimists."

We drank another glass of brandy each. I had not spoken to her alone since the night of the countess' party.

"Are you squiffed?" I asked.

"No, not yet."

"Good. I wanted to ask you something."

"Oh, did you? What?"

At the moment, I thought, she gave the least persuasive impression of a woman consumed by passion that I had ever seen. The tip of her cigarette had broken off in a glowing ember, and she was trying, with many little mincing expressions of frustration, to scoop it off the tablecloth with a teaspoon. She succeeded at last in depositing it on a bread-and-butter plate and poured a drip of brandy onto it from her glass in an effort to extinguish it. It burst immediately into capering blue flame. She started back with an expression of astonished delight.

"Good Lord; how exciting! I'd forgotten brandy was combustible."

"That's something you're very careless about."

"Do you think so?"

"It's very possible," I said, "that you'll leave this whole coast in flames behind you."

"If I do, it's because it was all tat and tinder to begin with."

"What's 'tat?'" I asked.

"Oh, all that junky, inflammable grandeur that they spread about on the stage when they're doing Shakespeare: painted palaces and alps and gardens and the rest of it. Trumpery."

"Well, that's very likely," I said.

"Not that I'd mind. I prefer a bucket of honest ash to all these tatty parliaments and palaces they've hung up all over the bloody landscape. I like wrecking things."

"You seem to be very good at it," I said.

"Yes. It's because I'm serious about it. You think I'm a wretched little mindless vandal, but I'm not. I don't destroy anything of value, or I try not. But I don't find that a very limiting scruple in this sort of a world. It could stand a good bath of flame, believe me."

"I didn't know you felt so strongly about it."

She looked up at me angrily. "No, I know. You didn't know I felt at all. The only thing you were wondering about was how tight a cunt I had. Well, let me tell you something: I've never in my life prostituted myself, which is a bloody sight more than most of the married women in this world can say."

"I didn't mean to offend you," I said.

"You respectable married bread-and-butter chaps give me a bloody pain occasionally," she said. "Mooning about hand in hand with your wives, murmuring your touching little devotions to them; and then larking off with the music hall girls the minute they've got their backs turned. Do you know what you get for nothing? Nothing. I should think you'd know that at your age."

"I don't want nothing," I said. "I'm sorry that's the impression you got. Why don't you just forget it?"

"Don't worry, it won't be difficult."

We sat in strained silence for some time. She gulped down the last of her brandy, refilled the glass, and then slowly separated the strands of yellow hair that fell across her forehead with a desolate little motion of her fingers. "Sorry. I may be just a bit squiffed, at that. Did you know I was raped once, by one of your chaps, in Greenwich Village?"

"My God," I said. "I'm sorry."

"Well, it's not your fault, I suppose."

We drank another glass of brandy each.

"Do you love your wife?" she asked.

"Yes."

"Do you get on well with her in bed?"

"Now how in the world can you expect me to answer that?" I asked.

"Well, perhaps you'd better, if you expect to get anywhere with me."

I raised my head to seek in silence for Margaret among the throng of dancers. After a moment I saw her, at the edge of the band platform, lifting her chin to laugh at one of Adrian's remarks.

"I like your wife, you know," Gwynyth said. "It's a funny bloody thing, but I seem to like everybody's wife that I go to bed with." She picked up one of the paper roses and tossed it high in the air, closing her eyes as it descended. When she opened them it lay in a coffee cup in front of her, as neatly as if placed there by hand. "All right, then," she said. "I'm going in to Cannes on Tuesday. There's a little family hotel there at the west end of the beach called the Atlantide, with a garden that runs right down to the avenue. I shall be sunning on the sand, just in front."

"When?" I asked.

"Oh, all morning. Unless Belmondo or somebody comes along and sweeps me off in a Ferrari."

"That gives me something else to worry about."

"Well, old son," she said, "if you want to stop worrying, you'd better stop living."

The music had stopped and Margaret and Adrian were making their way among the dancers to the table. I rose as they approached, to greet them with a smile.

"There's something the matter with the Citroën," I said to Margaret. "I think I'd better take it in to Nice in the morning and let them have a look at it."

"Oh, good," she said. "I want to get my hair done. You can leave me off at the coiffeur and pick me up on the way back."

"OK, fine."

We were having coffee on the terrace after dinner. It was still far from dark, and there were great flat panes of dusky, saffron-colored light dividing the pines of the forest behind our garden. To the left of the terrace, where the land bordered on the Chemin du Roy, a pair of nursery-aged children who lived in the villa opposite had invaded the garden and were crouched at the base of a mound of brown gravel, digging with tin spades and a brightly colored bucket.

"*Bonjour, enfants,*" Margaret called, waving her hand to them. The little boy stood up and waved his spade.

"*Bonjour, Madame.*"

"They love that gravel," Margaret said. It had been left from the landscaping operations of a previous tenant. I had been going to spread it on the garden paths, but Margaret would not let me, because the children enjoyed playing in it so. They came two or three afternoons a week, a little boy and girl, of four and five, in freshly laundered white playsuits and Buster Brown hats, to make tunnels and palaces and loaves of molded, damp fine pebbles. They had black hair and glittering brown eyes and the little girl wore tiny gold hoops in her pierced ears. The boy crouched down again and they went on digging, gossiping to each other in glasslike pealing voices, like the tinkling of wind-chimes.

"Aren't they adorable?" Margaret said.

"Yes."

The little girl was crouched in one of the panes of declining light, which shattered softly on her hair in many little chips of burnished topaz. Occasionally a strand of this dark, gem-littered hair would fall across her eyes, and she would raise her bare white arm, as slender, ivory-smooth, and moist as a branch of poplar from which the bark has been freshly peeled, and brush the hair away with the back of her wrist, her sandy fingers held daintily askew. They dug very earnestly, their delicate faces full of gravity and absorption.

"Suppose I have to leave it there?" I said. "You'll be stuck."

"Well, we can always take the bus back, can't we?"

"I suppose so. I don't know how often they run, though."

"Or a cab, then. I feel very extravagant today, anyway."

"OK. I thought I'd take it in early, so we'll still have some of the day left. How long will your hair take?"

"Well, about three hours in the States, so I'd say about four, here. Will you mind waiting all that time?"

"Oh, no, I'll find something to do. Maybe I'll take my trunks along and go for a swim."

"That's a good idea. Then we can have lunch together if I get through in time. I wonder if I ought to make an appointment?"

"Maybe you'd better," I said. "They're probably pretty busy this time of year."

"I think so, too. But, Lord, I hate using that telephone. Why don't you do it for me?"

"Oh, no; not me. I did the *Electrique* man last week; I'm still recuperating."

"All right, then." She sighed and rose, mumbling as she went in through the bead curtain, "Just what is a husband *for*? That's what I'd like to know." The beads swung tinkling for a moment after she had parted them, and in a moment I heard her speaking in the unnaturally high and harrowed voice in which we both attempted to communicate our needs by telephone. A blossom fell down from the bougainvillea arbor and landed lightly on the table. I picked apart the papery purple petals and blew them from my palm. Across the garden the little boy stood up and flung a handful of moist brown gravel into a rosebed.

"*Il pleut, alors!*" he cried.

"*Viens, petit,*" I called to him. He looked toward me uncertainly. "*Viens. J'ai un morceau de pâtisserie pour toi, pour tous les deux.*" They came running across the garden and up the terrace steps, their faces bright with shy, inquisitive expectancy. "*Regardez ça. C'est bon, n'est-ce pas?*" I pointed to a piece of French pastry iced with glazed sugar and almond slices.

"*Oui, Monsieur.*"

"*T'en veux?*"

"*Oui, Monsieur.*"

I sliced the pastry in half and set the halves on separate saucers, placing one in front of each child.

"*Merci, Monsieur,*" said the little boy. He lifted his slice from the saucer and began to nibble at it with a squirrel-like delicacy.

"*Mais moi, j'ai les mains sales,*" said the little girl, spreading her sandy fingers for me to see.

"*Oh, la la. Ça nous arrangerons tout de suite.*" I took her tiny hands and dusted them clean with a napkin, brushing the grains of moist sand from between her fingers. The exquisite little frail cool hands lay in mine as lightly as flakes of flint. I lifted and kissed them, feeling a ghostly tenderness toward the child.

"*Alors. Ils sont bien propres.*"

"*Merci, Monsieur.*"

She began to eat, her head tilted sideways, fastidiously and with a beautiful happy avidity, her temples hollowing and swelling with the movement of her jaws. A fine blue vein ran up her temple and forehead, disappearing into her smooth black hair. She smiled at me.

"*C'est bon, ça.*"

"*Oui, n'est-ce pas?*"

Margaret came out through the bead curtain and stood smiling. "*Ah, Monsieur vous a donné du gâteau, eh?*" she said.

"*Oui, Madame.*"

"I had to call three of them," she said. "Lord, what an ordeal. But I've got an appointment with someone named Charlus, of all things, for ten o'clock. At the Continentale. Is that all right?"

"Fine. That'll give us the afternoon."

The little girl had finished her slice of pastry and sucked the melted sugar from her fingertips with her pursed lips.

"*Tiens,*" I said, handing her the napkin.

"*Merci, Monsieur.*" She scrubbed her fingers, frowning with concentration.

"*Comment t'appelles-tu?*" I said to her.

"*Lisette.*"

"*Veux-tu me donner un baiser?*"

"*Oui, Monsieur.*"

She put her arms around my neck and clasped me tightly, kissing me on the cheek with warm, sticky lips.

"*Et toi?*" I said to the little boy. "*As-tu un baiser pour moi aussi?*"

"*Oui, Monsieur.*"

He embraced and kissed me also, very solemnly. I put my arms about him and held him against me for a moment, his small sun-warm head pressed against my throat. He smelled of bath talcum, freshly ironed cotton, and the hot fallow fragrance of child-breath.

"*Bon. Vous êtes très bons enfants. Allez-y.*"

"*Merci, Monsieur. Au revoir, Monsieur-dame,*" they cried, their voices chiming together.

"*Au revoir.*"

They went scampering down the terrace steps into the garden.

"What lovely children," Margaret said. "I love that sweet formality they have. It doesn't spoil their childishness at all."

"No. You ought to get out around one or two, then."

"I think so. Will that give you time enough, do you think?"

"Oh, it should. I don't think it'll turn out to be anything very serious."

At ten o'clock in the morning I let Margaret out in the circular driveway in front of the Continentale, with the agreement that we should meet in the lobby when we both were finished.

"If it gets too late, go ahead and eat," she said. "There's no sense in starving."

"All right. You too."

"I will. Good-bye, darling."

I kissed her on the forehead and she jumped out and ran up the steps, turning to wave to me as she entered the revolving door at the top. I drove out of the entranceway, along the Promenade des Anglais out of Nice and along the coastal road toward Cannes in the morning sunlight. It took me half an hour to reach the eastern end of the Croisette. The tamarisk trees along the sea were tossing in the morning breeze and the palms swayed gently against the white walls and balconies of the *grands hôtels.* I found myself beguiled by the luxury and exuberance of the street, the parade of expensive and exotic motor cars, glittering European convertibles with their tops down, inhabited by bronze-faced men and slender girls in sunglasses and clinging pastel-colored sports clothes, their sun-bleached hair blowing softly, breathing perfume and indolence and privilege as they presented themselves for envy and admiration; beyond them the bright red and yellow parasols and the brown sand of the beach and the hard blue morning sea; and on the crowded sidewalks, legions more of them, elegant, long-legged, cool, delicious people in sharkskin slacks, straw sandals, soft powder-blue and lemon-colored sweaters worn over bare brown chests or lively breasts, flickering in front of jeweled shop windows in which lay carelessly draped stoles of sable, emeralds scattered on white satin, jade figurines, black lace, and bracelets that glittered icily. The morning had the same intoxicating quality of luxury; the air was cool and sweet as sherbet; the green hedgerows, sprinkled with crystal; the soft clouds over the blue sea, voluptuous as ermine.

I was born slowly in the scintillating stream down the mile-long deluxe stretch of seafront, the grand hotels and expensive shop fronts and the promenading throngs dwindling gradually and yielding, in the shelter of a stone sea-wall at its western extremity, to a small municipal harbor where an atmosphere of the humble, the perennial, and the fundamental merged uneasily with the lees of the glamour of the Croisette. Here there were old-fashioned benches with cast-iron legs and arms set under gnarled plane trees on the stones of an ancient circular Place, and the nodding masts of yachts and fishing boats, berthed incongruously side by side, and old men in denim working clothes bowling in the sunlight on a space of thread-bare dusty turf. Beyond the Place the shore bent northward and the seafront became bourgeois; there were jumbled notion shops overflowing onto the sidewalks with rubber bathing sandals, beach balls, pneumatic mattresses, snorkeling gear, and portfolios of postcards; there were old modest family hotels, refreshment stands, and a long stretch of public garden with the straight, palm-lined boulevard between, running out of the city along the foaming edge of the blue sea. I found the Hotel

Atlantide and parked in front of the willow gardens which descended a hundred yards from its patio to the curb of the boulevard. On the beach there was a bathing pavilion where one could rent *pédalos*, parasols, and canvas chairs. Beside it a set of wooden stairs descended from the pavement to the sand. I went down them very deliberately, trying to limit the turbulence of my state of mind by counting them. There were eleven; a fact which did little to alleviate the turbulence. Beside the pavilion a group of young people had set up a net and were playing a noisy and exuberant game of volleyball. They had magnificent brown-skinned bodies, hard and lithe, clad in bright bikinis, and leaped and slapped at the leather ball with a ferocious animal joy, landing ankle-deep in the soft sand, their hair and jewelry flying. Apart from them there was a scattering of sunbathers, their bodies prone on beach towels in the white glare of the morning sun. My eyes roamed over them in a rapid, vehement way until they found Gwynyth, in her white bikini, lying on one side, propped up by an elbow, her face curtained by her hanging yellow hair, reading a book whose pages she held open with the spread fingers of her ragged-nailed, gnomish hands. I came and stood above her, my shadow falling across her on the sand. She looked up, rather solemnly.

"Oh, you've come, then, have you?"

"Did you think I wouldn't?" I said.

"I really didn't know."

She was wearing white-rimmed sunglasses, one of whose hinges had been broken and bound with flesh-colored adhesive tape. They had very dark lenses which concealed her eyes entirely. I sat down beside her on the warm sand.

"What are you reading?" I asked.

"*The Spy Who Loved Me.*"

"Is it good?"

"No, bloody awful. I found it in the Tube." She sat up, clutching her knees to her breasts, and stared at me. "I don't suppose you've brought any of that iced Cinzano along?"

"No. Shall I get some?"

317

"No, it doesn't matter. Did you have any difficulties?"

"Small ones," I said. "But not insurmountable, as you see."

"Yes. Still, it must have been a bind. You look just a bit haunted. You've not done a lot of this, have you?"

"No, very little."

She took her glasses off, squinted at me for a moment, then put them back on again. "So bright. How can you stand it?"

"I don't often wear them."

"No, I know. Funny, that."

"Why?"

"Well, most men never take them off anymore. Even at night. I d'know why, but that's one of the few affectations that drives me absolutely potty. Well, look here, had you anything in mind in the way of lunch?"

"No, I thought I'd leave it entirely up to you," I said.

"How'd you feel about a picnic, then?"

"Wonderful."

"I know rather a nice spot for one, just up the coast a mile or two, near Théoule. Do you know that place?"

"No."

"It's jolly nice there. There's a little private beach I know how to get to."

"Suppose we pick up a bottle of wine, then, and some bread and cheese? Or whatever you feel like."

"Lovely. Get away from these ruddy athletes." She stood and shook out the sand from the white chenille robe on which she had been lying, then laid it across her forearm, stepped into a pair of rubber bathing sandals, and bent to pick up a beach bag of woven raffia with circular plastic handles. Every step of this procedure filled me with an accelerating excitement, cold and fine as the *pétillance* that sprinkles upward from freshly poured champagne. We walked across the hot sand and up the wooden steps to the pavement, Gwynyth limping slightly.

"The toe still hurts," I said.

"Bit. Going down, though. I tried the Epsom salts, you know, and it was a jolly great help. I've got you to thank for that."

"I'm glad it worked." I took her arm and we scurried across the boulevard between the recklessly speeding cars.

"They're mad, these people," she said. "Automobiles are like alcohol to them. It's an absolute fact. I think the smell of petrol crazes them or something." I closed the door for her, got into the Citroën, and drove off the main boulevard up one of the narrow side streets to an *épicerie* where we bought a loaf of bread, a half pound each of pâté and blue cheese, and two bottles of dark-red Epernay which Gwynyth chose in a swift, impatient way. I also bought a paring knife and a corkscrew. While we drove, she opened one of the bottles, setting it on the floor and clutching it between the soles of her feet while she bent forward to draw the cork out with a liquid popping sound. She took a long drink of the wine and held the bottle toward me.

"Will you have some?"

"Not right away, thanks."

"God, that's lovely. I shall be drunk before you can count to ten; I've had nothing to eat but chocolate and one of those wretched croissants." She wiped her lips with the back of her hand and unscrewed the cork from the corkscrew, returning it meditatively to the neck of the bottle. "Do you eat a lot?" she asked.

"No, I don't think so."

"That's good. I can't stand people who're always thinking about food. I don't know why. It's the only sort of appetite that disgusts me. I don't mind if they drink themselves to death; it's just that constant shoving of food down one's gullet that puts me off."

"People are seldom at their best, eating," I said. "I've only known one who was."

"Isn't it the truth. When are they at their best, do you think?"

"I don't know. Listening to music, I suppose. Or reading. Or looking at things they find beautiful. There's a lovely humble look that comes into their faces. Absorbed. Outside of themselves. It's a look children have when they're playing."

"Yes, I know what you mean exactly. I've got a little brother, and I used to love to watch him making model airplanes. Such a sweet look he had. I'd sit in a corner with a book and pretend to be reading, and just watch his face. It leaves most of the films you see nowhere at all." She had another drink of wine. "Then, of course, you go into a restaurant and see some clod staring at a chunk of steak on the end of his fork."

"Yes. You'll let me know where to turn, won't you?"

"Yes. It's a good way. Just carry on for a bit." She stared out at the sea that swept by in unvarying sameness between the even-spaced trunks of the royal palms. "It's extraordinary, you know; I hate people, really, if I stop to think about it. And then if I don't stop to think about it, I find myself doing something like this. It's dotty, isn't it? Are you like that, at all?"

"I don't know," I said. "I don't really know very much about myself, apparently."

"Nor do I. And what I do know I'm jolly well unimpressed with. That's what's so bloody depressing, you know. I think I'm as good as most, and if that's the case, then we're in bloody bad shape, the lot of us." She held the bottle toward me again. "You'd better have some of this, hadn't you?"

"All right." I took the bottle in one hand and tilted down a mouthful of the cool bitter wine. It plunged down me like a bolt of acid. She laughed at my expression.

"What's the matter, don't you like it?"

"It's a little early in the day for me." I handed back the bottle and smiled at her. "When you laugh, you're an entirely different person."

"Yes, I know," she said. "I hate being angry all the time. And that's what people don't understand, at all. They think you're having a hell of a time, showing off or something. 'Being different,' as they call it. But what the devil is one to do: sit around talking about Mummy and God and Country, like the rest of them? I mean to say, you've got to be angry, haven't you; or you've got no self-respect left, at all."

"Don't you think you could manage to relax just a little, once in a while?" I said. "I think you'd be forgiven."

"Oh, now you're getting bloody patronizing again."

"No, I'm not. It's pure selfishness. I just want to hear you laugh more often."

"Go to blazes." She lifted the bottle to her lips again and at that moment I struck a piece of broken brick that had fallen from a truck onto the center of the boulevard. The wine splashed from the neck of the bottle onto her naked belly; she cringed and yelped with the shock of it.

"Sorry," I said. "There's a Kleenex in the glove box."

"I don't want a Kleenex. I'm going to rub it in." She did so, massaging her taut, sun-browned belly with the flat of her hand. "Oh, that's lovely. An alcohol rub."

"You'll stain your suit," I said.

"Well, the cold water'll take it out. We'll have a swim." She chuckled happily. "I've got an absolute navel-ful of it. I say, have you ever drunk wine from a girl's navel?"

"No."

"Would you like to try?"

"Not just at the moment," I said. "Or it'll be the last experience I ever have."

"Well, it would be rather a high note to go out on, don't you think?"

"Yes, it would; but I think we ought to stop somewhere short of total extermination," I said.

"Oh, do you?"

We had come now to the end of the formal boulevard, leaving Cannes behind, and the road departed from the immediate seacoast and began to climb the terraced green foothills of the Alpes Maritimes, winding upward in ascending loops between sprinklings of villas and deep folds of vegetation that were the soft bruised blue of grapes in the morning haze that lay upon the mountains. At every outermost bend of the loops we came above the sea and looked down over the tops of pines to the deep violet water, dark in the shadows of the hillsides, and beyond them, glittering in the sun.

"Have we got much farther to go?" I asked.

"Not a lot, no. A couple more bends, I think. There's an empty villa on the left, called Port l'Escale. You'll see the shutters on the windows and a sign in front that says *A Louer*. Just turn in the driveway and go right to the end."

"How do you happen to know this place?" I said.

"Andrea brought me." She turned to look at me fully after a moment of silence. "I hope you've not got any sentimental compunctions about that."

"I haven't got time for them right now," I said.

"Ah, well, that's very sensible. Perhaps we owe more to haste than we realize. It's only the fact that we're in such a bloody hurry through this world that keeps the humbug from being laid on even thicker than it is."

I laughed and turned to watch her take another long drink of wine, her throat rippling beautifully. She sucked the stain from her lips and scowled. "It's a good thing human beings aren't guaranteed immortality, or they'd be absolutely intolerable."

"On the other hand," I said, "haste may be what gets us into so much trouble."

"What sort of trouble? You don't look to me like a man who's been in very much real trouble."

"Well, I don't suppose I have. Not what you'd call trouble, anyway. Have you?"

"Oh, I don't know. I've been raped, I've had two abortions, I've had tuberculosis, and I've had all sorts of idiots falling in love with me all my life and threatening to jump off monuments and things. The usual amount, I suppose."

"I'd call that a little better than average," I said. I took my eyes from the road long enough to study her delicate figure with involuntary wonder. "How on earth have you managed to survive?"

"I'm tough," she said. "Just double your fist up."

"Why?"

"Hit me in the stomach, if you like."

"I haven't the slightest desire to hit you in the stomach."

"No, I mean it. Go ahead. You'll see." She tensed her abdomen and turned toward me defiantly. I clenched my fist and struck her lightly on the firm brown flat of her midriff; my fist bounced away as if striking cork. "There, you see. I can take a jolly sight of punishment, whether you believe it or not. I don't intend to go under for a good while yet."

"I don't think you will," I said.

"No, you can bet on it. Not till I've had my way."

"What is your way?"

"I'm not sure yet," she said. "I'm just working it out."

"Well," I said with great sincerity, "I'm glad it has included me."

"Don't be sure of that, either."

I saw the villa ahead of us, its red tile roof rising behind a blue stucco wall and a pair of blazing scarlet *flamboyant* trees. There was a rental sign fixed to the wall, with the words À LOUER and the name of an estate agency. The driveway was overgrown with waist-high grass and wild orange poppies.

"Is this the place?" I asked.

"Yes. Go right the way in and park at the back, by the guest cottage. You'll see it."

I turned into the unkempt yard, seeing that the huge wooden gate had fallen from its hinges and collapsed inward, breaking into weather-bleached debris. A pale gray cat fled through the grass, turning to look at us with burning fugitive eyes. I drove past the boarded-up villa to a small guest cottage at the rear and parked it in the hub-deep grass under a eucalyptus tree. We got out and stood looking at the silent, sunlit villa. It was like a small Moroccan palace.

"I think we ought to take the place," I said.

"Wouldn't I just love to. Look at that verandah." It ran the width of the villa's front, soaring out above the tops of the pines that fell almost perpendicularly to the sea. "Andrea and I climbed up there one day. You can see all the way to Nice. It's really breathtaking."

"Why do you suppose it isn't rented?"

"It belongs to some American millionairess widow who's very particular about her tenants. I actually called up about it. She wants something like eight hundred pounds a month. I asked how much by the afternoon, and they hung up on me. Bloody rude, I thought."

"Where is the beach?"

"Just down that path, through the pines. You've got the lunch?"

"Yes. Suppose someone comes and sees the car?"

"Well, they're not likely to come down to the beach. But if they should, we can always say we're looking for a little place for the holidays and wanted to have a look round. After all, it is for rent."

"All right, go ahead. I'll follow you."

She made her way through the tall grass of the yard and into the cool gloom of the pine forest that bordered it. We went down a narrow needle-carpeted path between the trees toward the welling and waning murmur of the surf below. The brown needles were slippery and the path so steep that I slid once and fell, landing on an elbow and clutching the parcel of food to my breast.

"Are you all right?" Gwynyth asked.

"Yes."

"You're not to spill the wine."

"I appreciate your concern," I said.

She laughed. "So you've got some vanity, after all. I'm so glad."

We went down cautiously, clinging to branches and tree trunks to brake our plunging descent. We saw now the deep blue of the sea between the pines, and in a moment came out of the forest and onto a knoll of boulders sprinkled with brown pine needles and packed all around their edges with dark, moist, spongy mold. In front of us lay a tiny private beach, a little basin of brown sand, walled at one end with a stone jetty and at the other with a sheer shoulder of hillside, silent, dense, pine forest, and gray boulders. The indigo water broke gently along the rim of the little beach, bubbling on the sand. Three shore birds of some kind, pipers or turnstones, ran swiftly along the edge of lapsing foam in a stiff-legged mechanical scurry, like wind-up toys of painted tin. Far out on the water a sailboat drifted toward Cannes, heeled sharply in the morning breeze. There was a smell of pine, salt, hot stone, and iodine, a smell of warm, primordial cleanliness, of elements freshly minted out of nothingness, almost like the smell of new-baked bread, hot virgin loaves of reality. Gwynyth stood breathing it in with a drowsy, rabid look of pleasure, a look almost of fatigue.

"Oh, Jesus," she said. "Do you know one of the lines of poetry that I really do love? One of your chaps wrote it: Robinson Jeffers. 'No matter what happens to men, the world's well made, though.' "

"This piece of it certainly is," I said.

"God, when I think of the Mersey: oil slicks and beer cans and turds and bits of floating corsets. And you don't dare even breathe in London anymore, the air's so full of poison. God, sometimes I wonder if we'll ever really beat those bastards down. We will, though, you know; we'll dance at their bloody wake."

"Whose wake?" I asked.

"All the bastards who're systematically blowing up and polluting our world for profit and power. It *is* ours, you know, just as much as theirs; though they've got the idea that they have exclusive title to it somehow." She sat down on the boulder and uncorked her wine bottle, staring with a kind of bitter pensiveness at the sea. "Do you know, when I was going to RADA I let one of those chaps take me down to Bournemouth for a weekend once, and I thought I was in heaven." She took a long drink of wine and finding that she had emptied the bottle, set it carefully on the stone beside her. "I'll tell you one thing: I'll never have another abortion. That's the only place I've gone really wrong, so far. That was truckling to them." Her face constricted slightly with the pain of shame. "That's the only thing I've ever done that was against nature. I cry about it sometimes. Honestly. Of course I was only a kid, and you get so scared, you know."

I sat down beside her and began to unwrap and lay out on the boulder the cheese and pâté and to slice the long loaf of French bread with the paring knife. She watched me idly, saying in a moment, "I'll get them for that; scaring me into doing a thing like that. God, I've so bloody much to settle."

"You're getting unhappy," I said. "You'd better stop talking about it."

"No, I'm not. Let's have the other bottle." I handed it to her. "Pity we only got the two."

"It's because we were in such a hurry," I said. "I told you haste led to misfortune."

"Yes, I know." She laughed, showing her white teeth. "I rather like you. You've got a nice decadent side to you that makes you interesting. Is that awfully common in the government of the United States?"

"I'm not really in the government," I said. "I can't speak for them."

"I thought you were in the Library of Congress."

"Yes, but it's fairly independent. We're not under Civil Service."

"Oh." She hugged the bottle between her thighs and tugged out the cork with a pleasant plop. "What does that mean? There's so much I don't know. God, I don't know hardly anything."

"Well, it means that we don't have to take their examinations or meet their requirements for employment or promotion, and several other minor technicalities."

"Oh." She cocked her head at me attentively. "That sounds rather a good thing."

"Yes. Listen, I wish you'd take those glasses off. I like to see your eyes."

"Do you? Well, it's so beastly bright, and I can't stand the light. Oh, yes, that's something else I forgot to tell you: I've got a wonky left eye. I got a draft in it, once, that made it go all wrong."

"How did that happen?" I asked.

"Well, there was this swimming bath in Hampstead where I used to go, and it had a row of wooden booths all round, where you changed. Someone had cut a hole in the side of one of them, and I was forever peeking through the wall to watch the boys undress. So I got this fearful cold in my eye, from the draft or something."

"You seem to have been thwarted at every turn," I said.

"Oh, it was worth it. I learned a lot, looking through that ruddy hole, I can tell you."

I spread a slice of bread with pâté and held it toward her. "Don't you think you'd better have a bite to eat?"

"Yes, I suppose I'd better. It's a good thing to have a bit of bread in you, I find, when you're drinking. Thanks." She took the slice of bread and began munching at it meditatively, her eyes on the burning blue horizon. "What sort of a man was Jeffers?" she asked. "Do you know anything about him?"

"Not a lot. He was a very lonely man, I guess. He built a house with his own hands, out of stone, on the coast of California, and spent most of his life there. I think he refused to send his children to the public schools or something. He only died very recently."

"Yes, I know. I saw an article about it. That's what made me look up some of his poems. I wasn't able to find much, though; just one or two bits in anthologies. I was down in this wretched little Midland town, in rep, and they hadn't much of a library. He seems to be one of your forgotten men, doesn't he?"

"Yes. He was never very popular. It isn't hard to see why."

"No, it isn't. I read that one called 'Shine, Perishing Republic.' I don't suppose that sort of thing goes down too well with your chaps."

"No."

"God, I thought it was marvelous. Do you know that bit where he says, 'Meteors are not needed less than mountains'? Lovely, that. Sort of a Jacobean ring to it. Do you like Jacobean things?"

"Yes, very much."

"Oh, you must come to London. We've got it all, there. Buildings, bedposts, breastplates, poison-boxes. I used to love going round the Victoria and Albert Museum on a rainy afternoon. There's a lovely musty, sweet smell in there, half rot and half perfume, from the tapestries and costumes and pomanders that ladies used to swing between their thighs with rose petals in them. It's funny, you know: I'd come out of there feeling so jolly good, so full of life, so confident, or something. How do you suppose that comes about?"

"I don't know."

"And then you go in one of these crashing great modern places like Festival Hall and feel as though you'd been in a fridge all night. No nourishment about it. I like a few potty old cupboards, I suppose, and a bit of dust and rubbish about. Not quite as much as the Mersey, of course." She lifted the bottle and drank, then passed it to me. "What it comes down to is that we're very much like garden plants, I suppose; you've got to spread a certain amount of dung about, if you expect them to do well; but on the other hand you've got to keep them cultivated. Roots in the dung and flowers in the air. I just wish one or two of them would realize that they'll have no flowers to cut unless the roots are jolly well fertilized. Still, they'd rather have that plastic rubbish about, I suppose. No mess involved, no odor, and no pollen to annoy them." She grinned at me. "Pollen, you know, is a bloody great inconvenience."

"You're a philosopher," I said.

"No fear. I'm a bloody, mad, tough Mile Ender with a bellyful of wine." She stood up and stretched, snarling with pleasure and plunging her elbows into the sky. "I've got to go and scrub my suit before this stain sets, or I shall be out forty shillings. Mind you leave me a bit of wine."

"I will."

She leaped off the boulder and into the soft sand, falling onto her hands and knees, then rose and ran across the twenty yards of beach to the shiny dark-brown lip of moist strand, howling and hopping.

"God, it's hot!" She sat down in the foam of the gentle surf and tugged her feet into her lap, examining their soles. "I've cooked my bloody feet." She splashed water onto them from her cupped hands, then rose and waded out into the sea until she stood waist-deep; there she crouched down, wriggled out of her bikini pants, and began to wash them vigorously, swinging them about in the water and scrubbing them with her knuckles.

"How are you doing?" I called to her.

"Not awfully well; they won't come clean."

"Try scouring them with sand."

"Oh. All right." She crouched down to dig up a handful of sand from the bottom and tried this, rubbing them briskly for a moment, then dipping and rinsing them. "That's a bit better. It'll have to do, anyway." She lowered the pants into the water and wriggled back into them, falling down backward in the process and disappearing entirely for a moment in a splash of white foam. She rose, drenched, her wet hair clinging to her shoulders in slick bright strands, and came galloping up through the shallow water to the sand, panting and screeching. "Blimey, it's wonderful! Why don't you come in?"

"Not right away. You come out."

"Shall I? All right, then." She ran back across the sand to the boulder and climbed up it, leaving wet hand- and foot-prints on the gray stone. She sat beside me, panting, smelling of wet hair and salty skin. She dug her fingers into her drenched hair and scattered it loose in the sun, sprinkling me with fine cool droplets. Her brown skin glittered. "God, I love water. Isn't it marvelous? Do you know, I read somewhere that the temperature band in the universe where water can exist as water—I mean not as ice or gas, but as liquid—is so tiny that it's practically infinitesimal. One million billion trillionth of the total area, or something like that. And here we happen to have arrived right bang in the middle of it. We're bloody lucky, don't you think?"

"Yes," I said. "In many, many ways."

Her eyes stilled and she lowered and folded her hands together and looked at them rather shyly for a moment. "No, don't put me on. I mean we're so *bloody* lucky to be here, at all, and to have this lovely water to splash about in; and we're missing it all, you know. We haven't time to appreciate it, we're so bloody busy learning the rules. And then groaning and beating our breasts because we find out we've got them all wrong. We ought to spend every ruddy minute we have praising the Lord, and all we do is sit about poking our fingers in our eyes so we can't even see where we are."

"You believe in the Lord, then?"

"Oh, well, no; not properly, I suppose. Not the way most people *claim* they do, at any rate. And still, I feel I ought to thank *someone*, you know; and who else is there to thank? I mean I'd like my life to be sort of a picture postcard addressed to Him, saying, 'Arrived safely. Having wonderful time. Wish You were here.' I don't suppose that makes much sense, does it?"

It made such a great deal of sense that I could think of no way to acknowledge it but to lean toward her and kiss her cool lips. She closed her eyes and dropped her wet head against my shoulder.

"There you are, you see. That's what I mean."

We did not move for several moments. A wonderful lucid fire was exchanged between us; something her words had been unable to communicate. She disengaged herself gently and stood up on the rock to strip herself out of her bikini pants, balancing first on one leg, then the other. Stamped onto her slender, sun-browned loins was a pair of ghostly, duplicate bikini pants of white, untanned skin. The bright golden hair of her mound sparkled with moisture in the sunlight. She crouched and leaped down onto the needle-matted earth behind the boulder, her thighs tightening to receive the impact, furrowing between their long flexed muscles with a beautiful plastic suavity under the tea-colored skin. She unfastened her brassiere and dropped it on the needles. Her small white breasts against her sunburned torso had a look of startling, double nudity; pearl-colored, cool, and as perfectly symmetrical as melon-halves. She was a strange particolored little jeweled figurine, half common chocolate-colored quartz, inset with precious sections of milky opal.

"Come down. Throw me the towel."

I did so, and gathered her against me: wet, blazing hair; slick shoulders; stippled, slippery, caramel-colored ribs; little swelling buttocks, hard and cool as alabaster. We spread the towel on the needles and lay in the lee of the boulders in the sunlight with the gentle wash of the Mediterranean below us and the cool breathing of the pines above. Her lovemaking had an astonishing simplicity about it; it was very much like the water she admired. It washed us quickly clean with a cool, elemental sort of congruity, like the gentle sovereign surge of the Mediterranean surf. There was nothing elaborate or ungoverned about it, which surprised me greatly, for I had expected an element, at least, of the ire and distemper of her personality. But here was a startling Orient delicacy and profundity and immemorial orderliness, like that of the sea, that laved, excited, and restored me, giving me intimations of a perpetuity and excellence of things to which only talent is capable of introducing us. I never saw Gwynyth act, and have to accept the assurance of those who had that she was very talented at it; but I have no doubt whatever as to what her greatest talent was. Talent, of course, is a very different thing from skill; that the two sometimes appear in concert is a testament to the zeal of the academy, but no proof of their synonymity. As a matter of fact, simple sexual skill, devoid of this delicacy and profundity of which I speak, would strike me as being one of the most offensive forms of virtuosity one could experience, and far from being dangerous or inflammatory, productive largely of moralists and celibates. A man might be expected to flee from its consequences—as he would from a burn, a wound, or any other type of affliction—considerably more cautious and discriminating than before his exposure to them; but I can't imagine him being enchanted or addicted. There may, of course, be certain pathological exceptions, but I don't think that people on the whole enjoy the affliction, abuse, or loss of dignity involved in the conscription of their bodies, minds, or spirits; and I hope it is understood that in this respect, at least, I do not consider myself to have been victimized. I do not believe Gwynyth to have been a criminal or a madwoman: she did not have victims. She was an artist: she had beneficiaries. Now this is not to say that these beneficiaries may not be badly shaken men; indeed they almost necessarily will be, just as anyone who stands before a Michelangelo statue and has a full, pristine experience of it will be a shaken man. His immediate interest in ordinary social tasks, and his capacity to perform them, may be a bit diminished, and his future behavior, a bit less predictable; this is inconvenient for society, no doubt, but indispensable to civilization. Which seems to convict me of the somewhat meretricious conclusion that Gwynyth was indispensable to civilization, too. And yet perhaps she was, and is. Perhaps, in either case, it is not the artist who is at fault, but the man who, confronted by his revelations, is capable of being demoralized by them. The artist does his work of intensifying, penetrating, and illuminating life; if mischief results, the indictment for it must be lodged, perhaps, in other quarters.

From the mischief that resulted in my case, therefore, I exonerate her (with the uncomfortable impression of hearing someone murmur, 'How very good of you,') and assume it as my own; *mea culpa*. I was not equal to her artistry. Whether she began her work of civilization upon me too late or too soon, I am unable to decide; as I was forty-one years old at the time, and an American, I think it may very possibly have been a bit of both.

In this shaken state, I sat, leaning against a boulder, and shared a cigarette with her, gazing through its pale violet fumes at the extraordinary world in which I found myself.

"Bloody ants," she said, slapping at her ankle and then scrubbing it vigorously with her ugly little fingertips. She looked up at me and chuckled. "I think perhaps we ought to move; we're attracting insects."

I was not surprised, the honey of her loins being spread so liberally about our nest of needles.

"Adders, more likely," I said.

"Oh, God, don't be Jewish."

"Jewish?"

"Oh, that solemn, philosophical Jewish humor. They try and get the whole of the Old Testament into every wisecrack."

"You don't like Jews?" I asked.

"I don't like anybody."

"Well, for a misanthrope," I said, "you certainly spread around a lot of good cheer."

She stood up and swung one naked leg across my shoulders, straddling my neck. "Come on, get me out of this. Can you stand up like that?"

"I doubt it very much."

"Oh, yes, you can. Actually, for a man of your age, you're not at all badly built, you know. Come on, I want a London bus ride."

I rose, rather unsteadily, bracing myself against the boulder with one hand, and stood, double-decked, with her brown legs hinged across my shoulders and her toes clasped firm against my back.

"That's it. There, you see. Now, right down to the water,

please." I carried her, staggering a little in the soft hot sand, down toward the shimmering blue sheet of the sea. "My dad used to walk me up and down Bournemouth Strand like this, stark naked, when I was a poppet. 'Come on,' he'd say, 'let's have a London bus ride, up the Strand. Upstairs you go.' Then he'd snatch me up and pop me onto his shoulders and walk me right up the shingle, tugging my toe and going, 'Ding! ding!' for the starting-bell, you know, with my mother screaming it was bloody indecent the whole time. God, I loved my dad."

"He was a butcher, you said."

"Yes. He had a shop just up the street from where I went to nursery school, and I'd run in every afternoon and hug him right round the legs and put my face right into his bloody apron; *literally* bloody, you know." She chuckled. "I guess that's how I got to love the smell of blood. I never associated it with eating, at all. It was just a sort of perfume that my dad smelled of. It's a bloody good smell, blood." She clenched my hair to steady herself, lurching suddenly backward as absorption in her recollection made her careless of her balance. "Do you know the part I always really longed to play? Hotspur. God, I did it marvelously when I was ten or twelve. I had the whole thing memorized, you know. I made him just like my dad: all smeared with raspberry jam, for blood; Northumberland accent, the lot. I'm going to play it yet, one day. After all, Bernhardt did Hamlet, so why shouldn't I?"

"I can't think of any possible reason," I said. We had reached the water, for which I was very grateful, for the soles of my feet were on fire. I waded in to my waist, then leaned forward, the two of us collapsing slowly, like an undermined totem pole, then, with gathering momentum, crashing down full-length, with a tremendous splash and cry of joy from Gwynyth, into the cool delicious lubricity of the blue water. She plummeted up out of it almost instantly through a shower of shattered crystals, glittering like a seal, her mouth a great red O of astonishment and delight.

"God, how wizard!" She seized me by the head, leaped up, and plunged me down until my forehead grated against the bottom, then trod on my neck and pushed herself away with a shove that ground my face into the sand. She crouched, grinning, up to her chin in the water, and watched me rise, gasping and tossing my head to clear my bubbling ears.

"You're a pretty rough customer," I said.

"Oh, you can expect no mercy from me. Come on, I'll race you to the jetty."

She swam ahead of me, with very little style but strongly and swiftly, her brown arms flashing like lacquer and her lovely little white bottom rolling through the splashing water of her wake. I had no desire at all to outdistance her. We clung to the stone wall, panting, and I kissed her wet face.

"My God, you're lovely," I said. I stared at her delicate, drenched, grinning face with a growing gravity.

"All right. You'd better let it go at that."

She pushed off from the wall and began to kick back lazily toward the shore, floating face up, her arms drifting, her yellow hair streaming in liquid sheaves. At the shore she rose and stood ankle-deep in the sheet of sparkling undertow that flew down over the smooth yellow sand, her bright wet body tilting backward as her heels were undermined, giggling at this experience. We ran up across the hot sand to the ledge of rocks and clasped the white, warm, puffy, sun-sweet towels against our faces and our chilled bodies, a sensation of infinite luxury and cleanliness. She struggled into her wet bikini, mincing and squeaking.

"God, that clammy thing. Like crawling into a fish-skin."

I buttoned my collar idly, dreaming of Eden, watching her toss her yellow hair in the white towel. She wrapped her chenille robe about her and sat down to smoke a cigarette. We looked at the sea. There was a little wine left, which we shared in sips, silently. Once, abstractedly, she bumped her teeth against the glass neck and drew her chin away sharply, scowling and saying, "Ouch. Ass."

"You look very happy," I said.

"Oughtn't I to be? I've got wine, water, sunlight, I've been jolly well screwed, and I've had the chance to run about naked for a bit. There's not a lot more that a girl could ask for."

"Still, people do," I said.

"Lord, don't I know it. My sister, for example. She's spent the last twelve years of her life trying to accumulate an eight-place setting of Louis XIV silverware, and she won't be happy till she gets it. Bloody fool. She's got a brain, too. That's what they're afraid of, you know: that if we do much of this sort of thing we'll lose interest in the wretched trinkets they're forever trying to sell us. Let down the old economy."

"But if we did," I said, "do you suppose anyone would ever do any work?"

"Work? Do you think I don't do my share of work? I played fortnightly rep for three years when I got out of RADA. Do you know what that means? Playing every night but Sunday and two matinees a week, and rehearsing all day for the new show that goes on in a fortnight. I'm just waiting for one of those corporation bastards to tell me something about work. *Or* morality."

"I don't think I'd want to be the man who does," I said.

"No. I'm my own bloody woman, and don't you forget it. I'd no more let one of them pay my way than I'd let one of them stamp his brand on me: his name, or title, or any of the rest of it. I've got just one chance at this universe: sixty or seventy years, if I'm lucky; and that's it. That's the lot. Do you think I'm going to waste it sitting about telling a lot of idiotic lies, or nodding and saying 'yes' to theirs? Not on your life." She finished the wine and tilted the bottle upward to catch the last few drops in her mouth, gaping like a goldfish. "Lovely stuff. What's the time? Ought you to be getting back?"

"Yes. It's after one."

"Right. I'll pack it up." She gathered together the empty bottles and scraps of cheese and breadcrumbs, rolling them into the sheet of brown paper. "There's a lovely bit of pâté left. I'll just take that along with me and have it for elevenses in the morning. No point in wasting it."

"No."

"Will you give me a lift back to Villefranche?"

"I wish I could," I said, "but Margaret's waiting for me in the Continentale in Nice. She's been at the hairdresser's all morning."

"My God. Really? That's cutting it a bit thin, isn't it?" She stared at me thoughtfully for a moment. "Look here, there's only one thing I insist on, about all this, and that's that no one's to get hurt. You understand that, I suppose?"

"Yes."

"I'm quite serious, you know. It wouldn't be worth it, otherwise."

"I know."

I took up her beach bag and the damp towels and we climbed back up the path through the pines to the villa. We paused at the top and looked down over the blue water.

"It's been rather a nice morning," Gwynyth said. "You were really very good for me. Thanks."

"Thanks to you."

We spoke hardly at all in the automobile. When we reached Cannes I said, "I'll take you on as far as Nice. There's a bus stop right across from the Ruhl, I think. Will that do?"

"Yes, lovely."

As we came into Nice I asked, "Can I see you again?"

"If you like."

"When?"

"When's the best for you?"

"Next Tuesday at the same time?"

"All right. I'll be there."

"If I can't make it, you'll understand?"

"Oh, yes. I don't get hysterical very easily."

I drew up to the curb along the Promenade des Anglais.

"Let me get you a cab to take you back to Villefranche," I said.

"Don't be an ass; it's a bloody extravagance. The bus will do perfectly."

"I'd feel better if you did."

"No. Look here, don't start being gallant, and all that rubbish. That's not what I'm after, you know." She jumped out of the Citroën and ran across the pavement to the bus stop, where she turned to wave to me and called, *"Ciao."*

"Ciao."

I drove on along the boulevard until I found a parking space across the street from the Continentale. I parked the Citroën, rented a *cabine* on the beach, changed into my swimming trunks, and for half an hour bathed and sat on the stony shingle in the sun. Then I changed back into my clothes, rolled my wet trunks into the towel, tossed them into the back seat of the Citroën, crossed the boulevard, and went up into the hotel lobby, where I bought a copy of the *Illustrated London News* and sat down in front of the Salon de Beauté to wait for Margaret.

They had done her hair in the bouffant style that was popular at the time, and it became her wonderfully, although it took me the better part of the afternoon to recognize the fact. It is a highly unnatural style, and when one is first witness to a familiar and beloved countenance in the transforming folds of art there is a period of considerable discomfort and indignation before one is able to concede that distortion sometimes has the power to enhance. Although my full conversion to the fact was still some while away, I lied successfully.

"Hey, they did a great job on you," I said. "It looks wonderful."

"Are you sure? I'm not at all. I feel sort of violated, or something. But I'm glad you think so." She touched the great airy tumulus of her coiffure with her fingertips and made a little creaky grimace of uncertainty. "I'm sorry I'm so late. Have you waited long?"

"No, not half an hour," I said.

"I thought they'd take forever. Have you eaten, darling?"

"Yes. I had a sandwich on the beach."

"Oh, that's good. They brought me one, too, under the dryer. Did they fix the car all right?"

"Yes. It was just the generator bracket; it didn't take very long. I went down to the beach afterward and had a swim for about an hour."

"Was it nice?"

"No. It's all stones here. But I watched the bikinis parading around, so it wasn't too bad."

"Well, now you can just buy me a martini for that."

"That's a deal. The most expensive martini in town. How about right here, in this Bar d'Algérie place they've got. It looks really extravagant."

"If you think I'm going to protest, you're dead wrong."

In the hushed, air-cooled, artificial twilight of this place we sipped our martinis through straws, surrounded by murals of bedouins with idyllic features wandering in caravans across sand dunes that were tinted by concealed lighting the most incomparable shade of mauve. I cannot tell you how sad I was. I hope sincerely, reader, that this strange sad tenderness which follows infidelity is a sensation unknown to you; it is a truly uncanny one and leads, as I have just attempted to indicate, to extravagances of many kinds. My second of the afternoon, following closely upon our pair of five-dollar martinis, was, on our way back to the villa, to park the Citroën along the most opulent stretch of the Promenade des Anglais, and taking Margaret by the elbow with an air of mysterious determination to lead her into the *galerie* in whose window stood the figurine of Italian glass which she had so incontinently coveted, and in spite of her astonished, horrified, and enraptured protests, to buy it for her on the spot. Yes, I did this. If you are revolted, reader, by the vulgarity, the abject ignominy of this act, you may consider my feelings when, for the remaining eight weeks of our stay, I was required daily— hourly, in fact—to look upon the wretched object where it stood, in all of its ignoble ostentation, in the center of the grand piano in our living room. I suppose there is a certain intrinsic value in mass; if I had been able, for example, to purchase title to the Grand Hôtel du Nord at Monte Carlo, or perhaps the whole of Cap Ferrat, it might have seemed a bit less shabby, an impulse of a slightly more heroic scale. I might have won the respect of one or two of you, at any rate. But that poor fragile little Venetian Harlequin, with his peppermint-striped pantaloons and curls of spiral glass—it was not enough; it would not do.

One evening Margaret came down with a virus of some sort, and was ill all the following day. She lay in a chaise longue on the patio, reading a bird manual, sipping iced tea and writing in a cloth-bound notebook she had bought in Cap Ferrat. We were to have joined our actor friends in Eze, where they were taking an excursion bus for the day; Margaret begged me to go without her.

"No, you're very ill; you need attention."

"Oh, don't be silly, Mickey. I'll just read and doze all day, anyway. You'll be bored stiff. Why shouldn't you go and have a good time?"

"I won't have a good time," I said.

"Well, that's sweet. It's silly, of course, but sweet."

"It will be fun to have a quiet day together, anyway. I'll make you broth and read to you and fetch you your medicine."

She smiled at me over the top of her glasses. This was one of Margaret's most attractive mannerisms; it gave her a rather severe, faintly pedantic, schoolmistress-like look which I found oddly appealing. I did not want to leave her alone. She was really quite ill, and I had that unpleasantly roiled visceral sensation of mild panic that the thought of illness in a foreign country, amongst heaven knows what sort of barbarously inadequate medical facilities, produces in some people.

"Well, you'd better call them, then. They'll be expecting us."

"Oh, God. I'll have to talk to the concierge; they've got no private phone."

"You see what you're getting into? You'd better just go along and meet them."

"I won't do anything of the sort," I said. "You're going to see the real order of my devotion."

After the usual number of surly and chaotic imbroglios, and a long unpromising silence, Gwynyth answered the telephone.

"Hullo."

"Hello. This is Mike."

"Oh. Where are you? What's up?"

"I'm at home," I said. "Listen, Mickey's not feeling well. We won't be able to come."

"Oh. What's she got?"

"I don't know. Some kind of a stomach bug or something. I'm sorry."

"That's all right. Listen, there's a thing called Blanc de Chine that's wonderful for that. You want to run down to the chemist and get some for her."

"All right, I will; thanks. Blanc de Chine?"

"That's it. It's dreadful stuff to take, but it works wonders. Tell her to take three tablespoonfuls. It only says two on the label."

"All right."

"I suppose we'll see you round the beach one day, then."

"Yes. You don't mind, do you?"

"Don't be dotty; why should I mind?"

"I don't know. Well, have a good time."

"We will. Cheer-o."

"Good-bye."

"You sounded rather curt," Margaret said. "Who was on the phone?"

"Gwynyth. She recommended a medicine for you. Something called Blanc de Chine. I think I'll go get you some."

"No, thanks. I've got the pills we brought. I'm perfectly all right."

"She says it's marvelous stuff."

"I can get along without it."

"What do you mean, I sounded curt?"

"I don't know. You sounded sort of brusque or something. Maybe it was my imagination."

"Well, maybe I did. She gets on my nerves a little, once in a while."

"Really? Why?"

"I don't know. Because she's twenty-two, I suppose. Anyway, she said to tell you she was sorry, and to get well."

"I intend to," Margaret said.

I made her a cup of broth from a bouillon cube and sat beside her in the shade of the bougainvillea arbor while she wrote in the green ledger. She would set it down occasionally and take up a pair of binoculars to watch a siskin or sparrow fluttering in the pines.

"What are you writing?" I asked. "An ornithological report?"

"No. I'm making notes. I'm going to write a play."

"Are you serious?"

"Yes." She evidently was.

"Can I read them?"

"Absolutely not."

"What's it about?"

"I'll tell you the title and that's all. It's called *The Sparrow Play*. That's probably as far as I'll get."

She would tell me no more about it. Around noon she felt tired and went into the bedroom to lie down. She slept for an hour—or at any rate was silent for an hour—while I sat on the terrace staring out at the shifting molten sea. It was very warm and still. After a while I went into the villa and took the electric fan from the kitchen into her bedroom, where I connected it to a wall socket and set it on the bureau so that it would play over her. The breeze from the fan stirred her hair softly about her temples, exposing occasionally a single glittering silver hair among the shifting strands of brown. I stood and watched her for a while, but she did not stir. I went back into the salon and fingered along the volumes on the bookshelves, where I discovered a book called *Spirit and Reality,* by Nicolas Berdyaev, which I carried back to the terrace and opened to its approximate center.

> . . . Many attempts have been made (I read) to solve the problem of evil. But evil is entirely irrational and without foundation, quite undetermined by any purpose or reason. It is useless to inquire into the origin of evil, because it is engendered by the world of necessity in which everything is subordinated to causality. But evil is initially related to freedom rather than to causality. It seems paradoxical, but there is an affinity between evil and spirit. They have a common attribute in freedom, although evil, of course, is destructive to both spirit and freedom. It is true that evil originates from spirit rather than matter. To say that freedom is the cause of evil is the same as saying that evil has no cause. In this case freedom does mean absence of cause. It is only at a later stage, in its consequences, that evil submits to the power of causality. Evil may be a cause, but it has itself no cause. Freedom is a definite mystery, an irrational element. It engenders evil as well as good without any discrimination, content simply to engender. There can be no rational interpretation of freedom; a rational definition would only kill freedom. That is known as a definitive conception (Grenzbegriff). Thus evil is born of freedom, it has neither cause nor foundation.

I set the book down and took up a manual called *Birds of the World* which lay beside Margaret's binoculars on her chaise longue. It was marked with a paper matchstick at a section entitled Old World Seed-Eaters, in which I read:

> With few exceptions the carduelines are tree-dwelling forest birds, much more so that the fringillines. All habitually sing during their peculiarly undulating flight, and their social instincts are highly developed. Few are strongly migratory, but most northern species move irregularly northward in winter. They travel compactly in unified flocks, and a number of

species nest in loose colonies. Unlike the other ploceids, they build compactly woven, open-cup nests, usually placed in tree branches well off the ground, except in the few species such as the redpolls that nest in treeless areas. Incubation is usually by the female alone, but the male feeds her on the nest and helps rear the young. A noteworthy aspect of their nesting habits which goldfinches share with the waxbills is their lack of nest sanitation. These are among the very few higher passerines that do not remove the nestling's fecal matter from the nest.

The European Goldfinch's neat beauty, its pleasant song, and the ease with which it is kept in captivity make it a popular cage bird, and thousands used to be caught for this purpose. A number of attempts were made to introduce the European Goldfinch to the United States during the nineteenth century, and releases were made in Oregon, Missouri, Ohio, New Jersey and Massachusetts, as well as in Bermuda. Though small populations still persist in favored spots along the south shore of Long Island, the species found conditions to its liking only in Bermuda, where it is now one of the common resident birds.

I closed this volume in turn, laid it back on the chaise longue, and returned to my contemplation of the sea. I was suffering from a peculiar kind of heightened sensitivity which gave to everything in range of my perception—including the two very dissimilar passages I had sampled—a freighted quality, a boding, a faintly sinister significance that created a cold, feverish tingle under my skin and in my mind, like the effect of too much sunburn. One of the most ominous of these elements was the silence of the afternoon. Ordinarily I regarded the silence of the place as benevolent and beautiful, but this silence had a clandestine quality, as if, behind or within it, negotiations of some primordial, unspoken sort were implacably proceeding. I was relieved to hear Margaret stir, and went in through the villa to see if she had awakened. When I reached the door of her bedroom I saw that she had; she had risen, put on her negligee, and was seated in front of her dressing table, combing her hair. The sight gave me a feeling of quite inexpressible sorrow. I suppose it was because she looked so lonely —although it is difficult to say exactly why—and so desperately proud. There was something about that gesture of prettying herself, determinedly, ritually, without express joy or hope, that was grave, sad, and yet incorrigibly feminine, immemorially lovely with the pride, the indomitable vanity, of her sex. I held my breath for fear of embarrassing her, and myself. In a moment she set down the brush, opened a drawer of her vanity and lifted out, clutched loosely in her fingers, a handful of costume earrings. She tried on four of these, one after another, fitting them to her left earlobe, examining the effect in her mirror with that grave, ritualistic look of invincible coquetry, and then discarding them in turn. The fifth—a luminous fuchsia-colored plastic hoop—she left in place, adding the matching one to her right ear; then she closed her eyes and for several moments sat absolutely still. I took advantage of the moment to retreat from the doorway and back through the salon to the terrace, where I sat down and picked up the Berdyaev, turning the pages sightlessly. In a few minutes Margaret came out through the bead curtain, humming "La Matinata," her hoop earrings glittering with a kind of importunate gaiety, as did the hummed notes of her song. This I saw as I lowered the book and raised my eyes to smile at her.

"Hey, you look pretty great," I said. "What have you done to yourself?"

"Combed my hair," Margaret said.

"Are you feeling better?"

"I think so. I *slept*. Goodness."

She sat down on the chaise longue, adjusting the hem of her negligee over her exposed knees with a strange matronly kind of fastidiousness that pricked at my heart. "What have you been doing?" she asked.

"Just sitting here reading."

"What is it?" She peered at the cover, narrowing her eyes

nearsightedly. The gesture suddenly recalled to me my mother entering a room, her hair astray, squinting her eyes in just that way in the effort to identify anyone who might be present.

"Berdyaev," I said. *"Spirit and Reality."*

"Is it good?"

"It's portentous," I said. "I don't know if that's good."

"Not usually," Margaret said. "It's what most bad books are." She smiled at me. "Poor Mickey; keeping his silent vigil. I've made you waste the whole day."

"Wasn't wasted at all. Full of study, rest, and contemplation. Everybody needs a day like this occasionally, to sort of sum up."

"Sum up?" she said. "Is that what you've been doing? Well, what have you decided?"

"I've decided that the sun will come up tomorrow, whether we're here to see it or not."

"I'd much rather hear," said Margaret, "that we will be here tomorrow, whether the sun comes up or not."

"You'll be here," I said. "I guarantee it. I'm going to make you some of that wonderful powdered watercress soup you like. That will keep you around for a while."

"Oh, that would be good," said Margaret.

I went into the kitchen to prepare it, but after searching among the shelves for several minutes I discovered that there was none left. I was about to return to the terrace to report this fact when the doorbell rang. The visitor was Alice Nesbit, the wife of an American naval officer in the Sixth Fleet, whose headquarters was Villefranche. Like most of the dependents of the commissioned officers of this command, she was quartered at Cap Ferrat. We had met her a few days before at the Plage Passable, where, with the help of a Danish *au pair,* she had been shepherding four unmistakably American children. She was a plump, pretty, good-natured woman of thirty-five or so, with a wry Service Cosmopolitanism spread over her bucolic Carolina personality like an improvidently chosen shade of makeup. We had invited her to visit us at the villa—her husband was away in the Mediterranean with the fleet—and although I think we were both surprised at the promptness of her acceptance, Margaret seemed genuinely pleased to see her.

"Oh, my goodness," Mrs. Nesbit said. "You must not be feeling well. I'd better come back another time."

"Please stay," Margaret said. "I've just got a little stomach bug. Mickey's been such an angel, taking care of me all day. Now we can have a nice talk, and it will give him a chance to get away for a while."

"Well, if you're sure. It's a blessing for me to get away from those kids for a few minutes. And I get so tired of playing bridge with the same girls every day that it's a real relief to see someone new for a change. There's about eight of us here on the Cape, you know, and we get so ingrown."

"I'll run down to St. Jean," I said, "and see if I can find you some more of that soup. Is there anything else you'd like?"

"I don't think so, thank you, Mickey."

"I'll make you some tea before I go."

"No; now you scoot," Mrs. Nesbit said. "I'll do the tea-making. Don't you go ruining my chance to be a good neighbor." She seemed to be exactly that. I stood in the foyer for a moment before I went out, and listened to them chattering and issuing merry housewifely cries of companionship which seemed very innocent, very touchingly mundane, very cloistered, like a glimpse of cornfield, a white farmhouse with its windmill and shade-elms, seen from a Pullman window.

I drove down to St. Jean-Cap Ferrat, as much to escape from the unnatural zone of silence that seemed to enclose the villa as for any reason. I anticipated, among the streets and shops of St. Jean, the resumption of a certain reassuring cacophony—the clatter of trade, the cries of children, the haggle of marketing—but it did not occur. It was a very still afternoon. The streets, the shops, the harbor, the whole Cape, seemed caught in a sunny, symphonic stasis, melodious and faintly ominous. In the *épicerie* I bought three packets of the powdered watercress soup, half a dozen oranges, and, on the strength alone of its anomalous presence in a dusty wire rack in front of me on the counter, a very old, soiled, sentimental greeting card, apparently intended as accompaniment to a remembrance of some modest kind, as it bore the inscription:

> *Voici un souvenir de notre jour*
> *Si bleu, si doux—si court!*

It was illustrated with a picture of a girl in eighteenth-century dress in a state of pretty reverie over a china *cache-pot* out of which issued a cloud of lavender-colored steam, painted, evidently, by that incredibly prolific artist whose work—largely thatched cottages with rose gardens in front of them—forms the foundation of the jigsaw puzzle industry.

I strolled back up the village street to where I had parked the Citroën in the shade of the *flamboyant* tree and, after staring for a while at the harbor, the tipping masts, and, far out on the sea, cloud-shadow blowing miasmally over the sun-sheen on the water, I started the car and began a leisurely meander around the Cape. The day was blue and sweet indeed (although so still!); I drove between cypresses, over dream-roads of talcum, through the purple, thrusting shadow of a lighthouse, over little lingering, reluctant lanes that took me—I imagined respectively as I pursued them—toward Margaret, away from Margaret, toward Margaret, away from Margaret, toward Margaret, away from Margaret, as if through an interminable, perfumed labyrinth of coral, ivory, and spikenard, with, here and there, a thrilling darkened vault, a chilling sense of stealth, a brutal phallic shadow on the stone. After a time I found myself at the end of the graveled entrance driveway of Quelques Saisons, and, with a very casual sort of impulse—nothing startled or spastic about it, at all—turned into it, feeling a sense of quite agreeable concurrence with this eventuality. It suited very well my mood of lyrical leisure. I should enjoy, I thought, an extemporaneous visit with the countess, a glass of vermouth, a half-hour of intellectual embroidery in the sunlight of the terrace amid the scent of rosewater and trichinopoly smoke. The thought that she might be resting, indisposed, or entertaining other visitors did not deter me at all, in the case of such a devotee of the unconventional, unexpected, and impulsive.

She was, in fact, entertaining Andrea; or, more exactly, he was entertaining her. They sat in the sunlight together on the stone-paved terrace in front of her villa, she sunken to her hips in chintz-covered cushions, a silk parasol tilted over her shoulder casting a pale-blue light on the faintly crocodilian flesh of her ancient face, her skeletal fingertips flittering about the ivory handle of the parasol, the coffee-colored lace inset at the bosom of her crepe de chine gown palpitating gently with little soundless spasms of amusement. In front of her on the metalwork table was a closed volume of Ronsard's *Poèmes,* a glass of bitterly sparkling blood-colored vermouth, and, resting on the lip of a crystal camellia-shaped ashtray, a panatela cigar from the tip of which blossomed writhing pale purple fronds of foliage. Andrea sat parallel to her in a matching cast-iron chair, his legs, crossed at the ankles, arrogantly extended to display a pair of wine-colored suede chukka boots, his hands plunged into his trouser pockets, lifting dashingly askew the hem of his magnificent English hacking-jacket of soft, saffron-tufted Irish tweed. His dark face took the sunlight beautifully, like finely tanned, subtly oiled leather, and with the same smooth glow and look of perfect fit as a calfskin glove worn over a delicate hand. His black eyebrows glistened almost as if —and indeed very likely—with pomade; beneath them, his eyes, like polished onyx, reflected the sun in seeds of fire. And amongst all this gleaming, swarthy splendor his teeth provided the perfect note of contrast and surprise; such whiteness, such astonishing emblems of purity and candor. Surprise, I reflected, as he approached me with these agents of my own glittering in a welcoming smile, is probably the chief component of all genuine beauty; to which I added the uncomfortable observation that for one man to assess another's physical attractions in such a comprehensive way must require an exigency of some unknown and considerable kind. He offered me a handshake in which there was not the slightest evidence of nervous deterioration.

"Mr. Pritchard! We are very glad to see you!" he cried. "Come and sit down. We shall have a drink together. Two or three, perhaps. We are delighted."

"Thank you." Without relinquishing his handclasp he placed his free hand in the small of my back and propelled me with gentle urgency toward the table. The countess lifted her hand to me. It was damp and cool. From her drink, I decided, a little surprised that I should require the comfort of this conclusion.

"How very nice of you to call," she said in a faint, dry, animated, locust-like voice. "But where is Margaret? Why haven't you brought her with you?"

"She's not feeling very well. She's got a digestive upset of some kind, so she's spending the day resting."

"Oh, dear. I hope it isn't serious."

"No; she's much better now. I've been feeding her bouillon all morning, and she's had a good nap. Then she had a friend drop in to see her; ones of the navy wives from the Cape, so I just ran out to get her some medicine. I passed by your driveway and thought I'd drop in for a moment."

"You've no idea how that pleases me. At my age one's great and constant fear is of being forgotten. But next time, of course, I shall expect Margaret as well. You must tell her that I won't hear of her being ill."

"I'm sure she won't dare to displease you again," I said.

"I know of a remedy," said Andrea, "which is extremely effective for this complaint. Blanc de Chine, it is called. It is really extremely effective, although very little advertised. I would recommend you to get some for Mrs. Pritchard."

"That's the very thing I've just bought," I said. "Miss Rees recommended it to me this morning."

"Ah. Really?" He smiled with a look of considerable private enjoyment. "It is good to have one's counsel supported from such unexpected quarters."

"What do you mean by that?" the countess asked.

"Miss Rees," said Andrea, shrugging genially. "One would not think, from looking at her, that she had been ill a day in her life. Or have advice of any particular value for a sufferer."

"That is impudent, Andrea," said the countess in a voice of mock severity. "The suffering of artists is something you know so little about that you would be much better off to say nothing on the subject at all." He inclined his head contritely. We had both remained standing. "Do sit down," said the countess. We did so, Andrea beside her as before, and I, facing them across the metalwork table. The countess set down her glass, lifted a little silver bell and tinkled it with a sudden convulsion of her pale hand. Andrea smiled at me, his legs thrust forward, crossed at the ankles, his elbows resting on the iron scrollwork of his chair-arms, his hands, bent idly at the wrists, tilted in toward his breast, the fingertips touching the pale blue silk of his handstitched shirt. The breast pocket was embroidered with a very small initial A, stitched in silk thread of a darker blue, and over this slightly raised monogram he stroked the fingertips of his left hand continually in a gesture of unconscious indolence.

"You have been feeding Mrs. Pritchard bouillon," he said. "Americans are so attentive to their wives. I have observed this frequently. It is very nice."

"With such a wife as Margaret, any man would be attentive," the countess said. "There is nothing remarkable in that."

"No, no, of course. But generally, I mean. I think it is true."

"More than among Europeans?" I asked.

"I believe so, yes." Both the countess and I regarded him in expectant silence for a moment, but apparently he had no inclination to expound the observation; he seemed content to have tossed it, like a small bouquet, at my feet. A bouquet which had, however, a slightly equivocal odor, or perhaps a sprig of thistle somewhere among its posies. The countess put the cigar to her lips and emitted from between them a languid plume of pearl-colored smoke.

" 'One of the navy wives,' " she said. "From your Sixth Fleet, here, I suppose."

"Yes. A Mrs. Nesbit. A very attractive little woman."

"Nesbit. I haven't met her. I have met a Mrs. Spurgeon and a Mrs. Lindquist. Neither could be called attractive. Which is altogether enigmatic. How a woman can manage to be young, pretty, rich, clean, respectable, well dressed, and at the same time eminently unattractive, I cannot make out."

Andrea's smile broadened, his mouth fell open slightly, the tip of his tongue appeared and touched the corner of his upper lip in a soundless mimicry of mirth.

"I suppose Mrs. Nesbit must have some redeeming qualities," I said. "I found her very pleasant."

"What sort of qualities?"

"Simplicity, sincerity, neighborliness." I listed them coolly, almost indifferently, with firm composure; but a certain amount of umbrage, of course, was expressed in the choice of the virtues themselves, and I could not help feeling a bit ridiculous at their unanimous and defiant ring of piety. I tried to dilute it a bit by adding, "They seem to be having a great time together. It was just what Mickey needed, I think: a long, bourgeois natter about haircurlers and recipes for risotto."

"Risotto," said Andrea mildly, his eyebrows lifting in a barely perceptible expression of acknowledgment. "She has a taste for risotto?"

"Oh, well, risotto, roast beef; whatever it happens to be."

"Ah."

"Periodically," said the countess, "your flagship puts into Villefranche Bay. I believe you will be able to see it from your terrace on the next occasion. It is large, sleek, beautifully designed . . ." She turned her left hand limply upward and on its fingertips, with the forefinger of the other, enumerated the qualities successively. ". . . expensive, silent, very clean, equipped with every sort of lethal machinery and I have no doubt, murderously efficient. Its advent produces regularly in Villefranche an invasion of prostitutes from Paris, pimps, gamblers, homosexuals, confidence men, and every other sort of panderer to human frailty; a disastrous—often treble or quadruple—rise in the price of goods, services, and real estate; crowding and confusion in public places that makes it impossible to procure a meal or make a purchase in comfort or dignity; public displays of drunkenness, fisticuffs, profanity, and every other sort of chaos that could possibly beset such a quiet, lovely, ancient place as Cap Ferrat, which I love. If your Mrs. Nesbit had the mark of God Himself upon her brow I should refuse to consider her attractive."

I managed to laugh. "I didn't realize she was responsible for so much unpleasantness," I said.

"Nor does she," said the countess, "with all her innocent neighborly natter about haircurlers and risotto. But to be innocent, in such a world as this, is no excuse for being irresponsible."

Andrea seemed very pleased with this conclusion. He plucked merrily at the knees of his finely welted faun-colored corduroy trousers with the tips of his thumbs and fingers.

"But what is mysterious to me," I said, "is how a shipful of American sailors—or their wives—can call forth all this wickedness and confusion in an ancient, benign, securely civilized world. It seems almost beyond their capacity."

"The power of innocence is inscrutable," said the countess. "One might as well ask how one slender, smiling, innocent girl, by eating an apple in a garden, could call forth all the wickedness and confusion of this earth. We must not expect answers to such questions. It is enough that we should be required to countenance such an abominable phenomenon, without having to provide an explanation for it."

Andrea's look of enjoyment waned; he gave the pleating of his trousers a swift disconcerted nip with his fingertips. The countess smiled. "Andrea considers me irreverent," she said.

She laid her hand affectionately on his knee. "He is such a dear, good, conventional scoundrel. He will not have the Lord or any of His mysteries taken in vain."

Andrea returned her smile with an even more dazzling one of his own. "I have my style," he said, "as you have yours."

"Indeed you have." She patted the knee upon which her hand rested, then returned her fingers to the ivory handle of her parasol, which they teasingly caressed. "And I must say, I have very nearly succumbed to it from time to time. What would you say, Mr. Pritchard, to the impudence of a man who tells a creature of my age that she has the charm of any dozen debutantes of his acquaintance, combined?"

"I would have to call it justified," I said.

"Ah, you are a pair. You would do well to throw in together. There is no telling what worlds you could conquer."

Andrea turned upon me a smile of wry delight at the irony of this suggestion.

"What do you say, Mr. Pritchard? Shall we make a combined assault on this lady's virtue?"

"My virtue?" said the countess with a little crackle of dry laughter, like the unfolding of a sheet of parchment. "Oh, you had better choose another prize entirely; you would scarcely find enough of it to divide between you." She turned her head toward the rustle of starched linen with which Amélie, in response to the ringing of the silver bell, approached us across the lawn.

"*Madame désire?*" asked the maid.

"Yes. What will you have to drink, Mr. Pritchard?"

"A glass of Cinzano, if I may."

"And you, Andrea; are you ready for another?"

"If you please," said Andrea, bolting the lees of his Pernod and setting the empty glass at his elbow.

"*Et encore pour Monsieur,*" said the countess. "*C'est entendu?*"

"*Oui, Madame.*" Taking up the empty glass, the maid retired swiftly through the sunlight toward the villa.

"Here one can relax," said Andrea, plunging his hands into his pockets and thrusting his feet forward as before. He sighed contentedly. "What a pity you could not have delayed being born by another fifty years. We would have made a marvelous couple, Countess."

"You are very simpleminded to believe it," said the countess. "If I were fifty years younger you would be very far from relaxed at this moment, you may be sure."

"Ah, it is true." He sighed more deeply, tossing his head to smile at her ruefully. "Then perhaps it is better that you were born when you were. But I am not so sure. Which would I have enjoyed more, ultimately? Your friendship or your love? It is interesting to consider. I ask myself this about almost every woman I meet. With some, of course, the answer comes much more readily."

"You don't consider it possible to enjoy both?" I asked.

"Unfortunately, no. As the countess has pointed out, they are not compatible. Not as I have experienced them, at any rate." He turned toward me a cautiously exhilarated eye. "Do you find that they are? I ask because of the bouillon."

The question bordered upon incivility, but having invited it with my own, I had very little grounds for indignation. I decided to smile.

"I don't dismiss the possibility," I said.

"Of course in America, as I understand it, you have this ideal of love between equals; of the absolute equality of women. That would make it much more possible to you."

"You don't regard women as our equals?"

"Not in every respect, no."

"How do you find them inferior?"

"Well, their physical strength, for example, is not equal to ours. That is very important."

"You think it should affect the relationship between us?"

"Oh, it must, of course." He shrugged good-naturedly. "Both for the good and for the bad. It may result in the abuse of women, but also it results in chivalry. If their physical

355

strength were equal to ours, chivalry would have no meaning. Oh, it makes many"—he groped in the air with his hand as if unscrewing a light bulb—"many nuances of the relationship."

The panel of lace at the countess' bosom palpitated merrily. "Nuances!" she cried softly, laying her fingers athwart the betraying lace. "Oh, it's very reassuring to hear you profess a respect for nuance in a relationship. I was beginning to fear that men were losing entirely the capacity to appreciate such things. I'm glad to hear that I was wrong. How fascinating your relationships must be, Andrea."

He smiled at her with perfect equanimity. "You have only to consider our own," he said.

"Indeed I must *re*consider it. I have taken you much too lightly, I see. I must look for far more interesting answers to such questions as why, at a party, a perfectly appropriate festive occasion, you do not permit so much as a single drop of alcohol to pass your lips, and yet, in the last half-hour, in the somewhat less gala circumstance of my exclusive company, you allow yourself to consume five undiluted glasses of pernod. There are mysteries here which I may have overlooked."

He turned toward me, nodding tragically and holding up his hands in a disconsolate appeal to me to bear witness.

"Do you see, Mr. Pritchard? This is a typical woman. I think I am enjoying her genuine hospitality, and I find that all the time she is counting the number of drinks she serves me."

The panel of lacework at the countess' bosom trembled appreciatively.

"How is it any the less genuine for being measured?" she asked.

"The only true hospitality is limitless," Andrea said, holding up a finger to her pedagogically. "If it is less than infinite it is not a full measure. You have cheated me."

She laughed wholeheartedly, crackling her sheets of parchment.

"I wonder how many ladies have heard that piece of wisdom from you? And been most disastrously moved by it? I'm afraid you are a very transparent rogue. But I will say this for you, Andrea: it would be a far more agreeable experience to be victimized by such a rogue as you than to suffer the benefactions of many of the virtuous men I know."

Amélie had now arrived at the table bearing a little gold-colored tray with glasses for Andrea and me, which she set before us. Andrea raised his in a toast, saluting the horizon.

"To my mysterious abstinence," he said. He drank the pernod in a single swallow and turned to wink at me. "That was number six."

The countess reached out to clutch a handful of his black curls in her frail fingers and give his head a tug.

"You are a sweet rogue," she said. "And very beautiful. I could almost wish I had a full measure of charity to offer you. If only I were young enough for it to be of benefit to either of us."

"It is a pity," Andrea said.

"Well, perhaps in heaven—where I understand we shall all be of the same age."

"No, not in heaven, madame."

"No, I'm afraid you're right." She loosed his hair and lifted her hand to unlatch her parasol, which she lowered musingly, binding the tips of its spines together with a little satin ribbon that dangled from one of them. "I have had a very enjoyable —and profitable—afternoon. It's all too seldom that I am awarded the attentions of two such very interesting young men on a single day. You must excuse me if I'm quite exhausted by the experience. I must go, now, and have my nap."

"Ah!" cried Andrea, bolting to his feet. "Forgive us for tiring you. I have stayed too long."

"Nonsense," said the countess. "You can't stay long enough to suit my vanity. You must have another drink or two together. It would please me enormously, and I have the feeling that you have a great deal to learn from one another." She rose, aided both by her parasol and Andrea's firm grasp of her elbow, and, escorted by one of us on either side, made her way across the lawn toward the villa. A sprinkling of tiny pepper-colored grass-hoppers sprayed up from the turf before our feet at almost every step. "Nicolas wants to kill these pretty creatures," she said, pointing with the tip of her parasol, "by spreading about some dreadful insecticide, but I forbid him to. I love the sort of effervescence they give to this patch of earth. It is almost like wading through champagne."

"But they spit on one," said Andrea. "And they will destroy your flowers."

"No doubt," said the countess. She was taken into custody at the villa steps by Amélie, who came down to the lawn to take her arm. "These gentlemen will require further refreshment," she said to the maid. "Will you see that they are taken care of?"

"*Certainement, Madame.*"

"Gentlemen, I have enjoyed your visit. Mr. Pritchard, I shall expect you to bring Margaret here to me no later than the day after tomorrow. If there is any further nonsense about her being ill I shall come round to your villa myself and see that she is properly taken care of."

"I hope you'll come in any case," I said.

"Perhaps I will. Andrea, why don't you tell Mr. Pritchard the story of your acquaintance with Madame Benoit? I think it would amuse him."

Andrea bowed to her.

"That is a great lady," he said as the countess was escorted into the cool obscurity of her villa by the maid. He smiled at me tentatively, as if to test my reaction to the opinion.

"She is certainly a fascinating one."

"Yes. She has three great mysteries about her: she is titled, she is rich, and she has avoided death for such a very long time. All this seems to be evidence that God has a special interest in her."

"Someone seems to have."

He turned to regard me inquisitively—we were walking

back across the lawn now, toward the terrace—and chuckled. "The Other One, perhaps? Well, it is possible. I have certainly felt the sting of her lash. Still, I feel sure that she is an affectionate person, on the whole."

"Oh, yes, very."

We had reached the chairs; Andrea collapsed into his with a kind of graceful, avid prostration, laced his fingers together across his blue silk shirt, and looked out across the boulder-strewn promontory, the dusky vineyard, and the dying olive trees. He nodded with baronial approval.

"I should like to own this," he said.

"Yes, it's beautiful."

"Beautiful. *Bellissima*. But the olives should be pruned. It is sad to see them like that." He raised his hand and tugged at the knot of his necktie. "I am going to loosen my collar just a little. It has been strangling me for the last half-hour, but I did not like to offend the countess. You don't mind, I hope."

"Not a bit."

"That is what I admire so much about Americans. Your marvelous informality. I am told by my cousin in Chicago that in your country one is able to dine in a respectable restaurant without a necktie."

"It is very often done."

"And to call someone by his Christian name at their first introduction."

"Yes, that's very common."

"It is astonishing. To most Europeans, of course, it would be distasteful. We put a much greater value on formality, on privacy. Perhaps because we have been crowded together so closely for so many centuries. But you, who have had so much space, and so few people to fill it, have quite the opposite desire—for informality, for intimacy." He had removed from a pocket of his jacket a small orangewood manicure stick and began to preen his fingernails as he spoke, raising his hand to flourish it

359

occasionally for emphasis, the white splinter flashing between his thumb and forefinger like a miniature baton.

"That sounds like a very reasonable theory," I said. "I never thought of it."

"I notice it in almost every American I meet. A certain hunger for friendship. It is the most distinctive thing about them."

"You're very observant."

"I am. I have a passion for people." He raised his head to smile at me magnificently. "They are my hobby." The phrase rang of quotation marks.

I smiled appreciatively. "People and automobiles."

"Not automobiles, no. They are my profession. About them I know everything, so I do not enjoy discussing them. I have lost my curiosity." He orchestrated his remarks with the orange-stick; the delicately uplifted instrument seemed to call for a particularly subtle passage from a flute.

I said, as melodiously as possible, "It's in those things of which he is an amateur that we find the true soul of a man." The phrase had a distinct taste in my mouth of rotten fruit; a kind of extravagant succulence.

"Ah, that is beautifully said. *Bellissima.* I cannot believe that you are not an artist."

"I'm an *amateur,*" I said.

"Oh, *ho! Perfetto!*" He kissed his bunched fingertips in reckless admiration, very nearly extinguishing one of his lustrous eyes with the orangestick. "Now I can believe what the countess told me about you. What I could not accept before."

"What was that?" I asked.

"That you are a government worker. A civil servant of some kind. Now I can understand. You exist outside of your work. It is my own case, exactly."

"Really? How is it your case?" I asked.

"I am obliged to instruct people in languages for my living. Which would be deadly, of course, if I did not have my hobbies, my passions, to sustain me."

"Oh, I see. Still, I understand you have some very interesting people as clients. That must compensate a good deal for the dullness of the work."

"Interesting people?" His smile broadened innocently.

"So Miss Rees says."

"Oh. Miss Rees has told you about my clients?"

"Yes. We were talking about you one day, and she said you had all sorts of glamorous ladies for pupils. A Russian princess, and a Lady—Trevellyan, was it?"

"Oh, yes. Lady Trevellyan. Yes, I have some extremely interesting people; and of course, as you say, that makes it much more endurable. *Ah, merci.*" Amélie had approached silently across the lawn and set before us fresh glasses of Cinzano and Pernod. Andrea raised the one containing the Pernod rather deliberately and smiled at me over the top of it.

"Cheers."

"Cheers."

He pressed his lips together and sucked a stream of air shrilly between them. "Ah. Lovely. Limes. It tastes of Sicily. There come beautiful limes from Sicily."

"Oh, do they?"

"Yes. Small, but very juicy, very sharp. Like the women." He blazed his teeth at me. "You find Miss Rees amusing?"

"Yes, very."

"She has a fascinating personality."

"Fascinating."

"And great talent. Or so I understand. But she is just a bit inclined to exaggeration, don't you think?"

"Not at all," I said. "I find her staggeringly candid."

"You do? Perhaps you enjoy her confidence to a greater extent than I." I drooped the corners of my mouth and raised my eyebrows deprecatingly. "I had no idea that she had ever given my welfare a serious thought. Perhaps you could tell me what her opinion of me truly is? I would be very interested to know."

I turned my head to regard him thoughtfully for a moment. "She has the opinion that you have considerable gifts," I said.

His own eyebrows rose in feigned astonishment. "Has she, indeed? I wish she would tell *me* such things. It would improve my self-esteem very much."

"Perhaps she doesn't feel that it needs improving."

"Perhaps." He laughed agreeably. "One never knows what women think of one. It may be just as well. There would be many less marriages if we did."

"You're probably right," I said. We had reached a sort of node, a moment of passive, tense preoccupation with each other. I focused my attention on his hands. They were very small, but not girlish nor delicate; short fingers with square tips to them; prominent, rather gnarled knuckles, the first two segments of each finger tufted with sproutings of black hair between the knuckles, a very short distal segment, naked of hair, terminating in flat thick nails, deeply grained with visible coarse ridges and festooned with large exquisitely decorticated moons of very pale purple.

"Speaking of your lessons," I said, "is your schedule full at the moment?"

"My schedule?"

"Yes. I wonder if you might have some time free for teaching." A certain amount of perplexity produced a slight flicker in his smile, the faintest twitching of his upper lip.

"You wish to study French?"

"My wife does."

"Ah." He gave one of his little bland gasps of acknowledgment, then stilled his head, frowning slightly, his mouth hung open, as if listening to some distant, unfamiliar sound. In a moment he closed his mouth and blinked, his smile instantly and faultlessly reborn. "I am very flattered that Mrs. Pritchard has so much confidence in me."

"Actually, it was my idea."

"Oh. Then I am doubly pleased. The confidence of men I value even more."

"I'm led to believe that you're a very capable instructor,"
I said.

"By Miss Rees?"

"Oh, by many people."

His features writhed with an amiably simulated humility.
"Oh, I am very pleased. I didn't know I enjoyed such a favora-
ble reputation."

"I'm sure it's well deserved," I said. "Do you think you
could accommodate me, then?"

"Ah." He allowed his smile to be extinguished by a tortured
look of regret. "I wish I could say with no hesitation whatever,
'Of course, my dear Mr. Pritchard,' because there is nothing I
would rather do than be of service to your charming wife; and
to yourself, of course. But I have a complication of a kind, that
my circumstances force me to consider. You see, at the moment
I have only two free appointments a week—on Tuesday and
Thursday afternoons—and this time I have more or less agreed
to give to an English lady who is very anxious to improve her
Italian. I will tell you frankly I am not enthusiastic about it,
because she is a terrible bore; but also she is very rich. She has
offered to pay me a really ridiculous fee, and unfortunately, as
I say, I do not feel able to refuse it." He tossed his hand abroad
in a grievous gesture of distress.

"Of course. How much has she offered you?"

He shrugged, grimacing with dismay at the lady's prod-
igality. "A really ridiculous sum. Fifteen thousand lire a lesson.
That is—how many dollars?"

"Roughly twenty-five," I said. "That seems rather a lot."

"It is, of course. Ridiculous. But money apparently means
nothing to her." He appealed to me with anguished eyebrows.
"How can I turn it down? I am a poor man. I cannot tell you
how much I regret it."

"Still, it isn't completely out of the question. I think
Margaret would be very disappointed not to have the best
tutor available. And judging from the enthusiasm of your
pupils, it seems to be evident that you're the very best."

He raised his hands in protest, their palms turned toward me.

"Oh, I could not accept such an exorbitance from anyone for whom I had a real regard, a real affection. This English lady is nothing to me, a stranger, a client; there is no feeling. But from you: no. No, no."

"If it added one degree to my wife's pleasure on this earth," I said, "there's nothing I would consider an extravagance. That is no concern of yours. You must simply decide which of them you would prefer to teach."

"You cannot be serious," he said.

"I'm very serious."

"For two hours of French instruction a week, fifty dollars is a very great sum."

"It is considerable."

He paused, studying me, his face fallen into utter and extraordinary repose; then shrugged at last, lifting his open palms to heaven. "As to which of them I would prefer to teach, there is no question. As I say, there is nothing I would rather do than to be of service to your wife."

"Then we have a bargain?"

"If you wish. I am delighted."

"Good. If you let me have your number, I'll ring you tomorrow, just to confirm it. What would be the best time to reach you?"

"At two." He took from the breast pocket of his jacket a little leather-bound appointment book with a pencil attached in a loop inside its spine. On a leaf of this he wrote down a telephone number, then tore off the page and handed it to me, every action meticulous, gay, full of the delight in contractual detail of the successful merchant.

"There. The crossed figure is a seven. Some Americans are not familiar with it." He wagged a short brown finger at the slip of paper, his face radiant.

"It's perfectly legible." I folded the leaf and slipped it

into my shirt pocket. "I hope this won't embarrass you with your English lady."

"No, no. I am used to making adjustments of this kind. After all, it is a small price for her to pay for being a bore."

"Very small," I agreed. There seemed to be little more to say, or do. In the rhapsodic silence of the afternoon I heard the distant scream of a peacock. A sudden little gust of breeze sent a shudder through the vineyard. I picked up my glass and stood up to drain its lees. "If Mrs. Pritchard should inquire about the fee, I'd appreciate it if you minimized it just a bit. She has an instinct for economy that might make her consider it an extravagance."

"Yes, of course."

"She might consider ten dollars a more usual amount. I don't want her feeling guilty about it."

"I understand. You are fortunate; that is a very fine quality in a wife."

I set the glass down with a clink on the metal tabletop.

"Good afternoon." He rose swiftly, baring his gleaming teeth and offering me his hand. It was soft-skinned, small, almost abject in its gentleness. I released it quickly.

"Good afternoon. And thank you very much, Mr. Pritchard. I hope my services will be satisfactory."

"I'm sure they will," I said. "By the way, it's Dr. Pritchard."

"Oh, I beg your pardon; I didn't realize. You are a doctor of philosophy?"

"Yes."

"I didn't realize. Will you express my regret to Mrs. Pritchard for her illness?"

"Yes."

"I'm sure she will find the Blanc de Chine very effective. Tell her to take three tablespoonfuls, although only two are recommended on the label. It is more efficacious."

"Thank you. I will."

I drove away over the molar-like grinding of gravel under

my tires and down those strange lanes where clouds of wild
talcum rose whirling in my wake, then gentled in a soft cumu-
lous coagulation and breathed a shower of moon-dust over the
bleeding rhododendrons. The zebra-stripes of shadow from
an avenue of poplars flayed me as I drove between them, and
having taken somewhere a wrong turning, I arrived again in
the purple pillar of shadow from the lighthouse, at whose
base I stopped the car and lit a cigarette. There was a parking
area for visitors, from which a stone-paved pathway led to
the entrance door of the lighthouse. The pathway was bordered with geranium beds, exact profuse rectangles of brilliant
and barbaric red. I got out of the car, walked between them,
and sat down on a wooden bench to smoke my cigarette. The
lighthouse stood on a promontory at the very tip of Cap
Ferrat; from here I could see, beyond the soaring columnar
mass of the tower, the blue sea spreading away, far beneath.
There was a stretch of railed observation deck surrounding
the base of the tower on the seaward side, but I did not approach it, because I was so delighted with my discovery of
the place and with the prospect of bringing Margaret here to
share my original enjoyment of it that I did not want to di-
minish that enjoyment by having already experienced the full
splendor of the sight alone. I turned my eyes deliberately
away from the seascape and contented myself with counting
the rows of huge stone blocks of which the tower was built.
They were rectangular, approximately one and a half by
two feet in dimension, their dazzling whitewash stained a
winish purple by the shadow of this northward side on which
I sat. I counted seventy-five rows of stone, the rows diminish-
ing in apparent breadth as they ascended, until, at the halfway point, they became too narrow for any further distinction.
From this fact I estimated the height of the tower to be two
hundred and fifty-five feet, of which two hundred and twenty-
five were accounted for by one hundred and fifty rows of
blocks, and the balance by a projecting, bulbous, glass-paned
structure at the top, whose additional height I judged to be

thirty feet. In this, the great electric beacons were evidently mounted, and a surveillance and communications area provided for the keepers. I took a strangely fugitive, desperate sort of pleasure in the precision and formality of my calculations.

In any case, Margaret and Mrs. Nesbit would not yet have finished their visit.

I smoked another cigarette, my head tilted back to rest upon the topmost slat of the bench-back, deliberately excluding from my vision any felicities of sea or shore or panorama, limiting my contemplation to the great uplifted cupola of glass and fretted stone which poured forth light, guidance, and salvation by night, and by day, the cool purple shadow in which I now refreshed myself.

In a little while a middle-aged couple with that faintly thirties look about them of continental bourgeoisie in holiday dress (Panama hat, wide, pointed lapels, chiffon blouse with flounces) came out of the lighthouse and after pausing to look up at it for a moment in murmurous, gesticulatory admiration, advanced along the path between the geraniums to my bench, where, with a little jerky bow of introduction, the man addressed himself to me.

"*Pardon, Monsieur. Est-ce que vous pouvez nous dire la route la plus courte à St. Jean-Cap Ferrat?*"

"*Non, je regrette,*" I said. "*Je suis perdu.*" I groped apologetically with my hand. "I'm sorry. I am lost."

"*Ah, vous aussi,*" he said merrily, a gold tooth flashing in his smile. "*Merci, tout de même.*"

I watched them walk up the path beyond me to the parking area, murmuring animatedly, comfortable, frugal, full of the humble pleasure of their two-week's *vacances,* beatifically commonplace.

After smoking another cigarette I made my way back along the unfamiliar roads to tell Margaret of the arrangement I had made for her pleasure and instruction.

. . .

When I came back to the villa Mrs. Nesbit's station wagon had departed. Margaret was dressed, seated at the grand piano and playing a Chopin *étude*. I heard the sad shivering clusters of notes come tinkling out between the scrolled black bars of the salon windows as I got out of the Citroën and walked up the path between the oleanders. I stood and listened for a moment outside the villa door.

"Where have you been?" she said. "I thought you'd never get back."

"On my errand of mercy. Seeing to your welfare. Where's Mrs. Nesbit?"

"She left, half an hour ago."

"How'd you get on?"

"Oh, she was nice."

She went on playing. I leaned on the piano to listen, setting my packages on the embroidered Spanish shawl. The glass Harlequin had been removed to a nearby tabletop. Behind Margaret's chair, in the open French doorway, gelatinous panes of heat went shivering up from the stone floor of the terrace. The wine-stain on the wall had darkened in the late afternoon light. She played only the treble keys, her crippled hand lying in her lap. With all the bass notes omitted, the music had a strange, ruptured, demented sound. Her face was grave and effortful. I had never heard her play the piano before.

"The advantage of my condition," she said, "is that when I play music I have to leave out all the somber notes. Isn't that funny?"

"I like it," I said. "It sounds sort of unearthly."

"What've you got in the packages?"

"Soup, oranges, and medicine."

"What medicine?"

"What Gwynyth recommended. You're to take three tablespoons immediately."

"I don't need it. Really. I'm all better."

"Don't be stubborn."

"I'm not stubborn. I'm just recovering. Never change a winning game." She closed the sheaf of music and sat up straight on the piano bench to look at me. "Is that where you've been all afternoon? Buying medicine for me?"

"Not all afternoon. I took a little tour around the Cape and then stopped by to see the countess for a while."

"To see the *countess*? Why?"

"I got lost on a strange road and happened to wind up at her place, so I thought I'd run in and have a drink with her. I thought you might like some time to visit with Mrs. Nesbit."

"Oh. It was for *my* benefit."

"Well, you're the one who suggested I should take off. I was just trying to accommodate you."

"By guzzling quarts of Cinzano all afternoon with the countess. That was very thoughtful of you. I appreciate that."

"You're jealous," I said.

"I'm jealous of *anybody* who was anywhere else in the *world* for the last two hours," Margaret said. "God."

"You mean you didn't have fun? Didn't you like her, really?"

"I don't know. I must be getting to be the worst snob in the world. Oh, she was nice, I guess. She was too nice. She made me nervous." She closed the keyboard, shuddering. "Do you want to hand me my Harlequin?"

"What's he doing over here?"

"I was afraid the vibrations would topple him over or something. I've been putting out some pretty strong vibrations for the last half-hour or so." She took the Harlequin from me and held it in her hands for a moment, touching its glass features with her fingertip. "This really is the most beautiful thing in the world. Only I live in terror now, that it's going to get broken." She set the figurine carefully on the piano top. The blue and scarlet panes of his costume twinkled in the half-dark of the room.

"What are you doing dressed, anyway?" I asked. "You should be in bed."

"I certainly should *not*. I'm so sick of this *house*. You've got to take me out somewhere, for a ride or something."

"Don't be silly, Mickey," I said. "You've got to rest."

"Listen, I'm not going to waste another moment of our precious time lying around here being liverish. It's absolutely ridiculous. Now, come on. You've got to take me out. It's the loveliest part of the afternoon."

"As a matter of fact, I found the most marvelous place you ever saw. You really will love it."

"Where?"

"I'm not going to tell you; just take you there. But listen, I don't think you're up to it, really. Why don't we make it tomorrow?"

"No, I've got to get out of here for a while."

She would not be put off. In the car I said, "What was the matter with Mrs. Nesbit, anyway? What did she do?"

"She got very confidential and started telling me about her troubles."

"What sort of troubles?"

"Oh, she has a son she's terribly worried about. They got him an appointment to the Academy, and then he dropped out in his second year and went off to California to work in a laundry or something, and they can't understand where they've failed. We were quite a pair: me with my enteritis and she with her wayward son."

"What did you do, load her up with martinis?"

"Nothing but tea, honestly. She had just reached that point, I guess. Of course it really must be awful: to think you've ruined your own child's life in some terrible mysterious way that you don't understand, and can't help, and can't ever redeem. God, that's a *real* problem. I'm glad that's one we don't have, anyway."

The dust billowed all around us in soft lime-like clouds. The violet stripes of shadow from the cypresses lashed our faces. A cock hurtled across the road in front of us in a mad, heraldic way, his plunged neck shimmering green and rust, his scarlet sliver of tongue spurting like a blood-jet from his gaping beak. Among the eucalyptus trees the still villas were gathered in the warm gold-dust of afternoon.

"Oh, Lord, how lovely," Margaret said.

The lighthouse enchanted her, as it had me. We got out and walked hand in hand between the red blossoms to its base, standing to look up at the stone-bound cupola reeling against the clouds.

"You discovered this?" she said. "This is a magic lighthouse."

"I think we should buy it."

"I do, too. I mean, it wouldn't really be an extravagance, would it? It's something we really need."

Inside the door, in a little circular lobby appointed with brass lanterns, there was a polished brass commemorative plaque set in the stone, on which, in bas relief, a beheaded, whiskered engineer stared at us above a gravely worded incantation. Beneath it there was a display case through whose glass panes were seen, as if in ice, fading photographs of stages of construction, an antique sextant, frayed, cinnamon-colored mariners' charts, and a tiny dessicated spider. An old man in a worn, pale military uniform sat at an oak table with a stack of pamphlets and a wooden cigar box, smiling a brown, rotten smile.

"What is the fee?" I asked.

"What you wish." He held the box toward me, in the same gesture opening and dropping back its lid to reveal a heap of coins and tattered franc notes. "One pays what one can afford."

I groped in my pocket and brought out two bright, freshly minted coins. "Is that sufficient?" He nodded. The coins dropped with a bitter clink into the box. He handed me a pair of pamphlets, his dark hand trembling.

"You will find it worth the price, monsieur. The view is magnificent."

It was bare and cold and clean. Everything stone was whitewashed; everything wooden, varnished; everything metal, polished. The blaze of sunlight from the panes of the observatory above rained on the bone-white walls, the stone steps that spiraled up against them and the hand-rail of burnished brass that writhed in a contracting spasm to the dazzle of sunburst at the top.

"Can you climb them?" I asked Margaret.

"Yes. I must see from the top."

Our footsteps rang in the still, stone-cool air. At intervals of twenty feet or so there were slotted windows in the tower walls with deep stone sills, a foot in breadth, through which, on the seaward side, the low sun sent almost horizontal shafts of light. At each of these we stopped, leaning into the sills, our heads bathed in the sauterne-colored light of the late afternoon, staring down through the fluted black bars to the gently seething silver of the sea. The lighthouse itself stood on a high cliffbound promontory, its sheer rock faces standing naked, cleft by landfalls, brazed by the low light that streamed across the water; at their base we saw the line of snow-white sea-foam, so distant it was motionless and soundless, and tiny boats with a white feather of wake behind them, everything frozen and exquisite, like a piece of porcelain chinoiserie.

"Can you see Villefranche?" I asked.

"Yes. There. It's even tinier than from the villa."

"The countess said we'd see the flagship soon. They anchor there. She was very bitter about it."

"Why?"

"Apparently whenever they're in port they bring in a flood of vice from Paris. Whores and gamblers and what-not."

"Oh, dear. Why do we cause so much confusion everywhere we go?"

"The Pax Americana, I guess. Over here they seem to regard it as the Pox Americana. Something very virulent and contagious. I guess they prefer their own diseases."

"They've built up an immunity to them. I wish *I* had."

"What do you mean by that?"

"I mean my Galloping Gastro-itis or whatever it is. What would I mean?"

"Is it getting bad again?"

"No, I'm better, really. But I had some beautiful moments. What else did she have to say?"

"She sent her regards and said for you to get well immediately, or she'd be around in person to see that you were taken care of. Stew up a pot of her bat-liver brew for you, I guess."

Margaret laughed. "Poor old witch. You're not kind to her."

"Andrea sent his regards, too. He was there."

"Andrea? Really?"

"Yes. He recommended the Blanc de Chine, too, by the way."

"He did?"

She was wearing a sleeveless dress. The cool damp air had chilled her arms. From elbow to shoulder the flesh was tinted a pale mottled blue, stippled with little chalky papillae of gooseflesh. I put my hand around her upper arm; it had the heavy, slightly swollen feeling of flesh that is past maturity. When I released it I left the livid imprint of my four fingers across the pale violet skin.

"Look what you've done," she said, turning her head to watch the white bars fade slowly.

"Are you cold?"

"A little."

"You'd better have my jacket."

"I don't want you to freeze."

"Don't be silly; you're sick. Here."

We went up to the second stage. Everything had grown more miniature, more stylized; the view was even vaster.

"I must say you have all the fun," Margaret said.

"What do you mean? You had Mrs. Nesbit."

"Oh, yes. And you're carousing with the International Set. I don't know why you went there, anyway. I thought you disliked them both intensely."

"Oh, I never said that. As a matter of fact, I got on very well with Andrea. We made a business deal."

"A business deal? What do you mean? What sort of a deal?"

"You'd never guess. I signed you up to take lessons with him."

"You *what*? *Why*?"

"I don't know. Moment of weakness."

"But that's crazy. We can't afford it. I don't believe you."

"Well, you keep saying you want to take lessons from somebody; and then he started this long pitch this afternoon about just losing one of his pupils and how desperate he was; so I thought, well, why not from him? You seem to admire the poor devil, and everybody says he *is* a good teacher. So I let him talk me into it."

"Well, honest to goodness. If you don't surprise me sometimes." She turned her head to look at me tenderly for a moment, her hair blazing in the mist of sunlight. "You really do."

"Why so surprised?"

"Well, it was very nice. Not only to me, but to him. It really was, Mickey."

"Probably the most foolish thing I ever did."

"But we can't afford it; you know we can't. It's extravagant. I don't need any silly French lessons. I was just nagging."

"Well, it's up to you. It isn't really so expensive: Ten dollars for two lessons a week. Just the price of a restaurant meal, really."

"Oh, that isn't so bad, is it? But still, it's an extravagance. The main thing is, you thought of it. That's what's so nice."

"There wasn't any particular altruism involved. That guy is a salesman. I thought he was going to fall sobbing at my feet."

"Oh, dear. Really? I suppose ten dollars means a lot more

to him than to us. You mean you actually told him that I would?"

"Well, I didn't sign anything. I told him I thought you might be interested, because you'd been talking about taking lessons; so I said I'd mention it to you, that's all, and let him know."

"Oh, goodness, you can't make *me* decide. That isn't fair."

"Well, it's not worth going into a flap about. If you think you'd enjoy it, and get something out of it, well fine. If not, forget it. I just thought it was an opportunity. I don't imagine he's going to starve. He'll always round up somebody, sooner or later, to fill in."

"I suppose so."

In the harbor of Beaulieu, bright-colored and immaculate, as if embroidered on a bedspread, we saw a trawler unloading at the quay. A heavy hemp net swung from her cargo boom, dripping mercury. We saw the glitter of sunlight on the catch, a shimmering shower of silver as the herring poured out of the net into barrels on the quay.

"Oh, that was beautiful," Margaret said. Gulls hovered and wheeled and plunged beneath us like white petals streaming in the wind, the debris of a bridal wreath. "If I worked in a place like this I'd go absolutely wild."

"Shall we go up?"

"Yes. Each one is more fantastic than the last."

She stumbled and tottered for a moment on the steps, her hand reaching out to clutch the coiled brass hand-rail. It trembled a little from the impact of her grasp, like a bright convulsive nerve. I caught and held her arm.

"Are you getting woozy?"

"No. I just hooked my heel." She looked up into the blaze at the top of the stairwell. "How many more stages are there?"

"Just two, then the top."

"*En avant,* then. How's that for French?"

"Just like Danielle Darrieux."

"You see, I don't need any lessons."

375

"No. I think you're right. We'd better forget it."

"Of course it would be wonderful to be able to pick up the telephone without getting paralyzed with fright. And to go home and natter away in French at cocktail parties like a mad cosmopolite."

"I'm not sure we should encourage that."

"Ah, you see! You're backing out now."

I smiled and denied it. From the next window the view was truly intoxicating. We seemed to have passed beyond some critical dividing line of altitude above which the charm, the simple novelty of unusual but still not unnatural height had become transposed into something of a different order, an unearthly sense of separation, a kind of transport. The boats, the tiny harbors, villages, and highways, all the works and ways of men, were lost in distance; lost, it seemed, almost beyond reclamation. We had slipped forever beyond the reach of their gravities, which we felt loosening about our hearts like dying fingers. The sea lay like the bottom of a gigantic bowl, a curving sheet of blue enamel, hard and brilliant, falling toward Africa; only this sea, and the Alps, streaming mist above the pathetic villages, survived the scale of our perspective. They were all we saw that matched in majesty our own hauteur, that did not provoke some soft ignoble feeling: pity, amusement, condescension: as did the neat toy hamlets, the ribboned highways, the tiny tidy patchwork fields, cultivated to such a frivolous, spurious symmetry. I don't know how to account for the grandeur of this sensation; it was something I had never experienced in any remotely similar form from treetops, mountaintops, airplanes, or the Empire State Building. It must have been the combined result of mood, circumstance, and the glamour of the place. There is a phenomenon called "the rapture of the deep," from which, I understand, divers sometimes suffer at great depths; perhaps there is a corresponding rapture of the heights, which afflicted Margaret and me in the lighthouse. She did feel it, as well as me. She shivered and pressed against me.

"Are you dizzy?" I asked.

"Dizzy or drunk, or something. It's just incredible, isn't it?"

"Yes."

"Why don't I feel like this in the Washington Monument?"

"I don't know. Maybe because it's the Tidal Basin underneath, instead of the Mediterranean; and what you see in the distance is the Pentagon parking lot and the Commerce Department, not the shores of Corsica and Sicily and Thebes."

"That could make a difference," Margaret said. "But I don't know about *this* much. I feel strange up here."

"Well, you said it was a magic tower."

"I really think it is."

Her head, outlined against the infinite blue sea, so far below, had a delicate classical look, winsome, wanton, and Grecian, like a Wedgewood goddess. I touched her cheek with my knuckles. Her skin was cool. She did not smile or stir at my touch. Her eyes fell. Below us the old doorkeeper coughed; the sound was given a strange animal intensity by the hollowness and cold of the stone vault. It rang up through the stairwell like the snarl of a panther. We looked up at the burning milky radiance that poured through the observatory panes. The hot golden nerve of the hand-rail wound through the white mist like a gilded serpent.

"Shall we go up?"

"I don't know if I can," she said. "I feel a little giddy. Maybe I've tried to do too much."

Her throat was stretched, looking up. I leaned toward her and kissed her throat. Still she did not smile.

"What was that for?" she asked.

"You have a pretty throat."

"Well, you're getting very fancy. It must be the height." She looked up, clutching the lapels of the jacket about her breast. The luminous explosion above drenched her eyes and lips with light. "I wonder if there's anybody up there? I've got an absolutely wild idea."

"Shall I see?"

She paused, her eyes strained. There was a tumultuous stillness in her that made her swallow suddenly. "No, I guess not. I don't think I could stand the height just now. I'm tired. We'd better go down."

"Are you all right?"

"Yes. I'm just a little weaker than I thought. I'll be better when I get outside."

I took her arm and we came back down the steps abreast. Margaret's hand, the fingers clenched lightly, slid down in a long caress over the smooth bright rail. She placed her feet in an absorbed and careful way, as I have seen children, walking on a beach, retrace their footsteps through the sand. The doorkeeper, his face turned up into the light, watched our descent with pale burning eyes. He was drinking wine out of a tin cup; a very dark red wine, which had stained his mustache unpleasantly.

"You did not go to the top," he said.

"No, not all the way."

"A pity. The view is unmatched."

"Madame was a little indisposed."

"You must come back. No visit to the South is complete, otherwise."

"Perhaps we will."

Outside, the warmth of the open afternoon air was very sweet. In the car Margaret took off the jacket and let the wind blow over her bare arms and through her hair. She held her eyes closed, and her face, bathed by the low light and the warm wind, had a lovely sculptured look of purity and composure. The wind forced the flesh back slightly against the bones and smoothed the faint cobwebs of lines about her eyes, and the late light flooded all the minor imperfections of her skin and features with an ivory wash that gave her face that look of passionless, idealized beauty of children or statuary.

I prepared the watercress soup for her supper and a bowl

of salad for myself, and we ate from the arms of our deck-chairs on the terrace through the twilight into darkness. The sea was flaming. Then there was a purple deluge out of the sky, pouring down like dark wine over the Grand Corniche and the hillside villas and the port of Villefranche. We spoke hardly at all; we were very tired. I asked her once if I should light candles, but she said no, she preferred the dark.

We went to bed very early, with the windows open and the night air blowing the curtains. The air was soft and jas-mine-scented and made the branches of the pines outside the window tremble so that the stars beyond them flickered, obscured intermittently by the black, shifting branches. After we had lain for some time in the darkness I heard her say questioningly, "Mickey?" but I did not answer. Almost im-mediately after, I fell into a fathomless, lightless, aboriginal sleep.

In the morning I said to Margaret, "I told Andrea I'd call him this morning. What shall I tell him, then?"

"I don't know," Margaret said. She was pouring coffee. I had asked her for a second cup, and she had taken the empty cup from me and turning in her chair extended her arm across the edge of the parapet and poured the lees into the flowerbed below. Ordinarily she set a deep saucer on the table at break-fast for this purpose. The small departure from our morning breakfast ritual disturbed me. The slight extravagance, the slight bravura of the unfamiliar gesture—holding her arm at full length, swinging the cup, then halting it abruptly to toss abroad a sprinkle of shining caramel-colored globules—upset some extraordinary impulse toward formality or ceremony which seemed to possess me at the moment. "Some people use coffee grounds for mulch," she said. "It's supposed to be good for them. The flowers. I don't know. What do you think I should tell him?"

"Whatever you like. As far as the money goes, ten dollars

a week isn't going to break us. Why don't you try it for a couple of weeks and see if you get anything out of it? You can always drop out, if you like."

"All right. If you really think I should."

"Well, it isn't a matter of what you *should* do; just what you *want* to do."

"All right, then. You can tell him. Yes, I think it would be fun, if you're sure we can afford it." She poured the cup full and handed it to me across the table, her eyes resting, unmoving, on my face as I raised the cup and sipped.

"What's the matter?" I said.

"I forgot to put the eggshell in this morning. That's why it tastes different. I was wondering if you'd noticed."

"No. Tastes just the same to me."

"Well, think of that. That's something I've been doing every day of my life for the last fourteen years, and now you can't even tell the difference." She folded her hands into fists and rested her chin on them, staring at me with no expression whatever. "Thank you for my lessons."

"Don't mention it."

Andrea was delighted. He arrived the following afternoon at forty-seven minutes after three in a bright blue Aston-Martin, carrying a textbook entitled *Nouvelles Causeries en France* and a sheaf of flash-cards on which were printed drawings of bears, kites, apples, penknives, shoes, and loaves of bread. He was wearing a Victorian-styled cotton jacket with a broad blue vertical stripe and blue piping along the edges of the pockets and lapels, white flannel trousers, and a necktie, handkerchief, and suede shoes all of pale powder blue. He smelled of a spice-laden cologne, and one springy lock of black hair trembled about his forehead when he laughed, which he did almost incessantly. He accepted a glass of sherry and wandered admiringly around the salon, pausing to stand and nod his head in silent approval before the volumes of Erasmus, at whose spines he waggled one short, brown, solemn finger with a smile which seemed to say, "So. All is said."

"They're not ours," Margaret confessed gently.

"But they are here," he said, his eyebrows raising cryptically.

We retired to the terrace, where he set his glass on the parapet and took up the binoculars to make a roving survey of the sea and shore below, in the course of which his head began to bob again in its benedictory way.

"Yes, this is the place for you," he said, setting the glasses down and turning to face us, leaning with crossed legs against the parapet. "I come to an imperative decision. You must come back every year and spend the summer here. We cannot do without you."

"I think it's a glorious idea," Margaret said. "But I'm afraid we're once-in-a-lifetime sort of people, as far as Cap Ferrat is concerned."

"No, you are not. I know that sort of people, believe me. I know almost no other type. But you are the sort of people who, when they discover something truly beautiful, can never be satisfied with anything less. If you do not come back you will not be content. Nor will we."

"I hope you're wrong," Margaret said. "That would be an awful outcome for such a lovely summer: a lifetime of discontent."

"It is very easy to avoid," he said, raising his open hands with a shrug. Margaret laughed, and although it was my turn to speak, I deliberately—and ignobly, on many counts—permitted the simplicity of the solution to go unchallenged. As a matter of fact, I compounded the ignobility by observing that there were many places that we had not yet seen, and increasingly fewer summers to see them in.

"But you are *young!*" he cried gallantly. I did not deny this, either. In a moment I finished my martini, set down the empty glass, and said that I had better go away and allow him to educate my wife.

"Will you wait for me on the beach, after?" Margaret asked.

"Yes. Maybe Andrea would like to join us when you've finished."

"I have not my costume," he said.

"There's one of Mickey's you can wear. The blue one; can't he, Mickey?"

"Yes, of course."

"You are very kind. Perhaps for half an hour, then. Unfortunately I must get back to Nice by six."

"I'll look forward to seeing you, then."

He straightened up from his reclining position against the parapet, smiled, bowed, and accompanied me to the curtain of the terrace portal, a handful of whose glittering glass beads he paused to drape and fondle across his carpenter's hands, making one of those few chimerical remarks which served periodically to temper my opinion of the man. "They are like rain, aren't they? A beautiful rain falling."

I left the villa and walked quickly down the Chemin du Roy—I was twenty minutes late—to a partially paved, weed-cracked, barricaded turnoff from the main road which had been the intended entranceway to an abandoned building project at a further extremity of the Cape. Here, several score of yards within its densely shielded bower of oleander, Gwynyth lay nude in the sunlight on a large flat slab of lichenous rock, blowing idle puffs of breath at globes of dandelion blossom that occasionally floated by. I sat beside her on the rock and kissed her lips, eyes, nostrils, nipples, navel, and the sweetly cleft nectarine buried in the blazing flax of her thighs.

"My God. You're hungry," she said.

"Yes."

"You're late. Where have you been?"

"I had something rather important to attend to. I'm sorry."

"Jolly important, it must have been. Is it secret, as well?"

"No. Andrea came to call. I couldn't very well dash off the moment he arrived."

"Andrea? How extraordinary. What did he want?"

"He's giving Mickey French lessons."

"You're not serious?"

"Yes."

She stared at me for some time with a quaintly reflective look, raising her hand to tuck back with a fingertip the bridge of her battered sunglasses.

"Well, that's rather an odd development, isn't it?"

"Why? It gives me a very legitimate excuse to get away two afternoons a week."

"Oh, I see. But why Andrea? There must be absolute pots of language tutors about."

"Why not? He was the only one we had any acquaintance with at all. And Margaret likes him."

"Oh, does she?" She reached out suddenly to clutch a floating globe of dandelion seed, shattering it in her clenched fingers, then opening them slowly to blow away the shreds of gossamer with that look of suspended petulance, of instantaneous reverie, with which such things as butterflies, silver balloons of dandelion seed, or the icy tinkle of glass beads transformed the somewhat bitter beauty of her face. She blew each silvery sliver of seed from between her fingers, then sat up and clutched her legs, resting her chin on her knees and narrowing her blue eyes in the glare from the sea.

"They're up there now, are they? Studying?"

"Yes."

"For how long?"

"An hour. Perhaps a bit longer."

"Then what happens? Have you to go back?"

"No. They're going to join us down at the beach. Or so they say."

"Oh. Then we'd better make the best of our time, hadn't we?"

"Yes."

She turned toward me and began undoing the buttons of the silk sport shirt I was wearing. When she was only half-finished I took her by the shoulders and began devouring in turn her sealed, fluttering eyes, her ears, and her shuddering brown throat. Her sunglasses fell and tinkled into ruins on the rock.

"My God, you're wild today. What's got into you, anyway?"

"I don't know."

"Lord, I love you like this. Oh, Lord, men are wonderful."

When we had finished we lay with our hands loosely clutched together, staring through our closed, sun-drenched eyelids into a crimson infinity, recovering our breath with long, lingering, narcotic drafts of jasmine-scented air, tremblingly inhaled and gaspingly expelled, with a sound almost of horror. Gwynyth giggled in a moment.

"We sound like two freshly caught flounders expiring on a pier," she said.

"So we are."

"Rubbish. I never felt better in my life. Just need to catch my breath a bit, that's all." She smacked me on the belly with the flat of her palm. "You're always being so bloody metaphysical about it. I'm absolutely certain you're a Jew."

"I am. A freshly caught, floundering, rapidly expiring Jewish metaphysician. Captured with just a sliver of apple for bait; or a nectarine, to be more accurate."

"Oh, Jesus. I should hate you if you weren't able to screw me within an inch of my life. Have you brought any drink?"

"No."

"No. There you are."

She sat up and began to gather fragments of her sunglass lenses from the rock, searching out the slivers of shattered colored glass and dropping them into one outspread palm.

"Just see what you've done to my glasses. And I've had them for ten years. I shall be a nervous wreck without them."

"It's time you had a new pair, anyway. *They* were a wreck."

"Nothing of the sort. I was just getting adjusted to the idea that the whole universe was a sort of lovely muck-brown color. It'll take me absolute centuries to get used to anything else. I shall have a collapse of some sort."

"Come over here and have it," I said.

"Yes, all right." She did so, very winsomely, laying her head into the hollow of my throat, her arm across my chest, and wedging one warm brown thigh between my own with a long sigh of content. "I shouldn't mind dying now, at all. I'm so absolutely still and warm inside. You make me feel dreadfully good, you know. I should like to thank you for that, in case I forget to, ever."

I clutched her close involuntarily with gratitude, and said in a moment, "May I ask you a rather impertinent question?"

"Yes, all right."

"What is the relationship between you and Adrian?"

"We're very dear friends. We love each other."

"You're not having an affair?"

"No. We did once, years ago, when we were at school together. But that's all done."

"What happened?"

"Nothing happened. Or rather, everything. We just moved on. We love each other, you see. Do you mean you don't understand that?"

"Not exactly."

"Well, what do you reckon is the greatest good you can wish someone else? I reckon it's liberty. We wouldn't dream of taking that from each other. It's so jolly simple, I don't understand why you're all muddled about it."

"But you don't go to bed with him any longer?"

"No, certainly not. But I don't think there's anyone in the world I should go further to help if he were in trouble, or whose unhappiness or death I should regret more. You really *don't* see, do you?"

"Not exactly," I said. "But I have glimmerings. I have glimmerings. Or perhaps it's just the light in this place. It makes you think you see things better; it's so strong."

"Well, it's jolly weak in Adams Mews, I can tell you," Gwynyth said. "Which is where I learned about love, living on cat food and spaghetti for two years, while we scrounged our way through RADA. And what I learned mostly is that you don't mention the bloody subject. You don't have to, if it's there. And that it has nothing to do with possession, with owning someone's body and soul, because you've got a certificate of title to them filed away in a drawer somewhere. But just the opposite: restoring someone to himself again; giving him back clear title to his own soul and body, after years of bondage to one person or another. That's what Adrian did for me. Along with cooking pots of absolutely marvelous spaghetti, and hearing me my words when I'd an awful part to learn, and saving crusts for me to feed the seagulls at the Round Pond, and watering my flowerpots when I went home to Mile End for weekends. And when it was time for me to go, letting me go without a single bloody question, and taking me to Scott's in Piccadilly that night for the most marvelous meal I'd ever eaten in my life, as his way of saying, 'Thank you.' That's sweet, you know. That's jolly sweet. That's why I love the man."

"I see."

"It isn't a word I like using, because most people don't know what one means by it, at all."

"Well, I'm glad you explained it to me," I said.

She lay still for a moment and then said with extraordinary gentleness, "I thought it might be a good thing, one day, if you knew about it, too."

She would not come down to the beach with me to wait for Margaret and Andrea, which annoyed me.

"It'll look bloody bad, you know," she said. "Even if Adrian and the others are there. How are we going to explain where we've been all this while? And if they're not, it'll look all the worse: the two of us larking about while she's been slaving away up there at the villa with Andrea. No, I shall walk down to the fork and hitch a ride to Villefranche."

"I don't like you hitching all these rides," I said. "It's damn dangerous."

"Then you shall jolly well have to get used to it, shan't you? Would you rather Margaret was hurt?"

"No."

"No. Nor would I. Zip me up, will you, love?"

She was getting into a pair of yellow Dacron slacks that clung to her hips like a coat of honey. Her yellow hair had fallen all about her throat and face, and in her haste to dress had been buttoned into the upper buttonhole of her blouse. She bit her lips and growled, snapping her loosely flung fingers in the Italian gesture of impatience. I felt in the warm masses of her hair for her ears and clutched them, kissing her ravenously, gone suddenly senseless with fresh desire.

"Oh, Jesus, please, darling," she murmured. "We're so late, and we'll get caught, and then what? Oh, Jesus, please don't start me off again, will you?"

"I can't let you go."

"I know. Oh, don't I know."

She broke away from me and went plunging out through the barricaded entrance to the Chemin du Roy, her slacks unzipped, her blouse flying loosely about her bare breasts, her yellow hair streaming.

I don't give a damn, I thought. I hope we do get caught, and then I can buy one of those beautiful Italian target pistols and shoot us all, and make arrangements for the newspaper clippings to be sent to all our friends and relatives, and that will be that.

"Listen," I shouted, "you'd better come back here or I'll start screaming. I'll tell everybody about it. You come back here!"

She fled down the road, gathering together her flapping clothing as she ran, until she disappeared where the Chemin du Roy bends to the right away from the imitation beach with its imported sand from Africa and the cluster of candy-colored villas, looking as if made of sugar-icing on a very elaborate anniversary cake.

I went bitterly down to the beach through the shaded lane and picked my way among the prostrate bodies in the lee of the bath house to the far end of the strand, where I lay face down in the brown sand until, perhaps twenty minutes later, Margaret poked me in the small of the back with the thermos jug and said in a brand-new, very ostentatious accent, *"Levez-vous, mon mari. Voici nous, alors."* I looked up and saw the four pillars of their legs standing side by side; Margaret's, slim, pale, shaven nude; Andrea's thickly, blackly haired, with calves of carved mahogany, above them a pair of Herculean thighs defined by the knitted border of my blue bathing trunks, which he filled, buttock and crotch, with a distinction wholly novel to them.

"Hi. How'd you get on?" I said.

"Oh, I learned so *much*! Honestly. In just an hour. Andrea's absolutely wonderful!"

"That's what I understand."

"Oh, no, she is the wonderful one!" cried Andrea, his brown face convulsed with appreciation. "Such intelligence! It astounds me. She will learn everything in a month." He raised his hands in awe.

Margaret's pleasure was obvious. She laughed and said, "Well, it's such a lovely language, and I have such a lovely teacher, that I don't see how anyone could *not* do well. Still, you'd have to say we're a pretty good team, I guess."

"Ah. Exactly," said Andrea. He bowed, then raised his hands to take the lapels of the white chenille bathing gown out of which she had begun to struggle, and lift it from her shoulders.

"We're going to have a dip right away, because Andrea has to get back to Nice. Are you coming?"

"No, I've just dried out. I'll lie here for a while and have some of the Cinzano."

"All right. I don't know what's the matter with you; you were in such a rush you left it on the kitchen table." She stooped to set the thermos bottle and her raffia bag on the beach towel I had spread on the sand. Andrea folded her robe and laid it beside them.

"We will swim once to the jetty," he said. "And then I will have a very small sip of your Cinzano, and then, unfortunately, I must go. But I have brought my clothing in the bag, so it is not necessary to return to the villa. I can change in the pavilion, and there will be no need to disturb you."

"Oh, that wasn't necessary," I said. "But it was thoughtful of you, Andrea."

"Come on," Margaret said. "I'll beat you to the jetty."

"I have no doubt of it," said Andrea. "I swim like a locomotive." This was true, I discovered, watching him flounder out toward the jetty in a really monstrous style, his arms thrashing back and forth like railway pistons, demonstrating very little more buoyancy and almost as much of the steam, uproar, and general turbulence as one of the old-fashioned six-eight wheelers of my youth thundering down a rural straightaway. There was something rather sad in his confession of the fact, because he swam, as a matter of fact, exactly as all poor children swim—never having been properly instructed in the art—or as they play tennis or golf. A few years ago there was an Italian tennis player named Giuseppe Merlo who played in exactly this way: with a flailing, graceless, but indomitable determination that managed to win him international standing and very respectful entry into such tournaments as Wimbledon and Forest Hills. Nevertheless there was something so grotesque, so depressing to me about his play that I almost never stayed to see one of his matches through. Watching Andrea swim gave me an almost identical feeling of discomfort. Apparently there was no limit to the mortification he was to work upon me.

They were back in a moment, laughing, panting, and scattering drops of water as they toweled themselves. We sipped Cinzano and smoked cigarettes, Andrea sitting cross-legged with his towel draped across his head and clutched beneath his chin like a burnoose, one eyebrow arched in a startlingly impressive parody of Rudolph Valentino. He tapped the tangled moist curls of his chest and murmured in a melancholy and lubricious voice, "Sheik. You recognize? Sheik."

"*Oui, oui. Très chic!*" said Margaret, and they both burst

into rolling, helpless laughter at the ingenuity of her joke. "One lesson, and already she makes puns!" cried Andrea. He clapped his hands and held them pressed prayerfully together in admiration. "This is a formidable woman! Oh, it is a delight to teach her! I should pay for the privilege."

A little later he went to the pavilion, changed into his street clothes, returned with my trunks and towel, expressed an almost Apostolic gratitude for the use of them, and departed, turning back just as he passed out of sight at the edge of the pavilion to wave good-bye to us in the curious Italian clutching gesture of the raised hand which seems to beckon rather than to bid farewell.

Margaret and I finished the contents of the thermos jug and then climbed lazily and a little unsteadily through the lacelike shadows of the Chemin du Roy toward the villa, pausing at the uppermost bend of the road to regain our breath and look down at the evening light on the sea. I stood behind her with my arms about her waist and she lay against me, resting her head on my shoulder.

"I take it you're satisfied with your tutor," I said.

"I *am*. You know that boy is intelligent, Mickey; really? He's more than just clever, I mean; he's really intuitive. He has a way of making you see things immediately and dramatically, somehow. I think it's because he has a basically theatrical nature. Those kind of people always make the best teachers."

"Also the best politicians, bullfighters, and prostitutes," I said.

"I suppose so." She twisted her head to peer up at me. "What does that mean?"

"Just an idle observation. That's all I have to offer anymore: just idle observations."

"What's happened to your famous *Weltanschauung*?"

"Dissolved," I said, " in alcohol and sunshine."

"Oh, dear. Just like my famous Kansas Articles of Belief. Who's going to keep up the moral fiber around here?"

"I don't know. We may have to learn to get along without it."

She giggled. "Improvising madly between thermos bottles." She twisted her head again, to lay her cheek against mine. "Do you know how I feel right now? Just like when we used to drink wine in Rock Creek Park and get absolutely stoned. Do you remember? Painting wild pictures and eating salami and kissing each other. Oh, my goodness. Oh, my goodness." She raised her hand and laid her five fingertips lightly against her temple, staring across the Mediterranean at the sycamore trees along Rock Creek. "Oh my goodness."

"Oh, your goodness," I said, kissing her on the ear. "Oh, your goodness. Oh, your goodness."

I have said that I never saw Gwynyth act; which is true enough, although the statement might be challenged, I suppose, in its strict sense. A little over six months ago, on the strength of my surpassing pallor, I was persuaded by a friend to attend a celebrated motion picture in his company. It cost seven million dollars to produce and I am sure was not as bad as it seemed. I was tired, had eaten a supremely discouraging meal of veal cutlet, and my friend, although a generous and compassionate man, held opinions about modern drama which were far too enthusiastic for entire comfort. We arrived, moreover, very near the end of the film, and had to wait until the theater was lighted, cleared, and reoccupied to see the initial two thirds of it. In this interim there was shown a preview of a coming attraction, a British film about a shipwreck and the subsequent adventures of its survivors on a desert island. I can't remember the name of it, for my attention was as desultory as these things generally deserve, until suddenly, in the midst of the jumbled scraps of passion and pageantry with which it hoped to lure us back to Loew's Palace, there was flashed on the screen a gigantic, colored, animated portrait of Gwynyth's face, her Mediterranean-colored eyes drowsing under their black brows, her yellow hair scattered, her red mouth, with its weary, opulent look of desire, drooping toward me like a wind-blasted rose, as once, on the little beach below Port l'Escale, she had bestrode my body, her knees dug into the sand, her hands clenched gently on my shoulders, the sunlight blazing through her hanging hair while, in rhythm with the oceanic surging of her hips, she murmured, "Good. Good. Good. Good. Good."

I don't believe I need to emphasize the state of shock into which I was thrown by the wanton exposure, before a whole theaterful of total strangers—most of them cynically eating popcorn—of this buried, blazing intimacy out of my life.

"You look ill," my friend said. "Is it your heart?"

"No, no. It's just a twinge of some kind. I get it periodically. Nothing to worry about."

He watched me anxiously, however, for the next half-hour or so, until satisfied that the histrionics of several hundred Cossack horsemen, by whom the screen was now occupied, had restored me. I did not fully appreciate them, however, although I clucked my tongue agreeably now and then, as one does to indicate respect for the Epic View of Life; I was occupied with devastations of a far more substantial sort:

Gwynyth, crouching in a rattan armchair at the sunny window of a hotel room we have rented for the day in Nice, peering out through the dusty voile curtains at the idle afternoon flow of events in a quiet, hidden, very clean, square park, paved with white stone, bordered with royal palms and surrounded by blazing white rococo *fin de siècle* hotels, like the set for a screen version of a Feydeau farce; nude, clutching her shiny brown knees to her chin, the rattan creaking as she shifts forward to follow the course of some especially appealing vignette in the street below, stirred to an occasional chirrup, chuckle, snort, or wearily ironic declination of her head, plucking periodically from the windowsill a glass of iced Cinzano which she sips, then clasps against her throat, shivering at its coldness; carrying on with me, meanwhile, a desultory yet curiously electric dialogue, scraps of opinion, narrative, observation, which range from the cosmic to the dazzlingly picayune, and which bring my eyes occasionally down to the nape of her brown neck from the garland of plaster cupids gamboling about the base of the porcelain chandelier under which, my body still wet from our lovemaking, I lie in the delicious breeze of an electric fan.

"I love those white tropical helmets the police wear. Will you get me one?"

"How on earth will I get you a policeman's helmet?"

"I've no idea. But you must. I've got to have one."

"What for?"

"To scrawl graffiti on. They absolutely scream for desecration." After a moment, "Do you know what I saw on the wall of the loo in the casino the other night? 'God is not dead; He is just very, very sick.' Isn't that marvelous?"

"Yes."

"I mean, what else is there left to say? God, I've read whole thumping great solemn novels that labored the point for five hundred pages, and didn't get half as much sense, or fun, out of it."

"I know. I've read a few myself."

"Well, there you are. It's time we routed those solemn, windy buggers out of the arts entirely. Take this room, for example. Only a very, very serious man could have designed a room like this."

"Still, we've had a lot of fun in it."

"Oh, you can have fun in it, yes; but it's rather an expensive joke. Sort of like building St. Pancras Station just for a laugh. Or writing *Die Walküre*."

"You think *Die Walküre* is funny?"

"I think it's an absolute howl. But of course it's not meant to be, and that's one of the funniest things about it."

"What else is funny?"

"Like that, do you mean; or really funny?"

"Like that."

"Well, American automobiles, and bowler hats, and the Albert Memorial, and Dryden's plays—especially one called *Aureng-Zebe*—and *Land of Hope and Glory*, and the whole city of New York, except for Harlem."

"I'm surprised you left out the Houses of Parliament."

"Oh, they're not funny. They would be hilarious, of course, except that they can hurt you. You can't laugh at the absurdity of anything that can hurt you; or you're a bloody fool if you do. The whole of life would be a riot, otherwise. But if you're dying of cancer, or happen to get your legs blown off by an atom bomb, you sort of stop chuckling about it all. That's when you get mad."

"When did you get mad?" I asked.

"Oh, I'm not always mad." She turned to grin at me. "I didn't act awfully mad just now, did I?"

"No, not just now."

"Well, there you are. Give me my due."

"I couldn't possibly," I said.

"Well, you'd better start trying. I mean to have a policeman's helmet, or I shall make a disturbance."

"You've already made a disturbance," I said.

"Nothing to what I shall do." And then she rises and comes toward me, the sunlight from the window behind her showering her slim body with a milky radiance, and curls up beside me on the bed, her head on my breast, her moist sauterne-colored hair scattered on our faces, her little witch's hands probing the bones of my cheeks and jaws and skull.

"Lovely head, you've got. All put together like a puzzle; one of those Japanese wooden apples you get in your Christmas stocking. I rather like men's heads."

"That's not all you like about them, is it?"

"No, not all. But the head's got to be right, or the rest of it doesn't matter. Funny, that." And, after a moment, "Do you know what else is funny? How people happen to hit it off, at all. You absolutely never know when someone'll be

394

right for you, do you? I can't make out at all, for example, what it is that you and I have; but it's there, you know."

"It's there, all right."

"I knew a girl once would have nothing but dwarfs. Nothing else got to her, at all: movie stars, football heroes, nuclear physicists, poets. Had to have one of these wretched dwarfs; and of course they're not all that easy to come by. Life was a perfect torment for her, scuttling up and down alleys looking for tiny men. There's simply no accounting for it."

"None at all."

"What is it for you, then?"

"Apparently, for me it's rag-tag butchers' daughters, drinking and swearing, wetting their pants, staring at butterflies, grinning and snarling, speaking poetry out of their mouths and eyes and ears, and out of this."

She rolled over, staring down into my face for a moment, and began to kiss me with quick little thirsty kisses, like the darting of a hummingbird.

"God, I love it when you talk to me like that. Really. It makes me itch. I love to know I've got you so stirred up. It's sort of like starting a bloody great fire and then flinging yourself into it."

"Well, come and get roasted."

"I think perhaps I will, you know."

Then, considerably later, "Well, look at me; your Roasted Apple." She very much resembled one: hot, brown, ripe, glazed with a syrupy patina, sweet juices boiling out of her, freshly removed—as I observed imprudently—from the mouth of the pig.

"Oh, Christ, there you go. I knew you would, sooner or later."

"Would what?"

"Oh, that bloody piety, bloody Anglican guilt. If you think you ought to pay for this—and I don't mean just with money;

with a couple of Hail Mary's or something—you've got the wrong girl, I can tell you. I won't have it."

"No payment intended," I said. "It was just an incidental comment on my own table manners."

"So what's the matter with pigs? We don't like the way they behave, we might not like to live with them, but we've no scruples when it comes to shoving them down our gullets. I should think we were half pig ourselves, many of them as we've eaten in our lifetimes."

"I don't like the subject," I said.

"Nobody likes it. That's why they wrote the bloody Bible." Then, after a rather freighted silence, having risen and begun indolently to whack ice cubes apart in the silver canister with the heel of her shoe, turning toward me with a level, articulate air, her voice gone cool and profound as the seawater of her eyes: "You give your Faith to Margaret. I don't want any of it. I'm not in the Business."

She could be very rough.

And very humbly, movingly sincere. Now (the Cossacks are still thundering about the screen, the village rooftops are still flaming in the sacked Ukraine) she is stretched out on a slatted bench, her head in my lap, staring idly toward Africa after a gloriously spontaneous experiment in a *pédalo* float, half a mile off the coast of Juan-les-Pins.

"I hope there's no one back there with binoculars. God, I suppose one day I shall actually go too far. Marvelous when it happens like that, though, isn't it? Such a sense of peace, afterward. God, I could sleep for six months."

I examine her ear with my fingertips, soothed and beguiled by its intricacy, delicacy, and, at the same time, its almost simian simplicity.

"Wasn't it ever like that with Andrea?"

"No. Oh, well, once or twice, I suppose, at the beginning. But it got steadily worse. Steadily and rapidly."

"And yet you said he was very good at it."

"Well, *expert,* I suppose I should have said. He was, yes.

And of course that can be terribly important, sometimes. But I got bloody tired of watching him comb his hair, I can tell you. D'you know when I packed it up with him, actually? Just before the countess' party; the very afternoon. I was watching him sitting on a stool in front of the bathroom mirror plucking his eyebrows with a pair of tweezers, and I suddenly realized I'd had it. Flung a martini at him and drenched all those glorious curls."

"I can't imagine a woman being attracted by that sort of a man," I said.

"Oh, can't you. Well, you've a lot to learn about women, let me tell you."

"Why?"

"Handsome beast like that? And skillful as he is? And he can talk, too, mind you, when there's something on the line. Lord, there's been a dozen or more millionairesses that *I* know of absolutely dotty over him; giving him clothes and cuff links and paying his club dues. Older women, mostly, of course, with not a lot to choose from. But some young ones, too. There are some types of women, you know, who like a certain amount of coarseness, and vanity, and cruelty in a man. Especially for sexual purposes. Do you mean you didn't know that?"

"I suppose I've suspected it," I said. "Do you think it's universal?"

"A jolly sight more than most of them admit. Well, just think of yourself; we're not so very different, you know, men and women. Do you mean to say you don't find a certain amount of indifference—or cruelty or perversity, even—stimulating in a woman?"

I smiled at her. "A certain amount."

"Well, there you are."

"You mean he actually accepts gifts from women for his —favors? Is he what you'd call a male prostitute, then?"

"Well, a rather sophisticated one, of course. A cut or two above a common beach boy. But I don't think there's much doubt about how he makes his living."

"I thought he was a language tutor," I said.

"Oh, well, that's his front, of course. That's what gives him entree to a good many of his clients. But you can't drive an Aston-Martin or play tennis at the Club de Monte Carlo on language lessons." She reaches up suddenly to tug at my hair. "You thinking of going into the business yourself? You're getting a bit cheeky, aren't you?"

"No. It's just reassuring to know that I can compete with a professional."

"You need a jolly lot of reassuring, don't you? You're doing all right, you know. I shouldn't be here, otherwise."

"It's not getting steadily worse?"

"No. Better, actually."

"With me, too. How much better do you suppose it can get? Is there a limit?"

"Oh, there's a limit, you can be sure of that. But I don't know that we'll reach it before we run out of time. Perhaps that's what keeps it going, actually."

"I hate to admit that," I said.

"Well, you'd be better off if you did. That's the mother of all poetry: time. Or the lack of it, rather. There'd be bloody little done in this world if we thought we had forever to do it in. I've said that before."

"I remember."

"I don't pretend to be wise, at all; but that's one thing I'm sure of." She lies for a time staring up into the hot blue sky, wriggling her nose occasionally to shift the weight of the battered sunglasses which slide constantly downward, and periodically raising her hand with a quick petulant gesture to shove them back against her brow. "Do you know one of the very profoundest things I ever heard said? 'A gentleman should know how to play the flute, but not too well.' Do you know who said that? Aristotle. It was quoted to me by that Spanish philosopher; what's his name? Madariaga. I met him on a boat once, coming back from America."

"What does it mean?" I ask.

"Well, I was thinking about Andrea. That's the trouble with him, of course. He's ruined the best thing in life by turning professional at it. I've done the same with acting, so I know. The minute you get paid for anything the joy automatically goes out of it. That's a warning to you, you know. Just be sure you don't get *too* good at it."

"That's the least of all my problems," I say.

"Well, you never know when it might come up. *I* would have been a whore, I think—quite literally—but I sort of realized in time that I would have lost the best thing of all, that way. So I decided to whore at acting, instead."

"You can't call that whoring," I said.

"Why not? It's exactly the same thing, isn't it? You've got to whore at something. Scientists sell their brains to an automobile manufacturer or a soap company or something; lawyers sell theirs to whatever client bids the highest for them. Everybody sells his skill, or talent, or intelligence to someone or other. I sell mine to a houseful of total strangers every night; stand up there and dance nude, while they throw pennies at me. It's exactly the same thing as a Windmill Girl, you know; only a bit coarser. Because if there's one thing they love more than a nude body, it's a nude spirit. The only part of yourself you can keep is what you give away; and that's bloody simple logic. No mystics about it."

"You don't much like mysteries, do you?"

"I do not. Jesus, how much manure has been packaged and pushed across the counter under that label." She lifted the glasses from her eyes for a moment and squinted at me. "I hope to Christ," she said, "that you weren't about to tell me that I was mysterious."

"Yes." I lifted the brassiere of her bikini and cupped my hands over her breasts. "These are very mysterious."

"They're mysteriously *small*, that's about all you can say. I used to work at them for hours with one of those toilet plungers when I was a kid, but all I got out of it was blisters. Oh, Lord, you're getting me going again. We shall wreck this bloody raft, you know."

Here this remembered reality merges into the scraps of melodrama that have been advertised a moment ago before me on the screen: the shipwreck, the tropic island, the coconuts bobbing in the surf, Gwynyth and I born shoreward clinging to the wreckage of a ruined *pédalo* with A. FOURNEAUX ET FILS, NICE stenciled on its battered paddlewheel, then eating breadfruit forever in the shade of a shack of woven palm leaves, staring into a Technicolor sunset that flushes our faces with what appears to be a wave of terrible and eternal embarrassment. This scene fades slowly to the shabby stairwell of Gwynyth's *pension* in Villefranche. I stand against the flaking wall of soiled plaster, looking upward through the iron banisters as I await a signal from Gwynyth, who has preceded me up the smoothly worn stone steps to the door of their flat, to follow her. There is no signal; but in a moment, chuckling softly and carrying her shoes by the heels, one in each hand, she comes pattering swiftly down the steps and whispers to me in a voice of muffled hilarity, "God, she's *in*! *Tessa*! And she's got a girl there. I heard them talking. Isn't it marvelous? I jolly near walked in on them."

"It's a bloody nuisance," I say (her style of speech is very infectious). "Where can we go, then?"

"I've no idea. There's no time left, that's the trouble. What do you make it?"

"Two twenty. I've absolutely got to be back by three thirty. Ian's coming for tea."

"Blast. We shouldn't have had that second martini. Well, there's only one thing to do. I can't wait, you know; I'm absolutely seething."

"So am I."

She sets her shoes down on the stone floor and lifts her skirt to her hips, standing in total nudity to that point. She almost never wears underpants; bare brown belly, with its un-

tanned strip of white about her loins, brown thighs, crinkled
gold hair of her mound glistening in the gloom. The children's
voices come tinkling up the stairwell from the hall. She bites
her lips and sighs swiftly with soft rabid impatience. "Oh,
please, Mike. Hurry."

"What about the children?"

"Never mind them. They won't come up."

"God, you're a mad thing."

"I am. I know."

Standing at the wall in an attitude of grotesque resolution
I gather her against me, guiding her lunging hips with worship-
ful hands, her skirt falling to shroud partially our feverish absurdity, until, after one of the briefest and most piercing of all
our moments together, we stand limply, in absolute exhaustion,
our heads hanging over one another's shoulders, panting in a
soft bewildered way while from the hall below a child cries in
a voice of crystalline outrage, *"Mais tu te trompes, alors! C'est
défendu!"*

"Oh, Jesus, that was good," she whispers weakly. "Oh, that
was good."

I stare beyond her shoulder at the balustrade, stroking her
head softly. "It was so good," I say slowly, "that I really don't
know what I will do without it."

She leans back, laying her hand against my face in a throe
of childish and extraordinary tenderness. "Do you love me,
Mike?"

"I don't know. I love something."

"I know. Let it go at that, will you? Can you do that for
me?"

And now (while a man in a bearskin hat with a bandolier
over his shoulder and an air of intense enthusiasm for his role
stares into the flames of a faggot fire and delivers a fearless indictment of evil) she is playing baseball on the beach at Port
l'Escale, swinging a branch of driftwood to knock far out into
the foam the cork float from a fishing seine I have pitched to
her, racing naked up the shining brown mirror of the strand

to the patch of seaweed we have placed for first base, so improbable a vision of grace, exuberance, and abandon that, wading back with the piece of broken cork, I stand for a moment to stare at her with a kind of pilgrim awe. And now, between the spears of the accredited, remorselessly documented holocaust before me, she is crouching beside the body of a dead gull, frowning through her scattered yellow hair at the ragged, blind, stiff-legged carcass, her sea-eyes gone gray with grief as she pokes one fragile fingertip through the sunlight to touch this memento mori that has been cast before us. A little later—with a bright red mustache from the Bloody Marys we have brought in the thermos jug which, with Rabelaisian jocosity, she holds clamped between her thighs like a gigantic phallus—she stares up into the blue sky of southern France and says quaintly to the private angel to whom are addressed so many of the remonstrations, remorseful looks, and Lost Tourist epithets of outrage with which her life is punctuated:

> "Dans le vieux parc,
> Solitaire et glacé,
> Deux ombres ont tout-à-l'heure passé.
> Et leurs yeux sont morts
> Et leurs lèvres sont moules
> Et comme deux ombres ils ont passé
> Sur les avoines folles."

Then she smiles shyly and murmurs, "The last couple of lines are wrong. I've forgotten them, so I just make them up. I love to make up famous poetry."

And now she is stretched out on our iron bed in the Hotel d'Egypte, plucking large green grapes one at a time from a bunch of them laid alluringly in the cleft of her thighs like a cluster of jade pubic hair, and, with astonishing velocity and accuracy, spitting their seeds at the plaster cupids who cavort above her.

"There! I popped him in the eye. That nasty little one there, with the leer."

"You'd leer, too, if you'd spent your life staring down at the sights he's seen."

"I shouldn't do anything of the sort. Cheer, perhaps; but not leer."

I laughed suddenly and loudly.

"Why are you laughing like that?"

"In my country the word 'cheerleader' has a connotation that you couldn't possibly appreciate. It's the last thing in the world I would think of you as."

"Oh, is it? Why?"

"Well, it's a college girl who puts on a little short pleated skirt and carries a colored pompon in each hand and does cartwheels whenever Our Side makes a score."

"Well, what's the matter with that? I'd be jolly good at it. It's just that I never get the opportunity, that's all; my side does bloody little scoring."

"I guess you're right," I said. It is perhaps the best possible description I could give of Gwynyth: an unemployed cheerleader. I began to kiss her passionately.

I was absolutely mad about her. I bit her once, very hard. It made her angry, and it was a great gamble; but I took it, because I wanted to leave my mark on the girl, permanently. I wanted the sign of my desire, and of my brief sovereignty over her, somewhere on her flesh, forever. So that if I met her again, in five years, or ten, or fifty, I would know that I had only to pare away her clothing (blue crepe? dove-colored chiffon? incredible gray watered silk?) to find on the highest prominence of her left hip a set of faded toothprints. Pritchard was here. His sign. Oh, reader, do not smile. Not if you are under fifty. It may be yet that you will one night prowl for hours about a silent house, consuming coffee, aspirin, and Cinzano alternately, arriving at no formula to relieve the cold excitement in your throat like the taste of cyanide as you watch the windows avidly for signs of a day that apparently will never dawn, which seems to be the first in some epoch of cosmic dislocation in which the sun is never again to shine, never to yield to you the vision of a girl in a knitted bone-colored dress, her blond hair burnished and burnt like wheat, bounding toward you on brown legs across a space of pavement glittering with mica like diamond dust (at two, exactly), carrying, perhaps, a bunch of violets swung on a ribbon to nuzzle with her sunburned nose as, later, in her murmurous, sleepy, after-love lassitude, she lies smiling at that private angel, whose forbearance must be the very model of that virtue. No, reader; if you are under that age it is not too late to conceive of you lying in a restless bed beside a troubled wife who is feigning sleep with very little more success than you, staring up into the darkness whose far shores now lap with amorous tongues the lids of those childishly sealed, black-lashed surly eyes, the long stippled tendril of brown spine, the tender fluting of the little ribs, the cinnamon of her armpits, the tangled yellow spikenard of her loins. You may well wake at one or two in the morning, as I have done, to watch this creature chasing butterflies for hours, naked, over the boulders by a blue sea, or lying propped against the brass rails of a baroque bedstead, reading Donne to you in a voice incongruously cloyed by maraschino cherries, a whole bottle of which she abstractedly consumes meanwhile, flipping the stained red stems recklessly abroad to make a curious pattern of tiny crescent cicatrices on the white sheet. Do not dispute the possibility. Older men than you, and wiser, no doubt, and with a bit less hair into the bargain, have paused in the midst of their morning coffee and clenched the tabletop or spread their lips against set teeth to weather a bolt of primordial fire that for no known reason (that shaft of birdsong, perhaps; that pattern of light on the breakfast table; that bowl of grapes which your wife, innocently humming airs from *Bittersweet,* has wedged between the toaster and the coffee pot) has suddenly blighted not only their heart, but their liver, pancreas, kidneys, spleen, adrenal glands, and every other moist, pulsating scrap of tissue the sum of whose functions, they realize, in a sad, nine a.m. epiphany, is Justin W. Myers, Realtor, or Roger Crabthorn Pratt, M.A., Assistant Professor of Romance Languages at Merryknoll State Teachers.

It is not too much to suppose that you will yet, one day at luncheon, engage in conversations like this one, with your wife:

MYSELF: Bloody peacocks. Why do they scream like that? Did you hear it last night?

MARGARET: Yes. Is that what kept you awake?

MYSELF: I guess so. That or the blintzes. Why, were you awake, too?

MARGARET: Off and on. I thought I heard you get up once.

MYSELF: Yes, I made some coffee. Why didn't you yell, then? I'd have brought you a cup.

MARGARET: Oh, I didn't want coffee. I was groggy. I thought I might have been dreaming. I went right off again, anyway. But thank you.

MYSELF: You're welcome.

MARGARET: (Fishing a chunk of avocado out of her salad with great absorption) Do you like to bring me things?

MYSELF: Yes. (There is a pause, during which I make it evident that my faint sense of indignation has been subdued by my indestructible goodwill, innocence, and faith in the equal goodwill, innocence, and faith of others.) You look as if you doubted it.

MARGARET: No, I don't doubt it; not after all the things you've brought me: a station wagon, the Côte d'Azur, my little glass Harlequin, these daisies. How could I doubt it? But I wonder sometimes—if it gives you so much pleasure, bringing me things—why you don't let me do the same for you.

MYSELF: (After another pause, this one of a humbler nature) I let you bring me everything I can. Everything I need.

MARGARET: Because I want to, you know. I think that's the greatest thing a man can bring a woman: his need. An empty basket for her to fill.

(No one could be more aware of the poignance of this remark than I, and yet some implacable fastidiousness in my nature is offended; I am aware of a vague sense of distress at what seems to me the faintly vulgar, banal, or undignified quality of the phrase—perhaps I have come to appreciate a gamier, less floral style of speech in a woman. At any rate, I cannot help wishing that she had worded the sentiment a little differently. I smile and lay my hand on her wrist.)

MYSELF: You're doing a pretty good job, Mickey. My basket is full. (I cringe slightly, inwardly, at becoming an accessory to the metaphor. She continues to regard me gravely for a moment, then becomes aware, apparently, that there is a certain unbecoming urgency about her look, and returns my smile.)

MARGARET: You're sure? Isn't there room for one more buttered croissant, maybe?

MYSELF: (With a really genuine smile of relief) Well, maybe one more. (I take one from the plate, butter and bite into it, grinning handsomely.) My cup runneth over.

MARGARET: I made the woman promise to save me half a dozen every day; they're always running out. I told her my husband would beat me if she didn't.

MYSELF: I would, too.

MARGARET: It's all right if I bring you croissants, then?

MYSELF: Absolutely. Anytime.

(We eat and sip coffee for a while in silence. Margaret licks the tip of her finger and begins to pick up crumbs from her plate with it, transferring them to her mouth and nibbling them between her front teeth.)

MARGARET: I think you're getting Europeanized. You said "bloody" just now.

MYSELF: I did? When?

MARGARET: Just now. You said, "bloody peacocks."

MYSELF: Really? Well, maybe I am. It's a very useful word,

actually; sort of in between "damned" and "God-
damned." We don't have anything for that area
in American.

MARGARET: No. Maybe that area isn't as extensive in America.
In Kansas, as I remember, there never seemed to
be anything out of range of "consarned," or maybe
"dadblasted."

MYSELF: Oh, it was there. We just weren't awakened to it.
We weren't sensitive to things in that category.

MARGARET: That's very sad. I always thought that when you
grew older the problem would be finding more
and better ways of praising life; it's sad to discover
that what you really need is a greater supply of
oaths to curse it with.

MYSELF: Well, you see, if we were brought up in a really
articulate tradition, that's one piece of disillusion-
ment we would be spared.

MARGARET: Or a really profane one. (She pours herself another
cup of coffee, drops into it one lump of sugar, and
stirs it meditatively for a moment.) There's really
a lot to be said for that. Because if children were
taught very early that things were pretty dismal
here—and supplied with a profanity to condemn
it all with—then the great surprise, the great
delight, that they'd have later on would be to discover that there's really quite a lot to be said for
this old world; quite a lot that deserves praise. And
how much more pleasant a surprise that is to get
when you're sixteen or seventeen. Or thirty-six.

MYSELF: Yes. (I am not particularly anxious to amplify this
point of view.)

MARGARET: I suppose that's the great advantage that Europeans have, really. They start with the *pièce de ré-
sistance* and have their dessert later, as they should;
we start with the dessert, and by the time we get
around to the meat and potatoes we're apt to be

so full of ice cream that we feel like throwing up. (She sips from her coffee cup, sets it down, takes a cigarette from the pack of Gauloise Bleu that lies before her on the table, lights it, inhales, shudders in a resigned way, and stares reflectively through the coarse blue smoke at the sparkling morning sea.) Yesterday when I came out of the *charcuterie* I walked back through that alley toward the post office, and a man urinated right in front of me, against the wall. I wish that had happened when I was six.

MYSELF: Why, for God's sake?

MARGARET: I think I'd be a better woman today; a better wife, even.

MYSELF: Oh my God, what rubbish.

MARGARET: No, it isn't. When I watch those children running around the streets in Nice, with their dirty dresses and little bright black eyes and quick hands, I know they're going to be better off than I am. They know something about life that I never knew; that I still don't know; that I never will know, perhaps. They're invulnerable, they can't be metamorphosed. They've already learned to praise the selfishness of life.

(I smile at her, unforgivably, out of a sense of unease that is produced not by the inconsistency of the remark—which seems to me quite agreeably romantic—but by the unexpected, unsentimental, almost uncanny appreciation of misfortune which it reveals. I do not like this in Margaret. It is maculate, unvirginal, initiate. It spoils something in her which I had come to regard as inviolable, and which, now that it is shadowed in this way, I begin to suspect how much I love, how much I have celebrated. And the boldness of the remarks I do not like. They bespeak a kind of courage, a kind of chrysalid daring or desperation, which alarms me. And I feel responsible for it.)

MYSELF: You talk like a woman.

MARGARET: That's the nicest thing you've said to me all day.

MYSELF: All you're really saying is that American children are spoiled, as far as I can see.

MARGARET: Perhaps. But that's a good bit to say, isn't it?

MYSELF: Well, it isn't really in the order of a revelation. In my opinion, those dirty little Niçoise kids of yours will live about half as long, on the average, as the spoiled American ones; they'll grow up with bad teeth and tuberculosis and rickety bones; they'll die of diphtheria or smallpox or assorted forms of malnutrition; they won't be anxious or able to read books or to add up figures or to appreciate music; they'll live their lives in poverty and abuse and overwork and illness, and they'll die, for the most part, without a single ideal or grace or inspiration to bless their lives. How you can call that "being better off" I don't quite see. (Some of my unease may be evident in the vehemence of this reply.)

MARGARET: But they'll be safe.

MYSELF: *Safe?* Safe from what, for God's sake?

MARGARET: I don't know. (I stare at her in astonished irritation. She draws deeply on her cigarette and exhales, coughing slightly.) Isn't there *any* way we can get some American cigarettes?

MYSELF: You mean some of those perfumed, tasteless, debilitated, affluent American cigarettes? You sure you don't prefer those wonderful rank Gauloises? You don't get a thrill out of that sawdust and cabbage leaf and horse manure?

MARGARET: Oh, I get a thrill out of them, all right; I tremble from head to foot every time I take a drag. But I'm not sure they're good for me. (She laughs suddenly.) How did this argument get so turned around, anyway? You started off talking like an Englishman and praising the "articulate tradition" of Europe, and all of a sudden you're waving Old Glory at me.

MYSELF: It got turned around when you started talking like Cassandra and going on about the splendors of poverty and child-abuse. It's a good thing to be able to appreciate Europe, but you ought to do it with your eyes wide open. My God. Michelangelo and Caravaggio I'm all for; smallpox and open sewage I can do without. (Margaret crushes out the butt of her cigarette. Her eyes grow stern and withdrawn. She blows crumbs of ash and tobacco from her fingertips and settles her chin into her hand, staring at the sea.)

MARGARET: Do you suppose she really killed that young man?

MYSELF: What young man? Who?

MARGARET: The countess. That young man she was talking about, who was drowned at the boating party.

MYSELF: My God, what put that idea into your head?

MARGARET: Well, Yvonne says she smells of blood. I wonder sometimes whether she's really a countess at all, or just some dreadful grimy old tobacco-stained fraud who's looking for a fresh set of victims.

MYSELF: That's a really wild idea. Do you mean to say you consider her capable of murder? That's fantastic.

MARGARET: She could be, for all I know. She's so civilized it's impossible to tell. I was always taught that refinement was such an invariable sign of virtue that I can't believe anyone who has good manners can be bad.

MYSELF: You're a very old-fashioned girl indeed.

MARGARET: Yes, I am. (I begin to eat my salad of orange and avocado slices. She watches me silently.) Don't

	those oranges taste wonderful? They're real Seville oranges, from Spain. And the avocados are, too, I think.
MYSELF:	They're great.
MARGARET:	I'm going to send some to Susie. (She takes a piece of lettuce from her plate and begins to tear it idly into strips.) What did you say you got in Beaulieu this morning?
MYSELF:	Tools to work on that icebox. Needed some masking tape and a pair of pliers.
MARGARET:	Do you think you can fix it? I mean with this funny current and everything? I don't want you to get electrocuted.
MYSELF:	Oh, it's just an open circuit on the power plug; not really an electrical job. I wouldn't try that.
MARGARET:	How did you happen to decide not to go down to the beach?
MYSELF:	Well, it looked like it was going to cloud up, and I thought it would be a good chance to pick up the tools. Tired of sour milk and soft butter.
MARGARET:	Thank you for the daisies. Did you get them in the market?
MYSELF:	Yes. Aren't they pretty? I got the whole bunch for ten francs.
MARGARET:	Flowers are so cheap here. But I think it's the funniest thing, the way they dye them. That's really French, isn't it? Really civilized: adorning nature so you can hardly recognize her anymore. (She cradles one of the purple blossoms in her hand.) You're never really sure what they are. What kind are they, do you think?
MYSELF:	Michaelmas daisies.
MARGARET:	Michaelmas daisies? I never heard of them. That must be what the English call them.
MYSELF:	I guess so. I guess the woman thought I was Eng-

lish. That's what she called them. So I'd understand, I suppose. (I realize that I have explained
somewhat too hastily and thoroughly.)

MARGARET: (Taking the flower thoughtfully by the stem and
lifting it from the vase) Is it all right if I take just
one of them; to use, I mean?

MYSELF: Sure. They're yours. Do what you like with them.

MARGARET: I'm going to use just one, for divination. (She begins to pluck the petals from the blossom one by
one.) Purple. I never saw a purple daisy before.
These must be dyed, too.

MYSELF: I guess so. That's a wonderful market, isn't it? I
love to walk around there. They had some fabu-
lous-looking melons this morning, that I never
saw before: sort of a striped cantaloupe. And
pomegranates. Those are really wild-looking things.
I was going to get some, but I decided it might
not be the best idea.

MARGARET: Why?

MYSELF: Oh, I thought they might be too exotic for your
taste. Upset you or something.

MARGARET: Really? Well, I might surprise you. I might get
addicted to them, and then where would you be?
Having to supply a ravening wife with pomegranates for the rest of your life.

MYSELF: Well, there you are. It's a good thing I decided
against them. (I watch her pluck the last petal
from the daisy and twirl the stripped calyx on its
stem, like a purple pincushion.) How'd it come
out?

MARGARET: (Raising her eyebrows with a look of mock desolation) It said he didn't. But it's a false, dyed flower,
so I suppose it lied.

MYSELF: Yes. It's overcivilized; you can't trust it in these
matters.

MARGARET: (Studying the artificial-looking purple remains)

Strange flowers. Everything seems so strange here
sometimes. Don't you think?

MYSELF: Well, yes; but that's what's interesting, of course.
That's what's so stimulating.

MARGARET: Does it inspire you?

MYSELF: Oh, I don't know about inspires. No, it's the familiar that inspires, I think.

MARGARET: Explain that to me.

MYSELF: Well, inspiration is an entirely different thing:
more nourishing, more permanent, more comforting. I don't know.

MARGARET: (She frowns, her frown transposes to a smile, then
a light laugh.) I've decided it's absolutely impossible to explain anything to people in words. It
really is. Sooner or later you've got to resort to
actions, to behavior. It's the only way you can
really understand people. Language doesn't work.

MYSELF: I suppose so.

MARGARET: Especially if it's French. Poor Andrea! I was trying
so hard this morning to explain to him that we
were going to have chicken for dinner. I kept saying, *"Poules,* we're going to have *poules* for dinner," and he looked absolutely bewildered. Then
when I told him what I was trying to say, he had
to explain that it doesn't mean "chickens" any
longer. Oh, it still means that, literally, I suppose;
but in ordinary conversation it means "whores."
He was terribly embarrassed, and tried to be so
delicate about explaining it.

MYSELF: You can't be too careful.

MARGARET: No. He wants to take me in to Nice one day soon,
to do some shopping. It's the only way to really
learn idioms, he says.

MYSELF: Apparently he's right.

MARGARET: Is that all right?

MYSELF: What? If he takes you in to Nice?

MARGARET: Yes.

MYSELF: Sure, I think it's a good idea. If you order anything by telephone we're liable to have a pack of whores showing up for dinner some night.

MARGARET: Would you really mind?

MYSELF: Well, I wouldn't want it happening every Friday.

MARGARET: No. If we could select some choice ones, personally, of course, it wouldn't be so bad. But if they sent around the common garden variety it might be a little unnerving.

MYSELF: (After a considerable pause) You still think he's a good teacher?

MARGARET: Oh, in his field, very. I'd never engage him to teach me philosophy. But then, he's not supposed to.

MYSELF: No; fortunately.

MARGARET: (Blowing off the table the scattered daisy petals she has plucked) We might go in to Nice next Tuesday, then. If it's all right with you.

MYSELF: Sure. Somebody's got to be able to order the groceries around here.

MARGARET: Why don't you take lessons from him, too? We could take them together. Then we could both manage it.

MYSELF: Not me; I can't stand the man.

MARGARET: Why do you hate him so much? I don't understand that.

MYSELF: I don't hate him; I never said that. I just think he's foolish and transparent. (I cast about for another word; then, shrugging, appear to compromise.) Lazy.

MARGARET: Lazy? Teaching languages seems to me a pretty difficult way of earning a living. Pretty *damn* difficult, if he has many pupils like me.

MYSELF: Well, I suppose so. I just don't like the way he

does things, I guess. He doesn't seem to have any values in life.

MARGARET: *Values?* You mean because he doesn't put on a seersucker suit and go to an office every morning? Or because he uses a different brand of cologne: Notte di Sorrento or something, instead of Right Guard? Or maybe because he prefers race-car driving to country club golf.

MYSELF: I don't care what kind of cologne he uses, or whether he goes to an office or how the hell he amuses himself. I just wish he wouldn't spin a lot of fantastic yarns about himself and bat his eyelashes all the time, and smile that damned sad *smile.*

MARGARET: You mean you just wish he had an Anglo-Saxon temperament instead of a Latin one. You'd prefer him if he were English, perhaps.

MYSELF: Oh, for God's sake. I'd prefer him if he were *simpler.* If he meant it when he laughed. If he weren't forever kissing women's hands.

MARGARET: Where do you think he ought to kiss them? On the foot, perhaps. Or on the cheek, like a nice American boy. I didn't know it made so much difference. (I do not reply to this.) As for those yarns of his, I think I'd need them too, if I had been born in Reggio di Calabria. They make the truth all the more valuable, all the more touching, when he does entrust it to you. It's almost the only thing of value that he has—the truth. Perhaps that's why he doesn't give it away, immediately, to everyone he mets.

MYSELF: I can't imagine him giving away anything of value, ever.

MARGARET: Well, you might be surprised. Only this morning he showed me a photograph of the house where he was born, in Calabria. Chickens in the doorway and Coca-Cola signs for a roof. It really was quite touching, to know he had that much confidence in me. I don't think he believes in the sympathy of very many people.

MYSELF: Well, that's one thing that's real about him, I'll admit: his poverty. (I am about to add that trading on the compassion that it arouses in certain people is perhaps his least attractive quality, but decide that I have said enough about the man.) Anyway, he speaks good French, which is all I'm concerned about.

MARGARET: It oughtn't to be.

MYSELF: (Involuntarily) Why?

MARGARET: We ought to be more concerned about people; about everyone, not just the ones we find immediately agreeable. Sometimes they deserve it the least. I don't know why it is that the people who most need our sympathy, our affection, are always the ones we're least willing to give it to. There's something really very perverse about the human capacity for affection, don't you think?

MYSELF: I suppose so. (She studies me for a moment with a look, which she manages to counterfeit, of irritation. I am aware, however, from its length, from the tension of her hands, from the ungovernable tremor of her voice, of the effort that has gone into producing this appearance of superficiality.)

MARGARET: Oh, it's so easy to say, "I suppose so," and just dismiss it like that. Because there's this terrible gentleman's agreement to be jolly about our sins, to chuckle over them—even to rejoice in them, I suspect sometimes. "Well, we're only human, after all," and the big grin. But I'd like to be different. I insist on being different.

MYSELF: Then you'll spend your life kissing the wounds of beggars.

MARGARET:	I might do that, too. There must be some way in this world to prove *something*.
MYSELF:	(I am much moved. I look at her as gently, as devoutly, as I dare.) What do you want to prove, Maggie?
MARGARET:	I don't know. That we're not all lying to each other all our lives, perhaps. Something. Almost anything. (She stirs, moves her feet restlessly on the stone, plucks a burnt match from her saucer, breaks it, and tosses it away.) Oh, that sounds so whiney. I hate to hear myself sounding like that. And amidst all this, too: sunlight and roses and wine. It's really dreadful. I'm sorry, Mickey. (She rises and goes to the parapet where she stands with her hands laid flat on the wall, looking down into the garden. Her beach towel is there, draped across the parapet, and the drawstring bag into which she has thrown the requisites of our daily descent to the Plage Passable.) Come and smear me, will you?
MYSELF:	All right. (I rise and go to the parapet, taking up the beach bag.) In here?
MARGARET:	Yes. (I open the bag, finding amongst its jumbled contents a tube of suntan lotion from which I unscrew the top and squeeze into my palm a cylinder of white cream. I lay my hand flat upon her back and begin to smear the cool mucoid lotion on her skin. She tilts her head back, wriggling luxuriously.) Oh, that feels lovely. My skin is so sensitive all the time. I don't think I'll be able to wear anything but silk for the rest of my life. (She bows her head, relaxing into languor as I massage the back of her neck and shoulder blades.) I love you to touch me.
MYSELF:	Silk and pomegranates. You're going to be quite a problem.

417

MARGARET: Why do I feel so sensitive all the time? It's weird, really. (She turns her head to me, dropping her cheek against her shoulder and rubbing it lightly along the greasy film of lotion I have applied to her skin.) My skin, my mind, my feelings, everything. I feel sort of—scalded—all the time. Or sort of peeled, or something. Like a snake in his new skin, or a soft-shelled crab.

MYSELF: Maybe you're getting too much sun.

MARGARET: Maybe I am. Too much sun. Too much lux. Luxury. Did you know it had an odor?

MYSELF: What? Sunlight?

MARGARET: Yes. It does. I can smell it, now. I can tell whether the sun is out, in the morning, before I even open my eyes.

MYSELF: There's a rare skin disease called lupus, that some people get. They become very sensitive to sunlight. They can die from light, I understand.

MARGARET: Lupus. That means wolf, doesn't it?

MYSELF: Yes.

MARGARET: What an awful name. You usually think of werewolves wandering around in the moonlight. But sun-wolves; that's dreadful.

MYSELF: We'll have to start limiting you to an hour a day, or something. (I replace the cap on the sun-lotion tube and drop it back into her beach bag, removing at the same time a pale blue Kleenex, with which I begin to scrub the palms of my hands.) There. You're well greased, anyway. That ought to protect you from the worst of it, for an hour or so.

MARGARET: Thank you. You're a wonderful greaser. (She takes up the beach towel from the parapet and begins to fold it.) Did it ever strike you how ridiculous it is that white people, who look down so much on Negroes and Asians, spend half their lives lying in the sun trying to get burned just as dark as they are? I simply don't understand the human race.

MYSELF: Well, it's artificial; that makes it exciting.

MARGARET: Yes. Like Buddha's poverty. Andrea's, of course, is merely contemptible.

MYSELF: I've admitted it's the only real thing about him.

MARGARET: I know. You didn't say that about his manners, though. (She moves from the parapet to the table and stands looking at the soiled luncheon plates and silverware on the littered tablecloth with an expression which curiously combines conscience with defiance. Conscience wanes.) The hell with it. I'll do it when I get back.

MYSELF: (Tossing my crumpled Kleenex amongst the litter) That's the spirit.

MARGARET: It's time these sparrows got a good feed, anyway. French sparrows are just about the shabbiest form of animal life I've ever seen. It must be French frugality that does it; they never get a decent crumb to peck it. (She points to one who sits bleating on a far corner of the parapet.) Look at him. Poor fellow. Poor little scavenger. (She plucks a piece of roll from the table and tosses it onto the stone floor of the terrace. The sparrow, with a swift predatory flutter, descends upon it hungrily. We watch him peck away a morsel of the bread and dart off with it into the shrubbery.) He's just like those Niçoise children: bright-eyed, hungry, shameless, wise. That's what gave me the idea for my play. I envy sparrows.

MYSELF: How is it coming?

MARGARET: Oh, I don't know. I've written a little more. (She takes up her beach bag and tosses the towel across the bend of her arm.) Would it please you to have a wife who was an artist?

419

MYSELF: Absolutely. We could retire on your royalties, and buy this place, maybe.

MARGARET: (She smiles.) I used to feel so cultured when we made those Sunday afternoon trips to the Mellon Gallery, or went to Constitution Hall; such an aesthete.

MYSELF: So you were; as aesthetic as the best of them.

MARGARET: No. Art isn't just for Sunday afternoon. (Holding the bag by its drawstrings she tosses it over her shoulder with an air of somewhat reckless resolve, as if to dismiss all that she has said to now.) Are you ready?

MYSELF: Yes. Just got to put the stuff in the jug. Won't take a minute; it's already cold.

(I rise and go in through the bead curtain and across the plum-colored rug of the salon to the kitchen, where I remove from the noisily purring refrigerator a pitcher full of iced Cinzano which I pour into the quart-sized thermos jug that stands open on the sink-shelf. Margaret follows me and leans against the door-frame, watching the procedure idly, standing with the heel of one foot on the toes of the other.)

MYSELF: I think I'll take a bottle of Scotch, too; Ian said he might drop by.

MARGARET: Is this Saturday?

MYSELF: Yep.

MARGARET: Good Lord, already? How the weeks fly. (She stares with a wide, idle look of retrospection through the sunlit window of the kitchen.) *Grit.* We used to get a funny old-fashioned country newspaper called *Grit.* Did you ever see it?

MYSELF: No.

MARGARET: I wonder if it's still published. I haven't thought of it in years.

MYSELF: I never heard of it.

MARGARET: I used to memorize all the jokes and tell them to my girl-friend when I'd go in to stay with her on Saturday night. She thought I was a riot.

MYSELF: We're going to have to get a new thermos. This top doesn't screw in right.

MARGARET: I know. Listen to this; do you want to hear a joke?

MYSELF: Nothing I'd like better.

MARGARET: Well, this farm boy goes into town for the first time, and he's just fascinated by the paved streets. He keeps banging his heels on the asphalt, and finally he shakes his head and says, "Well, you can't blame 'em for building a city here. Ground's too danged hard to plow anyhow." (I turn and stare at her.) I can still hear Leona giggling at that. Her mother had to come in and tell us to keep quiet. How in the world do you suppose I remembered that joke?

MYSELF: *Why* in the world did you remember it?

MARGARET: Didn't you like it? It's a *Grit*-type joke. You wouldn't understand.

MYSELF: I understand it; I just don't like to think about it. Here; you put this in the bag; I'll take the thermos. (I hand her the bottle of Scotch, which she puts into her beach bag, giggling at my look of scorn.)

MARGARET: You don't appreciate my flashing wit, my infinite sophistication, the swiftness and subtlety of my mind.

MYSELF: Your mind is fried, I'm afraid; it's all that sun. Come on, let's go and finish the process up. It shouldn't take long. (I take her by the shoulders and guide her, still giggling, out of the kitchen, across the salon past the grand piano, whose bass keys she strikes a tremendous booming blow with her fist as she passes, through the bead curtain, which she lowers her head to break tinklingly asunder, across the patio, down the stone steps and through the sun-steeped garden to the Chemin du Roy, where I release her and, with the plastic top of the thermos jug pressed against the small of her back like a rifle barrel, march her, like a captured soldier, down the steeply falling, bright-bowered avenue toward the sea. She is still giggling, full of a strangely abandoned, whimsical gaiety.)

MARGARET: Am I a prisoner or something? What are you going to do to me?

MYSELF: You're going to be buried up to your neck in the sand, until all those awful jokes are boiled out of you.

MARGARET: (Breaking into loud satirical song)

"I'm just a prisoner
Of loooove . . ."

(She swings her beach bag, flinching merrily as I prod her with the thermos bottle, her voice ringing out in the still, golden midday silence:)

"I'm just a prisoner
Of loooove . . ."

It is a perfectly natural thing for a woman in her mid-thirties to enjoy the undivided attention, for an hour or more, twice a week, of a handsome, well-mannered, multilingual young Italian desperado. (At any rate, I don't think I need fear any dispute about the fact from you, my lady; since the woman who would deny it has long ago, I feel certain, laid down this book.) It is not surprising, then, that Margaret—whose fundamental reactions to life I have never discovered to be anything less than natural—should give evidence of just that enjoyment. We used to joke about it on Tuesday and Thursday evenings —her lesson days—when I returned to the villa after having left her and Andrea to an hour or more of academic privacy while I went about my own somewhat less scholarly pursuits.

"Well, how'd you get on with Pépé le Moko?" I might say.

"Oh, marvelously! Do you know what it turns out that he's needed, all along?"

"Well, I'll guess: his own little tastefully upholstered Rolls Royce."

"No. Understanding. Just simple understanding."

"Which you are so well able to provide."

"Exactly. And you should see how he responds; like one of those wild poppies in the Lombardy fields, turning toward the sun."

"I am very moved."

"You are not. But you'll see, one day. There's something so *good* in that boy, struggling to get out."

"It's been struggling in that *boy* for the last thirty-six-odd years; I'm afraid it may never make it."

"Well, it doesn't really matter; I think he's contributed his fair share to this world already: he's beautiful, he's a matchless pedagogue, and he's broken every speed record that ever existed. Do you have to have goodness from him, too?"

"It may be too much to expect," I said. "Tell me about those speed records."

"Ah!"

"Ah, yourself."

All this, as I say, was natural (or nearly so; there may, to the perspicacious, be a faint note of hysteria, an air of deliberate and somewhat forged banality, about our banter); what was less than natural was that after her third or fourth lesson this attitude of predictable gratification on Margaret's part changed slowly to one considerably less festive. It declined— if that is the proper word—through the matter-of-fact, the pensive (sometimes even the melancholy), to the grave. I *say* it was less than natural, although I am far from certain of the fact. What is perfectly certain is that she began to hum a good deal while preparing dinner; that once she dropped an egg, and instead of swearing, bit her lip; and that at the height of what I call the Pensive Period it was possible for me to ask her a question in the course of a meal with very little expectation of a reply; if I glanced up inquiringly I might find her staring into her coffee cup while she stirred in an abstracted, automatic way, or nibbling a fingernail, her lip lifted in a delicate, savage expression of absorption, like the snarl of a dreaming lioness. Then there occurred one morning at luncheon the conversation I have recorded in the preceding chapter, that one in the course of which we spoke of the curious French custom of dyeing cut flowers, of the progress of her play, of the wisdom which is spawned and nourished in the gutters of Nice, and of Andrea's intention to squire her among those gutters one afternoon in the near future, the better to acquaint her with its idioms.

I don't know how much of that wisdom she acquired or how well she learned to speak in its vernacular, but she came back from the expedition—as she did from subsequent ones to the Musée des Beaux Arts, *les grands magasins, les casinos*— with an air which could be considered compatible with wisdom, I suppose, if for no other reason than its inscrutability. I don't mean by this that it was determinedly composed (which might indeed have produced conclusions of one sort or another on my part), or visibly agitated (all the more so), but rather, insolubly ordinary. Most occultly of all, she was Margaret, or so she seemed to me. She came back, not glittering with any exceptional air of mystery or enigma, but rather glowing softly with that familiar, diurnal (and eternal) ambiguity which was herself. If she had been walking all afternoon on the cobbles of the Vieux Carré there was nothing extraordinary in the fact that almost immediately upon entering the villa she should snatch off her shoes, collapse on the sofa with her forearm draped across her brow, and even after having a glass of gin and tonic solicitously wedged into her fingers, lie for a time with her eyes effectively hooded, replying to questions in a voice of bleak fatigue. (Or was there, after all? Was this degree of exhaustion unusual or feigned? Was there something inconsistent, perhaps, in the fact that after touring the museums or the *grands magasins,* she should wish, on the other hand, to take a very long cool shower, filling the bathroom and, through its open window, the adjacent garden with a merry contralto rendition of "La Donna è Mobile," after which she would appear in a fresh print dress, smelling of talcum powder and grinning like a schoolgirl, holding behind her back a package of Niçoise *saucisson,* which I was required to guess the identity of before I would be given any for dinner?) The fact is that I didn't know what to make of her behavior, any more than I do yet. In its careless and unstudied variety, it defied interpretation. A feverish volatility would have produced equally feverish speculations on my part; but Margaret's manner was much closer to what I can only call her traditionally miscellaneous one, and produced in me only a kind of traditional perplexity.

And yet I knew that there was something strange, something approaching distraction, even, in it. I could not have told you how I knew; such sort of intuition between people who have lived together for twelve years cannot be analyzed. It it, very simply, a feeling one has; something does not quite ring true; there is a slight air of the counterfeit about a mannerism, a tone of voice, a gaze held lowered too long, a reverie broken by a sudden self-conscious, apologetic laugh. I searched for such things in Margaret's behavior, I solicited them, even; and yet, when I discovered them—or thought I had—I could not quite believe them. After long, obsessive examination, I would dismiss them or discredit them. What I was searching for, I suppose, was evidence of joy; what I feared to find was evidence of despair. Any eccentricity which could have been construed as perturbation, fear, remorse, I rejected. I did not dare to accept as a true and valid incongruity in her nature anything which might have passed as a token of the vitiation of it. (Contentions to the contrary will be entertained, however.) All this, as you can imagine, put me in a very tenuous and equivocal frame of mind (I may, as a matter of fact, be in it still); if she laughed too much I felt a moment of strange content, a kind of ghostly comfort; then, almost immediately after, fear: the fear that her laughter was an expression of hysteria, not joy; had it not had, I asked myself, the hollow ring of desperation? The answer, of course, had to be no, for the sake of my own self-respect. I had to discredit its singularity entirely. There was nothing really very unusual about it, I would then assure myself; she often laughed that way; I was becoming too sensitive to her reactions, that was all—too concerned about them; it was understandable. It was certainly understandable.

By this process everything that she said or did went through a strange quadruple transformation at the hands of my somewhat tortured vision: it was, first of all, itself: a pure, innocuous "Margaretism"; then, an emblem of a secret ecstasy; then, of a secret agony; and then, with the swift reflex of fear and guilt, itself again, the original artless "Margaretism," expressive of nothing but her own unaltered innocence.

Now, while I was able more or less successfully to rationalize away individual instances of her growing distraction in this manner, I was not able to withhold from myself eventual recognition of the fact that it *was* growing. It was a very gradual and protracted process, of course, with so many reversals and remissions that I was for a long time honestly unaware of it as a continuous development; but I could not forever evade the fact that these demonstrations of hers were progressively more intense, progressively less disciplined, and more and more abundant. The sudden scowls, the unnaturally brilliant trills of laughter, the midnight impulses to wander about the garden for an hour in the moonlight smoking cigarettes: these had to be acknowledged, finally, as what they were; as symptoms of— of what, exactly? This, of course, was the question; the enormous question, in whose unanswerability there resided for me such fearful portent.

(The reader should recognize me by now as being incorrigibly American: I live by the Success Principle. If something "works," it is good and commendable; if it does not, it is bad and damnable. If the thing "worked," therefore, if the source of this distraction of Margaret's was joy, or anything approaching joy—as simple transient pleasure; the satisfaction of her vanity; *divertissement*; a mild, amused, or motherly affection; anything at all that her taste and conscience would permit— then I might expect to be congratulated. If it were anything less, I should have to face the consequences. The question of whether or not I had the right to make such an experiment, at all, did not enter into my considerations: one of the principles of pragmatism is that the right to perform a given action can be earned only after the performance of that action, the right to do so being determined entirely by its success.)

I'm afraid I have failed to draw an adequate portrait here of the complexity and ambiguity of Margaret's behavior at the time, of its bewildering little lapses and inconsistencies, its equally, if not more bewildering *consistencies,* or of its indefinably communicated impression of distress. Something that cannot be said of her husband. The reader must by now have a very clear picture indeed of this harrowed creature—starting, staring, giving his febrile attention to her every word and gesture, peering with narrowed eyes over the top of his newspaper, eavesdropping around corners, listening with hectic concentration to her telephone conversations and the murmurings of her sleep, stationing himself—as it became my habit to do— at the little barred window in the front door of the villa on those evenings when she was to return from an excursion with Andrea into Nice. I made a point of being home before her on these occasions, so that I could watch them taking leave of each other unobserved; but my cunning yielded only compounded uncertainties, because they parted with invariable decorum. The driveway was to the left of the villa, so that when Andrea brought the Aston-Martin to a halt just in front of the three steps of multicolored stone chips that led up to the front walk, Margaret would be on the far side, leaning forward in the shelter of the windshield patting together her disordered hair and laughing, almost invariably, as she expostulated on the excitement of the ride (the Chemin du Roy, with its many acute curves and close-bordering hedges of honeysuckle and bougainvillea, gave him an opportunity to demonstrate his skill and daring which apparently he was never able to resist). She would get out of the car, close the door with a firm gentle clopping sound (nothing so delights a man who loves automobiles), come around in front still exchanging pleasantries which reached me only as the unintelligible, merry, swiftly and radically inflected tones of small-talk; then when she had reached the top, turn and bid him good-bye in a slightly louder, slightly higher-pitched voice whose words I was now able to distinguish: "Thanks again, Andrea. I'll see you Thursday, then. If you don't kill yourself first."

(Sternly, scowling) *"En français, Madame, s'il vous plaît."*

"Ah, oui. À bientôt, alors. Et ne vous tuez pas."

"Que cela ne vous tourmente point. À bientôt, Madame."

He would raise and clutch together his fingers briefly in farewell, then twist his head and shoulders to watch behind him as he backed the Aston-Martin swiftly out of the driveway, pause when he had straightened it on the Chemin du Roy to wave again and call smilingly, *"À tout à l'heure!"* and with a snarl of the faultless engine, disappear beyond a cloud of golden allamanda.

There was just time to get back onto the terrace (carefully stilling the swinging bead strands of the curtain with my spread hands), into the lounge chair, and to snatch up the volume of Erasmus I had set by along with a half-empty glass of Cinzano before I heard the front door of the villa open, then close gently, then the tap of her heels across the tile floor of the foyer, then the sudden silence as the plum-colored salon rug devoured all evidence of her passage, then, after a moment of suspense, either the recession of her footsteps along the distant corridor toward the bedroom or the clash of glass beads from the archway immediately behind me which would tell me whether she had gone directly to her bedroom or come to greet me on the terrace. If the latter were the case, I would set down my book, look up tranquilly, say good evening, offer to make her a drink, launch into my habitual fatuous flow of bonhomie.

If she continued to the bedroom I would also set down the book and hold it negligently clasped against my stomach while I stared with expressionless attention through the blue veils of distance that hung above the sea, listening for what I should hear next: perhaps the splash and hiss of shower water against the plastic curtain through the bathroom window, the deliberately extravagant vibrato of her voice, singing an Italian aria, or only silence, pernicious and profound, after a quarter of an hour of which I would set the book down, rise, slip through the curtain, go quickly and quietly down the corridor to the bedroom, where, from behind her, through the open door, I would as often as not see her sitting at her vanity peering into the mirror in an attitude that I have variously interpreted as rapturous, remorseful, agonized, girlishly bemused, or stunned. Ordinarily I would turn and make back to the salon, from where I would call heartily, "Maggie! What happened to you? There's a great big gin-and-it waiting here for you." Once, however, she turned and saw me, and said immediately, in a composed, unhurried voice whose lack of pauses or inflections of any kind gave a startling impression of soul-lessness: "Oh you scared me standing there like that where did you come from."

"Down the hall," I said. "I wondered what happened to you."

"I thought you were down at the beach so I came straight back what time is it anyway?"

"Six."

"Oh I'm late." She glanced at her wristwatch, smiled, and resumed a much more normally inflected tone of voice, as if her sense of the present and her vitality were suddenly restored. "I'm sorry; I couldn't get Andrea out of the Galéries Lafayette. He's like a child, around a department store."

"Doesn't matter; I just got back myself, a few minutes ago. Can I make you a drink?"

"I guess so. Or maybe I better not. I've got an awful headache. No, I better not. Mickey, would you mind if I just stretched out here for a few minutes? I've got this awful headache."

"No. Sure." I stood for a few moments loitering uneasily, smiling quickly as her eyes found mine in the mirror. "Okay, I'll let you snooze for forty-five minutes and then I'll come and yell, and we'll go out to dinner. How will that be?"

"Heavenly. Can we really?"

"Sure. Only thing to do. You look beat."

"I am, a little. Thank you, darling."

I had an impulse to go and touch her hair or hold her lightly against me for a moment, but I decided it was a very mistaken one.

"I'll get you an aspirin."

"I've got some right here in my purse. Just get me some water, please."

"Okay." I went into the bathroom and returned with a tumberful of water which she took from me, still sitting at the vanity, and gulped down, clenching her eyes closed tightly, as she always did when she swallowed pills.

"Listen, you shouldn't let that guy get you so worn out. I mean, if this thing is getting to be a chore for you or anything—"

"*Chore*. I'm not *that* tired. It's just a little headache. Nothing that a forty-five-minute nap can't cure."

"Okay. Well, stretch out, and I'll give you a yell in a while."

"You're a wonderful husband. I don't deserve you."

"Yes, I know."

"I mean it."

"I know. Go to sleep. I'll call you in a while."

I went back to the terrace, resettled myself in the lounge chair, took up my glass of Cinzano, and spent the next forty-five minutes in the toils of what had by now become the joyless compulsion to reenact in all of its tormenting, insoluble detail whatever scene we had just played together; every word she had spoken I would recall and study, sometimes even to the

point of whispering or murmuring it aloud, the better to re-
duplicate and explore its accent, tone of voice, intensity, and
pace; every gesture I would reiterate and reexamine for its
hidden meanings; every silence I would try to fathom. I could
not stop the process; I would go to sleep at night with all the
appearances she had made before me in the course of that day
clipped out of the surrounding events, spliced together and
projected incessantly in my mind, like the endless rerunning
of a movie sequence. (It has even been suggested to me by one
or another of the personal demons assigned to my case that my
anxiety for Margaret to return can be largely accounted for by
my desire to have the hidden meanings for these actions of hers
at Cap Ferrat yielded up to me at last.)

I think it was after her third such excursion into Nice that
once, on a Thursday morning at breakfast, she asked rather
shyly, "What are you going to do this afternoon while I'm
studying?"

"I thought I might run down to the harbor and have a
chat with Ian."

"Oh, that would be fun," she said. "I wish I could come,
too. Could I?"

"How could you come? You've got a lesson."

"I don't feel like studying today, somehow. I could ring
Andrea and call it off; he wouldn't mind."

"What's this? You getting bored? You going to be a drop-
out?"

"I'm not in the mood, that's all. I'm entitled to a day off
now and then."

"I don't believe you," I said. "What is it, really?"

"That's all there is to it. I feel lazy. I want to play hookey."
She struck a match and let it burn almost to her fingertips,
blinking three times while she watched the quavering gelatinous slice of blue-and-yellow flame. "Would we have to pay him
anyway?"

"Oh, yes. Professional appointment. Can't have him missing
a meal just because you want to play."

She blew out the match and stuck it into a strip of melon rind on her plate. "You don't want me to come with you, do you?"

"Certainly I do. Thinking of you, that's all. You're the one who's always complaining about the lack of moral fiber around here."

"Well, I won't ever complain again, I promise. I'd much rather be with you and Ian today than work. Can I?"

It would not do to inquire too strenuously, and there was no logical reason to object. There was nothing to do but to leave Gwynyth languishing in our bower of oleander. She would not languish very long, I knew, nor would she make any particular fuss about the disarrangement; she did not "get hysterical very easily." Margaret went in through the bead curtain and called Andrea, but he had already gone out. I listened while she explained to his concierge (with really greatly improved confidence and fluency) that Monsieur d'Agostino's appointment with Madame Pritchard for the afternoon was to be canceled. In case he should not return to his hotel before coming to her lesson, she wrote out (in French, with the same new confidence and fluency) an explanation and apology for our absence and fastened it to the front door of the villa with cellophane tape. Then we drove down to St. Jean-Cap Ferrat and drank Scotch all afternoon with Ian aboard the *Victorious.*

He was going to take a short cruise up to St. Tropez the following Tuesday, he said, and invited us to come along.

"Oh, wouldn't I love to," Margaret said, "but it's my lesson-day, and I can't skip another one. I'm playing hookey today. Andrea would give me up entirely."

"Ask him along," Ian said, "and have your lesson aboard. He'd probably jump at the chance."

"I'm sure he would," Margaret said. "Is it really all right?"

"Lord, yes. All sorts of room, here. Ask someone else as well, if you'd like to."

"Do you mean it?"

"Shouldn't say it, otherwise."

"We know some lovely young English people," Margaret said. "Actors. I think you'd like them. And I know they'd love to come."

"Splendid," Ian said. We were all a little drunk. "I'll get a crate of champagne in, and we'll make a day of it. How many of them are there?"

"Five. Is that too many? I don't know if they'll all come."

"Doesn't matter if they do. I like young people. Ought to be jolly amusing." He was very fond of Margaret and very happy to have pleased her.

"I love that man," she said when we got home. "He's so terribly shy."

"You like terribly shy men?" I said. "I didn't realize that."

"I like there to *be* shy men."

"What does that mean?"

"Well, I mean whether I know about them or not. Like I like there to *be* bingo parties, and evening ceramics courses, and *Grit*."

"Would you like soda or water?" We had carried our final drinks back to the villa in waxed-paper cups so as not to interrupt our afternoon's revelry, and I was now refilling them.

"Water, I guess."

"What is the difference," I asked, "between ceramics courses and French courses?"

"Well, one is in a language, and one is in pottery-making. There's quite a lot of difference, really."

"I think you're drunk."

"That's very possible." She took the cup and smiled at me giddily. "Do you know, I used to think *you* were shy."

"And now you don't?"

"No, I don't think I do anymore. Maybe." She peered into her cup for a considerable time and then asked, "Would you like to hear another joke from *Grit?*"

"No, thank you."

"Well, would you like to play bingo?"

"No, I don't think so."

"Well, is there anything you'd like to do, especially? Because I'd be very glad to participate."

"No, I'm fine. Really. I like things just the way they're going."

"Are you sure? I could run down to Nice and get some clay, and we could spend the evening doing ceramics or something."

"No, I think I'll just stick with the Scotch and the boating party. I think that'll work out just fine."

"All right," Margaret said. "I thought I'd better offer you the choice."

The next evening while she was preparing dinner I drove down to St. Jean on the pretext of buying cigarettes, and from one of the *cabines* in the post office I telephoned Andrea. He sounded cautiously surprised: "Ah, Monsieur Pritchard. How delightful to hear from you. But I hope all is well. I have been wondering about the note I received from Mrs. Pritchard yesterday. Is she not well?"

"I'm not sure," I said. "I don't really understand why she did it."

"But I thought she explained this in her message. She was to visit a friend with you, on his boat. Or that is how I understood it."

"Yes, that's what she decided to do, but I'm not sure why. I thought perhaps you might have an idea."

"I? No, why should I have any idea?" There was a short pause which I left deliberately vacant. "I don't understand, Mr. Pritchard. Perhaps I am a little stupid. Could you explain?" His voice had become cautious, elaborate, artificially concerned.

"I don't know that we'd better go into it on the telephone," I said. "I wonder if I could see you for a few minutes tomorrow, before you come over for the lesson? I'll be in the café at St. Jean, if you'd like to stop by on your way up to the villa."

"Yes, of course, if you like. But I am really very much at a loss—"

"Well, we'll talk about it tomorrow," I said. "Say at one thirty?"

"Very well."

"Thank you, Good-bye."

"Good-bye, Mr. Pritchard."

I hung up and telephoned Gwynyth, who took a full ten minutes in getting to the phone and was airily detached.

"I'm sorry about yesterday," I said.

"That's all right. I got a lovely burn. What happened?"

"Well, I said I was going down to see Ian, so Mickey insisted on coming with me. There was nothing I could do."

" 'Mickey,' " she said. "Don't you think that's a bit fey?"

"What?"

"The way you have the same pet name for each other. Sounds just a bit like the *Woman's Day,* or something."

"It's just American cuteness, I guess. Listen, can you make it tomorrow?"

"If you're not there it'll be the last time."

"Are you angry?"

"No, not at all; but it's a bloody bind galloping up to Cap Ferrat every day for a bit of sunburn."

"I know. I'm coming in to Nice. We'll go to the Égypte."

"At two?"

"Say two thirty."

"Right. Cheer-o, then."

"Good-bye."

At one thirty the following afternoon I was sitting at one of the four outdoor tables of the Méditerranée, St. Jean's single café, drinking a glass of Pernod which I managed magically to sustain undiminished by diluting it periodically with warm water from a cracked pale-brown pitcher. After each drink I would remove from the top of the pitcher a prewar ten-franc saucer which protected it from the dust of the plaza and restore the level of the cloudy licorice-tasting fluid in my glass to its former mark, with no apparent effect on its flavor or potency, a phenomenon which delighted me both for its economy and its implications of the divine. I had been drinking the same glass of Pernod for twenty minutes. It was a very bright, hot, dry day with an intermittent warm wind off the sea that sent whirls of dust scurrying across the plaza and between the rattan legs of the café chairs, and that blew upright, against the grain, little tufts of the yellow neck-fur of a sleeping bitch who lay ten yards from me against the white wall of the café in the sun. Across the plaza and the ancient smooth stone blocks of the harbor jetty I could see the short mast of the steadying rig of Ian's cruiser swaying slowly as the *Victorious* tilted in the wind. I had started the day with coffee-brandy, in which I had persuaded Margaret to join me, had kept the spirit of the occasion alive by dousing our grapefruit in Benedictine and by adding an equal portion of rum to our prune juice, and now, at some indeterminate point in my inexhaustible Pernod, I was feeling very skittish indeed. In a moment I saw Andrea's sky-blue Aston-Martin descend the steep curve of asphalt roadway that wandered down into the village from the outer heights of the Cape, the blue enamel of its finish glittering intermittently behind the palm trunks and hibiscus blossoms that surrounded the post office, then idling down into the blowing dust and blanched walls of the plaza. He saw me immediately—I was the only tenant of the café at the moment—and raised his hand to wave, his teeth gleaming in his dark face, as he turned the car to park it in the municipal lot on the upper seaward side of the square, directly beside the Citroën I had left there twenty minutes before. He leaped out, clapped the door shut (his hand still on the handle, in the manner Margaret seemed to have adopted), and strode toward me across the cobbles, the hem of his jacket fluttering in the wind.

"Good afternoon, Mr. Pritchard," he cried, extending his hand to me as he came between the tables. I half-rose to accept it in the most perfunctory way possible, waving him into a chair. He sat down, smiling at me and smoothing back his wind-scattered hair with unpleasantly fastidious movements of his hands. "Ayy. It will be a mistral, I think. It is time. You know about the mistral?"

"I've never experienced it," I said.

"Oof." He tossed his hand upward despairingly, ducking his head. "For days and days it blows. A furnace wind, across the ocean, out of Africa. In Italy we call it the sirocco. It is a nightmare."

"So I understand."

"Of course, some people enjoy it. They claim it elevates the blood. Me it only makes very nervous. I detest wind. Do you?"

"I don't mind it particularly," I said. "Of course the dust must get to be a nuisance."

"Exactly. The dust. In everything. In the bed, the food, the eyes, the hair. Ayy." He flung his hand heavenward again, rolling his eyes. "But you have something of more importance to say to me, I believe. You have no idea how concerned I have been."

"Yes, I have, as a matter of fact. About Margaret."

"Mrs. Pritchard, yes. You say you do not understand why she canceled her appointment with me yesterday."

"No, I don't entirely. That's why I asked you to come. I thought perhaps you could shed some light on it." His eyes were narrowed slightly, fixed and brilliant with attention. It was evident that he was not at all sure of what his reaction should be, in spite of the conversational nature of my first few remarks. I managed a brief, very imperfectly formed smile. He returned it at once, lacing his fingers together on the table-cloth in visible reassurance.

"I wish I could," he said, wrenching his eyebrows upward in an expression of dismay. "You have no idea how it upsets me to learn that she is not entirely contented. I was so sure that she was enjoying her lessons. We got on very well together, or so I believed. She seemed to have great enthusiasm. To think that I may in some way have offended her, displeased her—" He disengaged his fingers, raising one hand in a gesture of contrition and concern, shaking his head abjectly.

"Oh, I don't suppose for a moment you've done anything like that," I assured him. "Certainly not knowingly. But I thought you might have noticed something about her behavior —some little thing she might have said or done—that would help me to make better sense out of it. You see, it isn't only her lessons that she seems to be dissatisfied about, but things in general. Cap Ferrat, the acquaintances we've made here—the whole vacation seems to have lost its flavor for her. Which causes me a good deal of concern, because she's looked forward to it for such a long time, and because it's the only one we're apt to get for quite a while. Naturally, I want her to have an absolutely wonderful time. I'd like things to be as near perfect for her as possible. I want her to have everything she's ever dreamed of—" I became suddenly embarrassed by the strenuousness of my own tone and raised my hand with a deprecatory smile. "Women, as you know very well, are romantic creatures. They dream these dreams about places and then, if they're disappointed, they live in bitterness and disillusion for years. It would almost be better if they'd never seen the place, at all."

"Exactly." He nodded in vigorous appreciation of the point, with a rueful and indulgent smile.

"Still, she *has* seen it; and I've got to do everything in my power to make sure that it meets her expectations." I ventured a swift confidential smile in his direction, an effort that very nearly nauseated me. "I don't know whether it's ever come to your attention, but living with a disenchanted woman is just about the most harrowing experience a man can have."

"Aaah!" He closed his eyes and dropped open his jaw, letting the word trickle out like molasses, smiling an amused conspiratorial smile. His ease was increasing to the point of opulence. Apparently he sensed that he had nothing to fear. In the dusty gloom of the café's interior the proprietor had taken note of him, and emerged now into the white sunlight of the plaza drying his hands on his blue shopkeeper's apron. Andrea, with magnificent restraint, feigned not to notice him.

"Will you have a drink?" I asked him.

"Oh, that is kind of you." He thrust his arm forward in his jacket sleeve, twisting his bared wristwatch into view. "Have I time?"

"Oh, yes. Margaret isn't expecting you till two."

"That is so. Good. Then I'll have a Pernod with you, if I may." He turned his face up to direct this decision to the waiter, who nodded and went back into the café. Andrea leaned back in his chair and hung his arm across the back of it, his apprehension apparently now fully dispelled. "What you say makes me very sad," he said. "It is one of the great quiet tragedies of life that things do not fulfill our expectations of them: places, people, works of art. Perhaps even heaven. It makes one afraid to live, and eventually, even to die." He turned up his empty hands, one behind his chair, one across the table, in a marvelously comprehensive gesture of irony. "It is the very thing," he added gently, fixing his eyes on mine in a mild but insistent encounter, "that has kept me from ever marrying."

"That's very well observed," I said, deciding inwardly that it was a little *too* well observed.

"But that Mrs. Pritchard should suffer from such a thing seems to me incredible. She has such *joie de vivre*, such *élan*. I would have thought that she was enjoying herself enormously."

"Of course she's very sensitive," I said. "About her handicap, I mean. She's apt to feel that she's not entirely acceptable to people. If there's the slightest suspicion that she is rejected by anyone, that she is regarded as anything but normal, then she withdraws very quickly. It becomes very difficult to put her at her ease. Perhaps I should have mentioned this earlier."

Andrea looked distraught. He raised his hands in protest, his face writing with sincerity.

"I assure you," he cried, "that no such thought has crossed my mind. It is impossible that I could have offended her in this respect. It has never occurred to me that she is anything but a lady of the greatest beauty and intelligence. Oh, I hope she has not received such an impression."

"I'm sure you've done everything in your power to accommodate her," I said. "And I appreciate it. This is just the sort of assurance that she needs, you see. And anything that you can do to give it to her, I'll be very grateful for. Extremely grateful."

He held his hands imploringly outspread. "It is my privilege."

The waiter reappeared with a glass of Pernod, which he set before Andrea. When he had disappeared again Andrea raised the glass and saluted me: *"Santé."*

"Et à la vôtre," I said, raising my own and nodding.

"Aha! Vous parlez très bien!" He was very genial.

I sipped at the cool licorice fluid and held my glass aloft for a moment, shaking it meditatively to tinkle the single cube of ice I had been allotted.

"It occurs to me," I said, "that you may have additional expenses that we hadn't counted on. When you go into Nice, I mean. I'm sure you must stop occasionally for refreshment when you're wandering around the city in this heat. A cocktail, or a Coca-Cola, at least. Or perhaps even a bite to eat in a restaurant." He shrugged, drawing down the corners of his mouth negligently. "No, no; there's no reason why you should be obliged to foot the bill. After all, it's customary these days for all professional people to have an expense account."

"That is very kind of you. There *are* times when I would like to invite Mrs. Pritchard to take a little refreshment at a café. It is very tiring, of course, so much excursions in the department store, so much walking in museums—" His voice had again become canny, voluptuous, full of the joy in negotiation of the dedicated merchant. His dark eyes shone.

"That's what I mean. You might even want to take her to a motion picture some afternoon—I understand that's an excellent way of learning languages—or to a cabaret, or something of the kind. It would all be part of her education. And in that case, of course, you should have a small account to draw on. That's only reasonable. What do you think would be adequate?"

"Oh, that I will leave up to you," he said. "Whatever you believe to be reasonable. Then, of course, if there should be some extraordinary expense—"

"That you could let me know about."

"Exactly."

"Well, suppose we say fifteen dollars a trip. Or perhaps twenty-five; after all, Nice is a pretty expensive place. That should cover taxi fares, a couple of cocktails or a bite to eat, admission fees at museums, and so on. I should think that would do it, wouldn't you?"

"It is very generous," said Andrea, nodding gravely. About money, it was impossible for him to be facetious.

"Good. And we'll have to make that retroactive, of course. I'm sure that you've already had expenses that you haven't mentioned. How many trips is it that you've made?"

"Three."

"Three. Well, that's seventy-five dollars; and twenty-five for next Tuesday—Is it Tuesday you're going in again?"

"Tuesday, yes."

"That's a hundred for expenses, and then two hundred for the months' lessons. That's three hundred altogether. Suppose I settle with you now; I've got some bills with me. That is, if you don't mind taking dollars. I can get them changed, if you like."

"No, no. As a matter of fact, I am able to get a very good rate of exchange."

"Good." I took out my wallet, counted out three hundred dollars in twenty-dollar bills, tapped together the edges of the little stack, and handed it to him, smiling with an air of great relief. "Well, that takes care of the business. I'm always glad to get business over with."

"Exactly. It makes a great *ennui*." He folded the money and slipped it into a trouser pocket, shifting himself onto one haunch for the purpose and settling back into his chair with a sigh which seemed to indicate that the pocketing of such windfalls disturbed him in more respects than one. His smile, half-regretful, half-congratulatory, seemed to reinforce the implication. "But I must say that in business matters you Americans are formidable people. It is your great *forte*. You combine a genuine disinterest in money with a great respect for what it represents. In this you are infinitely superior to Europeans. That is why I so much prefer to do business with you. With a European—particularly a Frenchman—a business transaction is an agony." He withstood an invisible oppression with the palm of his hand, closing his eyes and grimacing.

"I'm surprised to hear it," I said. "It was my impression that Europeans regarded us as irredeemably provincial."

"Oh, no. Certainly not in business matters. Not in anything! No, no."

"Well, I'm sure it's a justified opinion, in general. But I'm glad to hear that you don't share it. At least in my case."

"Certainly not in your case, signore." His eyes and teeth sparkled with complicity. "Your sophistication in all matters surpasses me by far."

"I hope not by too far," I said. His smile broadened disagreeably. His eyelids drooped to cover his glittering chocolate-colored pupils in an expression of ugly appreciation of my confidence. I stood up abruptly, dropping a ten-franc piece onto the table. "I've got to get in to Nice," I said. "And I mustn't make you late for Margaret's lesson." I twisted my wrist to examine my watch. Andrea rose with me, draining his glass.

"Yes, I must go, too. Thank you very much for the drink. And for the other—consideration. I hope I deserve it."

"I'm sure you will," I said, breaking into a stride between the tables and out across the plaza toward the parking lot. Andrea followed beside me.

"Ah, I parked right beside you; I did not notice."

"Yes." I paused with my hand on the door, looking across the harbor to the swaying masthead of Ian's cruiser. "Do you see that yacht, there: the old Dawn cruiser, with the Union Jack?"

"Yes."

"It belongs to a friend of ours: Ian Shillington. Do you know him?"

"No, I don't think so."

"He's asked us to go with him for a cruise next Tuesday. He suggested that you might come along and have your lesson with Margaret aboard. Would you be able to make it, do you think?"

"I believe so, yes. What a very nice idea."

"Good. Margaret'll give you all the details." I started to get inside the car, then paused again. "Perhaps you'd better not say that I mentioned it. I think she'd like to surprise you with the invitation herself."

"I understand."

"My wife is really quite an admirer of yours."

"It is mutual, I can assure you. Good-bye, Mr. Pritchard."

I nodded, got into the Citroën, and backed out from the lot into the plaza. At the turn of the road by the post office I looked into the rear-view mirror and saw a tiny image of him standing beside a sea-blue sports car, one hand on his hip, smiling after me.

I drove into Nice, found Gwynyth on her bench on the Promenade des Anglais, made love with her under the plaster cupids in that bone-white room with the grilled windows and the echo in its corners, brought her back to Villefranche, and left her under the great *flamboyant* tree at the bend of the corniche, and very late in the afternoon I came back to the villa, having paused first on a lay-by on the Cape to stoop and run my hands along the greasy front axle of the Citroën.

Margaret was cooking dinner and the kitchen was full of those culinary smells which are so supremely wholesome, fragrant, sane, and expressive, as nothing else in the world, of domestic felicity. She looked at me with a long bleak stare.

"Is everything all right? You're so late. I was worried."

"I had a flat, and then the car fell off the jack."

"Oh, I'm sorry. Did you get it fixed all right?"

"Yes. I'd have called, but I was miles from a phone. On the bend, there, just after you get onto the Cape." She did not reply to this. I kissed her on the forehead. "Can I wash up here?"

"No, you'll get the sink full of grease, and I'm just going to do the lettuce."

"Okay. I won't be a minute." I went down the hall to the bathroom, shouting to her through the open door while I scrubbed my hands: "How was the lesson?"

"All right."

"What?"

"I said it was all right."

"Did you ask Andrea about coming with us on Tuesday?"

"Yes."

"Well, what did he say?"

"He said he would come."

"Good. We ought to have a great day, then."

"Yes."

I came back into the kitchen, rolling down my sleeves.

"What do we have for dinner?"

"Ris de veau. It's a Provençale recipe I got—" She had started to tell me where she had got it, and then, in the middle of the phrase, had given up the intention (managing, nevertheless, to give the word "got" a more or less terminal inflection). Why had she given up? What had suspended the impulse to be comfortable, conversational, intimate, rattling off the little domestic details of her life to me? Ennui? Despair? Prudence? Something inauspicious, certainly; the broken sentence, and the broken sentiment it represented, left a small ragged hole in the atmosphere. She splashed lettuce leaves in a bowl containing a milky decontaminant, solemnly absorbed in the procedure.

"*Where* did you get it?" I asked.

"From the lady in the *crémerie*. Madame Perrier. She wrote it down for me, and Andrea translated it."

"Ah. So our investment is beginning to pay off already. He translates recipes for us."

She raised her eyes very briefly without fully encountering my own. "Well, we'll see. He understood *her* all right, but I'm not sure he put it into the proper English. You'd better be prepared for anything."

"*Smells* good."

"Yes, it smells good. Like Andrea." She dumped the bowl of lettuce leaves upside down into a colander in the sink, the disinfectant running in a chalky stream down the drain; then she set the colander under the faucet, turned it on, and began to rinse the leaves, lifting and spreading them separately under the splashing ice-blue water. She had retreated into herself.

"Shall I set the table on the terrace?" I asked.

"No, it's too windy. It'll blow everything all over the place. We'd better eat in the kitchen, I think."

"Okay. It's weird, that wind, isn't it?"

"Yes."

"Andrea said—" I managed to cut the sentence off, hot with sudden awareness of my faux pas. I pretended I had discovered something on my tongue, dabbed at it with my fingertip, spit daintily several times, scowled, and shook my head. "Hair in my mouth. I remember Andrea said one day that the mistral blows about this time of year. Maybe we're getting one."

"I hope not. That lasts for days, doesn't it?"

"I think so."

"I'll go out of my mind if it does. The shutters have been banging here all day. I had to tie them back with my twist-em things. And there're pine needles absolutely *every*where. I'll bet I've swept that terrace six times."

"You've had a pretty exciting day."

"Yes, too exciting. I'm not very good at contending with the elements." She was shaking the leaves now, dropping them into a dishtowel and patting them dry. "I needed you to help me. I didn't know you were going to be gone all afternoon. Why didn't you tell me?"

"I wish I'd known. It's kind of hard to predict when a tire's going to blow out."

"Those aluminum chairs in the garden blew all over the place, too. I managed to collect them, but I nearly got blown away in the process. It was like trying to hold down a giant-sized kite."

"Sorry. Did they do any damage?"

"I don't know. I had to fish one of them out of a rose bush, but I didn't stop to examine it."

"Why didn't you get Andrea to help you?"

"He'd gone," she said. She looked up, thoughtful and perplexed, as if trying to confirm the fact in her own mind. "He'd gone by then."

"I'm sorry," I said. "I got back as soon as I could. When the damn thing fell off the jack I had to walk all the way to St. Jean to have a man bring a hydraulic lift. I just couldn't jack it on that slope." I watched her arrange the salads of lettuce leaves and asparagus spears while I struggled desperately to amend the incongruity I was instantly and bitterly aware of. "I tried to use their phone at the garage, but it was out of order, the man said. I think he just didn't want me to use it; you know how perverse these people can be if they don't know you. And by that time the post office was closed and I couldn't buy a token for the *cabine* phone, so I gave up. Boy, this is one country that is not made for emergencies of any kind."

"You ought to carry tokens around with you," she said. "I have half a dozen in my purse that I keep for situations like that."

"I usually do; but of course when you need one you're always out."

"Well, you'd better sit down," Margaret said. "This is ready."

We sat listening to the wind shriek thinly in the pines outside the villa. Through the kitchen window we could see them swinging and plunging, and occasionally, scraps of yellow or blood-colored blossoms streaming by the panes.

"It's eerie," Margaret said. "I saw a play about it once. *The First Mrs. Somebody-or-Other*. With Elizabeth Bergner. There was a murder in it."

"If this keeps up," I said, "there'll be no cruise on Tuesday. Look at those whitecaps on the bay."

"Maybe we'll drown," Margaret said. She stared out at the wind-driven water, streaked with white foam, surging against the harbor jetties in Villefranche, far below.

"Well, you'll have to admit it would be quite a romantic way to go," I said. "Drowning in the Mediterranean. Like Shelley."

"Did Shelley drown here?"

"Yes. In the Gulf of Livorno. And there was an epidemic of some kind going on, so when they'd recovered his body it had to be burned on the beach. But his heart wouldn't burn."

"I don't believe it," Margaret said.

"It's true. It was huge, and it wouldn't burn; so they sent it back to England and buried it in Westminster Abbey." She stared out of the window at the raging sea far below, the whites of her eyes stained with a crimson flush from the rose twilight that streamed across the water. "We have a photostatic copy in the division, of the notebook he had in his pocket when he drowned."

"Are there poems in it?"

"Yes."

"From the bottom of the sea."

"Yes. They're all waterstained and strange-looking. You can't really make them out very well."

She ate in silence for a moment, then stood up suddenly, saying, "Oh, there's a letter for you; I meant to put it on the table."

"I'll get it."

"I'll get it. There's one from Susie, too. Do you want your glasses?"

"I have them."

She went quickly out of the kitchen and down the hall,

reappearing in a moment with the two envelopes and her glasses in a red leather case. We each put on our glasses, opened an envelope, unfolded a letter, and holding it in one hand and a fork in the other, began to read. The wind shrieked faintly under the windowsills.

My letter was written on Library of Congress stationery and was from Dr. Stornoway, our special consultant on American History. I had to read it several times before I was able to assimilate it fully.

> *Dear Dr. Pritchard:*
>
> *I hate to disturb you on your vacation, but a small problem of policy has arisen, on which I would very much appreciate your advice. Representative McGonigle of Texas has been using the Huey Long Papers for some research on pending legislation for a federal power project in his state. This, of course, is perfectly all right; but he has been making demands on some members of the staff—particularly Miss Crighley and Dr. Abner—which I feel are exorbitant. I think we should get it straightened out for the record as to just how far we should go in supplying and organizing such material for members of Congress. Dr. Threlkeld thinks that we should accommodate him, but I feel very strongly that this is a responsibility of the Legislative Reference Service and that our own obligations should be limited to making the material and the indices available, and perhaps supplying a certain amount of informal guidance in manuscript research procedures. We just don't have the staff to do any more, and I think the constant demand for such service is an imposition.*
>
> *I don't suppose the matter is going to get cleared up overnight, but your opinion would help to formulate a permanent policy position, and I would greatly appreciate your advancing it formally. If you could take a few minutes off to notify Dr. Threlkeld of your feelings in this matter I know it would weigh heavily in his decision. As you know, we have had a certain amount of friction in dealing with Representative McGonigle before, and I for one would welcome having a firm and established position from which to deal with him.*
>
> *I hope you and Mrs. Pritchard are having an enjoyable vacation. Many years ago I had the pleasure of visiting the Roman*

Amphitheater at Orange, not very far from your part of the country, and the experience has remained one of the high points in the memories of my younger days. But I suppose you will have much to occupy you. More than once since you left we have said to each other here, "Oh, for a beaker full of the warm south—the true, the blushful Hippocrene!"

I hope I can rely on you to give a few minutes of your precious time to this request.

Sincerely,
Aaron (Stornoway)

When I had reread it for the third time Margaret was still musing over her letter from Susannah, which was several pages long and included snapshots of little Margaret and Nicky. She nudged these toward me with her fingertip, and while I worked my way through the salad I studied them, noting the inscriptions on the backs and making appropriate grunting sounds of astonishment at the children's rate of growth.

"Do you want to hear some of this?" Margaret asked.

"Sure."

" 'Nick has gained thirty-seven pounds! And that's even since he started bowling regularly with me on Friday nights. I swear I'm going to give him a Vic Tanny membership for Christmas, and make sure that he *uses* it! It wouldn't hurt me any, either—since the children have come I really have to watch that spare tire. Maggie, I'm afraid your old pal is getting to be a Helen Hokinson type faster than you'd ever believe.'

" 'Oh, I mustn't forget to tell you the latest little Maggie story. (It's really what I've been working up to all the time.) When I picked her up at kindergarten the other day she came trudging over to the car holding this enormous clay figurine she'd made in her art class. It really was a monstrous-looking thing, all horns and humps and claws, like a gargoyle—but of course I said it was lovely, and I cooed and gurgled over it, the way I thought I was supposed to. She said, "Mommy, do you really think he's *pretty?*" So I said yes, he was absolutely lovely, just the prettiest thing I'd ever seen; and she said, "But,

Mommy, he's not *post* to. He's sick!" Honestly, a sick dinosaur, or whatever it was! So that's the kind of namesake you have, Miss Meg.' "

Margaret put down the letter and taking up her knife began to slice little bits of veal from the portion on her plate.

"Is that all?" I asked.

"No, there's more. You can read it if you like. Who was yours from?"

"Stornoway. He says Representative McGonigle has been making demands on Miss Crighley."

"Oh, my goodness," Margaret said. "That *is* news."

"I like you with your glasses on," I said.

"Why?"

"I don't know; you look like a schoolmarm."

"Oh." She took them off and holding them in her fingertips studied them gravely. "I wonder what she thinks she's doing?" she said in a moment. "Having all those children, and *bowling* and everything. I mean, my God, who does she think *cares?*"

"What in the world is that supposed to mean?" I asked.

"Oh, I don't know. Do you want some coffee?"

"Yes; coffee'd be good."

She rose to get it, but at that moment there was a sound of something breaking; a clear, sharp, penetrating, brutal sound of fracture, something between a rifle shot and the snapping of a man's leg—which I heard once, during a Fourth of July softball game, when the middle-aged father of one of my schoolmates stumbled over the second-base bag and collapsed immediately, clutching his dangling foot, puffing with agony, his thin hair blown astray, his blue serge vest popped open, a round, sweaty little man, rolling over and over in the red clay of the diamond, raising clouds of dust that powdered his long, loose-lobed ears with a fine carmine dust, as I saw when I picked up his gold pocket watch and came and stood above him, waiting shyly for his agony to abate before I handed it to him. ("Oh, thank you, sonny," he said, chuckling through his pain, his face gone livid,

"I can't afford to lose that, can I?") Margaret stood transfixed. There was now a muffled, shuffling, thumping sound, as of something wounded and brought low, flopping about on the ground or stumbling away to shelter.

"Oh, my God," she said. "It's my arbor. It's my moon-flower vine."

I don't know how she recognized it so immediately—it was the last interpretation in the world that would have occurred to me for that strange and somehow sickening sound—or why her reaction to it was so extraordinary, but both were true. She must have anticipated it, I thought; perhaps, during the melee with the garden chairs, she had seen some evidence of the arbor weakening in the wind and had been fearing its collapse ever since. But why she should stand with that pale and stricken look, lifting her fingertips to touch her lips in such a desolate and pathetic gesture, I could not understand; and for some reason I was very much annoyed.

"Well, my God, it's not all that serious," I said.

But it was to Margaret, apparently, for she turned and ran out of the kitchen and down the hall toward the salon, thumping her hip against the door jamb as she fled. When I followed her a few minutes later, having paused to remove the coffeepot from the burner to prevent its boiling over, I found her in the garden crouched beneath the kitchen window beside her broken, flopping arbor that swung and banged against the stucco wall of the villa in the wind. She held out her hands to gather together the crushed and deracinated tender vines with their limp, broken-necked bells of white blossom, crying like a child. I knelt down beside her, taking her by the shoulders, and kissed her hair, murmuring, as if she were a little girl, "Never mind, sweetheart. We'll get some more. We'll get some new ones. Some much prettier ones, Maggie. I'll get you some tomorrow."

The wind turned out to be not the beginning of the mistral, but only a two-day blow, so we were able to go on the boating party with Ian. I can't report it in any very great detail, however, because I don't remember it in any very great detail, or in any very reasonable continuity; I got far too drunk. But what I do remember, I remember vividly and with the kind of bitter clarity of things seen by lightning flashes on a stormy night: brief, stark tableaux, drenched in pallid light; immobile, fishbelly-white faces, frozen hands, floating hair; photographs of dreams.

For example, Adrian is sitting in a deck chair with his heels hooked over the teak guardrail of the afterdeck, his eyes washed almost white by sea-light, staring across an ocean of shuddering, gelatinous grape jelly in which dolphins, suspended as if in aspic, smile and soar. He is talking about murder:

"For example, when I was going to medical school in Sydney, there was this chap who killed his sweetheart. He took her bathing one night at Rose Bay and drowned her in the surf. Or so it was claimed. There were bruises on her throat and arms and shoulders—handmarks—and other evidences of a struggle —torn straps to her bathing costume, and so on—which seemed to indicate that she'd been held deliberately and forcefully under water. Of course it was all circumstantial, so they didn't actually charge him with murder, thinking they'd never get a verdict. He was found guilty of negligent homicide or something of the sort, and given five years, I think it was. A very interesting chap he was.

"For example, this is the sort of thing he used to say. We were having beer one evening in a hotel out at Bondi, and we were talking about this girl he knew—the one he was going to do in, later on—and he said, 'Well, I suppose there are none of them faithful in the long run, are there? If you want a love that will last forever, you'd better be in love with sorrow.' Well, it isn't often you hear a medical student making a remark of that sort, and you tend to remember it.

"And there was something else he said that I remember, although I never thought of it again until he'd done in the girl —or whatever it was that happened. This was just after we'd

452

finished final exams, the end of our first year. We'd gone along to his rooms to celebrate with a bottle of gin, and I remember he drank too much and got rather excited in a quiet, nervous sort of way. He had very wet eyes, this chap, anyway, and it always put me off a bit. He was afraid he'd failed, you see, and that he'd be sent down. Well, he had, as it turned out; and I suppose that had a lot to do with what happened afterward. 'I want to fight for something,' he said. 'I want to fight for something so badly that I don't know what I shall do if I'm not given the chance. Sometimes I feel as if I should do the killing now, and assign the cause later. Because later, when we find something to fight for, we may be too old to kill.' I'm not just sure of the words, but that was the sense of it, anyway. A jolly strange remark."

Adrian's shadow, which lies on the afterdeck beside his chair, lengthens with every starboard roll of the boat, stretching out across the pale teak planking until it covers the legs and thighs and belly and breasts of Yvonne, who lies on a rubber air mattress at our feet clad in two crosswise strips of tangerine-colored fabric; it creeps upward until she feels her throat stained by the cool penumbral flood, at which she blinks at last, complaining, "Adrian, you're blocking out the sunlight."

"Then one of us must move," he says genially, making no move to do so as he turns his head to regard her appreciatively. "I think you've had enough, anyway. Your navel's beginning to bubble."

"It's nothing of the sort," she says chuckling, laying her hand upon it, to be certain.

"Do you suppose he was mad?" asks David.

"I suppose he was, although I never thought so at the time: a bit moist in the eye, perhaps; but not mad. Still, he may not have done the girl in at all, you know. I must say he put up a bloody good defense, at the trial. He claimed he was trying to save her all the time, and that she got hysterical and struggled with him, and that's how she got the bruises and the torn straps and all the rest of it. Well, it's perfectly reasonable, of course;

people do get panicky when they're drowning; as a matter of fact you often have to knock them out before you can cope with them, at all. It was very convincing. If the charge had been murder they'd never have made it stick."

"Were you at the trial?" I ask.

"Yes, twice. I went every day, but I wasn't always able to get in, it was so crowded."

"Did you believe him?"

"I don't know that *I* believed him," Adrian says. He frowns and stares off at the sea. "But I had the feeling, you know, that *he* believed *himself*. That he'd literally persuaded himself that it was true, because it was so reasonable, and because he couldn't bear to think anything else. That's possible, I suppose." He sips from his drink and blinks several times, his frown deepening. "I must say he did it all very well, if he *didn't* believe it. I can remember him sitting there in the dock, very quiet, very intense—not hysterical, not out of control, at all—saying, 'I *loved* her. Why should I want to kill her? I would have given my soul to help her; I *tried*, to the very limit of my strength. But she didn't understand. She screamed and struggled with me. Why didn't she understand? Her eyes were so wild. I think the last thing she ever felt toward me was fear. Not love, but fear.' (He repeats the entire speech with the dramatic skill of an actor.) Well, he went on like that, you know, for a quarter of an hour or more. It was jolly moving. But the coroner insisted she'd been strangled, so it wouldn't wash. I went round, afterward, and took him some chocolate and fags and whatnot, and he was rather touched, and asked me if I didn't believe him. Well, of course, I said absolutely, you know, and clapped him on the back and tried to look the very picture of reassurance, generally. But I wonder if he believed me."

"I drowned once," says Gwynyth. "In a dream."

"I don't know why you've got to wait till we're on a boat trip to tell us about it," says Yvonne. She plucks about blindly for a stick of cocoa butter lying on the deck beside her, finds it, and without opening her eyes or sitting up, greases her bright lips.

Margaret and Andrea have gone below; they have taken their books and flash-cards down into the cool, old-fashioned saloon, with its teak and quilted ox-blood leather and constantly shifting light, to study French.

We are moving north, toward St. Tropez, with the coast on our right, or starboard, the successive tiers of verdure, separated by the ribbons of the three Corniches, stepping down to the glittering cobalt of the sea. We are making only about eight knots, so that this panorama slides very slowly past. A pair of renegades in a *pédalo* with a red-and-white-striped canopy wave to us. Gwynyth looks at me and smiles.

Signor d'Alessandro, Ian's guest, is the Italian consul at Nice and an amateur poet. He is magnificently handsome, with soft silver hair at his temples, a volatile leonine face, and exquisite hands, ornamented by a pair of massive baroque rings. He wears white flannel trousers and a shirt of striped blue batiste which is semi-transparent, and through which the luxuriant iron-gray hair of his chest is faintly visible, giving an impression of brutality very much at odds with the elegance of his clothing and manners and with his intelligence and charm. At St. Tropez he is to join his wife, who has motored up from Nice the week before to stay with friends. His hobby is "found" poetry, whose principles he is explaining to me:

"For example, I take the morning paper, I open it at random, I let my eye wander across the columns until I find an article that seems promising; there are several categories which I have found to be especially productive: articles on finance, politics, international affairs. They are apt to be sententious, full of pronouncements, and their language is splendid for the purpose: full of bureaucratic jargon, neologisms, barbarisms, such as 'overkill,' 'triggered,' 'hopefully,' 'GNP,' 'search and destroy.' Well, then I study it. I isolate passages from their context. I do not alter the wording, you understand—that is forbidden—but I sometimes allow myself certain liberties with punctuation. A comma, inserted for the sake of emphasis, can introduce a wonderful note of irony, or a sentence left suspended can have a very startling oracular effect. And then, of course, I arrange it to give a metrical effect, a look of composition.

"For example, there is one I found only last week in the *Guardian*—English-language papers are especially fruitful, for some reason—let me see if I can remember it." He closes his eyes and lowers his head, frowning with the effort; then, a moment later, he dismisses his intention, raising and shaking his head vigorously, his deep gray eyes alight. "No, but I must write it down. One does not get the full effect by hearing it. You must see it written to enjoy the irony. Have you a piece of paper, by any chance?" I grope in my jacket pockets. "Well, never mind. I'll go down in the saloon and take a piece of stationery. I think I saw some on the chart table there." He goes to the companionway, turning to raise his jeweled hand to me. "I won't be a moment." I nod to him and smile. I have scarcely had time to turn back to the rail before he has returned, looking somewhat grave; meeting my eyes, he bursts into an extravagant smile. "I have discovered an envelope, after all!" he says effusively. "It was foolish not to think of it. It will do very well. Now then." He places the envelope on the mahogany rail and removing a silver pencil from his pocket begins to write in a stately Georgian hand.

"For example," says Ian, passing close to us with Yvonne, whom he is conducting on a tour of the deck, "a boat of this type is what is called a displacement hull. That is to say, it has no planing capacity, at all; can't lift itself out of the water, so to speak. So its hull speed is limited. Go any faster and you start wave-making."

"Oh, I see," says Yvonne.

> A nuclear rocket on which
> The U.S. has so far spent
> *1.1* billion dollars
> Could be made ready to fly
> in *1976*
> And a year after that could be
> Carrying twice the weight

Into space now lofted there by
The giant Saturn 5.

A one-year delay in funds
Could result in two-years delay
In having an operational
Nuclear engine, he said.

It might even mean the end.

I am a little disappointed.

"Do you notice?" Signor d'Alessandro says, "that the article
—I have copied it verbatim—is written in absolutely regular
meter? Except for the caesura in the third-to-the-last line, which
makes an interesting break in the symmetry. Discoveries of that
sort are astonishing, I think."

"Yes." I smile irresolutely, wondering: Why did he come
up from the saloon so quickly? Why that extravagant smile when
he met my eyes?

The boat thrums under us; the two giant diesel engines
throb endlessly, imparting a kind of metabolic tremor to everything: our bodies, our voices, our vision. The surface skin of
the drinks in our glasses shivers unremittingly, a silver teaspoon quavers in a saucer, the far coast trembles in the blaze;
something inconsolable, a soft terror or chill, seems to possess
the earth. Even my thoughts are affected at last: they are tremulous, unstable, afflicted, like those of a man in danger or despair.
Perhaps I am drinking too much. I go across to the table and
lift a silver pitcher of ice water to dilute my drink. David
scowls disapprovingly and says, "Easy on that, cock; it'll rust
your pipes."

Gwynyth leans with her elbows on the aft rail, staring down
at the wake, her hair flying. She holds a glass in one hand, her
wrist drooping beautifully, like the neck of a swan with head
submerged. The wake is flat, moiling, green, glazed water,
marbled with threads of foam and bordered by two constantly
diverging medium waves, glassy and bright at their rounded
shoulders, pouring over into two white noisy runnels that

457

stretch out in an eternally widening V behind us. A gull follows, suspended on wires, his head twitching from left to right to left, hunting for garbage.

"Where is the lighthouse?" Gwynyth asks. She raises her eyes to search the shore.

"You can't see it from here. It's behind the Cape."

We stand in silence for some time while I study her face. It is clean as flint, almost incandescent in the ocean light.

"Tessa has gone to Greece," she says at last.

"So Adrian told me."

"Oh, did he? She's gone to Mykonos. She wants me to join her there."

"Are you going?" My breath is scalding in my throat.

"Don't be daft." She looks at me quickly, annoyed; then, noting what I am sure is the pallor of my face and the tremor of my voice, her look softens. "You'd better come off it, old son; you've got a wife aboard."

"Yes. And you have a couple of cast-off lovers."

"So I have." Her expression coarsens into a willful grin. "Well, we shan't want for amusement, shall we, if we get ship-wrecked?"

She raises and presses to her cheek a glass of ice-blue tonic and gin, smiling at me with moonstone eyes.

"Well, suppose we put it," says Adrian, "that passion must have expression. That it must either find public, mass expression in the form of periodic warfare; or private, individual expression in the form of licentious behavior. Then it becomes our responsibility to decide which of the two is the greater, or lesser, peril to society. It seems to me that society has been muddling along for centuries on a sort of compromise basis. It has allowed itself a certain amount of traditional Bacchanalian behavior—the fertility rite, the Mardi Gras, the Christmas office party, the football game—to let off some of the extra steam, but has found that these outlets are really totally in-sufficient. There is still a worldwide holocaust every twenty years, on the average. Now if we accept this as the case, then it seems to be inescapable that society has simply got to become more liberal, or with the means it has at its disposal now it will blow itself to bits."

"That is interesting," says the consul, "but oversimplified."

Inside the wheelhouse one of the Algerian crewmen is at the helm, his dark sardonic eyes narrowed against the glare. He wears a greasy black beret and carries a cigarette tucked behind one ear. All of his features come to sharp ridges: his brows, the bridge of his nose, the crests of his lips, the line of his jaw. As I lead Gwynyth past the port-side door of the wheelhouse he turns to watch us with a bitter smile. I have an impression of utter and implacable hostility. We stand and look straight down at the blade of the prow racing through the glittering, deep, plum-colored water. We are cleaving the earth apart. The bow wave falls away with a long ruinous sigh on either side. We look back at the great wound we have opened, its lips bubbling with froth.

Behind the Algerian helmsman there is a companionway of four steps leading down to the saloon where Margaret and Andrea are studying. They have a set of flash-cards on which are printed bold line-drawings of kites, typewriters, apples, loaves of bread, and bicycles. Margaret is wearing a short-sleeved cotton playshirt of white piqué and a white cotton skirt with a patch pocket in the shape of an enormous sunflower, embroidered in yellow thread. She has brought with her the cloth-bound ledger with lined and numbered pages in which she is writing her "Sparrow Play," and which, while she was in Nice with Andrea last Thursday, I discovered in the cosmetic fold of her suitcase. Of the notes and scraps of dialogue which cover the first eleven pages of the journal, I can remember these:

HE: What if I said that it was for my sake—or for the sake of the man I would like to become.

SHE: I would do it for your sake only. Not for a man you might become, a man I do not know.

HE: You are vain of your constancy. This, in itself, is a change in you.

459

SHE: Perhaps I am changing, then. To that degree.
HE: What changes you?
SHE: These blood-sports. This morning when I heard you fire, and saw the first bird fall, I was blooded. I began to change.
HE: That was only three hours ago.

The death of love. Or transformation. Or declension. (Not the Phoenix; that poor bird is already overcooked.) Avoid turgidity. Avoid Christopher Fry.

"He played the piano as if he were tickling it, and the music came out like a giggle."—Esther.

Robert sticks litmus paper in orange juice. Orange juice turns blue. Esther: "So you corrupt things by testing them."

Reserve this final irony for Robert: in the midst of his remorse, his grief, he discovers that the thing he mourns never really existed. Or at least not in the form he thought it had. That it was, ultimately, a sentimentality, a bourgeois absurdity. He has not even any right to the supposed magnificence of his remorse. The declension of tragedy to travesty corresponds to the supposed declension of his love. In the end we are denied legitimate grief as well.

ROBERT: Rhetoric is the great destroyer; we would do well to love in utter silence; never speak a word.

Or have Anne say: "If this was murder, where is the corpse you boast of?"

Death by water. The Drowned Man. The Tarot cards. "The unplumbed, salt, estranging sea."

In the scene where they are served ortolans, make Robert's horror very clear. He loves all sparrowlike creatures.

They have been studying in the saloon for approximately thirty-seven minutes.

In the center of the foredeck there is a canvas-covered locker, the size of a steamer trunk. We sit with our backs against it, watching through the bow rails the soaring and falling horizon. I lay my hand on her thigh, hot, brown, and firm as a loaf of fresh bread.

"Can that man see us here?" Gwynyth asks. "Bloody ruffian, he looks."

"No."

"What are you doing? You're mad as a hatter."

"I know."

I am playing chess with Ian. He leans forward across the board, his forearms laid along his thighs, his hands folded together, sucking on an old malodorous black pipe. Occasionally he plucks at his eyebrows or his mutilated earlobe, then looks up at me quickly with a most disarming smile. I do not understand the smile, since sometimes it appears to be vaguely congratulatory or encouraging and sometimes it precedes a devastation on his part. He is a brilliant and merciless player whose opening moves are rather leisurely and contemplative and whose end-game is paralyzingly rapid and exact. There is something hypnotic about the speed of his concluding moves; he establishes a tempo which I respond to recklessly, without conviction or strategy. I feel very callow at his hands.

"You are much too good for me," I say.

"Oh, no, not at all. You play very well, but you're just a bit impulsive, perhaps."

"Is Michael impulsive?" says Yvonne sleepily from her air mattress. "I say."

I comfort myself with the thought that I have very grave distractions, which is far from untrue.

The chess set is especially made for shipboard play; the board is of metal and the pieces have weighted and magnetized bases, to prevent them from sliding or toppling. They are made of a heavy solid plastic, cast in molds of a Gothic anthropomorphous design, elaborately detailed. The king and queen are clad in the costumes of early medieval sovereigns and stand in conventional attitudes with downcast eyes and lifted hands; the knights, in chain-mail and slotted casques, are mounted on rearing horses, swinging maces; the bishops, in miters and processional robes, stand with the solemnity of cathedral statuary; the pawns are pages; the castles have exquisite stonework and crenelated battlements, with banners flying from their keeps. I am drawn into the Gothic melancholy of the scene; I seem to sense the dampness of stone around me, the reek of moldy velvet from a lady's cape, the drone of plainsong from a chapel. A fragment of poetry comes into my mind:

> *I only, in such utter, ancient way,*
> *Do suffer love. In me alone survive*
> *The unregenerate passions of a day*
> *When treacherous queens, with death upon the tread,*
> *Heedless and willful, took their knights to bed.*

Ian raises his hand and with a studious but determined sweep of his arm removes my queen from the board. He holds the little figurine aloft for a moment and, apparently to ease the shock of the catastrophe, offers a verbal *nota bene*: "These pieces are exact reproductions of the life-sized effigies of Henry II and Eleanor of Aquitaine, at the Abbaye de St. Denis, outside Paris. She's rather beautiful, I think."

"She is indeed. I'll miss her."

He chuckles. I am demoralized; I have always considered myself a fairly competent chess-player—one, certainly, who does not permit his queen to be captured without redress.

"I'll have to resign," I say. "I'm sorry. I'm not concentrating. Why don't you take on Signor d'Alessandro?"

"Are you sure?"

"Yes. I'm afraid I've had a bit too much to drink."

The consul takes my place at the table. I wander across the deck to where Adrian and Gwynyth stand chuckling beside the rail.

"Did he beat you, then?" asks Adrian.

"Yes."

"I'm not surprised. He looks the sort would beat a chap at chess."

"Don't you like Ian?"

"Yes. So much so that I'd rather not have him for an adversary."

"Men worry about that, don't they?" says Gwynyth. "Winning and losing? They seem to perpetually have their self-esteem at stake."

"Men?" says Adrian. "Come off it, old girl."

She laughs and slaps him in the belly with the flat of her hand. Their ease and intimacy with one another creates a sense of dark indignation in my mind. This will go on, I reflect, this playfulness, this affectionate and familiar bantering—this and who knows how much more—long after I have said good-bye forever to the South of France. They will perform together on the stage, meet at parties with secret and tender glances, drink ale together on winter afternoons in London pubs, take summer holidays together in Greece, in Capri, in Dalmatia, while Margaret and I, in our wordless Collector's Trance, are gathering rocks along the coast of Maine, or reading desperately, in our respective armchairs, in the parlor of our quaint little house in Georgetown. "Do you remember that American chap you had the fling with, that summer in France? What was his name? Pritchard?" "No, Richards, wasn't it? Oh, I don't know." I turn away to face the companionway, from which, in a moment, Margaret and Andrea appear. They emerge in file, Margaret ahead, clinging to the grab-rail on the port side of the companionway. They both look somewhat somber. In his free hand Andrea carries, clasped together by their rims, a pair of empty champagne glasses. The *Victorious* rolls suddenly to starboard and Margaret lurches back against him, the full weight of her body falling back against his chest. He manages to support her, swinging perilously abroad the pair of champagne glasses, which tinkle with alarm. Still they do not smile. Having regained their poise they weave toward us, digging sunglasses from their pockets.

"Your wife has mastered the French language," says Andrea, breaking now into his customary smile. "I have no more to teach her." He bows his head to slip on his sunglasses, which are Italian, very dark, opaque, with massive black tortoise-shell frames.

"I haven't," says Margaret. "But I've learned one thing. That it's much easier to learn things when you're drinking champagne."

"I'm very glad to hear it," says Adrian. "I've known all along that I was following my higher instincts."

"Can I get you another?" asks Andrea.

"Please," says Margaret. "I have so much to learn."

He weaves away, bearing her glass.

"What have you been doing?" she asks. "Have we missed all the fun?"

"I shouldn't think so," says Gwynyth.

Margaret clutches the rail and leans back, staring at the green coast shimmering in the haze across the water. Apparently she has decided to dismiss Gwynyth's reply.

"Oh, this is heavenly. I love boats. Did you know that Mickey proposed to me on a boat?"

"No, did he really?" says Gwynyth. "How terribly romantic."

"On the Chesapeake Bay."

"The Chesapeake Bay. What a lovely name. Is it like this at all?"

"No," Margaret says. "The water is yellow, and there are stinging nettles. You can only swim there in the springtime."

"What a pity. It has such a pretty name."

Inside the saloon someone has put the Noel Coward records on the phonograph. Up through the companionway comes the tinny, glamorous sound of the twenties song, "I'll See You Again." The music stings me. I remember suddenly a phrase from a summer-theater production of *Private Lives* which Margaret and I saw once on a very hot Sunday afternoon in July, in 1948: *It's extraordinary how potent cheap music can be.* The actor who delivered it was very bad. He spoke with a transparently artificial British accent and a kind of hysterical urbanity whose fraudulence I have never fully appreciated until now.

"Where is the lighthouse?" Margaret asks.

"You can't see it from here. It's back around the Cape."

The boat rolls again to starboard, obliging us to clutch the rail. Our bodies sway in unison. The sea is still considerably rough from last week's gale. Andrea staggers toward us up the sloping deck bearing a brimming champagne glass in each hand. The dark hair of his wrists sparkles with tangled jewels: spilled wine. Margaret takes the glass from him demurely.

"You may be a devil behind a wheel, Andrea," says Gwynyth, "but you don't look much of a sailor."

"Unfortunately," says Andrea, smiling invulnerably, "I cannot pretend to be: Michael and Margaret have seen me swim." He salutes us with a nod and sips from his shivering champagne, then looks up portentously. "And sometimes it is a very useful thing, even for a racing driver, to swim well. One year—I think it was 1955—during the Grand Prix du Monaco, Alberto Ascari lost control of his machine and went off the road entirely. He plunged into the sea and exploded with a terrible roar and splash, like a volcano. One thought that he was dead, of course. The crowd was shocked. But a few minutes later he came swimming back to shore, very much refreshed." He laughs, nodding emphatically to forestall our disbelief. "It is absolutely true. He was an astonishing man, and the greatest of all drivers. Later that year—or perhaps it was the next—he was killed at Monza." He shrugs, raising his eyebrows and drawing down the corners of his mouth.

"Do these chaps want to die, do you suppose?" asks David. "I mean it's such a bloody dice, the whole thing, isn't it?"

"Speaking for myself, I do not," says Andrea. "I want very much to live. And yet, without the danger, you know, it would not really be living. I love danger very much." He tilts his head with a deprecatory grimace.

"I suppose," says Margaret, looking into her glass, "that it can very easily become the thing one chiefly loves."

"Exactly," says David. "And then where are you?"

"Half a mile off the coast of Juan-les-Pins," says Gwynyth. "Drunk, and full of itches." She tosses the lees of her glass into the air and stands under the shower of crystal droplets, yelping with delight. "I say, do you think we could get Ian to stop this thing and let us have a swim? I intend to try."

The boat rides at anchor, lifting smoothly to the swells. With the engine cut off, the silence is startling, profoundly natural, profoundly vast. It is as if we had opened suddenly a door into a huge storeroom, a huge cellar full of soundlessness which we had not known to exist, and stood staring with a compound sensation of dread, astonishment, and delight into this freshly discovered, limitless store of silence. As a matter of fact, it is not entire silence; what makes it more dramatic are the little natural noises which persist, or are revealed: the suckle of water under the hull, the tatter of loose halyards in the sea-breeze, the occasional plash of the tip of a gently cresting wave. We sit bemused, refreshed, by these soft sounds for several moments before anyone speaks or anything is done.

But the tremor abides; in my hands, my eyes, my voice. Something in me has been set vibrating and tingles remorselessly, like the pervading, body-wide titillation from a sore gum.

Ian has put down a swiming ladder; there are a pair of bronze brackets in the transom into which the ladder fits with a corresponding pair of metal latches. Each of the four pale ash-colored teakwood steps which are visible above the waterline is darkened at its center with a glittering chocolate-colored stain from Gwynyth's wet feet; she has been the first to mount them. She stands slick and wet, glistening like honey, snapping her fingertips to sprinkle us with water, laughing at our indignation.

"Don't be such a bloody clod!" cries Yvonne. She flees daintily across the deck to the shelter of the cabin-top.

"Right. You've had it now," says David. He chases Gwynyth, who howls with contrition, across the deck and up a metal gangway to the cabin-top, where he captures her against the mast. He picks her up and carries her, shrieking and flailing with her arms and legs, to the starboard side, from where he flings her ten feet down into the violet, bottomless sea. She strikes the surface with a great watery explosion, disappearing into what looks like a foaming bower of hydrangea, white, and pale blue, which ruined blossoms she parts in a moment to peer through, a drenched and blasphemous naiad. Margaret has gone below to change into her swimming suit. A few moments later Andrea has followed her. The men are to use the forward stateroom for changing; the ladies are to use the larger, owner's stateroom, under the afterdeck. It is six minutes by my watch since Andrea has descended.

Yvonne has flung her rubber mattress into the water, swum to it, and after many thrashing contortions, shrieks, and spills, has managed to climb aboard it, where she lies now, brown and burnished, in her invincible languor, trailing both her hands to the wrist. Signor d'Alessandro, holding the rear end of the raft and kicking idly, propels her in gentle circles around the boat. He is speaking to her quietly and apparently amusingly, for she drops her head back frequently and laughs with a bell-like chiming sound across the water. Ian sits in one of the canvas deck chairs, a floppy-brimmed white cotton hat on his head, massaging his hairy wrists while he listens with studious enchantment to Gwynyth, who sits at his feet, her knees clasped, directly a long, shy, murmurous discourse to him. From her buttocks, flattened against the deck in their white bikini pants, a sparkling puddle of water widens slowly. One of the bishops has fallen over on the playing board and rolls slowly in a pendulum arc, its weighted base stationary, from side to side with each alternate list of the boat; from port to starboard to port and back again, making a diminutive scurrying sound as the asymmetrical cylinder of the carved figurine casts back and forth across the board. No one adjusts it.

Margaret steps out, now, from the companionway, wearing her white chenille bathing robe and rubber sandals. She comes toward me at the rail and sets down the drawstring beach-bag she is carrying, on the deck.

"You're not changed," she says. "Aren't you going in?"

"No. I don't think you should, either."

"Why not?"

"It's too cold out in this deep water. You could get a cramp."

"Oh, don't be silly."

She unfastens the belt of her beach robe and opens the robe to lay it across a deck chair. She is wearing a blue bikini. I have never seen her in one before. It is skintight and very brief. I cannot suppress the feeling of astonishment I have at seeing her belly and navel bared publicly. Her small breasts, bound by the narrow band of blue cotton, are no larger than an adolescent girl's. What is the feeling I have at this sight? I am interested enough to inquire of myself. Is it distaste? No. Disapproval? No, not entirely. Indignation of any kind? I don't think so; not indignation exactly. Approval, then? No, not approval, either. Yet some very keen, some very vivid feeling. The nearest sensation I can relate it to is that of having once, while attempting to peel a particularly tight-skinned orange, given up and bitten through the skin into the flesh, tasting suddenly the cool, sweet luscious flow of juice mingling with the oily bitter pungence of the rind. It is a strange and absurd analogy, which causes my face to twitch with disconcertion.

"Well, that's quite a hot little number," I say. "Where did that come from?"

"I got it in Nice the other day. Do you like it?"

"It's great. When? When you went in with Andrea?"

"Yes. It's supposed to be a surprise."

"Well, that's just what it is."

She pulls her Ondine bathing cap over her head, tucking her ears into it.

"Are you going in?" I ask.

"Of course. You're being silly."

"Well, wait, then. I'll go change and come in too."

"All right." She frowns at me. "Why do I have to wait?"

"Well, don't, if you don't want to."

In the passageway to the forward stateroom Andrea stands before the mirror that hangs above the basin in the toilet com-

partment, very carefully combing his hair. He carries his left
hand cupped, just above the sweeping comb, lowering it behind
each stroke to adjust the freshly curried thick black curls with
skillful and fastidious patting and fluffing motions. He is wearing white-and-blue-striped bathing trunks and a matching
cabana jacket of white terrycloth, unzippered, which sways
open with the movement of his arms, revealing a lining of
bright blue glazed cotton and the black hair of his chest. He
smiles at me in the mirror and asks, "You are not going in?"

"Yes. I'm just going to change."

"Ah. Have you seen Margaret's surprise?"

"Yes." I stare at him levelly in the glass.

"Do you think it is becoming?"

"Yes, very."

"So do I. We are very fortunate." He lowers his arms
and tucks the comb into a pocket of his jacket, turning to nod
acknowledgment to me. The evident congeniality of his remark
is even more shocking than a conscious insolence would have
been. He slaps up the steps of the companionway in a pair of
rope-sandals, leaving in the passageway the fading fumes of
frangipani. Hanging from a hook in the back of the stateroom
door is his black mohair suit. I unbutton my shirt and sit down
on the bed to remove my shoes and socks, looking all the while
at the suit, which swings very lightly from side to side with
the movement of the boat. When I have put on my bathing
trunks I take the suit down, lay it on the bed, and systematically
go through its pockets, emptying the contents of each on the
bedspread, examining them in turn and restoring them to the
pocket from which they came before going on to the next. I
discover a personalized book of paper matches bearing in gold
leaf on its cover the seal of the United States Navy and the
legend, Captain and Mrs. Willis O' Donald, U.S.N.; a plastic
swizzle-stick in the shape of a poignard whose shaft is imprinted
with the words HOTEL RUHL, NICE; a very old-fashioned coral-
and-black-colored Waterman fountain pen; what looks like a
locker key, suspended from an elastic wristband; two red plastic

ten-franc gambling plaques; a picture postcard of a small Alpine *auberge,* bearing a Swiss stamp and a boldly written message which begins, *"Caro Fratello"* (from his sister); a leather key case which contains a pair of automobile keys and what appear to be three interior door keys; his wallet and the appointment book in which, several weeks ago, he wrote down for me his telephone number. In the picture-fold of the wallet I find three photographs; One, Margaret has described to me: a faded, proudly unsmiling matron of that class of urban peasantry made familiar by Italian naturalistic films—short, dark, poverty-blasted, with tightly drawn hair, a black dress, and folded hands —standing before a sort of concrete shanty made of cinder block with a roof improvised of metal advertising signs. Of the others, one is evidently a family snapshot—half a dozen people grouped in the sunlight of a dusty stretch of road around a highway sign that reads: ANCONA, 15 K.—and the other a sepia studio portrait of a very beautiful dark-haired girl in a wedding dress who resembles Andrea closely. In the appointment book I am chagrined to find that with one or two exceptions he has iden-tified people by initials only. For the Tuesday and Thursday afternoons corresponding with his meetings with Margaret I find only the codified inscriptions: *2 h.—M.P.,* in several cases followed by the parenthetical observation (*Nice*), or (*en ville*). Leafing backward in the book I find in greater or lesser pro-fusion the initials *C., C. de T., B., A.R.V., G.* (six times), and occasionally the fuller designations *Sga. Tomlinson, Baronesa Dhrost,* and *Dr. Di Calpo.* The only entry of unusual interest is the carefully copied address, *Crown Publishers, Inc., 419 Park Avenue South, New York City, New York, 10016, U.S.A.*

I replace the address book in the breast pocket of his suit and return the suit to the hanger, feeling a thrill of shame run up and down my throat and the backs of my arms, like a caress.

The portside boarding chain-gate has been unfastened, and in the gap between the stanchions of the rail Margaret stands poising herself to dive. She raises her hands and clasps them, the fingers of the gloved hand crumbled in the palm of the right,

lowers her head, and stands for a moment in apparent fear,
looking breathlessly fragile against the endless expanse of swollen purple ranges that succeed one another as far as the horizon.
Her very slender, very white feet, still bearing the pink intaglio
of her sandal-straps, are placed neatly side by side, the toes
bent to clutch the edge of the teak planking. She crouches
slightly, her knees bending, sighs suddenly with a little sob of
intaken breath, and plunges down into the sea. When she strikes
the water I shudder. I see her body slide down into the glaucous
violet depths, encased in a caul of silver bubbles. They foam up
and burst above her in a sprinkle of effervescent whispering,
like an exhalation from her flesh. When she reappears, gasping with cold, with a silver-plated head and stricken eyes, I call
to her, "Don't go too far. It's very cold. You'll tire." She shakes
her head and strikes out for the raft, from which Yvonne
indolently watches.

The Algerian crewmen are setting the table on the afterdeck for lunch. They have cleared away the chessmen, opened
the two drop-leaves, and spread a white linen cloth on which
they now arrange with bird-swift movements of their brown
hands a huge silver tray of poached salmon, over whose coral
flesh a faint pale iridescence plays, like that which shimmers over
mother-of-pearl; another, smaller tray of sliced tomatoes, lettuce
leaves, glistening black olives, and pale green disks of cucumber,
rimmed with ivory and inset with shining ivory seeds; a sauce-
boat of mayonnaise with a china ladle; a wicker breadbasket
filled with a loaf of finely sliced black Italian bread; and a bowl
of sour cream in which globules of scarlet caviar glow like
buried beads. The three champagne buckets have been re-
plenished with dark-green bottles of Piper-Heidsieck Triple Sec.

"Stone the crows," Gwynyth murmurs in her coarsest
Cockney. Stretching out her finger, she scribbles on the twinkling frosted silver of a champagne bucket a startled-looking
scrawny cat with arched back and enormous upright tail.

Out of the corner of my eye I see David, standing with
Yvonne on the narrow strip of deck beside the wheelhouse,

reach out to pluck open the front of her tangerine bikini pants and pour into them, against her convulsively withdrawn belly, a glass of cold champagne. She gasps, giggling; murmurs, "Oh, that's divine," and delivers to her mouth a forkful of salmon from the plate she holds in prayerfully bent arms, like a mantis.

"In a hundred years," says the consul. "Italy will catch up to Pirandello. You might call our nation Sixty Million Characters in Seach of an Author. We have never been created." He works a cigarette into an ivory holder, turning to his countryman for confirmation, but Andrea declines this opportunity to expound a romantic heresy. He nods, politely smiling. In the presence of the consul he is very circumspect about whatever convictions or activities may be responsible for his romantic exile. Circumspect to the point of deference, apparently; he produces a lighter and leans forward to ignite the consul's cigarette. Gwynyth turns her head and spits an olive stone into the sea.

"Of course that could be argued of any nation," says Adrian. "I don't know that England has been created, really. Or at any rate, to the satisfaction of very many people. If it has, where is it, at any given moment? Where is it now, for example? In Waterloo Station? In the House of Commons? In Selfridge's basement? In a miner's hovel in Nottingham? If any of these is true, then it seems to me that it is just as truly here, aboard the *Victorious*. Surely we are all busily forging our respective nationhoods at this very moment, just as truly as if we were sticking bayonets into Highland tribesmen at Culloden, or chasing Zulus through the bush in Africa, or playing whist in a bungalow in Kashmir. It's a pretty frightening thought, of course."

"It is indeed," says David, who approaches us from his position by the wheelhouse. "Makes one wonder if he shouldn't go a bit easier on the bubbly, perhaps."

"Not forging it, I shouldn't have said," says Yvonne. "Under*mining* it, more likely. It'd be closer to the mark to say we were a bunch of mutineers, not patriots."

"Well, of course, you know, that's what nationhood amounts to, really, isn't it?" says Ian agreeably. "Wholesale and continuous mutiny. Anything less would make a nation a prison, or a graveyard, or a sort of Home for Incurables."

Margaret raises her glass abruptly, splashing champagne on her fingers. "Here's to our jolly band of mutineers," she says. "One nation, indivisible." She pronounces it, "indivizzolble." Her wrists, elbows, neck, and jaw all give the strange impression of being overlubricated.

"Can I have some more caviar?" asks Yvonne. She leans over Ian's shoulder and spoons a great mound of it onto her plate. "I have twenty-three totally caviar-less years to make up for, so I intend to make a ruddy pig of myself."

"So you should," says Ian. "It's time someone started looking after you properly."

"You have a divine understanding," says Yvonne. "Can I sit on you?"

"I shall be very unhappy if you don't," says Ian. He dislodges a knee for her from beneath the table, and she perches on it, eating her caviar like pudding, by the spoonful. She pauses to pluck at her bikini pants, twitching and grimacing.

"Are you not comfortable?" asks Ian.

"Yes, it's just that I'm so beastly sticky. David poured a glass of champagne down my pants, and it's making me wretched."

"You said it was divine," says David.

"Well, so it was; but it's gone all sticky. I shall be sealed together for good, and then you'll be sorry."

"So shall you," David says. "It'll mean the end of your career."

She giggles, cupping her fingers to her lips to prevent the escape of a mouthful of caviar.

"Andrea, can I have some more champagne, please?" asks Margaret.

"Of course," he cries softly, moving forward from the rail where he has been leaning. He plucks the bottle from the bucket, sweeping the napkin about it as expertly as a waiter, and fills her glass.

"It sounds like a perfectly thrilling experience," Margaret says. Her lips twitch improvidently to form the words, as if she were speaking, very painfully, a foreign language. "I've absolutely got to try it for myself." She lowers the glass unsteadily toward her abdomen, fumbling at the edge of her bikini.

"I don't think you'd better," says Andrea from behind her chair, where he stands smiling. He reaches down to take her wrist and guide the glass back gently to the table. She drops her head back to look up at him, her eyes rolling upward in their sockets, like her limbs, too loosely.

"Well, Andrea! How solicitous you are of my dignity."

"I am willing to be scolded for it," he says.

"Why? Would you be upset if I got all sealed together forever, like Yvonne?"

His head moves very slightly in a nervous, reflexive way, and so swiftly and briefly that I am not able to decide whether or not it is an inadvertency, his glance brushes mine. Is there a hint of scorn in this glance? I ask myself; or perhaps of complicity? Does it express contrition at having overstepped? Or does it seek approval? Nothing, more likely. Tomorrow I will suggest to Margaret that we go to Rome.

She leans forward, laughing with undue hilarity at Andrea's disinclination to reply, the tips of the loose strands of her fallen hair dipping into the bowl of caviar.

"Oh, look, love; you've got your hair all mucked up," Gwynyth says. "Hold on a minute." She plucks the tips of Margaret's hair from the bowl and bunching them between her fingers strips them with a napkin of the blobs of sour cream with which they are gummed together; then, dipping the napkin into a glass of water, she strokes the strands of hair clean and pats them dry between a fresh fold of the napkin, nimbly, solicitously, almost tenderly, Margaret all the while bowed obediently across the table, submitting sleepily and smilingly to her ministrations, like a child being indulged, or perhaps a younger sister, or a lady with her maid. The sunlight casts broken silver lines of coruscation on both their moist heads and on their bare brown shoulders. Watching this scene, I have a sense of peace, of grave congruity, which is like a benediction; and for a moment the vibration stops within me; my St. Vitus dance is gone; I seem to enclose a cool quiescence, like that of drinking deer beside a stream. Gwynyth, her ablutions performed, leans down and murmurs to Margaret, and they chuckle, their heads together, like schoolgirls.

At St. Tropez the consul's wife is waiting at a harborside café. She leaves her party and comes down among the tables to the pier where she stands waving a brightly printed silk scarf as we glide in, our motors purling in reverse. She is a slender handsome woman with platinum hair and pastel slacks. Behind her the café is a gorgeous splash of spice-bright colors, like a Monet painting.

"Oh, how lovely," Gwynyth says. "Like a swarm of butterflies."

" 'C'est bruyant, animé, pittoresque, plein de couleur,' " says Margaret. It is a phrase she has memorized from her textbook; she gives the words a pedantically exact pronunciation, pinching together the tips of her thumb and second finger, the remaining fingers bristling fastidiously in the conventionalized parody of the connoisseur.

"Très bien," says Andrea. He nods deeply.

"Gorblimey," Gwynyth says. She and Margaret laugh and totter together in mischievous debility, their shoulders bumping. Andrea smiles cautiously.

"You are very gay," he observes.

We are invited to the villa of the consul's friends. It sits among a grove of pine trees on a rocky bluff behind the town, and is vast and incomprehensible, like an alabaster railway station. It was built, our host explains, by a British industrialist in the early days of the Côte, when the architectural standards of the region were those of Victorian Bournemouth and Torquay, which here have been uncompromisingly preserved.

Gwynyth and Margaret are delighted by it; they go wandering off together, carrying their cocktails, among the cavernous galleries and salons, where they can be heard chattering and hallooing to one another like school chums on a picnic. David, Yvonne, and Adrian join a game of croquet on the lawn in front of the terrace. I watch them for a while, then drift away along a gravel path that leads toward the sea, where I am joined in a moment by my hostess, who invites me to explore the formal gardens. These have been executed on the same scale as the villa; they are apparently infinite, labyrinthine mazes of cinder paths wandering between gigantic box and arbor vitae hedges, the tops of which are carved out in all sorts of rococo scalloping and crenelations. In places they are hewn into pillars with finials in the shape of onion-turrets, urns, globes, and sometimes gargoyles, green-scaled monsters sculptured out of living foliage, crouched, quivering, above us. Occasionally these corridors open into little square or circular flower gardens, laid out with geometrical formality, where beds of iris, peonies, and portulaca blaze in the sleepy silence; or sometimes into sunny green-walled chambers paved with shell or cinder and furnished with a pair of stone benches and a fountain, splashing with an eternal languid murmur. In one of these chambers we pause to smoke a cigarette. It is warm and still. A bird is piping somewhere behind a nearby hedge. The cigarettes are Romanian, and their sweet, perfumed smoke in the still air has a herbal smell, like rue or sage.

"The garden is a copy of a maze that was designed by Capability Brown, for Clarendon House in Berkshire." She pauses discreetly. "I don't know if you would have heard of him. He was a landscape gardener of the eighteenth century, who is supposed to have done the gardens at Hampton Court Palace." Her face is the kind which is invariably chosen by motion picture directors for patrician roles, but which, for some inscrutable atavistic reason, I associate with cornmeal, wooden privies, and incest. I calculate that she is fifty, but she has a slender, very interesting body which she still dares to encase in pale blue, clinging slacks of a semi-elastic material, like that of which ski pants are made. I make the reckless decision to kiss her. It is terribly embarrassing. She cringes and huddles her shoulders together to free them from the grasp of my hands, a gesture which I mistake for a convulsion of passion and which leads me to prolong and considerably embellish the kiss. This produces in her a gasp of now unmistakable indignation and a swift step backward to elude me. The calves of her legs collide with the stone bench, and only by twisting her body about with heroic agility is she able to avoid falling.

"I beg your pardon," I say. "I didn't realize the bench was so close."

"*Vous n'êtes pas sage, Monsieur,*" she murmurs angrily. "*Non, pas du tout.*"

She turns and walks quickly away across the cinder floor of the little atrium, disappearing into one of the four corridors which open into it. I smile with a kind of impervious bravado and with the back of my hand wipe the lipstick from my mouth.

For the next forty-five minutes I try to find my way out of the infernal labyrinth. I follow corridor after corridor, all demoralizingly identical, and eventually find myself back again in the circular chamber from which I have recently departed. I make a hazy, champagne-befuddled calculation of the direction of the villa and strike out again, arriving shortly at the flower garden—or one so like it that they are indistinguishable—which a short while ago I have visited with my hostess. From here, with elaborate, drunken care, I retrace what I believe to have been our route, and in a few minutes find myself again in the little circular chamber of my folly. All roads, apparently, lead to this scene of my confusion. A fresh attempt brings me very close to the outer perimeter of the maze, for beyond the dense high walls of box I can hear the distant sound of voices and the click of croquet balls. I cannot discover any exit, however; and—as I find after a scarifying scuffle—the hedges are impenetrable.

I consider calling for assistance, but some particularly perverse nicety of pride forbids me. I decide to smoke a cigarette. I sit down on the path with my back against the hedge and blow smoke rings into the mellow air. I try to remember the name of my hostess, for whom I have now developed a thorough hatred. Madame Fournier. Or Fourneaux. Or Fornicateur, more likely. I must remember to send her a Christmas card next year. To lead a man into a hellish maze, like this one, with what anyone in his right mind would consider a provocative invitation, and then to callously repulse his recognition of it, is apparently not indignity enough for this lady to inflict; she must then abandon him there, to starve and be forgotten in its depths. My indignation is a little overintense.

I realize in a moment that there are other persons than myself in the labyrinth. I hear the sound of footsteps on the cinder walk which lies adjacent to my own, separated from me by the six-foot breadth of the box hedge between us. It is accompanied by the murmur of voices, a man's and a woman's, approaching with the footsteps, growing clearer as they do so. The woman has very little to say. Her single comment—a very brief, somewhat expostulatory one—is made at a distance too great for me to identify her voice. The man's continues, fluent, persuasive, lyrically intoned, in a Mediterranean accent which, in a moment, I recognize as Andrea's. Not until they are directly opposite me on the far side of the hedge do his words become intelligible:

"—would be intolerable, of course. But some things are different. Some things need no justification. No, it is true. I know what you will say, and believe me I appreciate your right to protest, but it is true." There is a pause; the lady makes no audible response. Andrea begins again, in a freshly animated way, with a note of inspiration. "Look there. At those wonderful purple flowers—are they irises?" There is a murmur of confirmation. "Will you tell me who would deny those flowers the right to exist? What justification do they need? There are things which occur as spontaneously as those flowers, and as beautifully. No one could possibly—"

They pass on, his voice fading to a melodious murmur, their footsteps receding on the cinders. I crush out my cigarette, rise, and after waiting a moment or two longer, follow in the direction they have taken along the hedge, grinding my shoes in the cinders to make my footsteps very audible. In a little while I overtake them; I hear their own footsteps come to a halt. There is a moment of silence. I call out, "Hello! Is there someone there?"

Andrea replies, his voice risen slightly in pitch, "Signore Pritchard. Is that you?"

"Yes. Andrea? I've gotten lost in this bloody thing. Can you help me out?"

"But of course! I am always at your service!" He laughs, with unnecessary zest, it seems to me. Then, Margaret's voice, a little heavy with drink, a little incontinent in its surprise: "Mickey! What on earth are you doing in this *labbarumph?*"

"I was exploring," I say, "and I got lost. Do you know the way out?"

"I don't know. Do we, Andrea?"

"Of course we do," says Andrea. Then, to me, through the hedge, "Stay just where you are, Mr. Pritchard. We will be with you in a moment."

I stand looking up the aisle between the boxwood and in a moment, as he has predicted, they appear, smiling and waving as they approach. And now it is time for me to appreciate the prudence for which the countess has taken him to task, for he is the only one of us clear-headed enough to find his way out of the labyrinth.

It is late in the afternoon when we depart from St. Tropez, and when we are still an hour out of Villefranche the sun sets in the sea behind us, wild and red, showering the water, like the floor of an autumn forest, with scarlet leaves. I go down into the aft stateroom and try to waken Margaret to come and see it, but she is sleeping too heavily. She lies on her stomach, her face twisted to one side, her elbows out, her arms adangle, like a fallen marionette. I take her by the shoulders and shake her gently, and she stirs and twitches. I lean down and murmur into her ear: "Mickey, come see the sunset. It's beautiful." She mumbles and swings her face from one side to the other.

"What did you say?" I ask.

"Said I saw it."

"Not this one. You didn't see this one."

"Want to sleep. You tell me about it some time."

"I wish you'd come."

"No." She drifts back into sleep. I sit beside her for a while as we rock on through the sunset sea.

It is dark when we come into Villefranche, and the harbor lights glitter like foxfire in the black water. Standing beside Gwynyth against the deck rail in the dark (the others forward of us, looking shoreward so that they do not see) I lower my hand behind her to the hem of her skirt, then under it, to clutch gently the warm naked flank of her thigh, then glide my out-spread hand up slowly over the rose-petal flesh until I hold clasped in my enchanted fingers the swell of one small bare buttock, nude, hard and hot as a sun-warmed cantaloupe. I hear the sigh of her swiftly intaken breath.

"Oh, Jesus Christ," she whispers. "You'd better stop that, or I'll go off right here."

"Well, I'll go right with you."

"God, let's do. Can we?"

"Yes."

And with very little effort we manage it, standing not five feet behind our shadowy shipmates, pressing against the rail to keep our balance as we roll through the smoothly shining black seas.

At Villefranche all but Andrea, Margaret, and I disembark. There is no docking pier here; they must be taken ashore in the dingy, which is lowered from its chocks on the cabin-top by an electric winch. Gwynyth turns to murmur something to me that I cannot hear above the whine of the machinery. One of the Algerians rows them to the jetty, the while hull of the dingy dissolving gradually in the darkness. Their voices come with an eerie clarity over the water, as if spoken into a wooden barrel.

I wash Margaret's face with a wet cloth to waken her, sit her up on the bed, and guide her arms into a cardigan sweater she has brought. She is listlessly obedient, her hand hanging. Ian stands at the end of the boarding ladder to take her hand and assist her onto the jetty. She stands before him, smiling simply, her eyes downcast, their lids fluttering sleepily.

"There's a good lass," he says, and pats her on the shoulder. "Steady on."

"I must have a kiss from the captain."

"Oh, well. Yes. Right." He kisses her quickly and shyly, very pleasantly embarrassed. "Now, I've tucked a bottle of the bubbly in your gear. You'll want it in the morning."

"You're an angel," Margaret says.

"Oh, I wouldn't say that; no."

We thank him again, Andrea so profusely that he is embarrassed into silence. He stands watching quietly, hands in the pockets of his baggy white duck trousers as we walk slowly—one of us at each of Margaret's elbows—among the jumbled nets and coils of cordage and moonlit buckets of the jetty to the quay.

I follow the lights of Andrea's car as far as the fork of the Cape road, where he turns off toward the mainland, raising his arm in the open coupé to wave to us as he disappears into the darkness.

In the villa, I try to persuade Margaret to take some aspirin, but she pushes the bottle peevishly away. Nor will she accept my offer to help her into her pajamas.

"I'm going to sleep in my slip," she says. "Or slip in my sleep, maybe." She drops her skirt and peels her blouse off over her head, tottering about the bedroom, then collapses onto the bed and begins to breathe deeply.

But when I come out of the bathroom she has vanished. I search through the villa, but she is neither in the kitchen nor salon, nor on the terrace. I go down the steps into the garden, calling for her. The moon is out very brightly, sailing softly among pale rags of cloud. There has been a rainstorm during our absence, and there are pools of dark water standing in the gravel of the walks. I find her kneeling at the edge of one of these, peering down. The tips of her hanging hair trail in the water, deforming the moonlit face reflected there into a blighted brutal copy of her own.

"What are you doing out here?" I say. "Come to bed."

"Look, Mickey. I'm all of a piece now, anyway; you see? I have a kind of symmetry or something I never had before."

"Come to bed," I say, stooping to take her by the shoulders.

"Yes, all right; but aren't you proud? Aren't you proud of your wonderful new symmetrical wife?"

"Yes, very proud. Now come to bed."

When I have gotten her into bed and drawn the covers up to her chin she smiles at me sleepily and says, "What immortal hand or eye can trace my fearful symmetry?"

"Nobody's," I say. "Nobody's at all. Now come and rest."

Two days after the boating party Andrea arrived at the villa at two o'clock for his lesson with Margaret (I having neglected, meanwhile, to make my suggestion that we spend the balance of our holiday in Rome). I left them together and drove down into Villefranche through the mid-afternoon sunlight. I parked along the curb in front of the roadside café where the Corniche, descending from the hills, becomes for a moment part of a village street. After twenty minutes Gwynyth had not appeared. There was a *cabine* phone beside the café, from which I telephoned her, and was told by her concierge that she was ill, suffering from *"un gros rhume."* I sat down at one of the café tables and drank three glasses of Cinzano. It was then forty-five minutes after two. I drove back to the Cape and slowly past the villa on the Chemin du Roy. Andrea's car was still parked in the driveway. I drove on down the hill to the barricaded turn-in where I had once passed such a bountiful afternoon with Gwynyth, parked the Citroën and walked back up the road to La Fleurelle. I walked up the driveway past his car, carefully avoiding twigs and loose pebbles on the concrete, and onto the paved path of stone chips that circled the villa leading toward the garden. I passed under the kitchen windows, then stepped off the path and walked close along the wall of the house to the scrolled black iron grillwork which encased the floor-length French windows of the salon. The glass doors were opened outward, but behind them the transparent gauze curtains were drawn against the sunlight, shifting gently in the idle stir of air. There was a cool-jazz record tinkling softly on the phonograph inside the salon. I stood beside the window, straining my ears for the sound of voices—or of anything at all—but there was nothing to be heard but the muted thump and sibilance of the recorded music. In a moment it came to a stop, and after a brief pause there was the gentle clatter of the changing mechanism and the record dropping, then silence. Then, very close to me—apparently from someone on the ottoman just inside the open windows—the tinkle of ice sliding in a lifted glass. After another moment or two of terrible suspense I heard Margaret's voice calling from far inside the villa, at the end of the corridor that led into the bathroom, "Andrea, will you turn them over, please?"

"I don't understand this machine," Andrea said, almost into my ear.

"What did you say?"

"*I said I don't know how.*" His voice rose petulantly, as if the effort annoyed him bitterly.

"All right. I'll get them in a minute."

"Yes, you get them," he muttered in an ugly sotto voce.

In a moment, considerably closer now, and stationary, as if she were standing in the arch that led into the salon from the hallway, I heard her voice again:

"Don't you like progressive jazz?"

The tone of his reply had a shrug in it, a sound of dismissal; he did not want to be led into a conversation: "Oh, yes. It is all right."

After a pause Margaret said. "I think you're very hard to please, Andrea."

"I have certain tastes," he said. "In poor people that is considered being too fussy, giving yourself airs. In rich people it is called discrimination."

"I don't know why you're always making remarks about rich people to me," Margaret said. "I'm not rich, at all."

"Oh? That is not the impression I get," said Andrea. "Not from the way your husband spends his money."

There was another, considerably longer, pause; then Margaret said with a strange little laugh, "Then I'm afraid you're putting too much faith in your impressions. We're very ordinary middle-class people."

"Perhaps. By American standards," said Andrea.

"By anybody's standards. Mickey is a government worker. We have barely enough money to pay for this holiday. As a matter of fact, we'll probably be in debt for it for years. So I'd appreciate it if you didn't make any more allusions to my vast wealth."

I heard the mechanical snapping and clicking as she turned the records over on the phonograph. Then, very close—she had either advanced directly to the window or sat beside him on the ottoman—she asked unexpectedly, "Andrea, do I look any different to you?"

"Any different? Different from what?"

"From before. From the way I looked half an hour ago."

"No. You look no different. Not to me."

"Are you sure?"

"Of course I am."

In the hall the telephone rang shrilly, startling all of us, apparently, for I heard Margaret's distinct soft gasp.

"I won't be a minute," she said.

"I have to go, anyway," said Andrea. "I have many things to do."

"Oh, wait just a minute, please." Her voice was receding rapidly as she moved toward the telephone in the hall. I gathered that Andrea had followed her, for in a little while I heard the alternate murmur of their two voices, now indistinguishable, from the forward regions of the villa; then, shortly afterward and much clearer, unconfined by walls, the snap of the iron latch as the front door of the villa was opened and the sound of Andrea's shoes descending the stone steps to the driveway. Being in the direct line of sight from his automobile, I crouched down to shield myself behind the intervening shrubbery and saw, through the tangle of foliage, the blur of his bronze-colored sports shirt and the flash of blue enamel from the opening door as he got into the Aston-Martin. Margaret apparently stood on the front steps watching, for there had been no subsequent sound of the door-latch; when he had started the motor and put the car in gear, I heard her call, "If I made it three or four o'clock, Andrea; would that be better?"

"I'll have to see," he replied. "It may be difficult. I don't know." He revved the motor, waved, and backed out hastily, turning uphill, I was glad to see, in the direction of St. Jean; if he had taken the beach-road down the hill he would almost certainly have seen the Citroën standing in the turn-in where I had left it. A moment later, after I had heard the front door close, I went back along the wall of the villa, through the driveway to the Chemin du Roy and down the hill to the parked automobile. I drove in to St. Jean-Cap Ferrat, drank two more glasses of vermouth, and returned to the villa to find her gravely writing in her journal on the terrace.

That evening after dinner when she stood at the parapet in the dusk with a cup of coffee and a liqueur glass of Cointreau on the stone ledge in front of her and a cigarette held unlit and forgotten between her fingers, staring out across the cool sea with a look beyond my understanding, I took a cigarette lighter out of my pocket, ignited it, held it toward her and by its flame, as she turned her face toward me, I saw in her startled eyes a nude bright flash of naked ore, a glimpse of such an unshielded and blinding white lode of her spirit that for an instant I thought—I *feared*, perhaps—that she would speak at last; that she would yield up to me at last, uncompromised by any vestige of modesty or guilt or by the shadow of any covenant, some sovereign scrap of truth that by long deed and imprecation I had conjured out of her to meet my need. I was startled, and dropped the lighter with a clatter to the stone floor. As I stooped to pick it up she said, "You drink too much. It's beginning to show in you."

I said that I knew that, and for a while we talked about the condition of my liver.

In the morning I asked if she would like to ride into Villefranche with me to pay the rent and buy a fresh supply of batteries for the little portable radio we had bought.

"How long will you be gone?"

"Oh, an hour or two."

"I don't think so. I want to work in the garden this morning. But, Mickey, you could do me a favor, if you would."

"Sure. What?"

"If you wouldn't mind going on into Nice, you could pick me up a copy of this week's *Match*. Alice Nesbit called me yesterday and she said there was a wonderful article in it about Provence, that I'd like to have. Would that take you too long?"

"No. Glad to."

"You'll be back for the beach, won't you?"

"Oh, sure. But go on down, if I'm late, and I'll meet you there."

"All right. Be careful driving through that tunnel."

Those are the last words Margaret ever said to me. The first, as you can hardly be expected to remember, were, "Oh, never mind. It was my fault, anyway." What I think is an understandable concern for harmony and an equal one for comfort suggest to me that by inverting the order of those two speeches I might well have gained an effect far more cogent, far more reassuring, and no doubt far more exhilarating in an aesthetic sense. But that would have been the way of the artist, and I am no such creature. I am a simple chronicler, whose career, you will be glad to hear, begins and ends with this single work; I lack any further ambition to tamper with the natural order of things. Again, I think, understandably.

"Be careful driving through that tunnel." (Placed even where they are, they have a certain ring about them.)

"All right. I'll see you later on."

I drove to Villefranche, paid the rent, picked up Gwynyth at the café on the Corniche, proceeded through the tunnel with suitable caution, and saw before me Nice, the White City, burning in the sun.

We spent an hour and a half in our accustomed room in the Hôtel d'Égypte, and afterward, walking through the vast rococo lobby with my usual uneasy effort at dignity, I forgot Margaret's magazine. I did not think of it until we entered the tunnel that delves into the mountain which drops down to the sea to form the eastern arm of the Bay of Nice; at this point Margaret's parting admonition echoed in my mind.

"Oh, damn," I said. "I've got to go back."

"Why?"

"Margaret wanted a *Paris Match;* I forgot it."

"Well, why go back to Nice? You can get it at Villefranche."

"Are you sure?"

"Well, certainly. You can get it anywhere."

"Oh. Oh, well I will, then."

When I let her out of the car in Villefranche she clutched the edge of the door and pointed back along the street to a row of shops beside the café.

"There's a place there where you can get the *Match.*"

"Thanks." I plucked her hand from the door and kissed her fingers.

"What's that for?"

"That's for having such curly hair."

"You bloody man."

"Will I see you on Tuesday?"

"If you like."

I watched her swing across the little *Place,* turning when she reached the steps that went down to the Old Town to wave to me with her boyish grin. A dirty little gray kitten came running to her across the stone, and she bent down to pluck it up and clutch it to her throat. She was wearing a black beret that day, with a little twig of heather pinned to it by a tiny silver clasp in the shape of a wishbone.

I walked back to the shop she had pointed out, bought the *Paris Match* for Margaret, and drove to Cap Ferrat, looking down over the red tile roofs of the old gray afternoon-silent town. When I parked the Citroën in the driveway of the villa I looked at my watch and saw that it was twelve minutes after two. Margaret would very likely have gone down to the beach. I called to her when I opened the front door, but there was no reply. I went into the kitchen, took a bottle of ice water out of the refrigerator, poured out and drank a glassful, poured out another, and sat down to take off my shoes and socks, rejoicing in the feel of the cool tiles against the bare soles of my feet. The golden stillness of the afternoon poured palpably through the open window, like melting metal. I love this place, I thought. I opened the magazine on the kitchen table and leafed through it while I drank the second glass of water. There were splendid photographs of the medieval hill-town of Cagnes, of the university at Aix-en-Provence and of the ceramics studios at Vallauris. I finished the glass of water, closed the magazine, and carrying my shoes and socks walked back through the foyer and along the hall to the bedroom, where I sat down on the bed and began to unbutton my shirt. My eyes roamed idly about the room as I did so, pausing at her dressing table, where some strangeness about its appearance held them in vaguely disconcerted attention. It was several moments before I realized what this strangeness was: the dressing table was bare. Her comb and brush, her cut-glass atomizer, her silver tray of hairpins, her cosmetics bottles, the photographs of Susannah's children which she kept wedged into the lower corner of the mirror-frame, all were gone; all that remained to decorate the pane of glass which covered the kidney-shaped surface of the table was a small cloth-covered blue button and a little mound of face powder, spilled, apparently, in the haste with which it had been cleared.

I got up quickly and went to the closet. It was empty of her clothing, except for two outworn summer dresses (one torn, the other stained with wine), a pair of badly scuffed kid pumps, and a white patent-leather belt with a frayed tongue, which hung by its buckle from a wire hanger, like a dead snake. I went out into the corridor and opened the hall closet where we stored our luggage. Her two blue suitcases, her hatbox, and her leather cosmetics case were gone; there were bare rectangular patterns in the dust of the floor where they had stood. I went back into the bedroom and dragged out from under the bed the steamer trunk which we had shared on our passage over; it contained mostly articles which we used in common— towels, bedsheets, books, and so on—but she used it as well to store the few gifts she had purchased to take back to friends and relatives: these, too, were gone.

I sat for a few moments in a kind of catalepsy, then closed the trunk, went out through the hall into the foyer, opened the front door, and stood on the steps of the villa looking up and down the road, in what expectation I don't know—perhaps of seeing her standing in the middle of the Chemin du Roy surrounded by her luggage, waiting either for a taxi or to be cajoled back tenderly into the house to put on a pair of chops for dinner. In a moment I became aware of the absurdity of my standing there, and was suddenly and hectically possessed by the necessity of taking some kind of action. I went back into the foyer, snatched up the telephone, and dialed Andrea's number. A concierge answered; I heard the clatter of the telephone as she set it down and then her voice distantly hailing Andrea, up a stairwell, apparently. In a moment I heard his footsteps approach, pattering down a flight of stairs; then, with milky gentility, he murmured, *"Pronto?"*

"Andrea, this is Michael Pritchard. Where the hell is Margaret?"

"Margaret? What do you mean, where is Margaret? I don't know where she is."

"I want to speak to her. I know damn well she's there."

"But that is ridiculous. Why would she be here?"

"Where else would she be?"

"I don't have any idea. You are excited. Why don't you tell me what has happened?"

"Margaret's disappeared, that's what's happened. Do you mean to tell me you haven't seen her?"

"No, I have not seen her since yesterday, when I came to give her lesson."

"Have you spoken to her?"

There was a brief pause. "Yes. She called me this morning. At about ten o'clock."

"What did she say?"

"She wanted to change the day of her next lesson. She wanted me to come today instead of Tuesday."

"Why?"

"How do I know why? I assumed she would be busy."

"What did you tell her?"

"I said I could not possibly come. I had a previous engagement." There was a somewhat longer pause in the course of which his voice changed tone. It became now very cool and formal, verging upon arrogance, "As a matter of fact, Mr. Pritchard, I will be frank with you; I told your wife I could not handle her lessons anymore at all."

"You told her what?"

"I told her I would not be able to instruct her in the future. Something very urgent has arisen. I must go to Biarritz next week."

"Why didn't you tell me about this?"

"I did not know of it until this morning. It is a very important opportunity for me."

"Something that involves a bit more money, no doubt."

"Naturally it is a matter of business. I am not so fortunate that I can neglect a business opportunity. Perhaps you are."

"And how did she react to this?"

"She was noticeably disappointed."

"What did she say?"

"I don't remember what she said."

"I advise you to try."

There was another pause. "She did not seem willing to accept my explanation. She questioned me." There was a gathering petulance in his voice. "I am not used to having my motives questioned by these great ladies whenever they are disappointed. I want you to understand that you do not own me, Mr. Pritchard, in spite of the money you have paid me. My life is my own."

"Did you say that to Margaret?"

"I don't remember what I said to her exactly."

"Now look, my wife has packed up and left because of something you said to her this morning, and you had damn well better remember what it was, or I'll come over there and shake it out of you."

There was another considerable pause, during which his voice went through yet another transformation, this one appalling.

"You seem to have quite a passion for truth, Mr. Pritchard," he said. "I wonder how much of it you would like to hear?"

"What I want to hear is exactly what you said to my wife this morning."

"I told her that in any case the arrangement was quite disagreeable to me. That I could no longer tolerate the obligation you imposed upon me."

"What obligation?"

"Naïveté does not become you, Mr. Pritchard. You are one of the very few Americans in whom it is ridiculous." He gave me a moment to reply, then continued tranquilly, "The obligation to make love to a deformed woman. A thing which revolts me. Which revolts me as much as it does her husband, apparently. I am happy to say that I am now liberated from this degrading obligation."

"You said that to Margaret?"

"More or less. I don't remember my exact words, but I made it quite clear that the situation could not continue."

"Because you've discovered an even more lucrative one."

"What is that word, lucrative?"

"Did you tell her how much money I'd given you?"

"Yes I did. She was quite surprised."

"And yet you promised quite specifically not to."

"I don't remember what I promised. At any rate, why should I be concerned about saving your dignity when you go on heaping degradation on me every day? Do you think you are sacred or something? Do you think an Italian's dignity is not as important as yours? Or is it just something else to be bought? Like his lovemaking."

"You dirty, greasy, cheap, bloody gigolo."

"That is very insulting language, Mr. Pritchard. If I am a gigolo, then what is a man who employs one, for his wife? Would you like to hear what we call that kind of a man in Italy?"

"What I'd like to hear is that you're out of that place inside the next hour, or neither one of us is going to have much of a future."

I hung up the phone and sat trembling. The silence in the villa was terrible, an inhuman ringing void. I picked up the telephone book and began looking through it for the numbers of the international airlines. I had to call only one, Air France.

"Mrs. Michael Pritchard," said the reservations clerk. "Yes. She reserved passage on Flight 017, arriving in New York at eight P.M."

"What time does that leave Nice?" I asked.

"In fifteen minutes, at two-thirty p.m."

"Does it stop in Paris?"

"Yes. It arrives in Paris at three fifty and departs at five p.m. There is no change, however."

"Is there any way I can get to Paris before five p.m.?"

"No, monsieur."

"Can you deliver a message to Mrs. Pritchard during the stopover in Paris? It is very urgent."

"Yes, monsieur. We can even have it radioed to the plane in flight, if it is very urgent."

"Thank you. I would like her to call this number collect." I gave him the number of the villa.

"I will see that it is delivered, monsieur."

"Thank you very much."

I sent another cable to the airport in New York and a third to our house in Washington, then I began to pack. When I had got all my things into the suitcases and the steamer trunk I made a survey of the villa in search of forgotten items and discovered the glass Harlequin lying on the carpet at the foot of the grand piano, its head broken off. I took the two pieces out onto the terrace and threw them as far as I could into the pines behind the garden. The body of the figurine struck one of the pine trunks and broke apart with a glassy tinkle. I went back into the salon and found, forgotten on one of the bookshelves, Margaret's copy of Yeats' *Collected Poems*. I carried it into the hall and sat down beside the telephone to wait, discovering, as I leafed through the volume, the verse of "The Lady's Second Song" which she had underlined with violet ink (the pages fell apart at this point, marked by a pair of pressed violets she had picked among the rocks at Antibes).

> He shall love my soul as though
> Body were not at all.
> He shall love your body
> Untroubled by the soul.
> Love cram love's two divisions,
> Yet keep his substance whole.
> The Lord have mercy upon us.

The phone did not ring. I sat beside it for an hour, reading the poetry of Yeats. At five thirty I went into the kitchen and made myself a bowl of onion soup from a packet of the dried concentrate I had bought in St. Jean. I took it back into the hall and drank it, sitting at the telephone table, then washed and put away the dishes and cutlery, and returned to the salon to settle down with the copy of Yeats in an overstuffed armchair. By eight o'clock—the time of her arrival in New York—I had read half the volume and had learned more about the nature of poetry than an entire university education had previously yielded to me. From eight until nine I smoked a pack of cigarettes and drank a pot of coffee. The phone did not ring. At nine o'clock, on the possibility that she might have gone on directly to Washington from New York by the Air Shuttle, I placed an overseas call to our house in Georgetown for twelve o'clock, then began to read again. By midnight I had read all the poems that Yeats had ever written, and was temporarily diverted by the miracle that the wisdom of a man's entire life could be distilled into six hours of reading time. My own, I thought, would make one fairly substantial limerick.

At twelve fifteen the phone rang. I was shivering from head to foot when I answered it. An excruciatingly efficient voice announced that my party did not answer.

"Will you place the call again at three-hour intervals?"

"Certainly, monsieur. Until what time?"

"Until further notice."

"Very well, monsieur."

I returned to my armchair. There is this to be said: after that night, in that silent villa, there is little left in this life for me to dread. Twice again, at three and at six, the phone rang to inform me that my party was still unavailable. After the last call I went out onto the terrace to watch the dawn. The sea was gray and gleamed dully, like cold silver. The stone floor of the terrace was wet with dew. Finches had begun to chirp among the pines.

At nine o'clock I rang the estate agent in Villefranche and told him that we were leaving unexpectedly. My wife's father had died very suddenly, I said, and it was necessary for us to return to the States at once.

"There will have to be an inventory, monsieur," he said.

"Can you send someone this morning?"

"I will come myself, at once."

He arrived at the villa within half an hour and for the next forty-five minutes prowled about with a clipboard, estimating the damage we had wrought in terms of cigarette burns, broken crockery, wine-stains, and the like. I paid him for this, for a domestic to clean up after our tenancy, and for a pro rata charge for telephone and electricity. He seemed very pleased and offered me his card, in the eventuality that we should return some day and require his services again.

Shortly after he left, the telephone rang again and I was informed that my party was still unavailable.

"Thank you," I said. "You'd better cancel the call."

I rang the Air France office, reserved a place on a ten thirty flight to New York, drove in to Nice, surrendered the Citroën, and took a taxi to the airport. By nine o'clock that night I had returned here, to this room, where I am sitting now, and had begun the vigil which is three years old as I write these concluding pages.

I don't know that I expect it ever to be rewarded; it is a habit, I suppose, and no doubt a desperate one. Still, it may be that my great-grandmother's advocacy of hope has not entirely been lost on me; how, otherwise, can I have gone on for three years in the apparently immortal anticipation of one day hearing Margaret's latchkey in the lock, or the tinkle of her keys against the cloisonné vase on the hall table that will announce her entrance, or of finding her coat thrown across the back of the sofa one winter evening when I return from work. Or of one day hearing from her lips (or possibly reading from her pen) words whose meaning is, "I can bear what you have done to me, because I know you did it out of love." That it would be impossible to prove the truth of such a statement seems to me a very good argument for making it out of mercy, and Margaret was always merciful. Perhaps it is not so much that I believe in the possibility of her doing so as that I would rather not die until I have assigned to that possibility every available moment of my natural life.

Therefore I get up every morning at seven, fry myself an egg and bacon, go to work (where I perform no worse than any other government employee, and better than many that I know), come home in a crowded bus to this house, at whose door I knock and stand waiting for a moment before inserting my key (part of my same habitual rigmarole), enter, hang up my coat and hat (in winter), take off my shoes, and go into the kitchen in my stockingfeet to cook myself a chop and set a bowl of Hap-E-Kat beside the table leg for the stately companion of my declining years. I subscribe to *The American Scholar, The Atlantic, The Scientific American, The Saturday Review* and the *Hudson* and *Kenyon* reviews. I play chess by correspondence (and sometimes in person), dine occasionally with friends, and very infrequently, as you have learned, attend a concert or a motion picture. Sometimes on Sunday morning, if the weather is fine, I take a long walk through the neighborhood, which is changing rapidly. There are, as well, the other diversions I have spoken of: arranging ticket stubs in a pattern on the bedspread, and dusting, cleaning, and repairing Margaret's possessions—her paintings, photographs, clothing, books, and furniture (last Saturday, for example, was given over entirely to mending the legs of her boudoir chair, which the hot-air heating system had loosened badly). It is not at all a bad life, really. There is this to be said for an obsession: it produces in its victims regularity, predictability, and calm; virtues which governments are eternally seeking to encourage in their citizens. (In this respect, I think, I deserve the congratulations of those of you whose chief enthusiasm is law and order.)

Nor is this obsession of mine quite as irrational as it may appear; I have a couple of little mysteries to nourish it. They are humble enough, and I suppose as much a product of my own despair as of any genuine obscurity of nature. But this could be said of any mystery; and, humble as they are, I cherish them, for while they remain unsolved I continue to escape damnation.

There is, first, the parcel which I discovered on her bed when I came back into this house three years ago. I did not understand it; or perhaps I misunderstood it; or perhaps I did understand it. My first reaction was to cry triumphantly to myself, "She has come back! She has left this here for me as a reconciliation gift! She will be back shortly!" I dropped my suitcase to the floor and plunged toward the bed. Then, almost instantly, a second, and totally reactionary thought halted the outward reaching of my hand: "No. She has been here and left this as a parting token. She will not return." I picked the parcel up and held it in my hand. Then, as I weighed it (it is very light), the thought occurred to me, "Perhaps she placed it here before we went to France. For me to find—as I have—on my return." I saw then that there was a small white envelope tucked under the ribbon, but I was afraid to open it: afraid that the darkest of these possibilities would be confirmed. For months I did not dare to open that envelope. It lay there, sealed, until the day, just over a year ago, when I began this manuscript. Well, reader, you have seen it for yourself; you are as able as I am to interpret it, and welcome. My only advice is that you keep your opinion to yourself.

And what is in the package? Perhaps the contents will clarify the meaning of its message, if you have any doubts about it. Shall we see? No, reader—again, I fear it. (It is not really solutions that I seek, but time for miracles.) I am afraid that the contents of my little silver parcel must remain a mystery to you, as to me. Oh, it is possible (barely so) that some day—another three years from now, perhaps—overcome by curiosity, remorse, or simply, at last, fatigue, I may be driven to open it; but that will be a long time after you have laid down this book and forgotten the matter forever. It is only barely possible, at any rate. My present plan—duly noted in my will—is to have it buried with me in some suitably emblematic manner, perhaps like a knight's sword or a sovereign's scepter, clasped to my breast beneath my folded hands.

I suppose I could well be considered insane for putting so much value on such a meager little mystery as this, if it were not given a certain amount of added substance by a second—equally humble, to be sure, but to a man of my need, equally propitious.

I had sat for perhaps half an hour on the bed with my mysterious parcel in my lap, on this evening of my return, when the thought presented itself to me very strongly that I had better engage myself in physical activity of some sort. I opened windows, drawers, and closets. I turned on the radio for company and began unpacking my suitcases. As I was hanging up a suit I heard, at the bottom of the stairs and through the bedroom door which I had left open for just this blessed contingency, the three-toned pealing of the front-door chimes. In a swift reckless gallop I descended the stairs, flung open the door, and beheld a small plump man with thick glasses and a mottled nose—Mr. Dunthorpe, our next-door neighbor.

This gentleman had arranged to collect our personal mail and forward it to us during our absence, holding the balance —circulars, subscriptions, and so on—for our return. His face was badly wrinkled with anxiety.

"Oh, Dr. Pritchard," he said. "I'm so glad it's you. I just came over to collect your mail, and I saw the light on upstairs and thought I heard the radio in here, and thought I'd better check, because I knew you weren't due back till the end of August. Has something gone wrong?"

"Yes. Mrs. Pritchard's father has been taken ill very suddenly, and she had to fly out to Kansas to see him. So our holiday has been interrupted."

"Oh, dear. Oh, what a pity. I'm sorry to hear that. Is there anything I can do?"

"No, I don't think so, thank you. I'm getting along pretty well."

"Why don't you come over and have a little supper with us? It must be pretty dreary, coming back to an empty house, like this."

"Oh, I ate on the plane, thanks. I think I'll just unpack and get to bed. I'm a little tired." I saw that he had a yellow Western Union envelope in his hand. "Is that for me?"

"Oh. Yes, it is. That's all there was today. I have your magazines and things next door. I'll just go get them."

"Thank you."

He left me tearing open the envelope with trembling hands. It was an international cable, preceded by five encoded lines of jumbled hieroglyphic numerals and letters, beneath which I read:

PLEASE UNDERSTAND STOP I LOVE YOU STOP WAIT FOR ME
AT HOME STOP BE THERE AS SOON AS I CAN MICKEY

Reader, I cannot tell you how my heart soared. Or how, immediately afterward, it fell. Then rose. Then fell again. Then rose again, in an alternating pattern which it has followed unremittingly for the past three years. At first, you see, I did not recognize the cable as my own; then, immediately afterward, I did. Or thought I did. Then, a second later, I perceived that the wording was just sufficiently dissimilar to my own (as well as I could remember it; I had after all composed it extemporaneously, never writing it down) to make it possible that it was indeed from Margaret. But no, it was too great a coincidence. Then, somewhat defiantly, I thought, "Well, why not from her?" If she had *had* anything to say to me, it could very well have been in these words, too. As a message from either of us to the other it made good sense. Blessedly good sense. There was no denying it. The signature, of course, was no help. Nor was the address. With the conventional brevity of international telegrams it was directed simply to "Pritchard, 1613 34th St. N.W., Washington, D.C." I examined the coded garble above. Amongst the procession of symbols I could make out only the time (234 P EST), the date (JUL 22 62), and the word NICE. I had placed my own cable at approximately two fifteen, immediately after making my call to Air France. I concluded that what was given as the time of origin was in fact the time of transmission of the message, not of its reception from its author; because no matter who sent it, it was datelined four minutes after her plane had left Nice for New York. Obviously there had been a delay between the time of placement and the time of transmission. Either of us might then have sent it— myself by telephone from the villa, or Margaret from the airport. The date and place of origin would have been the same in either case.

None of this, of course, serves to explain what—if the message were from Margaret—had happened to my own. Why was it not in the mailbox with hers? There are many reasons (I have had three years in which to consider the matter), of which the most eminent is that the American office of RCA (the transmitting agency), on receiving almost simultaneously two nearly identical messages from the same point of origin and directed to the same address, would very naturally have assumed that one of them was a duplicate, and would have delivered only one copy to the addressee. Such errors after all must be very common. (If it does not seem quite so natural to you, reader, it is because you do not have my emotional investment in the possibility.)

These, then, are the pair of very modest mysteries on which my hope is founded. These and her silence. Their modesty may amuse certain pragmatists, who will no doubt invite me to dismiss them altogether and found my existence on some much more practical estimate of reality—that Margaret is gone forever, that I will receive from her any day a request for a divorce, that she is very probably, at this moment, considering remarriage. This is conceivable, of course. It is also conceivable that she may die before I do, but as I am not particularly anxious to confirm any of these things, I have stopped soliciting information about her from anyone. She will speak to me only if she wishes, and in time.

Meanwhile, she continues, as I say, as joint owner of this house, as beneficiary of my life insurance and as sole inheritrix of the estate with which you are now so tiresomely familiar: the furniture, the books and paintings, and my great-grand-mother's diligently spelled out exhortations to Pity, Charity, and Love. Perhaps it would be just as well if I survived her: it is not a legacy anyone would welcome.

A Note on the Type

The text of this book was set on the Linotype in a type face called
Baskerville. The face is a facsimile reproduction of types cast from molds
made for John Baskerville (1706-75) from his designs. The punches for
the revived Linotype Baskerville were cut under the supervision of the
English printer George W. Jones. John Baskerville's original face was one
of the forerunners of the type style known as "modern face" to printers—
a "modern" of the period A.D. 1800.

This book was composed, printed, and bound by The Haddon Crafts-
men, Inc. Typography and binding design by The Etheredges.